SUCCESS STORIES

Success Stories

*Literature and the Media in
England, 1950–1959*

HARRY RITCHIE

faber and faber
LONDON · BOSTON

First published in 1988
by Faber and Faber Limited
3 Queen Square London WC1N 3AU

Photoset by Parker Typesetting Service Leicester
Printed in Great Britain by
Mackays of Chatham Ltd Kent
All rights reserved

British Library Cataloguing in Publication Data
Ritchie, Harry
Success stories: literature and the
media in England, 1950–1959.
1. English literature — 20th century —
History and criticism
I. Title
820'.9'00914   PR471
ISBN 0–571–14764–X

Contents

Acknowledgements

The author and publisher wish to thank the following for permission to quote from copyright material:

Kingsley Amis and Victor Gollancz Ltd for permission to quote from *Lucky Jim, That Uncertain Feeling* and *I Like It Here*; the BBC for permission to quote from files held in the BBC Written Archives Centre (Caversham Park, Reading); the Estate of Cyril Connolly for permission to quote from *Enemies of Promise* © 1938; the *Daily Telegraph* for permission to quote from verses by Peter Simple; the *London Standard* for permission to quote from Philip Oakes; the Estate of the late Sonia Brownell Orwell and Secker & Warburg Ltd for permission to quote from *Inside the Whale* by George Orwell; Faber and Faber Ltd for permission to quote from *Look Back in Anger* and *The Entertainer* by John Osborne; V. S. Pritchett and A. D. Peters & Co Ltd for permission to quote from *These Writers Couldn't Care Less*; *Times Newspapers Ltd* for permission to reproduce the contribution by Somerset Maugham to the *Sunday Times* of 25 December 1955; the *Observer* for permission to quote from Kenneth Tynan; Victor Gollancz Ltd for Permission to quote from *The Outsider* by Colin Wilson.

Preface

This book studies the making of a literary generation in England in the 1950s, a generation represented first by the Movement and then by the Angry Young Men. It was a time when several young writers were front-page news. New authors inspired a series of controversies and scandals and countless commentaries and analyses, for their books and their own biographies were thought to be of great cultural and social significance.

I have focused on the careers of four new writers in the fifties – Kingsley Amis, John Osborne, Colin Wilson and Alan Sillitoe – and tried to show when, how and why they achieved success, because I believe their works and their receptions evoke important literary issues of the time. But for considerations of time, space, money and energy other young writers could well have been added to this list. This is not an attempt to give comprehensive coverage of all the literary events and developments of the fifties; the names of, for example, Father Trevor Huddleston and Rowena Farre do not appear, and other writers, who made quiet débuts in the 1950s and now receive greater attention and praise than many of their once-celebrated contemporaries, are conspicuous by their absence or make only brief appearances. This is not a general survey but an account of the promotion of what was and has been seen as the distinctive and representative new writing of the decade. I should also point out that this is a study of certain developments in English literature. 'English' does not mean 'British'.

Many people have helped me in the research for this book with correspondence and interviews. I would like to thank Kingsley Amis, Malcolm Bradbury, the late John Braine, William Cooper, Daniel Farson, Barbara Fearon, Paul Ferris, William Golding, Helen Griffiths, Michael Hastings, Thomas Hinde, the late J. W.

Lambert, Doris Lessing, Tom Maschler, Blake Morrison, Iris Murdoch, Alan Sillitoe, Jon Silkin, Keith Waterhouse and Angus Wilson.

I am grateful as well to the staffs of the Bodleian Library, Lincoln College Library, the City of London School, the John Rylands Library, the National Library of Scotland, the Newspaper Library at Colindale, the BBC Written Archives Centre in Reading, and the *Daily Mirror* newspaper cuttings library.

I greatly appreciate the assistance and advice I received from David Bradshaw, Stephan Chambers, Stephen Gill, Andrew Gotch, Alan Jamieson and Kate Whitehead. But by far my greatest debt of gratitude I owe to Anne Millman, for all her help.

Harry Ritchie
Edinburgh 1986

'In the Movement'

Modern English literature has a commonly accepted chronology. Definite periods have been marked by the reigns of monarchs and the spans of decades and characterized by 'generations' of new authors. So, in this century, the Edwardians are followed by the Georgians who are replaced – after the necessary interruption of the War Poets – by the Modernists and the Bloomsbury Group in the twenties. Then on to the political commitment of the Auden generation in the Pink Decade of the thirties. The war and the disappointing turn-out of War Poets help to make the identity of the forties far less certain but that decade can just about be saved from anonymity by the Neo-Romantics.

Between those days of Dylan Thomas and *The New Apocalypse*, and the swinging sixties with its pop poets and 'happenings', there is the fifties, a decade with a literary identity firmly established first by the Movement and then by the Angry Young Men. The decade of John Osborne, Kingsley Amis, John Braine, Arnold Wesker, John Wain, Alan Sillitoe . . . All those young men who described the unsmart reality of life in the provinces and who were angry about . . . well, no one was quite sure, but they must have been angry about something. The class system probably, or Suez and the Establishment, or maybe even the H-Bomb. No matter. *Look Back in Anger*, *Lucky Jim*, *Room at the Top*, *Chicken Soup with Barley*, *Hurry on Down*, *Saturday Night and Sunday Morning*, all those kitchen-sink plays and novels of social protest seem to belong to and identify the fifties, like skiffle and Teddy Boys and furniture with splayed spindle legs. This is English literature's Angry Decade.

One of the more obvious objections to the notion of a literary period which a moment's thought might raise is that it ignores the uncertainties and confusions, the developments and conflicts at the time. This objection certainly applies to the 1950s. The decade's literary reputation would have astonished commentators in its early years. It seemed then that the one distinguishing literary feature of the fifties would be an anxiety to find distinguishing literary features. The new decade began not with any signs of invigorating new literary energy but with all the symptoms of the post-war malaise. The significant events in 1950 for the literary pundit would have been the deaths of Orwell and Shaw and the closure of the two most important literary periodicals in England – John Lehmann's *Penguin New Writing* and Cyril Connolly's *Horizon*. In his *New Statesman* obituary of *Horizon* on 10 December 1949, T. C. Worsley noted the symbolic importance which Connolly's magazine had maintained since its launch in January 1940. Now its demise was equally important in highlighting the general infirmity of English literary life: 'Five years after the war there is still no sign of any kind of literary revival; no movements are discernible: no trends.'

There was a natural desire in 1950 to reject the writing of the previous decade and hope for a fresh start. In that year Alan Ross declared in his potboiler survey, *The Forties*, that the war and its aftermath had ensured a bleak decade for English literature with 'a dearth of real talents'. On 25 August *The Times Literary Supplement* produced a special section on the contemporary literary scene with articles which shared the view that the forties had been a fallow creative period which was really best forgotten. Auden, Isherwood and Huxley had abandoned England before the war to live in the United States, Joyce and Woolf had died in 1941, Wells in 1946. T. S. Eliot, Edwin Muir and Dylan Thomas were still alive and writing, but despite their individual achievements and the vogue for Neo-Romanticist poetry, English literature in the forties still seemed to have lacked a centre. This had only made the poor show of new writers even more disheartening. Three of the most promising poets – Sidney Keyes, Alun Lewis and Keith Douglas – had been killed in the war, and few other new names had arrived in compensation.

The problem for commentators in 1950 was that only the sudden emergence of startling new authors could prevent their lamentations about the forties becoming lamentations about the fifties. And in those *TLS* surveys of August 1950 no promises could be made of a literary revival. One writer describing 'The Immediate

View' found comfort in a hope common at the time: perhaps this was not so dire a creative period after all, perhaps there was some latter-day Blake or Hopkins around, an unrecognized genius whose great work would be acknowledged by envious admirers in the future. . . For the present, though, Cyril Connolly's final editorial in *Horizon* seemed to sum up the prospects for literature with appropriate pessimism: 'it is closing time in the gardens of the West and from now on an artist will be judged only by the resonance of his solitude or the quality of his despair.' This was not an auspicious start to the new decade.

There was no alternative but to continue the depressing post-war practice of looking for explanations for the lack of literary thrills. Convincing reasons were not hard to find. A common view in the later forties was that new work had been stunted or killed at birth by hostile social and political conditions. These conditions persisted into the fifties and continued to be blamed for the gloomy literary outlook. For a start, victory in the Second World War had not secured 'the gardens of the West' against the threat of destruction, but had been followed by other conflicts. The Cold War developed dramatically in 1948 and 1949 with the Berlin blockade and airlift, and international tension increased when the Soviet Union undertook its first atomic bomb test in August 1949. Britain's involvement in the Korean War, from June 1950 to July 1953, only confirmed that the victories of 1945 had not led to an assurable peace. Orwell's *Nineteen Eighty-Four* (1949) is the period's classic expression of the sense of civilization lost and similar premonitions are voiced by, for example, Roy Fuller in poems like 'Meditation', '1948' or 'The Lake' which appeared in his 1949 collection, *Epitaphs and Occasions*.

'I might have cut a better figure/When peace was longer, incomes bigger', Fuller complained forlornly in the 'Dedicatory Poem' to that volume. The years of post-war austerity had also made it all too clear that the country was not to enjoy the rewards of victory but pay the price of war. Labour's landslide victory in the 1945 election, the promise of post-war reconstruction and the evolution of the Welfare State, might have been expected to provide an inspiring environment for a literary renaissance, especially from writers who had been associated with left-wing sympathies in the thirties; but the realities of economic hardship overshadowed any vestiges of socialist enthusiasm. As John Lehmann recollects in *The Ample Proposition* (1966), 1945 seemed a 'time . . . of hope and confidence' with the prospect of 'a great epoch' lying ahead for the arts, promising 'a magnificent harvest', but such hopes had been quickly dashed. In *Horizon*'s editorial for April 1947 Cyril Connolly vividly described the effects of the aftermath of war and Stafford Cripps's austerity programme following an economically crippling winter: 'most of us are not men or women but members of a vast seedy, over-worked, over-legislated, neuter class, with our drab clothes, our ration books and murder stories, our envious, stricken, old-world apathies and resentments – a careworn people.' It was self-evident to Connolly that new art could not be expected to flourish amid such drabness and privation: 'there is no deterrent to aesthetic adventure like a prolonged struggle with domestic difficulties, food shortages, cold, ill-health and money worries. Art is not a necessity but an indispensable luxury; those who produce it must be cosseted.'

Roy Fuller's portrait of the character of George Garner, novelist and man-of-letters, in *The Second Curtain* (1953) could have been drawn to Connolly's specifications. Garner is struggling in the 'fag-end time of the forties' to make ends meet, performing the menial tasks of ghost authorship, tinkering with his long-delayed novel. He rejoices at the sight of a chocolate biscuit and indulges in a special breakfast treat with the weekly egg allowed by his ration book. A cosseted lifestyle and aesthetic adventure had both been unattainable luxuries for Garner and many of his real-life colleagues.

The fall of Attlee's Government in 1951 is usually taken to mark the end of post-war austerity, but the grim conditions of the forties improved only gradually. Rationing and price controls extended well into the fifties: it was not until May and July 1954, for instance, that basic foodstuffs were finally derationed and brand-names could appear again in the shops. If one particular year has to be chosen as marking the end of the 'age of austerity' and the beginning of the consumer society, it would be 1957 – the year of Macmillan's often-misquoted announcement that 'most of our people have never had it so good', and the year which saw the launch of the consumer magazine *Which?* The first years of the 1950s offered hints of emerging affluence but not the effective

4

reality of prosperity. (Hence the celebrity status of Lady Docker with her gold-plated Daimler.)

Just as in *Brideshead Revisited* (1945) Evelyn Waugh recalled a longed-for splendour during the hardships of war, so in the early fifties the continuing effects of deprivation are revealed in similarly indulgent depictions of the good life. Readers of C. P. Snow's *The Masters* (1951) would envy the gluttonous routine of Snow's Cambridge dons, who enjoyed astonishingly large and persistent appetites. Snow proffers a catalogue of lunches, suppers, High Table dinners, presentations of bottles and offers of morning Madeira, all of which conveniently provide occasions for arguments about college business which must have been conducted in an atmosphere of hungover indigestion. If conspicuous consumption is partly excusable as a by-product of Snow's plot, a desire for excess is central to *Room at the Top*. Although the novel was published in 1957 – and has been regarded as depicting the new materialism of affluence – John Braine began to write it in 1952, and it evokes the mood of prolonged austerity. Here, for example, Braine's hero, Joe Lampton, drools at the sight of a dodgily procured party buffet:

> There was lobster, mushroom patties, anchovy rolls, chicken sandwiches, ham sandwiches, turkey sandwiches, smoked roe on ryebread, real fruit salad flavoured with sherry, meringues, apple pie, Danish Blue and Cheshire and Gorgonzola and a dozen different kinds of cake loaded with cream and chocolate and fruit and marzipan.

But this would be frugal fare in the world of Ian Fleming's James Bond, who rose to stardom after the publication in 1953 of *Casino Royale*, where he first displayed his enviable familiarity with ultra-expensive exotica. 007 was licensed to spend.

If the social conditions of the late forties did not improve miraculously during the early fifties, neither had new talents yet appeared to disprove the well-established theory that this Welfare State was hostile to quality art. On 29 August 1952 the *TLS* carried a special survey of young authors: the depressive tone of the various articles had hardly changed from the accounts of two years before. As one commentator admitted, the topic of the present supplement might seem odd because no inspired and inspiring young talents seemed to be around. Articles on current poetry and drama concluded that a few individual poets were doing reasonably well and that there were no new playwrights. The article on younger prose writers, 'Uncommitted Talents', managed to cite fourteen competent or promising authors but none gave cause for real celebration. The age-limit for qualification as a 'young writer' had to be raised to a generous forty; two of these new talents, Angus Wilson and Doris Lessing, described themselves as middle-aged in 1955.[1] Wilson and Lessing would now be regarded as prominent exceptions to the rule that the late forties and early fifties produced no face-saving new major writers, but although both were well reviewed, neither made a decisive enough impression to effect a literary revival single-handed.

The same is true of William Cooper, whose *Scenes from Provincial Life*, published in March 1950, is often thought to have inaugurated a distinctively 'fifties' fiction. Despite puff reviews from Cooper's friends, C. P. Snow and Pamela Hansford Johnson, and several favourable shorter notices, *Scenes from Provincial Life* made a very limited impact at the time. Cooper compares a novel's usual reception to the effect made by a stone thrown into the sea: a few ripples are visible but they vanish all too quickly.[2] *Scenes from Provincial Life* may seem to have escaped this fate – John Braine, Malcolm Bradbury and Kingsley Amis have all said that the novel made a deep impression on them – but Cooper, like contemporary observers, remained unaware that a few ripples were still spreading. The immediate reception of *Scenes from Provincial Life* is described in its sequel, *Scenes from Married Life* (1961); here Cooper's fictional *alter ego*, Joe Lunn, is disappointed by the poor sales of his novel in 1950 and cannot be consoled by his friend's curious prophecy that the book will be acknowledged as seminal in years to come. In any case, 'William Cooper' was neither particularly young nor new to the literary world in 1950: he was a forty-year-old writer who had already published four novels under his own name, H. S. Hoff. Hoff adopted his pseudonym mainly to protect people he knew from any attempts to identify the supposed 'originals' of characters in *Scenes from Provincial Life*, a novel daring for its time in mentioning pre-marital sex and homosexuality. Hoff's precaution proved unsuccessful. *Scenes from Provincial Life* was read with dismay by one young woman who believed she was identifiable as Myrtle, Joe Lunn's lover. When she learnt that Myrtle would reappear in a sequel, fear for her reputation led her to threaten an injunction for libel. A fortnight before publication in 1951 *Scenes from Metropolitan Life* was withdrawn and the career of 'William Cooper' suffered a depressing setback.[3]

Unaided by hindsight, the author of 'Uncommitted Talents' could find no signs of real inspiration. S/he had to adopt the manner of someone whistling in the dark to stay cheerful: 'it is possible to feel a genuine enthusiasm for much that has been written since the war, and to recognize at the same time the checks and hesitations that limit the achievements of our young writers.' Still, the conclusion had to be faced: this was 'a difficult and confusing decade'. Confusing mainly because the fifties, in depressingly marked contrast to the thirties, had yet to be defined by a distinctive new trend or school of writing. The introduction to the *TLS* surveys of 1952 bore a headline that was only too apposite – 'A Generation In Search Of Itself'. With no new impulses in sight this article had to be devoted to more explanations for the rarity of new authors. One theory was that the war and socialism had destroyed the networks through which promising talents had once started successful literary careers. The congenial encounters in London squares and country houses were no longer possible, the days of the literary hostess had gone; the successors of Lady Ottoline Morrell and Lady Colefax would now be 'far too busy at the sink' to introduce young poets to benevolent editors of literary reviews.

Even the reintroduction of cheap domestic labour would not have improved young poets' chances for there were very few editors around, benevolent or otherwise; *Horizon* and *Penguin New Writing* were only the two most distinguished of the magazines to disappear before 1950. Paper shortages and the harsh economic climate had seen off many other periodicals, including the *New English Review*, *Politics and Letters* and *Polemic*. In 1950 an observer lamented, 'literary periodicals are dropping like November leaves'.[4] A couple of younger writers resorted to self-help. Dannie Abse edited the short-lived *Poetry and Poverty*, and another young poet, Jon Silkin, began his own magazine, *Stand*, in 1952 when he was sacked from his job as a lavatory cleaner. Silkin received a day and a half's holiday pay which he used to subsidize *Stand*'s first issue of four hundred copies.

In rather different circumstances from Silkin, John Lehmann

returned to literary editorship two years after the closure of *Penguin New Writing*. This new contract was with the BBC where he had been appointed editor of a Third Programme series, *New Soundings*. Lehmann said he intended his radio anthology to 'rescue creative writing from a dying-off of literary magazines that threatened to become a total extinction'.[5] There were twelve programmes in the series, which ran from 9 January 1952 until 11 March 1953. *New Soundings* was enthusiastically reviewed and thought within the BBC to be a resounding success, but Lehmann's anthologies could only reflect the sorry state of English letters. The recurring themes of his editorial introductions were the current literary stagnation and writers' distressing prospects. In the preface to his first broadcast, he blamed the false post-war peace, the country's ruined economy, and the threat of nuclear destruction for preventing the development of fresh talent. He spoke of recent young writers suffering the literary equivalent of 'bud blast'; promise and potential were just not being realized.

It seemed inevitable that Lehmann should rely on well-known, older authors for contributions to *New Soundings*. In his last programme he stated that he took particular pride in his promotion of Edith Sitwell, George Barker, Vernon Watkins and Charles Causley during the series. Only the thirty-five-year-old Causley could possibly qualify as a representative of the new writers Lehmann alleged he had also been proud to present. Significantly, that final editorial was followed by a contribution from the thirties surrealist poet, David Gascoyne, and a dramatized extract from Philip Toynbee's experimental novel, *The Garden to the Sea*.

The unfortunate truth was that *New Soundings* had revealed how little invigorating new work was being written in the early fifties, especially about contemporary life. There had been often dramatic social adjustments since the war, but most established novelists seemed oblivious of the fact. One exception was Evelyn Waugh, but uninformed readers of his 1953 novella *Love Among the Ruins* would have wondered how dramatic those social changes had been. The ruins are those of England in the near future, an utterly joyless country ruled by complex hierarchies of bureaucrats working for an all-powerful State which has exterminated the old values and traditions. Christmas has become 'Santa-Claus-Tide' when children sing 'old ditties about peace and goodwill', and strikers return to work to qualify for their seasonal bonus. Waugh's 'hero', Miles Plastic, works in the uniquely flourishing Department of Euthanasia. Among the eager customers of this addition to the National Health Service is Parsnip, a poet who made his mark in the thirties. Parsnip eventually reaches the refuge of the gas chambers to rejoin his friend Pimpernell, erstwhile supporter of the Left Book Club, who had seen the errors of his once-radical ways and was lucky enough to be an earlier 'patient'.

Waugh's outlook may be jaundiced but at least he was prepared to deal with post-war society in his fiction. Other established novelists appeared to cultivate the art of avoiding the present. The vogue was for evocations of a more amenable past, often the Edwardian era of the writers' childhoods. L. P. Hartley, Nancy Mitford, Rosamond Lehmann, Anthony Powell, Angela Thirkell – all were specializing in nostalgia. In drama as well as fiction a cherished setting was the country house, symbol of the good old days of prosperity and stability and servants. More disturbing still was the willingness of young writers to revel in the same anachronistic conventions: 'The paddock and fire-lit nursery, the tweedy homespun aunts, the curate's bicycling mishap, the rebel's brush with the vicar ... it is all too familiar,' sighed one exasperated critic.[6]

By the early fifties impatience with country house conventions was growing. The *Observer*'s young theatre critic, Kenneth Tynan, embarked on a critical crusade against 'Loamshire' plays, and a handful of other writers began to show a similar reaction against the fiction of refined nostalgia. One of these was Angus Wilson, whose collections of short stories – *Such Darling Dodos* (1949) and *The Wrong Set* (1950) – were notable for depicting current social changes, particularly as they affected a section of the middle class, the '*nouveaux pauvres*'. In his criticism Wilson began to attack the country house school and call for novelists to come to terms with the new realities of the Welfare State.[7] Pamela Hansford Johnson was another who condemned the escapism of post-war novels; like Wilson, she associated these novels of 'specialized sensibility' with the self-indulgences of Modernism, thinking that readers had been alienated by work which had been boringly experimental as well as socially irrelevant. The 'prestige side' of English fiction had been diverted from the mainstream and lost its readership to the 'popular entertainment side'.[8]

Wilson and Hansford Johnson shared this reaction with two other reviewers – J. B. Priestley and C. P. Snow. Snow was taken on as a book reviewer for the *Sunday Times* at the end of 1948, replacing the woefully bland Charles Morgan. Snow was not yet very well-known as a novelist, but he had impressed the *Sunday Times* Literary Editor, Leonard Russell, when they met at the Savile Club. Russell admired Snow's forceful opinions, especially after reading a summary Snow had prepared of his anti-Modernist views. Russell took a chance and appointed Snow as a lead reviewer in the hope that he would provide a much more vigorous column than Morgan. He was not disappointed. For four years Snow contributed fortnightly reviews which regularly lambasted the 'moment-by-moment' novelists who, at great cost to their work he thought, had ignored traditional forms and that hallowed figure on the Clapham omnibus, the 'ordinary cultivated reader'.[9] Another middlebrow spokesman, J. B. Priestley, expressed similar anti-Modernist opinions in various magazines and newspapers. For example, a review of *Dubliners* for the *Sunday Times* on 2 January 1955 gave Priestley the chance to write off *Ulysses* and *Finnegans Wake*; these works marked the end of experiment and anyway Joyce's style was nothing special – 'gems choice in fuchsia yaws' was Priestley's off-the-cuff demonstration of how easy it had all been.

To these anti-Modernists, James Joyce and Virginia Woolf were primarily responsible for 'prestige' literature losing its way. *Finnegans Wake* was the culmination of obscure and arid experiment, while Woolf's novels maintained the tradition of genteel impressionism. Angus Wilson thought Woolf had not only failed in her formal experiments but also failed to overcome her snobbery; evidence for the prosecution could be found in the condescending portrayals of working-class characters like Mrs Levy in *The Years* and the self-improving Charles Tansley in *To the Lighthouse*. The Woolfian sensibility was all the more regrettable to Wilson because he saw it becoming adulterated and hackneyed; the contemporary descendants of Mrs Ramsey and Clarissa Dalloway could be found in the novels of Elizabeth Bowen and Angela Thirkell, or even in the character of Mrs Miniver and in the clichéd values of 'high-class women's magazines'.[10]

To complement these revaluations, Wilson, Hansford Johnson, Priestley and Snow all tried to replace the literary values of sensibility and experiment with ones which embodied social relevance and entertainment value. Angus Wilson looked to the examples set by the Victorian novelists and Priestley valued the comic tradition of Fielding and Dickens; Pamela Hansford Johnson tried to relocate the true English tradition in the middlebrow novels of Priestley, A. J. Cronin and C. P. Snow. In his reviews for the *Sunday Times* Snow promoted the work of novelists who favoured more traditional, realist forms of fiction – William Cooper, Doris Lessing and Thomas Hinde.

There were signs, then, of changes in the climate of literary opinion in the early fifties as several writers spoke out against conventional assumptions. However, most of the literati were, by contrast, still very anxious to find a new, experimental avant-garde. Suddenly, in April 1953, an announcement was made that the decade had produced a distinctive new literary trend. To the dismay of many members of the older generation it seemed that this would not be the kind of exciting new group which they had awaited so keenly, but one which shared the views of J. B. Priestley & Co.

The impresario for the new writers was John Wain, a busy young man-of-letters – academic, critic, poet and novelist-to-be – and the stage he found for his show of young talents was a radio series on the Third Programme, *First Reading*. Wain had become known in the BBC as a contributor to *New Soundings* when he impressed John Lehmann and the series producer, P. H. Newby. Now, in one of the BBC's tactlessly performed reshuffles, he was chosen to replace the aggrieved Lehmann and briefed by Newby to liven things up by selecting young contributors. He took this instruction to heart, and in his introduction to the inaugural broadcast of *First Reading* on 26 April Wain made it clear that he would in fact be promoting a certain kind of young writer. His policy was going to be open bias in favour of a trend he detected among his contemporaries of 'consolidation' after experiment, writing which was more traditional in form. To disgruntled fans of Modernism 'consolidation' was a euphemism for 'regression'. Wain opened *First Reading* with a contribution which he thought best represented his preferences, a long extract from a 'novel in progress' – Kingsley Amis's *Lucky Jim*.

Wain repeated his aims in *First Reading*'s third broadcast on

1 July. He was so keen to advertise his young contributors (among whom were Geoffrey Hill, Donald Davie and Philip Larkin) as leaders of a new generation that he invoked the newspaper cliché, inspired by the recent coronation, of a 'new Elizabethan era'. But his announcement had a feeble peroration: 'At the moment there is a quite widespread feeling among young writers, and particularly poets, that the decks are going to be cleared and a special effort made.'

Wain's statements and his selections now incited Hugh Massingham, in the *New Statesman* radio column, to attack what he thought had been 'deplorable broadcasts'. Massingham was incensed by the idea of enthusing about what he saw as the dreary safety of 'consolidation'. The following week (25 July 1953), he lamented the loss of John Lehmann's *New Soundings* and advised the less gifted Wain to include foreign writers in place of the dull talents he had presented so far. His conclusion was emphatic: '*First Reading* ... will, I fear, only convince the average listener that modern writing is a bore.'

Massingham's hostility was not shared by others if only because, as Wain commented in the 30 July broadcast, reviewers either misunderstood his intentions or ignored the programmes altogether. He thought his efforts to publicize a new emphasis in current writing had failed; in his opinion 'no manifesto had ever cut less ice' than his editorials. Wain therefore tried in this fourth introduction to define more clearly the kind of literature, particularly poetry, which he wanted to promote. Introducing poems by Burns Singer, Dannie Abse and others, Wain stated that he was advocating verse which rejected the sociological fashion of the thirties and the 'loose romanticism' of poets in the forties. The closest he came to specifying distinct characteristics was to repeat his bias towards writing which 'roughly speaking ... involves discipline and detachment rather than luxuriance and emotionality'. Of John Wain's many talents, cutting ice with manifestos was apparently not one.

Although these announcements were less than clear, other attempts to define what was now being accepted as a new literary fashion began to appear in the correspondence columns of the *New Statesman*, where arguments were brewing over Massingham's remarks. On 1 August, the poet and critic G. S. Fraser rallied to the defence of *First Reading*. He was not entirely keen on

Wain's idea of consolidation but he still spoke up on behalf of the young contributors – understandably enough, since he was one of them. Noting the occupations of Amis, Davie and Wain himself, Fraser described his *First Reading* colleagues as being 'most typically . . . young dons, and often young dons in provincial universities', who 'think metropolitan urbanity rather hollow and metropolitan smartness rather vulgar'. Fraser's letter made a crucial contribution to the promotion of a new trend at a moment when it was badly needed, because after the sixth broadcast on 24 September Wain was replaced as editor of *First Reading* by the reliably unperturbing Ludovic Kennedy. Fraser not only supplemented Wain's vague literary definitions with a set of social characteristics but provided the material for a literary controversy into the bargain: the opposition he outlined between young provincial academics and suave metropolitan men-of-letters sparked off heated exchanges in the *New Statesman*. It was the first real literary dispute of the fifties, and like many literary disputes before and since, in its meandering progress resembled nothing so much as a badly supervised classroom debate. First John Lehmann stepped in to deplore 'provincialism' in literature as a 'blight', then Fraser replied by citing George Eliot, John Bunyan, Thomas Hardy and others as fine provincial writers; other correspondents sounded off about the merits or demerits of writers being academics, the London literary scene, the difference between 'dons' and 'lecturers', how much or how little lecturers should be paid, and then there was the inevitable letter parodying other letters as the arguments were wound up. Finally, V. S. Pritchett reflected on the whole affair in the *New Statesman*'s section on the season's books in his 3 October article, 'First Stop Reading!'.

The only clear conclusion was that 'metropolitan' and 'provincial' were literary adjectives loaded with prejudice but little definite meaning. Was 'provincialism' part of the 'provincial tradition'? What were 'metropolitan' literary values? If academics opposed the metropolitan literati, were Oxford and Cambridge provincial centres? The disputants had used the key terms of the debate in the cavalier manner of Humpty Dumpty: 'When *I* use a word . . . it means just what I choose it to mean – neither more nor less.' The result was that, as Donald Davie said, 'Half-a-dozen different quarrels seemed to be going on at the same time' and they finished only in 'a flurry of innuendo'.[11]

Still, the quarrels over *First Reading* had strengthened the impression given by Wain that a new literary generation was about to make its mark. On 16 October George Scott took up the theme in *Truth*, claiming he detected among his contemporaries

> a profound feeling that amounts almost to knowledge that a literary renaissance *is* about to take place, or is taking place now, in Britain. There is a great urge towards creative expression, an impatience with the verbose outpourings of sterile criticism. There is a belief that this creative drive will find new things to say; if not new things then at least old things worth saying again and important to the times in which we live.

It looks as if Scott was just struggling for good copy that week. However, he was able to be much more specific in response to a letter from Stephen Spender who said he had failed to find any 'flowers' among the 'ruins' of the *First Reading* scripts. On 30 October Scott again followed Wain's lead in predicting that the new writers would reject the formal experiment of their predecessors but prove to be their equals nonetheless. Scott went on to provide his own list of these future luminaries: A. Alvarez, Kingsley Amis, Arthur Boyars, Charles Causley, Hugo Charteris, Hilary Corke, Donald Davie, Iain Fletcher, G. S. Fraser, W. S. Graham, Thom Gunn, Thomas Hinde, Elizabeth Jennings, Iain Scott-Kilvert, Francis King, James Kirkup, Philip Larkin, Derek Lindsay, Mairi MacInnes, Jean Morris, John Raymond, W. W. Robson, Paul Scott, Richard Sleight, Sydney Goodsir Smith, Desmond Stewart, Frank Tuohy and John Wain. Again the influence of *First Reading* was obvious. Many of Scott's names – such as Fraser, Graham and Hinde – were already quite well known, and the newcomers in his list – Amis, Larkin and Mac-Innes, for example – had been presented by Wain on his radio series as unknowns. The list also reveals the variety of the contributors to *First Reading*. There was, *pace* G. S. Fraser, no 'typical' *First Reading* author – only a small minority, led by Wain himself, fitted the provincial and academic specifications. The inclusion of writers like Geoffrey Hill, Jon Silkin and Burns Singer in the series also guaranteed a range of aims and styles which explains why Wain had difficulty in defining the group identity.

George Scott had written his earlier article to complain that none of these new talents had been included in the first issue of

Encounter, co-edited by Spender and Irving Kristol. This appeared in October 1953, to be followed by the launch of the *London Magazine* in February 1954. Only now did it appear that English letters might recover from the epidemic of closures which had hit literary magazines in the late forties. The revival of the London literary scene was in fact being financed from two very unlikely sources – Daily Mirror Newspapers Ltd., whose chairman, Cecil King, sponsored the *London Magazine* as a 'useful piece of do-gooding' at the suggestion of Rosamond Lehmann (and appointed her brother John as editor), and the CIA, which funded *Encounter* under the cover of the 'Congress for Cultural Freedom'.[12] In March 1949 Spender wrote in *Horizon* that the best literary periodicals gave young writers the chance to be noticed alongside their elders; however, neither the *London Magazine* nor *Encounter* seemed at all inclined to provide this service. John Lehmann started, as he was to continue, by relying on established contributors and the *London Magazine* soon became known as ideal reading for those who enjoyed literary memoirs. As for *Encounter*, Spender stated in the second, November 1953 issue, that it would be the magazine's policy *not* to publish the young contributors to *First Reading*. His article was titled 'On Literary Movements', but it was the most recently arrived movement which occupied his depressed attention. The new group consisted, he thought, of writers-cum-lecturers who regarded literature as merely part of the curriculum, 'teachers who equate literature with sanitary engineering'. Spender detected the dark hand of F. R. Leavis manipulating puppets striking attitudes of 'provincial puritanism'. It was 'a rebellion of the Lower Middle Brows' and Spender, for one, would not be supporting it.

The surprise is that he could be so detailed in his prejudices by the end of 1953, for he could not cite any individual authors or publications as examples. Although many of the most significant contributors to *First Reading* had been writing and publishing poetry, fiction and criticism since the late forties, they were still starting out on their careers and their work had appeared mainly in outlets which could not have attracted critical attention, such as private presses. R. A. Caton's Fortune Press in London published, among others, Larkin's *The North Ship* (1945) and his first novel, *Jill* (1946), as well as Amis's booklet of poems, *Bright November* (1947). There was also the Fantasy Press run by Oscar Mellor from his home in Eynsham, near Oxford. Between 1952 and 1954 Mellor produced twenty-six eight-page pamphlets of verse, mainly by students or ex-students of Oxford University, including Larkin, Amis, Elizabeth Jennings, Geoffrey Hill and George Steiner.[13] Some of them had found a national audience on *New Soundings* (which broadcast poems by Donald Davie, Thom Gunn and John Wain among others) before Wain advanced the idea on *First Reading* that his contemporaries had some kind of collective identity. But six months after the series ended, *First Reading* was still the only available point of reference in the controversies started by Wain's declarations. This was the first literary group to have been promoted on the airwaves rather than in print; as a result, public awareness of this group preceded public recognition of individual works belonging to it.

Because examples of the new prose were even harder to find, it was the new poetry which first prompted reviewers' attempts to make their own generalizations about the trend Wain had been advertising. Of the characteristics originally described by G. S. Fraser, the 'academic' label became firmly attached to descriptions of the fashionable poetry. On 10 July 1953 the *TLS* reviewer of the *Springtime* anthology followed the editorial comments of G. S. Fraser and Iain Fletcher in singling out Amis, Wain, Alvarez and Davie as young poets who shared an 'academic mind'. The description appeared again, nearly a year later, on 2 April, when the *TLS* reviewed Fantasy Press pamphlets by Thom Gunn, Anthony Thwaite, Arthur Boyars, Donald Davie, Jonathan Price, Philip Larkin and Kingsley Amis; the critic saw the worrying prospect that the best poetry in England would be 'written by dons for dons'.

From 1953 headquarters of the promotion campaign for the new poets was the *Spectator*, which had acquired new personnel for its literary pages. J. D. Scott was appointed Literary Editor, where he joined the young Anthony Hartley who had become, in effect, Poetry Editor. Hartley had known Wain, Larkin and Amis at Oxford and had had a short story broadcast on the fifth of Wain's *First Reading* programmes. Encouraged by Scott, he began to secure regular contributions from the young writers he knew and admired and did his best to give their books favourable reviews, often at the expense of established figures. He also helped Wain and Amis to become the *Spectator*'s principal book reviewers.

Hartley's efforts meant that the *Spectator* was soon identified as *the* magazine for fashionable new writers: on Christmas Day 1954 a contemptuous *New Statesman* carried a spoof advert for its rival, satirizing the stridently youthful new look of the *Spectator*'s literary pages. One young writer who benefited from Hartley's activities was Philip Oakes; Hartley praised his first booklet of poems, *Unlucky Jonah* (1954), and helped him to find work on another magazine, *Truth*. Oakes was struck by the 'slight and bespectacled' Hartley's relish for the mischief of literary infighting: 'he made no attempt to disguise his glee when a malicious paragraph in the *Spectator* irritated some venerable elder. And when we met now and then for a drink he would hint at great plans afoot to create further embarrassment and upset.'[14]

Hartley found the best way to publicize the new poets was to group them together in general reviews. His first promotional survey, 'Critic Between the Lines', appeared in a hostile review of Edith Sitwell's *Gardeners and Astronomers* published in the *Spectator* on 8 January 1954; here he heralded the arrival of 'young academic poets' like Amis and Davie who were 'ironic, intellectual, rigorous, witty'. His second attempt at literary copywriting was published on 27 August, when he advertised his friends as the new literary generation – the 'Poets of the Fifties'. He claimed that these 'young university poets' shared a common social and cultural outlook, egalitarian and influenced by Leavis in an opposition to London literary circles. As before, though, Hartley relied mainly on Wain's *First Reading* contrast between the new poets and the poets of the forties. It was a useful and provocative technique – both Hartley's articles made further publicity for the new writers, with the *Spectator* publishing a selection of irate letters to the editor.

The technique also served to conceal the fact that there was still no definite membership of the new school; Hartley had managed to add only Wain and Gunn to his second list after naming Amis and Davie in the first. The problem was that too many young writers could be enlisted in the ranks of the new poetry. The literary specifications were too vague and the poets' work too thinly spread for Hartley to pick out the most suitable from the contributors to *First Reading*, the Fantasy Press series and the *Spectator*. He had had to draw up the briefest of lists and hint at other candidates, and this nebulous group had not yet been given a definitive label. Hartley had tried the 'University Wits' and the 'Metaphysicals', Donald Davie suggested the 'new Augustans', and the 'Empsonian' tag was also enjoying a brief currency.[15]

However, the identity of this new tendency changed when commentators began to discuss its fiction. John Wain's *Hurry on Down* is usually taken to be the first example of the new fiction, but it was not hailed as such when it appeared in October 1953; it had to wait until after the publication of *Lucky Jim* in January the following year to receive the attention of the pundits. Helped by its *First Reading* reputation, Kingsley Amis's novel was the first individual work to be noticed as a product of the new writing. Arguments about the group could now contain at least one specific reference. This development can be seen in the ultimately farcical correspondence in the *Spectator* in January and February 1954, following Hartley's article 'Critic Between the Lines'. Hartley's strategy of writing off 'forties' poets like Edith Sitwell in order to forward the new poetry had incited an indignant reply from his most prominent victim. Sitwell derided 'Little Mr Tomkins' or whoever was the latest fashionable poet of the week. Hartley was defended by John Wain and Elizabeth Jennings, and a pseudonymous 'Little Mr Tomkins' who made a facetious attack on Sitwell. In her third letter on 19 February Sitwell conceded one shared opinion with Hartley and that was an admiration for *Lucky Jim*, a 'most remarkable, most distinguished first novel'. The following week Amis replied that a writer beginning his career could not hope for such generous praise; adding that he should also point out that in fact he was 'Little Mr Tomkins'.

Lucky Jim entered the debate on a more serious level after Walter Allen in the *New Statesman* and George Scott in *Truth* identified Jim Dixon as a representative new hero and compared him with Charles Lumley of *Hurry on Down*.[16] When Iris Murdoch's first novel, *Under the Net*, appeared only four months later in May the critics were only too eager to shove it into the same pigeon-hole; if the similarities of two novels had been worth comment, the addition of a third was enough to establish a definite trend. 'In fiction the fashion is now for the picaresque eccentric,' wrote John Raymond in the *New Statesman*. Three weeks later, on 26 June, the *New Statesman* carried J. B. Priestley's announcement that the 'New English Novel is now emerging'. Priestley assumed that the coherence he perceived was not the product of a common manifesto, but proved that 'the *Zeitgeist* is at work'. While he did not name any individual writers, it is clear that he had Wain, Amis, and particularly Murdoch in mind, as he extracted details from *Under the Net* for his own account of the new anti-heroes. The influence of Murdoch's novel explains Priestley's choice of a London setting for the new literary type, but other critics persevered with the established assumption that the new fiction was provincial. Anthony Quinton, for instance, described the heroes of Wain and Amis as sporting a regional accent, and Spender's misgivings about the value of 'novels of provincial life', which he had assumed existed from the *First Reading* broadcasts, were repeated in August 1954. Wain's own Potteries background and the setting of *Lucky Jim* were enough to confirm Spender's worst fears: young novelists were regressing to realism and writing about the 'provincial North of Arnold Bennett, or about the Red Brick Universities'.[17]

'Provincial' had become the catchword to describe the new fiction just as 'academic' was the accepted label for the new poetry. The characteristics which had been bandied about in 1953 were still being applied a year later, however haphazardly and irrelevantly, in the attempts to see a definite coherence. However, these different accounts of current verse and prose were still bringing confusion rather than clarity, and an acceptable membership and label for the grouping both seemed even more difficult to find.

The various problems and confusions were overcome – or rather ignored – in another *Spectator* article about the new writing. J. D. Scott's anonymous literary leader, 'In the Movement', appeared on 1 October 1954, proclaiming the change in literary fashion: 'Who do you take with you on the long weekends in Sussex cottages? Kafka and Kierkegaard, Proust and Henry James? Dylan Thomas, *The Confidential Clerk*, *The Age of Anxiety*, and *The Golden Horizon*? You belong to an age that is passing.'

The importance of Scott's effort at identifying the new trend did not lie in his own description of the young writers' attitudes or in the moderately provocative tone he adopted. Nor did he supply an authoritative list of writers – he named only Davie and Gunn as poets and the obvious trio of novelists. Instead he gave the group a label which was to stick. Previous tags had been too exotic and too specific. The 'donnish new Augustans', the 'more-or-less Metaphysicals' and the 'provincial', 'picaresque' novelists were all accommodated in one title which had to be as bland and inclusive as possible. Scott had not invented the idea of a new movement, but he *had* invented the 'Movement'. His contribution was a capital M.

Looking back on his article and the heated arguments it provoked, Scott was inclined to dismiss his 'frivolous little piece' as 'a Madison Avenue promotion'. He wrote the article to liven up the literary pages of the *Spectator*, whose editor, Walter Taplin, had asked for more sensational content to halt a fall in circulation. Scott decided to follow up Hartley's 'Poets of the Fifties', and to include the latest novelists as well. He had not been trying to address posterity: 'I had an idea for a box of fireworks – fireworks that would startle with a sudden coruscation, cause a gasp, illuminate a wide scene momentarily and perhaps deceptively, and of course die at once and be forgotten.'[18] The effect was quite different, but Taplin could not have asked for better short-term results. There was yet another lively literary correspondence in the *Spectator* which published letters from, among others, Evelyn Waugh, G. S. Fraser, and a postgraduate student named Malcolm Bradbury. Like most of the correspondents, two young poets, Anthony Thwaite and Alan Brownjohn, were anxious to deny the existence of Scott's 'Movement'. Such objections were to have little effect; the idea, and now the label, of the group had arrived to stay. From now on the arguments over the Movement would be about not the validity of the grouping but its literary worth.

The Movement aroused only disappointment or hostility in such contemporaries as Dannie Abse and Jon Silkin, and in many older writers too. Spender, for example, feared the new writers were too 'complacent', John Lehmann scorned the value of 'consolidation', and Cyril Connolly thought the new breed of academics had failed to rescue English writing from the doldrums.[19] To these commentators the 'new Elizabethans' had yet to arrive. Pessimism especially about the state of English fiction continued regardless, culminating in the *Observer*'s 'death of the novel' symposium. The debate began on 29 August 1954 with Harold Nicolson arguing that 'the age of fiction is dead', a proposition which, after years and years of such obituaries, seemed just a bit clichéd. Nevertheless the topic was discussed in following weeks by Philip Toynbee,

Alan Pryce-Jones, Louis MacNeice and Edwin Muir. Some critics obviously still took gloomy pleasure in bringing news of the novel's imminent demise. 'Fiction, by general consent, has become the "Sick Man of Literature",' wrote John Raymond in May 1955; the novel would shortly suffer the same fate as 'the ballad, the Nō play and the Greek hexameter'.[20]

But Raymond had to admit that others were proclaiming the new vitality brought to English fiction by younger novelists. The writers who had earlier criticized Modernist and 'country house' writing were welcoming the arrival of new authors who had answered their call for a return to traditional forms and contemporary social material. On 10 October 1954 in the *Sunday Times* Priestley repeated his claim that Movement novelists had shown that the English novel was 'Alive and Kicking': 'Not only is the Novel not dead but it offers us now a livelier show of new talent than other literary forms.' Writing the same month in the *London Magazine*, Angus Wilson said that his own preferences for the virtues of observation, characterization and social setting had come back into favour; he even felt the reaction against experiment and sensitivity had gone too far. No such qualification was made by C. P. Snow. On Boxing Day 1954 in the *Sunday Times* Snow applauded the 'quiet and effective counter-revolution' against the 'novel of total sensibility' and selected *Lucky Jim* as a welcome replacement for 'obsolete' works of 'mindless subjectivism' such as (almost inevitably) *Finnegans Wake*. Others also expressed support for the new tendency at the expense of the older generation. To risk using the terms of a *Spectator* article published on April Fool's Day 1955, support for the 'New Provincialism' seemed to mean rejection of 'Bloomsbury'. Both T. R. Fyvel and J. D. Scott, for instance, praised the batch of newcomers for showing older writers that it was possible to deal imaginatively with contemporary society.[21]

A generation gap had appeared in the English literary scene. Philip Oakes's contention that the new writers were radically different from their predecessors was relatively commonplace by the time his article on 'A New Style in Heroes' appeared in the *Observer* on New Year's Day 1956. He described the contrast between the two generations by comparing two pairs of representative figures: Wain and Amis versus Lehmann and Spender. Having paid lip-service to the particular, Oakes devoted the rest of his article to a series of sweeping statements. He claimed that the new 'movement' in writing was more widespread than was usually believed, and extended it to include 'Theatre, film and television critics, mostly around thirty'. (Presumably he had in mind people like Kenneth Tynan and the film director and critic, Lindsay Anderson.) Even more confusingly, he hinted that this 'movement' might or might not be identifiable with the *Spectator*'s 'Movement'. But he was adamant that publicity had not created the group: it 'merely drew attention to its existence'. These (unnamed) 'like minds' publish in the same magazines and journals but 'deny allegiance to any kind of school'.

Oakes's generalizations show that there were still very few writers who could be confidently named as Movement members. The limited number of authors J. D. Scott had instanced as being 'In the Movement' in October 1954 was not really supplemented during the following year. William Cooper had occasionally been added retrospectively to the 1954 triumvirate of Wain, Amis and Murdoch. D. J. Enright was briefly included as a new provincial novelist by a few reviewers of *Academic Year* in 1955 – despite the novel being set in Egypt. The appearance of this fourth 'provincial' novel had in fact persuaded reviewers like the resolutely unimpressed John Raymond that the new trend had already declined into the predictability of convention.[22] But Enright's status as a Movement writer was still uncertain and his name was not used regularly afterwards in 1955 and 1956 in general surveys of the new writing.

In fact, the growing emphasis on current fiction meant that the number of regularly named representatives of the new generation actually dwindled in 1955; Davie and Gunn, for example, two of Scott's five Movement names, were no longer listed by other commentators. More significantly, Iris Murdoch had begun to lose her representative status: the appearance of *The Flight from the Enchanter* in 1956 marked the end of her reputation as a leader of the new literary generation. Pundits had to rest content with *Under the Net* as a significant 'fifties' work and treat subsequent novels by Iris Murdoch simply as novels by Iris Murdoch.

Final membership of the Movement would be decided by anthologizers. The critics missed the first collection of Movement writers, since D. J. Enright's *Poets of the 1950s* was published in Japan where Enright was teaching English. He consulted Robert

Conquest about which poets to include and settled for eight contributors: Kingsley Amis, Donald Davie, John Holloway, Elizabeth Jennings, Philip Larkin and John Wain, as well as Robert Conquest and himself. Meanwhile Conquest was preparing his own anthology of Movement poems. He added only Thom Gunn to Enright's selection, and when *New Lines* was eventually published by Macmillan in July 1956 the nine contributors were accepted as the official members of the Movement. Anthony Thwaite, Philip Oakes, Jonathan Price and other potential candidates would be remembered as allies or associates of the 'genuine' Movement writers.

A year earlier, though, it looked as if the Movement needed a recruiting drive, for at that time it had only two obvious members – John Wain and Kingsley Amis. Even this pairing looked vulnerable after both authors published their second novels in the summer of 1955. Unlike *The Flight from the Enchanter*, neither Wain's *Living in the Present* nor Amis's *That Uncertain Feeling* was taken as an upsetting departure from their first works. However, Wain's reputation suffered with his second novel, a trite and lacklustre effort which, in his own words, received 'savage attacks or contemptuous dismissals' from its reviewers.[23] *That Uncertain Feeling* fared much better and on the whole avoided the disappointed comparisons which are a common fate of the eagerly awaited second novel. Amis had consolidated his reputation, and his prominence increased throughout the following year as *Lucky Jim* continued to provoke heated reactions, with the result that he was coming to represent the Movement on his own.

By the beginning of 1956 there were signs that the arrival of the Movement was starting to be reported to a relatively large audience. Previously, the proclamations and debates had reached only the smaller readership of the quality magazines and periodicals. Oakes's *Observer* article and the controversy over *Lucky Jim* in the *Sunday Times* (see chapter 4) helped to give the Movement a greater public presence. A feature on Amis by Daniel Farson then appeared in the *Evening Standard* on 4 May. But such interest from a popular newspaper was still very rare; as Edmund Wilson remarked, the impact which even Amis had made was on 'the higher level of British journalism'.[24] At the beginning of May 1956 the publicity which the Movement attracted was generally of the same degree as had existed two years earlier when J. B. Priestley put the initial controversies into perspective: 'Compared with the vast ballyhoo of mass communications, all this may seem on a very small scale indeed, a tiny flurry in the review columns and the bookshops.'[25]

Nor had the Movement made an overwhelming impact even within the literary world. Claims by writers like Philip Oakes that a definite coherence had emerged and that this 'movement' was widespread seemed increasingly contentious. The social identity of the new generation established by G. S. Fraser was still current in descriptions of the group as 'academic' and 'provincial', but the number of its reliably mentionable representatives had slumped to one or two. In the absence of another manifesto after Wain's *First Reading* introductions, the literary identity of the grouping also remained very vague and depended on assumptions of some kind of opposition to older, established writers. The leading literary critics of the older generation were reacting in turn by discounting the importance of the group.

The result was that on 14 April 1956 it was still possible for Rayner Heppenstall to write in the *New Statesman* that the young authors would not be able to displace the literary image of the decade established earlier; with more than half the decade already passed, Heppenstall thought the fifties would still be associated with the nostalgic literature of an older 'Right-wing orthodoxy', 'a butlers' and antique-dealers' cult of gracious living and more spacious ages'. He also predicted that 'The names of Mr Wain and Mr Amis are unlikely to figure in the stereotype. If, individually, their work comes to anything and, even more, if they become *chefs d'école*, they will be claimed by the Sixties themselves.' The arrival of the Movement had neither transformed the literary scene nor, in the opinion of those like John Lehmann, revived it. In his foreword to the May 1956 issue of the *London Magazine* Lehmann was still looking for a new writer or a new group to reinvigorate English writing: 'It is difficult not to feel that the present is a moment of peculiar confusion in literature, with the impulses of twenty, or even ten years ago fading out, and no new impulses of sufficient force and inspiration taking their place.'

2

'The Angry-Young-Man Club'

In May 1956 startling 'new impulses' suddenly appeared with the force which John Lehmann had been looking for. Within three weeks of each other, two unknown authors in their mid twenties arrived with first works which were to transform the literary scene. The débuts of John Osborne and Colin Wilson sparked off extraordinary media interest which placed young writers in the forefront of public life. The hype involved controversies, scandals, and the creation of a definitive literary image for the decade – the Angry Young Man.

Look Back in Anger is usually remembered as the work which started this sequence of events, but it was Colin Wilson's book *The Outsider* which first enjoyed decisive acclaim when it was published on 28 May. The opening night of *Look Back in Anger* on Tuesday 8 May, has understandably been regarded as a turning-point in the history of English theatre, but at the time it hardly seemed such a momentous event. Osborne's play was selected as one of the new works for the first season of the English Stage Company, at the Royal Court Theatre in Sloane Square. The ESC's Artistic Director, George Devine, looked on John Osborne as a real find, but neither the first-night critics nor the public showed any great enthusiasm for his play. It seemed likely that it would be taken off after its initial three-night run. The play's prospects revived on Sunday 13 May, when Kenneth Tynan hailed it in his *Observer* review as 'the best young play of its decade' and claimed that Osborne was 'the first spokesman in the London theatre' for the young generation. Tynan's eulogy and the flop of Ronald Duncan's *Don Juan* and *The Death of Satan* helped to reinstate *Look Back in Anger* for another three performances, starting on 24 May. Business at the box-office was still slow, however, and Osborne was indebted to the perseverance of George Devine who fitted in two week-long runs of the play in June, despite the fact that it was still failing to break even.

While Osborne was making a precarious start to his literary career, Colin Wilson enjoyed a wonderfully successful début with *The Outsider*. With hindsight, his success seems much more surprising than Osborne's lukewarm reception. Considering the feeble condition of English drama, the rarity of vehement new talent such as Osborne's, and the relatively prestigious staging of his play, an eager welcome might have been anticipated for *Look Back in Anger*. No such expectations were held for *The Outsider*; Colin Wilson was completely unknown and his book appeared to be a forbiddingly recondite study of literature and philosophy about the human condition. That Gollancz offered it as a trade book was surprising enough. But the acclaim for *The Outsider* was immediate and sensational. The book was a tremendous critical and financial success, making such an impression that the popular press at once took a keen interest in the astonishing new writer. Colin Wilson was launched on a brief but heady career as the media's very own celebrity philosopher, a startling prodigy who could be lauded by intellectual critics and gossip columnists alike. Coverage of Wilson's début led *The Times Educational Supplement* to remark on 13 July that the daily papers had evidently begun to 'poach' on traditionally highbrow territory. The comment was premature. This press attention was not so much a lightning raid as the start of a full-blown invasion.

Back at the Royal Court, interest in *Look Back in Anger* had been growing slowly and not very surely. But by the second week in July the signs were that the play's fortunes were about to change. This was the result of an unintended masterstroke of arts publicity – the invention of the literary catchphrase of the fifties, the 'Angry Young Man'. It is usually assumed that the creator of this slogan will remain forever anonymous, like the originators of jokes or football chants. The conventional account is that the catchphrase was somehow inspired by the Christian writer, Leslie Paul, who had published an autobiography of that title in 1951. In fact, the phrase was 'invented' by the Press Officer of the Royal Court Theatre, George Fearon, who was having great difficulty in publicizing *Look Back in Anger*, a play he loathed. Quite inadvertently, he came across the promotion gimmick he badly needed when a journalist asked for his opinion of John Osborne. Fearon replied, rather despairingly, that he supposed the new playwright was 'a very angry young man'. The chance remark caught on and Osborne suddenly acquired a glamorous reputation in the press as an enraged protester and rebel.[1] The first major promotion of the tag, though, was by Osborne himself when interviewed on BBC TV's *Panorama* on 9 July. On the assumption that both writers were spokesmen for the young generation's social protest, the interviewer, Malcolm Muggeridge, asked Osborne and George Scott (whose autobiography, *Time and Place*, had just been published) about their views on class and culture in the Welfare State. Scott denied that he was 'angry', but Osborne preferred to dither: 'You see, if one recognizes problems and one states them, immediately people say – oh this is an angry young man.' It would still be a while before *Look Back in Anger* found assured financial success, but Osborne's *Panorama* interview had brought him and the new catchphrase to the attention of a wide public – and more journalists.

Struck by Osborne's new reputation and Colin Wilson's spectacular reception, a young freelance journalist, Daniel Farson, decided to write about the latest young writers. In two features published in the *Daily Mail* on 12 and 13 July, Farson announced that literature's 'Post-War Generation' had suddenly emerged. It was a classic example of a journalist being in the right place at the right time; Farson had already developed a friendship with Colin Wilson after happening to meet him the day *The Outsider* was first acclaimed, and had just written his feature on Amis for the *Evening Standard*. Having noticed the growing interest in *Look Back in Anger*, Farson arranged for Osborne and the eighteen-year-old Michael Hastings (whose first play, *Don't Destroy Me*, was about to open at the New Lindsay Theatre) to attend Wilson's celebration party. Hastings got into a fight and was sick and Mary Ure, who was playing Alison in *Look Back in Anger*, drank a great deal of the host's brandy and informed him that Osborne was a far superior writer. Unabashed by the results of his social introductions, Farson then grouped Osborne, Wilson and Hastings, plus Kingsley Amis, together in print as a new 'movement'.

In his introductory article he chose to take a disparaging view of the new literary 'generation'. His main angles were the regrettable emphasis on squalor in 'kitchen-sink' writers like Amis, and the baleful influence of James Dean's 'rebel without a cause' image on the plays of Osborne and Hastings. He was much more enthusiastic in the second article where he proclaimed the advent of a young genius in Colin Wilson. He also reported that the new prodigy disliked *Look Back in Anger*, just as Amis disliked being compared with Osborne. Nevertheless, Farson managed to give the general impression that the four writers were leaders of a new literary group – and to show his colleagues that profiles of the new authors as spokesmen of the post-war generation could make good copy. A fortnight later, on 26 July, the *Daily Express* responded with a rival feature by John Barber, who recalled Fearon's catchphrase and described the same four writers for the first time, and for no good reason, as the 'Angry Young Men'. Barber's starting-point was to compare the new authors with George Bernard Shaw, since the feature appeared on the centenary of Shaw's birth. The outcome was a forced and entirely unconvincing suggestion that the 'Angry Young Men' were reviving the spirit of Shavian iconoclasm. Following Farson's example, Barber depicted the AYM as vaguely non-U and hostile to gentlemanly culture and convention.

In the July issue of *Books and Bookmen*, Peter Forster added Osborne to the Movement duo of Wain and Amis, thinking that the three writers forwarded the same 'prototype-hero', a lower-class, left-wing scholarship student who sneered at upper-class authority. In Farson's and Barber's profiles, however, the new AYM group had no firm identity and its features tended to be determined by whichever new writer was being discussed. Consideration of *Look Back in Anger* led Farson to portray the new generation as cynical and self-pitying, without political or religious beliefs; Barber's focus on Colin Wilson produced a picture of the AYM as Bohemian enemies of the bourgeois. Only the sense that the group was vaguely lower-class seemed certain.

But middlebrow newspapers had discovered that these 'Angry' writers carried definite news value as indefinite representatives of a new Welfare State generation. Two years earlier J. B. Priestley had attacked the popular media for ignoring young writers who as a result could no longer find an effective public presence.[2] Now that situation was changing dramatically: soon Fleet Street editors were eagerly seeking articles by and about these angry young authors. The press coverage was all the more remarkable for being based on the importance of the new writers' works. Authors as such are very rarely seen as newsworthy; if they attract popular press interest at all, it tends to be as vaguely recognizable highbrow figures who have got up to Bohemian antics, or won a prize, or died. The literary foundation of the media's initial interest in the AYM can be appreciated by observing the more conventional qualifications for newsworthiness acquired by two other writers who hit the headlines in June and July 1956 – Brendan Behan and Arthur Miller.

Behan first suffered the attentions of Fleet Street after appearing on *Panorama* on 18 June to discuss his play *The Quare Fellow*. Behan's contribution to the programme was somewhat limited since he was incoherently drunk. It was a performance which won him immediate notoriety. Despite the efforts of a BBC spokesman to convince reporters that the unfortunate interviewee had merely been 'extremely nervous', the truth came out when Behan happily admitted that he had had several too many. A protest to the BBC from the Church of England Temperance Society and front-page headlines the following day in the *Express*, the *Mail* and the *Herald* were the results. The press coverage of Arthur Miller during his visit to Britain in the summer of 1956 for the opening of *The Crucible* at the Royal Court, had even less to do with his literary status. Despite the controversy Miller could have attracted in his own right, as a current victim of the House Un-American Activities Committee, he was lauded by Fleet Street only as 'Marilyn's Boy', the lucky man who was to become 'The new Mr Monroe'.

The creation of the Angry Young Men coincided with the culminating promotion of the Movement when Robert Conquest's *New Lines* anthology eventually appeared late in July. During the following months, reviews of the anthology continued to debate the merits and significance of the Movement. Profiles of Larkin, Wain and Gunn (as well as Christopher Logue for contrast) appeared in *The Times Educational Supplement* in July and August. In his *Encounter* review of *New Lines* in October, David Wright noted the ascendancy of the Movement on the Third Programme and in the 'booksy periodicals and newspapers', and the general welcome the Movement writers had received from 'the London literary racket'. Wright concluded that 'There hadn't been anything like it since Mr Deeds came to town', but the impact the Movement had made within literary circles was now being overshadowed by the far greater publicity campaign for the Angry Young Men.

The result was a confusing shift in literary fashion in the latter half of 1956. In September the Scottish commentator, W. A. S. Keir, viewed the recent changes in London's literary world with bewilderment. He acknowledged that the 'apocalyptics' of the forties appeared to have been replaced by the Movement, but it seemed that the whims of literary chic had soon ended the prominence of these 'Cambridge wits' as well. Now Osborne, Wilson and company were all the rage.[3] By the time of Keir's survey there were two very different accounts of contemporary writing in circulation. In highbrow periodicals the Movement was still being treated as the only new group of the fifties; in a *TLS* survey of 'Experiment in Prose' on 17 August the terms of reference were those established in discussions of the Movement. When Stephen Spender described Osborne as an 'Angry Young Man' in 'Notes from a Diary' in the August *Encounter*, the label remained in the singular. Richard Wollheim's account of the 'new conservatism' in the October *Encounter* ('Old Ideas and New Men') still took only Amis and Wain to be the prominent new authors.

In Fleet Street memories as well as deadlines were much shorter. In fact, as far as the newspapers were concerned, the Angry Young Men had not even replaced the Movement; for a journalist like Daniel Farson the highbrow debate about the Movement might as well never have existed: the post-war generation 'suddenly arrived' with the appearance of Osborne and Wilson. In his first *Daily Mail* feature Farson mentioned in passing that Amis was a leader of the only new literary 'movement', but this vague reference to the Movement was carried no further. By September he had simplified this version of post-war literary change to produce a conveniently striking chronology: 'Immediately after the Second World War no one of importance appeared on the scene. Ours really does seem a Lost Generation in so far as it never emerged at all. Only now, with people like Colin Wilson and John Osborne . . . has the new post-war generation arrived.'[4]

The Movement had not made a definitive impact and after so many years of waiting for a distinct and inspiring new generation, announcements such as Farson's were far too appealing to be questioned, especially in the popular dailies where literary copy had to be presented as sensationally as possible. On 4 September the *Daily Express* presented Wilson and Hastings as members of 'The Angry-Young-Man Club', with an excited introduction designed to banish any thoughts that these writers were a bunch of boring highbrows: 'A bright, brash, and astonishingly bitter new crop of Angry Young Men has pushed up into the London scene this year; writing plays and books bristling with fresh if feverish ideas and opinions.' On the same page Hastings obliged his unlikely patrons by announcing that he was indeed very angry – about working conditions for tailors. (Hastings was an apprentice tailor at the time.) An article by Colin Wilson followed ten days later, and then Osborne contributed a feature to the *Express* on 18 October, titled 'The Things I wish I could do . . . by the Theatre's Bright Boy'.

It was an appropriate headline because *Look Back in Anger* had just received an invaluable boost when an excerpt was broadcast by the BBC on 16 October. Nearly five million people watched the programme. The broadcast alarmed directors of the English Stage Company, for they assumed it would kill the show. They prepared to take *Look Back in Anger* off the stage, but the chairman, Neville Blond, persuaded them to keep it on. As it turned out, of course, the BBC excerpt finally assured a widespread public awareness of *Look Back in Anger* and new interest in the play was reflected by the great increase in business at the box office. Several weeks later, on 28 November, *Look Back in Anger* was televised in full when it was networked at peak viewing time on ITV by Granada (with a tantalizing warning before the programme that the play used 'very direct language'). ITV also screened a play by Ted Willis that same week; the two programmes led the disgruntled television critic of the *Sunday Times* to remark: 'In the electronic theatre it was benefit week for the Angry Young Men.'

Considering the date of this second broadcast of *Look Back in Anger*, it is very tempting to see the rise of the AYM as part of a reaction to the current political crises. 1956, like 1968, has become one of the key post-war years – momentous, even mythic, the year of a cultural and social watershed.[5] The myth of '1956' centres on the fiasco of the Suez Crisis which began in earnest on 31 October with the British and French military action against Egypt. The attempt to reclaim the Suez Canal, which had been nationalized by Colonel Nasser, was to end in humiliation for the Prime Minister, Anthony Eden. In a week which also saw the Russian invasion of Hungary, it became clear that Britain's gunboat diplomacy would have serious long-term effects. 'Suez' has become a powerful catchword, evoking the end of Britain's delusion of global importance, the loss of Britain's opportunity to exercise a moral leadership in playing Greece to America's Rome, or the shattering of the Butskellite consensus in domestic politics.

The emergence of the AYM at roughly the same time as the Suez Crisis has led those who mistake wishful thinking for self-evident truth to claim the young writers rose up in protest against the 'Establishment'. One recent account, for example, has presumed that 'The Angry Young Men . . . opposed the Suez campaign, since it represented for them the mindless and bullying arrogance of the Conservative ruling class.'[6] In more considered commentaries the AYM have been treated as a myth which was created to express the feelings aroused by events in Hungary as well as Suez, or a group which was rescued from an imminent slide towards obscurity by finding an obvious target for political rage.[7] Actually, neither the writers labelled as AYM, nor their media coverage, were noticeably affected by the Suez Crisis. That image and reception would probably have been the same if the invasion had never happened. For a start, any claim that the AYM were seen as active opponents of the Establishment after Suez, or even manufactured symbols of protest and discontent, has to come to terms with the fact that the writers themselves did not offer any conspicuous protest. Nor were they assumed to do so. Granted, Osborne does portray the decline of post-imperialist England in *The Entertainer* and Jean Rice does attend the anti-Suez rally in that play, but Osborne's views and reputation were much less 'political' than this suggests. Colin Wilson and Michael Hastings had even less informed interest in current social and political issues than Osborne; Hastings' political analyses were confined to his diatribe about working conditions in the rag trade, and Wilson preferred grand utterances about forming a new civilization based on religious awareness. Kingsley Amis went so far as to attend a Labour Party meeting after Suez, but his own reaction in print was to play down the effects of the affair on English intellectuals. (Amis's reluctance to proclaim a more definite commitment was attacked by the then left-wing Paul Johnson.)[8]

Just as the 'Angry' writers did not openly oppose the Suez campaign, no views were developed at the time which ignored this and promoted them as rebels inspired by Suez. The AYM did not receive any crucial impetus from the Suez débâcle because journalists did not at first connect the literary fashion with the political aftermath of the invasion. As a result, when Marshall Pugh declared in the *Daily Mail* on 13 December, 'This Is The Year Of The Angry Young Men', he had to make a series of general announcements about the young generation all over the planet looking for new values and ideals, a search apparently led in this country by John Osborne. Pugh had to see the new generation as apolitical, and made only one reference to Suez as an affair which would convince young people that the older generation could get itself into a bit of a muddle now and again.

In any case, public and press reaction to the Suez Crisis was not simply the outrage at the Government's disastrous venture which hindsight likes to assume; Suez appears a much more potent cause of disillusionment and protest in retrospect than it was at the time. Initially, popular feeling seems to have been very much in favour of Eden's initiative. Then, after the Labour Party decided to denounce the invasion and the anti-Suez rally was held in Trafalgar Square on 4 November, opinion polls reflected party loyalties rather than any more sweeping condemnation. This is revealed in the fact that the two quality newspapers which opposed the government's handling of the crisis – the *Manchester Guardian* and the *Observer* – both suffered a marked drop in circulation. The one popular newspaper which came out against the Government – the *Daily Mirror* – lost 70,000 readers as a result. Most of the popular dailies eagerly supported the attempt to teach Nasser a lesson. And it was in these newspapers that the AYM had been promoted, and continued to be promoted after Suez. Considering the pro-Government line taken especially by the *Daily Express* and the *Daily Mail*, any assumption that the AYM represented a Suez-linked sense of protest would surely have counted against them. When more jaundiced accounts of the AYM began to appear in 1957 they were reactions to, or part of, the publicity process itself, not politically motivated recriminations.

By the end of 1956, then, the media interest in the AYM was still founded on the sensational portrayals of a few writers as representatives of post-war youth. Beyond this, the identity of the group was still wonderfully vague, for the AYM had as yet attracted publicity, not attempts at analysis. This had given the new grouping the appearance of a large membership; already by 25 August 1956 Nancy Spain was writing in the *Daily Express* that

'There have been enough Angry Young Writers discovered this year to sink an aircraft carrier.' However, towards the end of the year only Osborne, Wilson and Amis, and possibly Hastings, could be named as young Angries. The promotion of the 'group' in the popular press also meant that coverage could be based on the cult of just a few personalities. Osborne and Wilson both seemed particularly eager to provide Fleet Street editors with reliably contentious material and were now installed as favourite *enfants terribles* of the popular press; they had graduated from being mere authors to fully-fledged media celebrities. Osborne was voted the most controversial 'personality' of the year, alongside Liberace, Yul Brynner and Diana Dors. In the *Sunday Times* 'Atticus' listed Wilson's *The Outsider* and the Angry Young Men as two popular fads of 1956, a nomination which placed book and group together with skiffle, records of *My Fair Lady*, and tortoiseshell-tinted hair.[9]

Osborne and Wilson soon learned that life in the media limelight had its drawbacks. Colin Wilson was the first to suffer derisive press coverage when scandals about his private life broke in the gossip columns in December 1956. This was the first real sign that his meteoric rise to fame was going to be followed by an equally spectacular downfall. (An account of Wilson's brief spell as an accident-prone celebrity is reserved for chapter 7.) Popular newspapers took a more prurient interest in Osborne as well when he filed a petition for divorce in February 1957. In those less permissive days, when a desire for smut had to stop well short of soft-core pornography, divorce suits were given regular and prominent coverage by the popular dailies – these cases were, to use a favourite adjective of the *Daily Sketch*, 'sexational', especially if a participant was already well known. Osborne's divorce petition received front-page attention in the London evening papers on 27 February and eight column inches in the *Express* the next day. Rumours about his relationship with Mary Ure were also surfacing in the *Daily Mail* and the *Evening Standard*. When the couple were married on 11 August 1957 gossip columnists reported the event under banner headlines.

Although these stories were obvious intrusions into Osborne's private life, they did help to sustain his public presence and to advertise his second play, *The Entertainer*, which opened at the Royal Court on 10 April, the day after Osborne was granted his divorce. With his uncanny knack for self-advertisement, Osborne had become a press officer's dream. George Fearon was having no difficulty at all with advance publicity for *The Entertainer*, especially after it was announced that the leading role was to be taken by the greatest celebrity in the English theatre, Sir Laurence Olivier. (Such was Olivier's popular fame in the mid-fifties that there was even a brand of cigarettes named after him.) It was a bold step for Olivier to ask to play the lead role of Archie Rice, and one that meant that the opening night of *The Entertainer* would be a media event. Both the *Express* and the *Mail* devoted half of their third pages to the play's first performance, with both carrying large photographs of Olivier as the faded music-hall comedian. (The *Express* stole a march on its rival by commissioning its pictures from the fashionable society snapper, Anthony Armstrong-Jones.) Publicity for *The Entertainer* continued when it started its second run at the Palace Theatre on 10 September. Three days later, for example, an article about 'obscenities' in 'Sir Larry's Play' was the leading item on the first page of the down-market London evening paper, the *Star*.

Fleet Street's literary craze brought an unprecedented degree of publicity to other young authors in 1957. One writer whose career was obviously changing as a result was Kingsley Amis. Before 'Anger' began to be hyped, Amis's books had received a good deal of attention, but from sections of the media – the Third Programme and the quality Sundays – which would be expected to take an interest in literary developments. By the beginning of 1957, though, Amis found that a work which might otherwise have received only passing highbrow attention, his Fabian pamphlet *Socialism and the Intellectuals*, had been given a great deal of popular press coverage. Amis became even better known after the film of *Lucky Jim* was released in September 1957. Another writer whose work found an unexpected reception at this time was Richard Hoggart. On 21 February the *Daily Herald* included a lead review of his book *The Uses of Literacy*, labelling him an 'angry young man' to ensure readership interest. This was followed the next day by a quiz-cum-questionnaire, inspired by Hoggart's book and intended as a survey of contemporary social attitudes.

With such publicity it is not surprising that the Angry Young Men found fortune as well as fame in 1956 and 1957. Indeed, as far as Osborne and Wilson were concerned, their royalties were so remarkable that these became the topic of more stories, although they were liable to exaggeration. Osborne recalled that he made £300 in the first six months from *Look Back in Anger*, but one report had him earning a sum one hundred times this figure.[10] Certainly *The Outsider* had already made Colin Wilson a wealthy man by the end of its first year and *Lucky Jim* went through eighteen impressions in its first three years. Plans for a film of *Look Back in Anger* were also well under way by January 1957. In his *Encounter* 'Diary' for March, Stephen Spender was able to note that the AYM's earnings were far greater than those of the thirties writers when they were young and could be better compared with the wealth gained by the young Noël Coward.

The financial benefits of the AYM label became even clearer after John Braine's first novel, *Room at the Top*, was published in March 1957. Any account of the contemporary reception of *Room at the Top* has to be a case of life imitating art. Here, after all, is a book dominated by its hero's desire for wealth and luxury, which made its author rich and famous. A success story indeed, and one which Braine had worked long and hard to find. He first tried his hand as a freelance writer in 1951 when he gave up his job at Bingley Public Library and moved to London. He published a few poems and articles and had a verse drama, *The Desert in the Mirror*, performed in Bingley. The play flopped badly, then Braine fell ill and was admitted to hospital suffering from tuberculosis in January 1952. He spent a year and a half in Grassington Sanatorium and it was there that he returned to work on a novel which he had been encouraged to write by his agent, Paul Scott. An early draft of the novel, then titled *Born Favourite*, had already been rejected by the *New Statesman*'s Turnstile Press, and when Braine tried again with the rewritten version in 1955 it was turned down by four more publishers. Paul Scott finally had the novel accepted by Eyre & Spottiswoode where the managing director, Maurice Temple-Smith, took it on despite a great deal of opposition.[11]

Temple-Smith's judgment was vindicated when reviewers seized upon *Room at the Top* as a work which was firmly in the literary fashion. In the *Evening Standard* Richard Lister announced: 'Mr John Braine steps right up beside Kingsley Amis and John Osborne as a leading member of the new school of young writers.'[12] Other critics agreed. Here was a realistic novel with a contemporary, provincial setting about an aggressive young lower-class character, so both Braine and his hero, Joe Lampton, were automatically categorized as Angry Young Men. That reputation and the relatively frank sex scenes in the novel brought *Room at the Top* to the attention of reviewers in popular newspapers; the *News Chronicle* critic combined both features in labelling Braine one of the 'Lecherous Young Men'.[13] Once again, though, it was television coverage which really mattered. Twelve thousand copies of *Room at the Top* were said to have been sold as a direct result of Woodrow Wyatt's interview with Braine on *Panorama* on 8 April.

Just as the *Evening Standard* took a special interest in John Osborne (as a London-based playwright who guaranteed good copy for the gossip column), so Braine received particularly enthusiastic coverage as 'the new apostle of success' from capital-ism's dedicated publicists, the *Daily* and *Sunday Express*.[14] The first feature on Braine in the *Daily Express* appeared on 23 March, only days after *Room at the Top* was published. A second article followed on 13 April in preparation for the newspaper's forth-coming serialization of the novel. The feature dropped Braine's Angry reputation and concentrated on angles more suited to the Beaverbrook philosophy – 'sex and success'. The first excerpt from *Room at the Top* appeared in the *Daily Express* on 22 April, under the caption 'Ambition and women: Right to the end it was to be explosive stuff!' For ten days half a page of the *Express* was devoted to extracts from Braine's novel.

As *Room at the Top* became a bestseller journalists transferred their attention from Joe Lampton's story to Braine's own rags-to-riches tale. (The novel still came in handy, though, if only for its title: 'It's cash, cash, all the time for the man at the top'; 'Mr Braine finds life good at the Top'.[15]) The *Daily Express* commis-sioned Braine's account of his early struggles as a writer and *Reynolds News* carried three articles by Braine about his 'Way to the Top'. The *Express* gave details of his first prosperous Christ-mas, and readers of *Books and Bookmen* were assured that des-pite his winnings Braine still bought his pyjamas from Marks and Spencer.[16]

By the time of Braine's arrival, the personal notoriety of Osborne and Wilson and the still-growing interest in their 'group' meant that the AYM had become such a familiar part of mid-fifties life that the *Daily Mail* could have their cartoon adventurer, Flook, spend a month as a Bohemian Angry. (Flook's rebellious phase began on 26 March and ended on 24 April when he decided that he had had enough of life as a 'displeased nonelderly male'.) Another indication of the general impact made by the leading Angry Young Men is the appearance of their books' titles as slogans and headlines. The change of title of Braine's novel turned out to be opportune, for adverts were currently claiming that 'Top People Take *The Times*'; 'room at the top' came to signify social mobility, the quest for money, status, power. Two books dealing with the 'Establishment' in 1959 took their titles from Braine – James Leasor's *War at the Top* and Clive Jenkins' *Power at the Top*. At the other end of the social scale Noel Woodin's novel about Bohemian poverty was called, with a stunning absence of originality, *Room at the Bottom* (1960). Occasionally this social and political emphasis was retained in the media use of the title catchphrase; as early as 27 April 1957 a Vicky cartoon appeared in the *New Statesman* showing a queue outside an emigration office with the surtax class climbing up a ladder to a window marked 'Room at the Top'. For the most part, though, the title became merely a recognizable pattern of words, a convenient headline for features on subjects from football (there was 'Very Little Room at the Top' of the First Division in 1959) to fashion (comfortable collars and shoulders in the Balenciaga Collection of 1958 offered 'Room at the Top').[17]

Sub-editors also took a liking to the other AYM titles. *Look Back in Anger* was particularly useful for any piece involving reflection or summary. Surveys of the year at the end of 1956 included 'Look Back in Sorrow', 'Looking Back in Anger', and 'Look Back in Calmness'.[18] *Lucky Jim* could be applied as a headline to any story involving good or bad fortune, especially if it involved someone whose first name was James or just abbreviated; even the new Prime Minister, Harold Macmillan, managed to acquire an Amis-based nickname as 'Lucky Mac'. So well known was Amis's novel in the mid-fifties that its title was used for the back pages of popular papers. A *Daily Mail* report about England cricketer Jim Laker missing a chance to repeat his record haul of wickets against the Australian team was headlined 'Anything But Lucky Jim'. When Sussex's Jim Parks made an unbeaten century after narrowly escaping an early dismissal, *Reynolds News* declared 'Lucky Jim punishes Kent'.[19] *The Outsider* actually expanded an entry in the *Oxford English Dictionary*; the established meaning of a person with little chance of victory was now accompanied by Wilson's coinage denoting an alienated artist or intellectual, which became a fifties catchword in its meaning of a social misfit, reject or rebel.

The most popular literary catchphrase of all was, of course, 'Angry Young Man'. A collection of exotically varied figures attracted the AYM formula; James Joyce ('Angry Young Dubliner'), J. B. Priestley ('The Mellow Old Man') and Algerian authors ('Angry Young Muslims') were only a few of those whose protest or lack of protest, youth or age, meant they were described in variations on what had rapidly become a very clichéd theme.[20]

When the AYM slogan reached the height of its press popularity in 1957, it seemed that almost any youngish contemporary author could be enlisted as a (temporary) member of the 'group'. Other writers who suffered Hoggart's fate included George Scott and J. P. Donleavy, as well as Colin Wilson's two friends, Bill Hopkins and Stuart Holroyd. John Osborne complained that the AYM label was even pinned to Nigel Dennis, 'the most charming, kindest and mildest of men, who is over forty and the father of teenage children'.[21] The necessary qualifications for AYM-hood were conveniently vague and various. Youth (Michael Hastings), a non-upper-class background for either the novelist or his main character (Braine), and if not social protest something that promised something like it (Hoggart, Donleavy) could all mean an AYM classification that was sure to enliven an ailing article or review. Nor could publishers always complain about the slogan's misuse. Macmillan cannily promoted John Wain's books with display cards which announced, 'John Wain Is *Not* An Angry Young Man'. The unfortunate Correlli Barnett was less respectfully treated by Wingate who released his first novel, *The Hump Organization*, in 1957 with a dust-jacket declaration that Barnett should definitely be added to the leading Angry trio of Amis, Osborne and Wilson.

These three remained the most frequently mentioned AYM throughout 1957, with Osborne the most prominent Angry of them all. This was reflected in the results of a *New Statesman* competition which required entrants to update Chaucer and describe an 'Angry

Young Clerke of Oxenford'; on 1 June the summary reported that 'Most of the Clerks were type-cast as Jimmy Porter, but a few Colin Wilsons and Lucky Jims crept in' (an account which also shows how authors and characters were being mixed up in the muddle). To Ritchie Calder in the *News Chronicle* on 13 August the 'professional AYM' were undoubtedly 'Kingsley Aimless, Colic Wilson and John Heartburn'. Discussion of the Movement had survived on only two generally agreed representatives in Amis and Wain. Now, with three figureheads, there was far greater publicity for the AYM and Amis found himself lumbered with a reputation as leader of another new literary trend.

A year after *First Reading* the Movement had acquired some sort of identity as a group of writers who came from the provinces, and taught in universities, and used traditional forms. Over a year after the first appearance of the AYM an even less certain collective image had emerged, with journalists conglomerating titles, slogans and reputations. Any literary hack stuck for a feature could always concoct something along the lines of the new rebels and outsiders who were looking back in anger but becoming lucky Jims when they married the boss's daughter and found there was room at the top.[22]

The one obvious characteristic of the Angry Young Men appeared to be a lower-class background. This was usually specified as lower-middle-class, but the addition of Braine's Joe Lampton often influenced commentators to describe the new writing as working-class. This development may have encouraged the more socially prejudiced accounts of the AYM hero as 'ill-mannered' and 'foul-mouthed', a 'literary hooligan', no better than a drunken 'educated thug'. Osborne's Jimmy Porter was considered to be nothing more than a Teddy Boy and he and Amis's Jim Dixon were said to present 'the shabby under-side of civilization'.[23] It was not very easy to maintain this line, if only because the new hero was also generally agreed to be on the make, venturing into higher social strata.

A popular opinion of the time held that this social-climbing had been sponsored by the Welfare State; these characters were 'products of [the] social revolution . . . who have been able to take advantage of the new educational ladder'.[24] Joe Lampton's vocational training might have deterred such generalizations but the biographies of Porter and Dixon seemed to sanction the view that the AYM heroes were graduates of the redbrick universities, and the most common account of the new heroes therefore placed them, in Tynan's phrase, as 'state-educated lower-middles'.[25] As such, they were presumed to be representatives of a new class which had apparently emerged from current social reform. J. D. Scott inferred that the fuss the writers had aroused was part of the 'screaming noise made by the stiff joints of England in taking another painful step towards social equality'.[26] (This opinion appeared to coexist quite happily with the view that the new writing articulated the attitudes of the young generation as a whole.)

Beyond this general consensus on the social background, and hence the social significance of the Angry Young Men, lay confusion and argument about the outlook of the group. What were the reasons and targets for these young men's anger? Some sort of class conflict was usually thought to be involved, but other explanations were offered as well; a few commentators even tried the H-Bomb as the underlying cause of this literary protest, a theory which merely shows the absence of any obvious common grounds for the writers' alleged rage. A *TLS* editorial decided that the latest literary fashion for 'fury and disgust' was 'largely unmotivated'. Similarly, other critics looked at Jimmy Porter's declaration that there were no 'good, brave causes left' and offered the ingenious explanation that, in an unexciting political and social climate, the AYM were angry about having nothing they could be angry about.[27]

It might seem strange that commentators did not solve their problems by questioning the validity of the AYM catchphrase itself. The capacity for independent lateral thought was evidently rare, though, and the anger of the literary young was taken for granted. Instead, the lack of obvious reasons for anger from writers who had supposedly been pampered by the Welfare State led some unsympathetic journalists to see the AYM as spoilt, petulant, self-pitying; the post-war generation was 'so busy being sorry for itself and angry with other people', to a *Reynolds News* critic, and full of 'moaners' not protesters, to Christopher Chataway.[28] The undeviating ambitiousness of Joe Lampton made others, like V. S. Pritchett, see the AYM as out for what they could get rather than committed to any ideas of social reform: 'The irony is that the successful diffusion of socialist or welfare ideas in the West has created a generation consumed by personal quirks, suspicion and self-interest, and of people committed to themselves.' For Pritchett as for so many of his colleagues, the AYM label was simply too intriguing to be ignored. From the welter of opinions and explanations which it produced, an image emerged which more or less followed Pritchett's cliché-ridden account of the typical AYM character:

> the hero and his friends are half-working class. By state aid and the luck of the war they have gone from the grammar school to the university and from there to some anxious little job in the safe provincial civil service. They are still shut out from the world open to the richer public school boy – or so they think it necessary to believe.

He described the creators of such unadmirable specimens with a similar fidelity to received opinion:

> These novelists regard the Welfare State with cynical detachment, revel in the bad manners, the meanness, the slackness, the caddish behaviour and self-pity of their characters and have a chip on their shoulders. They like the limited horizon. Why (exclaim their elders) when the state has given them everything? They have been called the Teddy Boys of literature.[29]

The ill-fated climax of the AYM's contentious reputation as social rebels and protesters came when *Declaration*, an anthology of essays by some of the publicized new authors, was published by MacGibbon & Kee in October 1957. Although the editor, Tom Maschler, condemned the AYM label, *Declaration* was naturally assumed to be an anthology of 'anger', just as *New Lines* had presented the new poets of the Movement. It could hardly have come as a surprise to Maschler to find that *Declaration* was regarded as 'a manifesto of the AYM', providing an 'official' list of AYM membership.[30] In that case the 'official' Angry Young Men would be John Osborne, Colin Wilson, John Wain, Kenneth Tynan, Bill Hopkins, Lindsay Anderson and Stuart Holroyd, with one angry young woman, Doris Lessing. Kingsley Amis was missing from the line-up because he had rejected Maschler's invitation to contribute to the anthology, and in no uncertain terms:

> I hate all this pharisaical twittering about the 'state of our civilization' and I suspect anyone who wants to buttonhole me about my 'rôle in society'. This book is likely to prove a valuable addition to the cult of the Solemn Young Man; I predict a great success for it.[31]

It was a safe prediction. In contrast to the highbrow reception of *New Lines*, *Declaration* was guaranteed widespread media coverage as an AYM event. Advance publicity started on 16 August with a preview by the *News Chronicle*'s gossip columnist and continued with press coverage of the publisher's launch party. Although this was attended by celebrities like Rod Steiger and Nye Bevan, it attracted media attention mainly because of the growing controversy about John Osborne's essay, 'They Call It Cricket'. Osborne had produced a wide-ranging attack on contemporary English society. The Church, Fleet Street, the H-Bomb, theatre critics – all were targets for Osborne's vitriol, but it was his attack on 'the Amazing Windsors' which proved most provocative. The 'Royalty symbol . . . is dead', claimed Osborne, 'it is the gold filling in a mouthful of decay'.

Coming as it did at a time of press idolatry of the Royal Family, remarkable even by Fleet Street standards, it is only surprising that Osborne's essay did not create a greater storm of protest than it did. Two other writers who hinted criticism of the Queen at the same time each suffered a dramatic backlash. After Lord Altrincham offered a few objections to the Royal entourage in his *National and English Review* in August 1957, he received threatening letters and a well-publicized punch in the face. Malcolm Muggeridge was dropped by the BBC from his appearances on *Panorama* and sacked by the *Sunday Dispatch* when he made several tentatively critical remarks on the monarchy in an article in the American *Saturday Evening Post*. The result of Osborne's diatribe, on the other hand, was to increase his lucrative notoriety; the *Sunday Express* recounted his adolescent rebelliousness (he had slapped his headmaster) and gossip columnists reported the *Declaration* launch with the news that the English Stage Company had dissociated itself from Osborne's opinions and refused to host the pre-publication shindig.

Nor was *Declaration* adversely affected by Osborne's anti-Royalty remarks. Excerpts from several contributions, including Osborne's, were published in *Encounter* as well as *Tribune*. As for the reviewers, they tended not to focus their attention on Osborne's piece, but on the general quality of the anthology. James Cameron's treatment of Osborne as the leading exponent of controversial 'Angry Young Mannery' was also exceptional for admiring *Declaration* as a collection with a coherent and relevant sense of protest. Most critics rightly treated the anthology with disdain, regarding it as a hotch-potch of unformulated or misguided attempts at social analysis. The *TLS* reviewer valued *Declaration* only for offering 'a study of middle-class psychology formed in a declining economy', Henry Fairlie thought the protests were 'fundamentally reactionary', and Angus Wilson concluded that 'the total content is trivial'.[32]

Particularly as an anthology of 'Anger', *Declaration* was an unqualified failure. In fairness to Tom Maschler it should be pointed out that he did not present his contributors as members of a united movement and introduced the volume as 'a collection of separate positions'. However, from the muddle of opinions and schemes which littered the book it was clear that Colin Wilson, Bill Hopkins and Stuart Holroyd formed a quite separate faction, propounding the same very peculiar aims and attitudes which revolved around their notions of a religious existentialism. (The split between this trio and the other contributors was not difficult to detect since Tynan, Anderson and Lessing all attacked Wilson in their essays.) Whatever their thoughts on the anthology as a whole, reviewers were unanimous in panning the contributions of Wilson and his two colleagues. Unfortunately for Colin Wilson *Religion and the Rebel*, his sequel to *The Outsider*, was published at the same time as *Declaration*. The combined effects of the extremely hostile reception of his second book as well as of his *Declaration* piece meant that he was summarily dismissed from serious attention.

The pattern and timing of Wilson's rise and fall in the literary world reflected the changing fortunes of the AYM grouping in general. It had taken only seven or eight months for the press to turn from hailing the Angries as an exciting new band of literary rebels to holding them up as targets for ridicule and condemnation. By October 1957 the reaction was complete.

Despite its terrible reviews *Declaration* was still a commercial success; 25,000 copies had been sold by the end of the year and sales were further helped when the BBC's new television arts programme, *Monitor*, broadcast a discussion about the anthology on 16 February the following year. Nevertheless, it is hard not to agree with Daniel Farson's view that *Declaration* 'marks the death of the "Angry Epoch"', just as Blake Morrison sees the publication of *New Lines* as ending the effective coherence of the

Movement.[33] Certainly, the attacks on *Religion and the Rebel* as well as *Declaration* did encourage a wholesale revaluation of the AYM phenomenon; in the *News Chronicle* the disastrous flop of Wilson's book alone was enough for the books editor, Gerald Barry, to insert a stop press notice beneath Wolf Mankowitz's scathing review of 23 October: 'From now on, the phrase "Angry Young Men" will not be used on this page in any context whatsoever.'

3

'When the Angry Men Grow Older'

The Angry Young Men did not suddenly vanish after *Declaration*, but there was a dramatic decline in the literary prestige of the 'group', a decline which was reflected in the more sporadic and dismissive popular press coverage after October 1957.

Above all, *Declaration* had ended the illusion that the young writers offered coherent, committed social protest; even Osborne's republican outburst could not make Anger really convincing any longer. But rather than deride the original hype for the AYM, commentators preferred to retain the images of that hype and deride the AYM themselves for having sold out. This was easy enough; after all, just look at the money those young writers were making . . . In May 1958 David Watt noted in the theatre magazine *Encore* that 'It is hard, of course, to be angry on fifteen thousand a year.' The *Spectator* competition on 17 January 1958 was based on the already familiar assumption that 'The Angry Young Man has become Established' and invited readers to compose the laments of the once-rebellious authors. In Roger Longrigg's novel *Wrong Number* (1959), a musical adaptation of *Faustus* has Wrath appear as an AYM, now a 'plump middle-aged figure'.

One way or another, the AYM had lost their threatening reputations. The main challenge they now presented to literary commentators was that of accounting for such unprecedented public prominence. Critics began to look back on Anger to find explanations for the young writers' phenomenal success and their supposed rage. Even *Good Housekeeping* published a retrospective – James Gordon's 'Short Directory to Angry Young Men' appeared in the issue for January 1958. By then Gordon took it for granted that 'the uneasy concept of AYM has already served its purpose and is flying apart'. The first book about the AYM appeared as early as May 1958 when this post-*Declaration* period of reassessment reached its peak. Kenneth Allsop's study was called

The Angry Decade, but a chronologically more accurate title would have been *The Angry Eighteen Months*. Allsop himself had assumed he would be able to summarize the achievement of the AYM by the autumn of 1957, when he began to write his account. In an introduction added to the 1964 edition he reflected confidently that his book had not, after all, been premature: 'the angry school of fiction that seemed in the middle Fifties to cleave ahead into the far distance, inexorably decisive as the M1 . . . petered out in the mud of abandoned country.'

Now that the AYM had lost their way and their credibility, their previous success seemed all the more undeserved. Intellectual snobbery helped the *TLS* reviewer of *Declaration* to dismiss the AYM simply because of their popularity: the writers had co-operated with the media whose values they must have shared, and obliged journalists by exaggerating their 'contrariness' and supplying newspapers with articles and scandals. According to this critic, the publicity campaign had given the AYM's books the sales figures of mass-produced 'consumer goods' rather than the appropriately limited sales of 'prestige ware'.

How and why had such popular success been achieved? Few critics showed the gumption of J. G. Weightman who offered the simple and sensible explanation that Anger had been an 'advertiser's gimmick, provided free by the Press'.[1] This was a time for recrimination and soul-searching analysis and matters could not be allowed to rest at that. Now that the hunt was on for explanations, the AYM were often granted importance only as products of a social and cultural malaise which they had previously been supposed to be rebelling against. As their success came to be examined in this light, the opinion grew that the AYM had been promoted not because they were 'angry' but because they were 'young'.

The emergence of Osborne and Wilson had prompted anxious searches for other new talents. Even the BBC went out of its way to court young writers: in August 1957 the head of television drama, Michael Barry, invited a dozen young authors to a party to entice them into writing scripts for him. In October 1957 a new monthly magazine from Beaverbrook newspapers, *Books and Art*, was launched to cash in on the AYM's success. As it turned out, the launch was ill-timed and *Books and Art* folded after six monthly issues, but the initiative was a sign of the times. The first issue carried a competition to find new authors: 'A new generation of writers is taking over from the long established lions and stalwarts of the pre-war era,' it announced. Budding authors were offered £250, and other cash prizes, for works on the obviously fashionable theme of 'Living As I Do'. If young hopefuls failed to find success with this project, they could always turn to the opportunities given by New Authors Limited, a venture sponsored by the Hutchinson Publishing Group to discover unpublished novelists.

Disenchantment with this AYM-inspired vogue for young writers was increased by the current fad for spotting talents even younger than the Angries themselves. This press craze for the literary child-prodigy reached absurd heights in the latter half of 1957, thereby coinciding with the publicity surrounding the AYM. The two literary fashions were understandably regarded as interrelated at the time, but the prodigy craze had its own roots and could well have prospered without the additional impetus which the arrivals of Osborne and Wilson undoubtedly gave. The first prodigies of the fifties were, in fact, imported from France where '*l'époque des jeunes*' had begun in 1954 with the début of the nineteen-year-old Françoise Sagan. Fleet Street interest in Sagan began to grow after the English translation of her novel *Bonjour Tristesse* was published in May 1955, and peaked in 1957 and 1958 when her car crash and her marriage were front-page material. This newspaper publicity was mainly based on the fact that Sagan was an attractive young Frenchwoman, attributes which automatically signalled sex-appeal for the popular dailies. However, the 'literary' emphasis was much more evident in the coverage of the other prodigies who were too young to offer journalists more prurient angles for their features.

The prodigy craze began in earnest in England on 9 December 1956 when another French writer arrived in London to promote the launch of her book – the nine-year-old poet, Minou Drouet. Was she a genius? Were the poems genuine? Did she have a little boyfriend? The public had a right to know. Honours went to the *Daily Mail*, which discovered that Minou's hobby was solving algebraic problems and found 'The Boy Minou Left Behind'. The authenticity question was answered when Minou appeared on *Panorama* on 10 December and, in a closed room during the broadcast, produced a poem to order about her visit: 'London, my

fingers have turned your pages,/Like a disturbing fairy tale . . .'
began the on-the-spot translation. The interviewer, Richard
Dimbleby, was impressed. When he reviewed her *First Poems*
Peter Quennell thought, on consideration, that Minou was not a
genius but a sort of medium who had picked up poetic vibrations
from her adoptive mother.[2]

With the fashion for juvenile authors set by the French, English
adolescents had to be found who could string a few words
together. The first home-grown teenage author to arrive was Jane
Gaskell. Appropriately, it was the 'William Hickey' column which
scooped a warning to Sagan of her rival on 2 February 1957.
Gaskell was an elderly sixteen when her novel, *Strange Evil*, was
published in August, but the *Evening Standard* could still acclaim
her as 'the youngest of the young novelists who have lately sprung
into the limelight'.[3] Within a week of publication, *Strange Evil* had
sold out and Jane Gaskell had appeared twice on TV. Ten thousand copies of her book were sold by the end of the year, and plans
for a translation meant that the French would have a taste of their
own medicine.

Following young Jane's breakthrough, two other teenage girls
published children's pony tales in October – Lindsey Campbell
with *Horse of Air*, and Helen Griffiths with *Horse in the Clouds*.
'Where are the schoolboy novelists?' cried Amanda Marshall in
the *Evening Standard* on 15 October, but two male 'Angry Tinies'
were about to make their mark that month as well. Kenneth
Martin's *Aubade* and Michael Hastings' *The Game* (written with
the help of an Arts Council grant) could be added to the list of
adolescent novels.

Helen Griffiths recollects that the media interest in her book led
to several television appearances and an invitation to join the
newly-launched *Honey* magazine, together with Gaskell and
Martin. As Amanda Marshall said, 'Business is booming for the
under 21s' in publishing.' It was a boom which produced the
curious opportunity for *Books and Bookmen* to report that a
romance between Jane Gaskell and Kenneth Martin was languishing . . . because they were not allowed to stay out late at night.[4]

The prodigy fad was obviously rich material for satirists. Towards
the end of 1957, *Punch* published a series of skits on the pubescent
literati and a cartoon which showed a teacher explaining the high
level of absenteeism in her class: 'Three absent with 'flu, one

having a novel launched, and two swimming for England.' Not to be outdone, *Books and Art* carried Alex Atkinson's news that he had discovered his own 'Peckham Prodigy', Dympna Hardinge, three-and-a-half-year-old author of *What's For Pudding?*[5]

The ridiculous vogue for these 'Angry Tinies' only encouraged the post-*Declaration* reaction against the AYM. By the end of the year both the AYM and the adolescents were being lumped together in attacks by the media which had, in fact, created both of these literary fads. *Books and Bookmen*'s summary of the previous literary year in January 1958 reflected this reversal: 'We are tired of: Angry Young men: literary prodigies.'

The reputations of the AYM were further devalued when sceptics began to look at the earlier promotion as part of a more general cult of youth by the media, since the AYM had emerged just when Fleet Street began to publicize the appearance of a distinctive youth subculture. The first news of this had come with the press coverage (which amounted to another invention) of the Teddy Boy gangs in 1954.[6] However, the national press really started to notice the new youth when the film *Rock Around the Clock* was released in 1956. Shocked headlines reported 'riots' in cinemas throughout the country as youngsters danced to the film's anthem by Bill Haley and the Comets. Fleet Street heralded the arrival of a new phenomenon – 'teenagers' – and publicized their showbiz idols like James Dean, Elvis Presley and Tommy Steele.

Comparisons with these new stars had been made from the moment that journalists first publicized the AYM. In his first *Daily Mail* article on the 'Post-War Generation', Daniel Farson had likened Osborne and Hastings to James Dean; Hastings had dedicated *Don't Destroy Me* to Dean, and then there was the irresistible cross-reference of the slogans associated with Jimmy Porter ('There aren't any good, brave causes left') and James Dean (known principally for his role as the *Rebel Without A Cause*). A year and a half later the glamour and controversy of this association had evolved into contempt, on the assumption that the AYM were merely another product of the media's discovery of youth as a successful gimmick. 'This youth cult makes me sick,' complained Tom Baistow. 'Today fame apparently awaits any youngster with a modicum of talent for the guitar, the microphone or the typewriter.'[7] To many critics the AYM were no longer serious writers but just another batch of young media celebrities, literary equivalents of the new rock 'n' roll singers. (Indeed, the publicity for the AYM had been so great that a pop star's career could be measured in terms of a young writer's fame; a *New Statesman* article stated that Tommy Steele had enjoyed a success even more extraordinary than Colin Wilson's, and concluded that 'Mr Steele might prove to be the Bill Hopkins of the music hall'.[8]

The AYM's latest reputation as literary spin-offs of the 'youth cult' was temporarily replaced by a flurry of highbrow interest in their rebelliousness in the summer of 1958, when Jack Kerouac's novel *On the Road* was published in Britain. Subsequent attempts to equate the AYM with the Beat Generation could only be confused and confusing; that such comparisons were made at all only indicates the continuing absence of a definite AYM identity. The Beats were a much more closely linked group, whose shared outlook and vocabulary showed how very little they had in common with any young English writers. Only the forty-four-year-old Colin MacInnes, with his hip novels of London street life, *City of Spades* (1957) and *Absolute Beginners* (1959), could stand comparison with the Beats. When Andrew Sinclair tried to use Beat attitudes and expressions in his second novel, *My Friend Judas* (1959), the embarrassing result emphasized how alien the literature of Kerouac, Ginsberg, Burroughs and the rest really was.

Nevertheless, the temptation to link the two groupings was strong enough for the Beats to be greeted in England as 'More Angry Young Men' and for the AYM to be attacked in turn as whining members of the home-bred Beat Generation.[9] In 1959 an American anthology, *Protest*, tried to present the Beats and the AYM as allied groups of anti-bourgeois rebels. An exhilarating notion, but the juxtaposition of Ginsberg's 'Howl' or William Burroughs' description of life as a junkie, with extracts like the Merrie England lecture scene in *Lucky Jim* and the openings of *The Outsider* and *Hurry on Down*, only revealed the gulf between the two sets of writers. The efforts of Gene Feldman and Max Gartenberg, the editors of *Protest*, were shown to be even more ill-advised when the Panther paperback edition of the book was published in June 1960. Writing by the AYM now appeared under a cover depicting a group of tight-jeaned, crotch-thrusting dropouts gathered in a back alley. The caption read: 'Rebels without a cause, they are shocked by nothing, defying society, conventions, the world, the "beatniks" and the "angries" speak their minds.'

Perhaps it was just as well the popular press did not develop such comparisons between the two groups. By this time, though, Fleet Street's interest in the AYM as a group had dwindled and journalists' residual attention focused on the writers whose names were already familiar to the public. The most familiar name of all was John Osborne. Despite his controversial attack on Royalty, Osborne's reputation had actually improved by the end of 1957, according to the *Evening Standard*'s Thomas Wiseman, who voted him the 'most transformed man of the year' on 21 December. In Wiseman's opinion Osborne had proved himself to be a serious playwright with *The Entertainer*. His personal image was still appealing enough for his opinions to be aired in magazines not usually known for an interest in the theatre. The 'men's magazine' *Lilliput* invited Osborne to be one of their 'eight headline men' who would select a favourite article of clothing. He accepted and cut a very dapper figure in the issue for December 1957, modelling his choice of a Norfolk jacket. Nor were Osborne's female admirers left out, for the same month *Woman and Beauty* published his insights (together with those of current Italian heart-throb, Rossano Brazzi) on the topic of 'Twentieth Century Woman'. At first he seemed keen to live up to his reputation as a fearless speaker of his mind: 'I don't like a too-knowledgeable woman,' he confided, 'I feel it is against her sex.' But in general it was a suitably bland piece which ended in fine school-essay style: 'Let's finally say I do admire today's woman.'

Back in the theatres, 1958 was a good year for Osborne. In February both *Look Back in Anger* and *The Entertainer* were being performed on Broadway and proving that he could arouse controversy in the United States as well. They had a mixed reception from American critics and provoked often emotional responses from American audiences. On one occasion in the New York run of *Look Back in Anger* a woman jumped on the stage and slapped Jimmy Porter (played by the puzzled Kenneth Haigh). 'He left me! He left me!' she explained. Reactions were less heated in London where Osborne was marking time with a production of *Epitaph for George Dillon*, an early work co-written with Anthony Creighton, which opened at the Royal Court on 11 February. By this time he was also enjoying a quite staggering financial success. Just how staggering continued to vary from one newspaper estimate to the next. An *Evening Standard* article on 19

September preferred to list the signs of his affluence: twelve suits, handmade shoes, a Buick, a Jaguar XK and three different companies, with his earnings given as around £1,000 per week. Osborne's winning streak continued when he brought a successful libel action against the *Daily Mail* for an article in the 'Paul Tanfield' column on 10 November which described him as 'the original Teddy Boy'. Exactly the same phrase had been used about him a year earlier in the *Sunday Express*, but he had not sought legal redress; the impression that the court case against 'Tanfield' was not unconnected with the publicity campaign for his forthcoming musical satire about gossip columnists was only strengthened when Osborne did not seek damages from Associated Newspapers. He settled for the defendant apologizing and paying costs.

For the other leading AYM, 1958 was not particularly memorable. John Braine fared better than most, gaining £5,000 for the film rights to *Room at the Top* and a four-month stint as the *Spectator*'s television reviewer. Kingsley Amis, on the other hand, who until now had been the most reputable of the writers labelled as AYM, saw his literary standing decline after the dreadful reception of his third novel, *I Like It Here*, in January 1958. Many reviewers thought Amis had merely repeated the formula which had won him earlier praise ('Find A New Joke, Mr Amis,' advised Quentin Crewe in the *Evening Standard*). Penelope Mortimer considered that Amis's reputation had slumped so far that he could be unfavourably compared with the author of medical farces, Richard Gordon.[10] As for Colin Wilson, the damage to his reputation was such that he had been relegated from serious literary concern to the uncertain status of a recognizable 'personality' whose name might occasionally be found in newspaper snippets.

As 'Atticus' reflected in the *Sunday Times* on 28 December, 'The Angry Young Men had an unusually quiet year' in 1958. Collectively and individually they were now less significant than the legacy of their lost prominence, which showed publishers and directors – and other writers – that young authors producing realist work could find great success. This influence was most evident in the revival of the English theatre with the emergence of a number of young, socially-concerned dramatists. Writing in *Partisan Review* in autumn 1959, Angus Wilson judged that the 'angry young novels' were 'passé': to him the AYM 'have been already revealed as the New Establishment knocking at the door' and could be contrasted with the 'patently sincere rebels who form the anti-Establishment theater'.

The institution which did most to sponsor this revival was the English Stage Company at the Royal Court. At first George Devine's dream of a Writer's Theatre seemed to have been just that – a dream. Despite the growing success of *Look Back in Anger*, his project with the English Stage Company was on shaky ground by the end of its first year, which had been a financial disaster. Neville Blond considered asking industrial companies to sponsor new plays, and Devine was forced to fall back on a production of Wycherley's *The Country Wife* to help ease the ESC's debts. Then, as royalties from *Look Back in Anger* and *The Entertainer* began to come in during the second year, the ESC gained enough financial security to allow Devine to continue taking risks with new dramatists. Among the new playwrights introduced at the Royal Court during the 1957 season were N. F. Simpson, whose *A Resounding Tinkle* was first performed there on 1 December, and John Arden, whose *The Waters of Babylon* was one of a series of new works given rehearsed readings on Sunday nights. Also in this second season were Nigel Dennis's *The Making of Moo* and Michael Hastings' second play, *Yes, and After*.

In the next two years a fine array of new talent appeared at the Royal Court. One of the more celebrated arrivals was Arnold Wesker. His first play to be produced was *Chicken Soup with Barley* which had a week's trial at the Belgrade Theatre in Coventry before opening at the Royal Court on 14 July 1958. The same transfer was used for the second and third plays in Wesker's trilogy – *Roots* in 1959 and *I'm Talking About Jerusalem* in 1960. Similarly, Willis Hall's *The Long and the Short and the Tall* was brought to the Royal Court in January 1959 after it had been presented first at the Edinburgh Festival and then at the Nottingham Playhouse.

As the experience of Hall and Wesker shows, a significant feature of the theatrical revival in the last quarter of the fifties was the new-found vigour of provincial theatres. Venues such as the Belgrade in Coventry, the Oxford Playhouse, the Royal Court in Liverpool and the Arts Theatre in Cambridge, were now able to present young dramatists' new plays which could then be brought to London. Robert Bolt, Peter Shaffer and Harold

Pinter were among the other new playwrights whose work was transferred to the West End from the provinces.[11]

The level of public enthusiasm for the new plays was shown when Penguin launched its extremely successful New English Dramatists series. The man behind the series was Tom Maschler, who had been head-hunted by Allen Lane for Penguin after making his name as editor of *Declaration*. A great theatre-lover and friend of many of the new playwrights, Maschler had grown impatient with Penguin's stolid drama list and suggested to the editor, E. Martin Browne, that they publish young playwrights. Maschler brought in as a sample three of the typescripts he had been reading at home and Browne promptly decided to publish them. The plays were Doris Lessing's *Each His Own Wilderness*, Bernard Kops's *The Hamlet of Stepney Green* and Wesker's *Chicken Soup with Barley*. When the collection appeared in 1959 it sold several hundred thousand copies. (Maschler would have been even more delighted had Browne not credited himself as editor of the volume.)

The most remarkable contribution to this resurgence in English drama was made by Joan Littlewood's Theatre Workshop. Founded in 1945 by Littlewood and Ewan MacColl, Theatre Workshop had only enjoyed a permanent base since 1953, when it took over the Theatre Royal in Stratford-atte-Bowe, in the East End of London. Until 1958 Theatre Workshop's socialist commitment had not attracted commercial success. Exceptions were *The Good Soldier Schweyk* in 1954 and Brendan Behan's *The Quare Fellow* in 1956, which both moved to the West End. Then, in 1958, two plays brought Theatre Workshop to general public attention – *A Taste of Honey* by Shelagh Delaney, which opened on 27 May, and Behan's second play, *The Hostage*, first performed on 14 October. Both plays had very successful transfers to the West End the following year. In addition, Frank Norman's *Fings Ain't Wot They Used t'be* had a successful seven-week run in Stratford after it opened on 15 February. Even the *Daily Telegraph* had to acknowledge that 1959 had been 'Joan Littlewood's year'.[12]

Of all the new playwrights to arrive after Osborne it was the Theatre Workshop's Behan and Delaney who received by far the greatest press interest. The main reason Shelagh Delaney attracted media attention was that she was only nineteen years old when *A Taste of Honey* was first produced, so she was initially treated as a late addition to the group of adolescent writers. The *News Chronicle*, for instance, classified her as 'the Françoise Sagan of Salford'. As 'the teenager of the week' whose play qualified her as 'the latest authority on love', Delaney was interviewed in the *Evening News* fashion column about the proprieties of adolescent romance.[13] However, her precocity was by now guaranteed to provoke highbrow scorn; in his *Spectator* review of 6 June 1958, Alan Brien was in no doubt as to how he should treat *A Taste of Honey*: 'Twenty, ten, or even five years ago, before a senile society began to fawn upon the youth which is about to devour it, such a play would have remained written in green longhand in a school exercise book on the top of the bedroom wardrobe.'

Brendan Behan attracted even more publicity than Delaney when Hutchinson timed the publication of his autobiography, *Borstal Boy*, in October 1958 to coincide with the opening of *The Hostage* at Stratford. Of course, Behan was already well known as a roaring-boy personality from his drunken *Panorama* interview two years earlier; 'William Hickey', for example, had described him as 'the Dylan Thomas of Ireland'.[14] *Borstal Boy* and *The Hostage* reinforced Behan's media reputation as a larger-than-life rebel, a man with a sensationally chequered past. The *Evening News* reviewer of *The Hostage* hailed Behan as 'a true Bohemian. He is a Borstal boy, IRA bomb-planter, house-painter, poet, toss-pot . . .' *Sunday Express* readers were warned that 'Mr Behan . . . makes the potted plants shake'.[15]

Coverage of Behan's play and his autobiography dominated the dwindling press attention given to new writers towards the end of 1958. One new author who appeared at this less fervent time was Alan Sillitoe, whose first novel was published by W. H. Allen in October. *Saturday Night and Sunday Morning* is now seen as one of the key works of the fifties, as important and significant a novel of the period as *Lucky Jim* or *Room at the Top*, but it failed, for reasons I shall explore later in this book, to make a comparable immediate impression.

By the end of 1958 the English literary scene was returning to relative normality after the hullaballoo over the AYM. The residual press enthusiasm for new writers had latched on to a few individuals. Neither the spate of new dramatists nor the October launching of some of the novelists discovered by New Authors Limited encouraged the media to promote another new movement.

Describing the mood of literary London in November, A. Alvarez was relieved to see that there were 'no crazes, no cocktail party manias'. In an astute summary, he noted that the Old Guard seemed to have reasserted itself, a development symbolized and strengthened by the success of John Betjeman's *Collected Poems*. He recognized too a developing opposition to the cultural right-wingers in the 'stirrings on the literary left', which he saw coming mainly from the journal *Universities and Left Review* (and its new coffee-bar social centre in Soho, the 'Partisan').[16]

Alvarez could also have mentioned two recently published books which were associated with this New Left. *Culture and Society* made Raymond Williams well-known as a radical literary historian. (Or rather, vaguely well-known, for he tended to be paired and confused with another adult education tutor who had published a successful cultural critique; one reviewer even managed to refer to '*The Uses of Culture* by Raymond Hoggart'.[17]) Also published in September 1958 was Norman Mackenzie's anthology for MacGibbon & Kee, *Conviction*. As the title indicates, *Conviction* was intended by the publishers to cash in on the popular success of *Declaration*. In fact, Mackenzie's contributors – who included Peter Shore, Paul Johnson, Iris Murdoch and Raymond Williams – made his anthology much more authentically radical than Maschler's damp squib.

The rediscovery of a sense of radicalism was also fostered by the emergence of a new pan-political organization in 1958. The Campaign for Nuclear Disarmament was launched on 17 February that year at a public meeting at Conway Hall in London, chaired by Canon Collins of St Paul's. Speakers included J. B. Priestley, Bertrand Russell, A. J. P. Taylor and Michael Foot. Five thousand people turned up and four overflow halls had to be used. CND gained national media coverage in Easter 1958 when the first march was organized from London to the atomic research establishment at Aldermaston. Although John Osborne, Alan Sillitoe and John Braine took part in Ban-the-Bomb demonstrations, CND was not thought to be associated with the AYM. CND had its own powerful identity as a protest movement, particularly of the young generation; in some ways it replaced the AYM in the public arena.

Writers could still be major news towards the end of 1958 and in 1959, but it was an indication of the declining press interest in young home-bred writers that the two authors who now claimed the liveliest media coverage were the Russians Boris Pasternak and Vladimir Nabokov. It was also a sign of a return to normal press priorities that neither of these internationally renowned writers was publicized on the basis of his literary talent. Pasternak and Nabokov hit the headlines because they found themselves involved in the highly newsworthy issues of the Cold War and sex.

Pasternak came to worldwide attention in October 1958 when the furore over *Doctor Zhivago* reached its peak. Banned in the Soviet Union, *Doctor Zhivago* had been published to great acclaim in Milan in 1957. The English translation appeared in September 1958 and became a bestseller after Pasternak was awarded the Nobel Prize a month later, but the Soviet authorities denounced his novel and then forced Pasternak to decline the award. The affair made him front-page news.

The controversy surrounding Vladimir Nabokov's *Lolita* had started in January 1956 after Graham Greene praised the novel in his contribution to the *Sunday Times* round-up of 'Books of the Year' on Christmas Day 1955. Readers who were impressed by Greene's recommendation would have found great difficulty in obtaining copies of *Lolita*, which was then available only from the Olympia Press in Paris; the likelihood of prosecution under the current obscenity laws had deterred British publishers from giving *Lolita* the respectability of a conventional place in the bookshops. One reader who was definitely not impressed by Greene's recommendation was the reactionary columnist of the *Sunday Express*, John Gordon, who had followed up Greene's remarks and procured a copy of the book. On 29 January Graham Greene and Vladimir Nabokov were added to the list of work-shy strikers, birchable delinquents and traitorous reds who were the usual victims of John Gordon's profitable outrage. Gordon denounced *Lolita* as 'the filthiest book I have ever read' and attacked Greene for publicizing a work of 'sheer unrestrained pornography'. This difference of opinion developed into a feud when Greene wrote to the *Spectator* to announce the formation of the 'John Gordon Society' which would campaign for the virtues of wholesome family entertainment. Readers entered into the spirit of the venture; one enthusiast suggested that the fan club commission a portrait of its idol as Diana, Goddess of Chastity, holding an expurgated copy of the Old Testament in one hand and *The Tale of Squirrel Nutkin* in the other. Other proposals included the suggestion that measures be taken to censor games of Scrabble.[18]

This vendetta functioned as advance publicity for *Lolita*, which Weidenfeld & Nicolson announced they would publish in 1958. That announcement caused even more advance publicity since Weidenfeld & Nicolson faced prosecution if they did issue Nabokov's novel. Censorship in the fifties was still under the stringent control of the century-old Obscene Publications Act. The result was that a novel like *Room at the Top*, which describes sexual relationships in a manner that now seems coy, could be received as a very frank account of lechery and adultery. The movement to liberalize the censorship laws was led by A. P. Herbert, President of the Society of Authors, and supported by MPs Roy Jenkins and Norman St John Stevas. Five years after Herbert started this campaign the Obscene Publications Bill finally gained Royal assent on 29 July 1959.

In the meantime, *Lolita* had become the focus of attention for the issues of permissiveness and artistic freedom which Herbert's lobbying had raised. In effect, *Lolita* was a test case and prepared the way for the more famous challenge to the censorship laws by Penguin Books in 1960 when that firm printed 200,000 copies of the banned *Lady Chatterley's Lover*. Weidenfeld & Nicolson were more cautious and delayed publication of *Lolita* until 6 November, over three months after the new Act had been passed. However, there was still great uncertainty about the extent to which legal restrictions had been relaxed and publication of *Lolita* was a tense and newsworthy affair. According to one report in the *Evening Standard*, George Weidenfeld did not know until the last minute whether or not official action would be taken against the book. In the event *Lolita* was not published to the accompaniment of police raids or bookshop queues. The novel was said to be selling well, but not very well, in a front-page *Evening News* item which would surely have been spiked had not *Lolita*'s publication been news enough in itself.[19]

Meanwhile Nabokov discovered that he had become something of a celebrity in the English press, with the dishearteningly predictable result that he had to deny that he shared his protagonist Humbert Humbert's passion for nymphets. Nabokov's own standpoint at the time became famous enough to be referred to in the *Evening Standard's* fun page. A cartoon appeared on 13 November 1959 which showed a painter busily drawing a helpless victim of cannibals. The painter justified the strange priorities of his concern: 'If I may quote the author of a much publicized book: "I am an artist. I am not interested in the social or moral aspects." '

The only English writer who could match the popular press coverage of Nabokov and Pasternak as the fifties came to an end was not one of the original Angries but Shelagh Delaney. Journalists briefly revived their flagging interest in young authors in 1959 after Delaney received £20,000 for the film rights to *A Taste of Honey*. The play itself appeared at Wyndham's Theatre on 10 February, but journalists were mainly concerned with her financial success, an angle which recalled their interest in the Angry Young Men rather than the Angry Tinies. The AYM link was strengthened by the fact that it was John Osborne's newly-established company, Woodfall Productions, which bought the film rights. Delaney's wealth, rather than her age or the content of her play, provided regular stories for the popular press. In the *Evening News*, for example, the West End opening of *A Taste of Honey* was mentioned as the occasion when Delaney paid a large bill for a first-night party. Even the 'news' that she had decided *not* to buy an expensive American car was faithfully reported.[20] But her publicity was exceptional. Even the politically or socially committed playwrights like Arden and Wesker failed to rekindle popular press interest in literary protesters. An indication of this was the apathetic public response to Arden's play, *Serjeant Musgrave's Dance*, which had to be taken off after twenty-eight ill-attended performances in November 1959.

As for the writers originally branded as AYM, 1959 was an even less distinguished year than its predecessor. Colin Wilson's third book, *The Age of Defeat*, was generally ignored when it appeared in September 1959. John Braine published his second novel, *The Vodi*, but failed to repeat the success of *Room at the Top*. A reaction was now setting in against Braine as well; *The Vodi* was published amid rumours that Eyre & Spottiswoode thought the novel so bad that they were afraid of releasing it. Another story was circulating that *Room at the Top* was not Braine's work at all but had been written by his agent's literary adviser, John Raymond.

The reaction Braine suffered was paltry compared to John Osborne's harrowing experience when his musical about Fleet

Street, *The World of Paul Slickey*, had its London opening at the Palace Theatre on 5 May 1959. According to Milton Shulman's report in the *Evening Standard* the following day, the first-night curtain fell to 'the most raucous note of displeasure heard in the West End since the war'. Shulman's article was accompanied by a large photograph of the disconsolate author alone on an empty stage, evidently reflecting on this disastrous opening night. Worse was to follow. Osborne has recalled that the audience's reaction was so bad that he was assaulted by irate first-nighters when he left the theatre: 'there was this mob of about eighty people and I had to run through them and they chased me down Charing Cross Road and I had to fight. Fortunately I got a taxi.'[21] The audience's displeasure was shared by the critics; the reviews of the musical were vitriolic enough to be front-page news in the *Evening Standard*, which also reported the consolation Osborne had found in contempt: 'It's a distinction,' he reflected, 'to be booed by some people'; 'not one daily paper critic has the intellectual equipment to assess my work or that of any other intelligent playwright.' *The World of Paul Slickey* was taken off after six weeks.

It is very tempting to take the response to Osborne's musical as finally marking the demise of the Angry Young Men. The grouping had lost prestige and credibility as early as October 1957, and the new lower-class novelists and playwrights who might have been allied to the group did not, on the whole, attract media interest and were rarely seen as late additions to the cult of Anger. As for the individual writers who had been publicized as AYM, all had suffered a critical backlash. With some, like Wilson, Holroyd and Hopkins, the effect was irreversible, while others like Amis, Osborne and Braine continued, with varying degrees of critical success, to pursue literary careers. Throughout 1958 and 1959 even the popular press lost interest in exploiting the catchphrase. Osborne, Wilson and others were upstaged by authors who offered journalists the chance of fresher or more sensational copy – Behan, Delaney, Pasternak and Nabokov.

Even so, the ascendancy of the AYM as a new cultural force was in some ways probably more influential in 1959 than ever. Despite the fact that public awareness of new 'fifties' writers had been secured by the remarkable media coverage of 1956 and 1957, the young authors were still known to most people only by the reputations sponsored or manufactured by the media. Sales of their work had been impressive, of course, but it was not until 1959 that the writing, rather than the writers, began to reach the wide audience which the AYM were supposed to be addressing and, indeed, representing.

This vastly increased access was achieved by the combination of the cinema and paperback publication. *Lucky Jim* had already been made into a popular film in 1957, but the screenplay had turned Amis's book into an innocuous farce which bore little relation to the novel. The distortion was partly rectified in 1959 when Four Square Books published a paperback edition before Penguin followed with their paperback of *Lucky Jim* in 1961. However, it was John Braine who was the first AYM writer to make an effective impact on a far wider audience. The film of *Room at the Top* was released in January 1959 with a marketing campaign aimed at popular success. Advertisements proclaimed that 'John Braine's Scorching Best Seller' was 'A Savage Story of Lust and Ambition'. Fleet Street reviewers responded in kind. 'The sex is there, in torrents', announced the *Sunday Express* reporter, with a less than fortunate choice of phrase. In the *Evening Standard* this film about 'brass and brassières' was said to have put 'an X in Yorkshire'. *Reynolds News* readers were titillated with the news that the film offered 'an unblushingly frank portrayal of intimate human relationships'.[22]

Penguin Books timed the paperback publication of *Room at the Top* in late February, to capitalize on the film's success. Priced at half-a-crown a copy and with a picture of Laurence Harvey as Joe Lampton on the cover, 'the book of the film'[23] sold 300,000 copies within three months of publication. In comparison, the highly successful hardback edition had sold 40,000 copies after two years.

The film of *Look Back in Anger* followed soon after the general release of *Room at the Top*, being premièred in Leicester Square on 28 May 1959. Although Nigel Kneale's screenplay gave Richard Burton a less vehement part as Jimmy Porter than the play itself offered, the film was still sensationally presented; its X-certificate was apparently more than justified according to the advertisements which showed two images of actresses Mary Ure and Claire Bloom in bed.

This film confirmed that the influence of the new works by the 'fifties generation' would survive and increase despite the decline in media promotion. The screenplay may have muted Osborne's own voice – the significance of the film of *Look Back in Anger* lies elsewhere. *Room at the Top* was justifiably regarded at the time as a breakthrough in English cinema, but the film of Osborne's play was the starting-point for other productions. The director, Tony Richardson, went on to produce Karel Reisz's film of *Saturday Night and Sunday Morning* (1960) and to direct films of *The Entertainer* (1960) and *A Taste of Honey* (1961).

Collectively and individually the Angry Young Men could no longer arouse the astonishing highbrow and popular interest of 1956 and 1957, but paperbacks and the 'New Wave' of the English cinema were bringing a handful of their key works to the general public. Meanwhile, the Angry Young Men had already been preserved by the myth-making process: the fifties had its own literary identity as 'The Angry Decade'.

4

'Beginning with Amis'

Leading young writers of the thirties have been grouped together as members of the 'Auden generation'. There is no comparably eponymous author for the fifties, but among the collection of usual 'fifties' names, one does stand out as a continuously influential presence – Kingsley Amis. In the light of his later reputation as a maverick reactionary and curmudgeon, a literary incarnation of Disgusted of Tunbridge Wells, this claim may seem surprising. Yet it would be difficult to overestimate the importance of Amis's literary career in the fifties. It was one which helped to precipitate the major shifts in the contemporary literary scene; a career which spanned the period of publicity for the new generation of writers, with Amis appointed first as a leader of the Movement and then as leader of the Angry Young Men; a career of challenges and controversies involving essential literary, cultural and social issues of the time.

His output was prolific. Between 1953 and 1959 he published three novels, two volumes of verse, one political pamphlet, a handful of stories and a great many articles and reviews. But his early career was dominated by his first major published work, one of the most popular post-war novels, a book which has been adapted for radio, television and cinema and which, despite Amis's many subsequent successes, probably remains his best-known – *Lucky Jim*.

Kingsley Amis was born in 1922 in Norbury ('it had to be called something'), a 'non-place' in South London. Amis has always emphasized that his were very ordinary, lower-middle-class origins; his father worked as a clerk for Colman's Mustard. Amis was educated at local schools and progressed to a large, fee-paying secondary, the City of London School, where he was awarded a scholarship in his second year. He then attended Marlborough

College for five terms (as a wartime evacuee) before going to St John's College, Oxford, to read English. He arrived in April 1941, got to know Philip Larkin and, later, John Wain (both fellow students at St John's), but was called up by the Army after only four terms. Amis spent three and a half years in uniform, mostly as a Lieutenant in the Royal Corps of Signals, before returning to Oxford in 1945. Two years later he took a First Class Honours.

He also had his first book published in 1947 – a slim collection of undistinguished poems, *Bright November*, which was put out by R. A. Caton's Fortune Press. In 1949 he co-edited the *Oxford Poetry* anthology with James Michie. Married a year before, he was completing his B.Litt. thesis (a study of late Victorian poets and their audience). Then he suffered several setbacks. He failed his B.Litt.; the University of Tucumán failed to return, far less publish, the manuscript of his critical study of Graham Greene; and his first novel, *The Legacy*, was rejected by fourteen publishers. (In later years Amis would express relief at the failure of *The Legacy*, dismissing it as a juvenile effort, affected and experimental.)

Compensation for these various failures came in October 1949 when he started an academic career as a lecturer in English Literature at University College, Swansea. Amis's literary fortunes improved in his first years at Swansea, as his poems began to appear in little magazines and anthologies. (His second collection, *A Frame of Mind*, would be published, on the advice of John Wain, by the University of Reading School of Art in December 1953.) Amis also found modest success when he teamed up with his friend, the composer Bruce Montgomery; their one-act opera *Amberley Hall* was broadcast on the BBC's regional Home Service in 1952 and their 'coronation ode', *The Century's Crown*, was performed by the Glasgow Choral Union a year later.

But since the late forties his main project had been a new novel. He had concluded from the unqualified failure of *The Legacy* that he had to stop dabbling in experimental trickery and start afresh. His first vague ideas for a new attempt had come to him late in 1946, but these notions only took a firmer shape in 1948 when he visited Philip Larkin, who was working as a librarian at University College, Leicester. One Saturday morning Larkin invited Amis to the Common Room for coffee:

I looked round a couple of times and said to myself, 'Christ; somebody ought to do something with this.' Not that it was awful – well, only a bit; it was strange and sort of *developed*, a whole mode of existence no one had got on to, like the SS in 1940, say. I would do something with it.[1]

He started tinkering with ideas for a comic novel about a likeably ordinary young chap being oppressed by the inhabitants of that odd university setting. Two years later he sent a sprawling first draft of the new work to Larkin, whose pruning and advice helped a great deal. Another important aid was the windfall of a real-life legacy: Hilary Amis had inherited two thousand pounds – enough to buy a house with a small study, a luxury for her husband after years of trying to work without a room of his own. In these improved conditions Amis began the final rough draft of what was to be *Lucky Jim* in February 1951, finishing the fair copy by September the following year.

In contrast to his first venture into the commercial publishing world with *The Legacy*, Amis did not have to endure the humiliation of rejection slips. He had taken the opportunity of a biographical note to his contribution in *New Poems 1952* to announce that he had written a novel. The ploy succeeded, for the note attracted the interest of a Gollancz director, Hilary Rubinstein, who had known Amis slightly at Oxford. Amis sent the final draft of his novel to Gollancz at the end of 1952 but a final acceptance was delayed. Amis recalls that Victor Gollancz was 'very much against publishing it' because he thought the novel was 'vulgar and anti-cultural'. (Gollancz later preferred to remember that he had been greatly attracted to the book by its witty irreverence.)[2] Gollancz was opposed by Rubinstein and Livia Gollancz, who were both enthusiastic. Unknown to Amis, the future of his novel was still undecided as late as April 1953. Even the title was posing problems; neither *Lucky Jim* nor Amis's original choice, *Dixon and Christine*, was thought suitable. Eventually, Gollancz decided to accept *Lucky Jim*, manuscript and title, but publication was delayed again. Amis was more than a little put out to learn that his novel would appear early the next year, at traditionally the slackest time for the book trade, but one often chosen for publication by Gollancz in the hope that their books might attract more attention. *Lucky Jim* finally came out on 25 January 1954.

It seems that it was destined for controversy. The arguments within Gollancz had been accompanied by public disputes well before *Lucky Jim* appeared in the bookshops, after John Wain chose an extract from it to open his *First Reading* broadcasts. The excerpt was over twelve minutes long and from a section of the novel that was to become notorious – the description of Jim's hungover breakfast and discovery of his burnt bedclothes. P. H. Newby was dismayed when he read the passage, finding it 'corny and adolescent', but Wain assured him that one day Amis's novel would be famous.[3] *First Reading*'s critics agreed with Newby; the extract had been introduced as the representative of Wain's contentious new movement and Hugh Massingham singled it out for attack. In his *New Statesman* article 'First Stop Reading!', V. S. Pritchett remarked on Amis's 'clumsy style' and regretted that Wain's exemplary young author appeared to be 'writing with his boots'.

This did not augur well for publication day, but when *Lucky Jim* did eventually appear it was very well received. A few reviewers frowned on what they saw as the vulgarity of Jim Dixon, but only Julian Maclaren-Ross of the *Sunday Times* echoed Massingham's hostility, concluding that Amis had confused 'farce with comedy, schoolboy grubbiness with wit'. Most critics, though, were won over by Amis's humour: 'most enjoyable reading', 'genuinely comic' (*The Times*); 'a very funny book' (*Spectator*); 'extremely amusing' (*Punch*). John Betjeman praised *Lucky Jim* as the funniest novel he had read since *Decline and Fall*.[4]

Helped by the legacy of attention from *First Reading* and Gollancz's tactic of January publication, *Lucky Jim* had wide and almost unanimously favourable review coverage. But good reviews do not always sell books. British sales picked up very slowly, and the book flopped in America where it was launched by Doubleday with a money-back offer if buyers failed to find it uproariously funny. Copies flooded back. Still, by the end of its first year in print it had sold over 10,000 copies in Britain. On Boxing Day C. P. Snow announced in the *Sunday Times* that it was one of the three or four greatest critical and popular successes of the previous twenty years. But, staunch admirer of the novel though he was, Snow was anxious to correct this 'overstatement' and added the following week that he had meant to write 'three or four *first* novels'. Even with this qualification, Snow was still guilty of exaggeration. 1954 had been a good year for first novels. Iris

Murdoch's *Under the Net* had been published to great acclaim, as had William Golding's *Lord of the Flies*, which received high praise from E. M. Forster in the *Observer*'s round-up of the year's fiction, whereas *Lucky Jim* was not mentioned once in either of the quality Sunday newspapers' surveys.

Even so, *Lucky Jim* was already beginning to overshadow its rivals by the end of 1954 in discussions about the 'new novel' and the new 'Movement'. It had also begun to attract attention as a work with intriguing social relevance; the first claim that Amis had created a new and representative social type in Jim Dixon was made by Walter Allen in his *New Statesman* review of 30 January. 'Is he the intellectual tough, or the tough intellectual?' wondered Allen. Whichever way round, this 'new hero' marked a clear departure from the sensitive young men who seemed to populate most recent first novels. Amis's new protagonist was 'consciously, even conscientiously graceless', with 'nerve-ends . . . trembling exposed' to 'the phoney':

> In life he has been among us for some little time. One may speculate whence he derives. The Services, certainly, helped to make him; but George Orwell, Dr Leavis and the Logical Positivists – or, rather, the attitudes these represent – all contributed to his genesis. In fiction I think he first arrived last year, as the central character of Mr John Wain's novel *Hurry on Down*. He turns up again in Mr Amis's *Lucky Jim*.

This was the first sign that Jim Dixon was to be seen as a potent symbol, a personification of a new post-war outlook. It was also the first of many attempts by critics and commentators to supply their own speculative details in profiles designed to stress and clarify Jim's social and cultural significance. A week later George Scott gave a similar account of *Lucky Jim* in *Truth*, comparing the heroes of Amis and Wain and providing his own characterization of what he took to be a representative of 'hundreds of thousands of young men of the post-war world':

> [Jim] is a lad who obviously came from a home where the *Daily Mirror* was more familiar than Kafka or Joyce . . . He is the kind of man so moulded by environment and heredity that he will never, in upper-class company, cease mentally straightening his tie and polishing his shoes on his trousers.

Jim Dixon's growing reputation as the hero of his time did not concern his creator. Amis was pleased to see his novel attracting publicity, just as he was pleased to see the promotion campaign for the Movement, saying to himself: 'if this means another five hundred dollars on my American advance, I'm all for it.'[5] He was far more concened with a new novel which he had started to write the previous summer so that he would not be too discouraged if *Lucky Jim* turned out to be a flop. And he was determined not to be influenced one way or the other by current opinionating about the great significance of his first novel.

In the event, when Gollancz published *That Uncertain Feeling* in August 1955, it confirmed Amis's existing reputation. The main character, John Lewis, evidently had much in common with Jim Dixon: both came from ordinary, lower-class backgrounds and both were placed in recognizably contemporary, unglamorous, provincial circumstances. The setting of *That Uncertain Feeling* is 'Aberdarcy', a Welsh industrial town, where Lewis toils in the public library. Lewis, like Dixon, holds left-wing opinions, and he bristles at signs of social privilege, but is nonetheless lured into adultery by Elizabeth Gruffydd-Williams, a member of Aberdarcy's Anglicized upper crust. Like *Lucky Jim*, *That Uncertain Feeling* received good notices. One detractor was Rex Warner who complained that the novel provoked 'a general distaste, a sort of queasiness in the stomach'. Equally exceptional was Philip Oakes's eulogy in *Truth*.[6] The consensus was that it was slightly flawed but still commendable. Most of the criticisms were directed at the ending, where Lewis renounces his socialite temptress and is reconciled to the virtues of his lower-middle-class home and hearth.

Several reviewers held up this finale as clinching proof that issues of class and class conflict were central to Amis's second novel.[7] *Lucky Jim* had given the general impression that Amis's new hero was something of a lower-class social misfit, but the novel's university setting meant that critics had assumed Dixon's plights were caused by problems peculiar to the enclosed world of academia. Conveniently, Dixon's university was redbrick, so *Lucky Jim* could be categorized under the two headings for the Movement – 'academic' and 'provincial'. In *That Uncertain Feeling* the social background was more orthodox and reviewers were now confident that Amis was a novelist of class-based comedy. One consequence was that social prejudices were also starting to infiltrate their accounts of his fiction. John Connell, for example, decided that Lewis was 'an outrageously common little bounder' and Elizabeth Bowen felt she had to point out that the Aberdarcy gentry were not *really* posh but 'staggeringly common'.[8] The most objectionable piece of snobbery in these reviews came once again from Julian Maclaren-Ross, whose suspension of disbelief collapsed when faced with the characterization of Lewis's father. Ross could not accept this 'proletarian parent' since he was inexplicably described as working-class *and* addicted to the *Observer*'s Ximenes crossword.[9]

Social prejudice was also leading some critics to question the appeal of Amis's comedy. 'One holds one's nose occasionally, not always when he means one to,' wrote the *New Statesman*'s Richard Lister on 20 August; 'The world his characters inhabit is smelly and mean; its values are non-existent.' Lister found compensation for the fact that Amis showed a 'lack of refinement' and that 'there is nothing subtle or civilized about him' since these attributes allowed the young author 'an uncanny understanding' of 'the Teddy-boy mentality' of his characters. But it was still time Amis moved on, thought Peter Quennell: 'he must enlarge his outlook, I think, if his literary talent is to continue to grow. It cannot hang about indefinitely, skylarking and scuffling on the back-stairs.'[10]

Amis's preference for the unrefined material of the Welfare State seemed baffling or perverse to many older writers, including some of those who had been famously left-wing in the thirties. Now they found the reality of a more egalitarian society not just uncongenial but positively harmful to the values they held dear. In *Time and Place* (1956), George Scott remarked that it was odd that 'so many of the contemporaries of Lehmann and Spender are becalmed on what they seem to regard as the dead sea of the welfare state'. Past enthusiasms had been forgotten: 'Where now is that worship of the Worker, with whom they strove so passionately to identify themselves?' A particularly remarkable political turnabout was performed by Stephen Spender, who now considered that the Welfare State had brought about 'an unprecedented spiritual malaise'.[11] In June 1956 an editorial in *Encounter* gave a very bleak account of 'This New England'. Prosperity and equality were not to be celebrated for this was a society of the 'over-employed' which had produced terribly unaesthetic effects:

In an overcrowded country approaching the condition where the majority receive almost equal shares, there is little vivid variousness, a spreading grey of suburbs which make up in quantity of dimness for the more concentrated intense ugliness of nineteenth-century slums. Everywhere the price paid for diffused facilities is sacrifice of quality ... Universal Welfare, it is beginning to be realized, casts a long, wide shadow over green, bright fields.

It was just such an attitude which led David Wright to describe Amis as 'the apostle of triumphant mediocrity', an author who dealt with the 'dinginess' of contemporary life.[12]

Now that he had created a young, ill-paid, lower-class redbrick graduate as his protagonist for a second time, Amis began to be attacked for representing a specific feature of 'Universal Welfare', the emergence of a new generation of graceless and ungrateful scholarship students sponsored by the Butler Education Act. Evelyn Waugh led the way in December 1955 with a diatribe on the 'primal man and woman of the classless society'. His observations were published in *Encounter*, apparently as a reply to Nancy Mitford's hugely successful survey of 'U and Non-U', but that was merely an excuse, not a reason, for his display of satiric contempt. Waugh's tirade included an attack on the new Movement writers who were, he implied, typical graduates of 'L'École de Butler' and portents of a 'new wave of philistinism': 'we are threatened by these grim young people who are coming off the assembly lines in their hundreds every year and finding employment as critics, even as poets and novelists.'

At the same time Amis's fiction was inspiring Somerset Maugham to contribute a more seriously presented condemnation of young people who were being educated beyond their station. Amis wrote to thank Maugham after *Lucky Jim* received the Award he had founded for first novels: a simple act of courtesy which Maugham appreciated. His reply was very friendly and full of praise for *Lucky Jim* but it took Amis aback; it commended him as a man of like-minded cultivation (had not Amis been at Oxford?) who had performed a vital social service in satirizing the new barbarians.[13] Maugham was obviously pleased with his part in the correspondence, for he adapted his letter as an extended contribution to the *Sunday Times* 'Books of the Year' supplement which appeared on Christmas Day 1955. Maugham's seasonal tribute to Amis is worth quoting in full:

Lucky Jim is a remarkable novel. It has been greatly praised and widely read, but I have not noticed that any of the reviewers have remarked on its ominous significance. I am told that today rather more than 60 per cent. of the men who go to the universities go on a Government grant. This is a new class that has entered upon the scene. It is the white-collar proletariat. Mr Kingsley Amis is so talented, his observation is so keen, that you cannot fail to be convinced that the young men he so brilliantly describes truly represent the class with which his novel is concerned.

They do not go to the university to acquire culture, but to get a job, and when they have got one, scamp it. They have no manners, and are woefully unable to deal with any social predicament. Their idea of a celebration is to go to a public house and drink six beers. They are mean, malicious and envious. They will write anonymous letters to harass a fellow undergraduate and listen in to a telephone conversation that is no business of theirs. Charity, kindliness, generosity, are qualities which they hold in contempt. They are scum. They will in due course leave the university. Some will doubtless sink back, perhaps with relief, into the modest class from which they emerged; some will take to drink, some to crime and go to prison. Others will become schoolmasters and form the young, or journalists and mould public opinion. A few will go into Parliament, become Cabinet Ministers and rule the country. I look upon myself as fortunate that I shall not live to see it.

Not surprisingly, Maugham's farrago of misreadings and prejudices provoked a heated response. The following week the *Sunday Times* printed a few of the many letters sent in protest, including one from the whodunnit novelist 'Edmund Crispin' (the *nom de plume* of Bruce Montgomery) who satirized the peculiar strategy of Maugham's 'vulgar insult'. A week later another defence of Amis, and the new class he was supposed to have described, came from C. P. Snow, who preferred to see Amis's characters as 'the present-day guardians of the puritan conscience'. Maugham's praise did little to promote a better understanding of *Lucky Jim*, but it did help to advertise Amis's fiction as works of great sociological interest. This was the angle for Philip Oakes's *Observer* article describing 'A New Style in Heroes'. He claimed that both Amis and Wain were representatives not only of the new 'movement', but of their generation as a whole, since they had the appropriate 'personal and social characteristics'. Oakes then gave his own profile of the background and outlook of the producers as well as the products of the new writing, in what he called a 'blueprint of the hero of our time and also of his biographer':

> Born: Coketown, 1925. Parents: lower middle-class. Educated: local council school, grammar school and university (after three years' military service). Married. One or two children. Occupation: Civil Servant/journalist/lecturer/minor executive. Politics: neutralist. Ambition: to live well. Interests: people, money, sex. Worries: money, sex. Enthusiasms: George Orwell, jazz, Dr Leavis, old cars. Antipathies: Dylan Thomas, provincial culture, European novelists. Future: indefinite.

Perhaps it is as well that Oakes stopped short of clairvoyance because the fortunes of Dixon and Amis were about to change as they were both thrown aboard the bandwagon of the Angry Young Men. However, this change was one of degree rather than kind. Amis had already made his mark in literary circles as a young writer with a variety of controversial reputations. The objections from *First Reading* opponents had existed alongside the descriptions of Amis as one of the clique of 'academic' poets. Initially, *Lucky Jim* had reinforced Amis's donnish reputation, but as leader of the Movement and creator of a Welfare State comedy in *That Uncertain Feeling*, his public image had changed. By the end of 1955 he was being categorized as a presenter and member of a new Butler-educated class. The donnish category had been submerged, only to resurface in the new catchword 'redbrick'.

As the supposed chronicler of the rise of scholarship graduates, Amis was the obvious writer for reviewers of *Look Back in Anger* to mention. Kenneth Tynan, for example, introduced his *Observer* review with a reference to Maugham's attack on the 'non-U intelligentsia', who had found another spokesman in Jimmy Porter. According to the *New Statesman*'s T. C. Worsley, Osborne was describing 'the seamy side of the Kingsley Amis world'. Comparisons between Amis and Osborne were encouraged by the happy coincidence of their protagonists' names – Osborne's hero was obviously an 'unlucky Jim'.[14]

In the two months between the opening of *Look Back in Anger* in May 1956 and the creation of the Angry Young Men in July, Amis's reputation suffered again when reviewers linked him with two more young writers, W. John Morgan and George Scott. Morgan's novel

The Small World appeared in May, furnished with a dust-jacket recommendation from Amis. Reviewers could not resist comparing Morgan's comic tale of a Welsh student's troubles with *Lucky Jim*, and the *Daily Telegraph*'s 'Peter Simple' could not resist passing satiric judgment on the new batch of redbrick heroes. On 7 and 8 June 'Peter Simple' gave his own vision of Oxford University in 1966, dominated by boozing, belching, spitting dons from 'South Shields, Swansea and Walsall', apparently in the Amis–Morgan mould. George Scott's *Time and Place*, published early in July, proved to Colm Brogan that society in general would have to face the rise of these 'Lucky Jims' from the 'proletariat'. Brogan tried to outdo Maugham in his denunciation of Amis' hero: 'Lucky Jim is a loafer, a sycophant, a vulgarian who has taken advantage of State bounty to secure a university post when he is mentally and morally unfit to be a school janitor. If Redbrick has many like Lucky Jim, that institution may be written off.'[15]

Now that critics had established Amis as the creator of a Welfare State oik, the pundits of Fleet Street had no difficulty in press-ganging him into the Angry Young Men. First of all Daniel Farson followed up his *Evening Standard* interview with Amis to name him as a leader of the literary 'Post-War Generation'. Farson's original feature described Amis respectfully as a successful novelist whose work was discussed in universities. His *Daily Mail* article on 12 July conveyed a rather different impression: 'Kingsley Amis . . . writes about adultery, nappies and washing-up. His new type of hero, Lucky Jim, dislikes anything that smacks of culture and has been bitterly described by Somerset Maugham as "scum".' A similar image of Amis was conjured up by John Barber in his presentation of the Angry Young Men in the *Daily Express* a fortnight later. Barber hailed him as 'the sort of man who likes billiards, bars and progressive jazz clubs' and loathes 'sham' and 'suave politeness'. The account of Jim Dixon and John Lewis followed suit: 'His heroes prefer beer and blondes to brains. They are unashamed lowbrows.'

Once he was burdened with AYM status, Amis became a household name. Only six months after the invention of the AYM, a review in the *Daily Worker* announced that 'Kingsley Amis is as much a part of the world of 1957 as television, rock 'n' roll and the FA Cup.'[16] Previously the popular press had shown very little interest; the *Evening Standard* had managed to carry Farson's feature on Amis in May but Farson had had to introduce him as 'a figure in the intellectual world'. The introduction would look odd and unnecessary in the following three years, a period in which Amis appeared on television and was featured in papers like the *Sunday Dispatch* and the *Daily Express*. Of course, the degree of literary interest in Amis varied now that he was a celebrity; for example, readers of the *Daily Mail* were able to enter into the confidence of Hilary Amis who divulged that her husband was a 'very good kisser'.[17]

Amis's new-found fame was soon causing anxiety at Gollancz where anticipation of the great profits their controversial young author might bring was dimmed by rumours – incorrect, as it happened – that he was dissatisfied and thinking of moving to another publisher. In an effort to keep their lucrative asset Gollancz took the unusual step for them of issuing a book of poems – Amis' third collection, *A Case of Samples* – in November 1956. Two months later his next work did appear under a different imprint, but it was a pamphlet issued by the Fabian Society, *Socialism and the Intellectuals*. Besides receiving fairly comprehensive coverage in the quality press, the tract was also reviewed in the *Daily Worker* (which went to the trouble of featuring a reply from Amis), the *Daily Express* commissioned an article by Amis on his political views, and *Reynolds News* serialized 'The Pamphlet Everyone Is Talking About'.[18]

In September 1957 *Lucky Jim* began to reach a far larger public after the general release of the film. Early reports that Hitchcock would direct and that the young Cambridge Footlights comedian, Jonathan Miller, might play the part of Dixon, proved to be unfounded. It seems a pity that this intriguing combination was not involved, especially because the Boulting Brothers' production and Patrick Campbell's script created a vapid, knockabout farce. Ian Carmichael (soon to play the upper-class twit in *I'm All Right, Jack*) was pitiably miscast as Jim Dixon and struggled to produce a sporadically northern accent. Amis put on a dutiful front in public, saying that he was pleased with the film, but privately he was very miffed. He complained and offered to help with re-writes, but to no avail. However, he decided against open protest:

> You say to yourself, 'Is there a matter of principle here?' Which is another way of saying, 'Is anybody whose opinion I care about going to be misled or disaffected by this?' Answer, 'No.' So then you might

as well make the best of it and take the money. Wasn't much of that. Still, you take it.[19]

The screen version of *Lucky Jim* was actually premièred at the Edinburgh Film Festival but with its scrapes and japes storyline it was clearly aimed at popular success. Reviews appeared in newspapers such as the *Star*, the *Daily Herald* and the *Daily Sketch* ('Lucky Jim! It's Fun, Fun, Funny') which had remained oblivious of the novel.[20] The *Daily Herald* critic claimed he had cried with laughter, but most reviewers recognized the film for what it was – a witless failure. Nevertheless, the adaptation acquired a life and success of its own. The adulteration of the original work reached an absurd level in the first week of October when the *Evening Standard* published Philip Oakes's serialization of the story of the film of the book.

Amis's media prominence in the fifties was at its height between September and December 1957, four months which overlapped with the period of greatest fame and notoriety for the AYM in general. While *Lucky Jim* was being screened in cinemas throughout the country, extracts from Amis's third novel, *I Like It Here*, were being serialized in *Punch* (from 16 October to 4 December). Amis had a radio drama, *Touch and Go*, broadcast on the Third Programme on 6 November, and there was talk of his writing a musical with Bruce Montgomery about beauty contests.

In common with the other Angry Young Men, Amis discovered that this success was to be short-lived. His refusal to contribute to *Declaration* had helped him to avoid the notoriety of Osborne or Wilson, but he still experienced a critical backlash when Gollancz published *I Like It Here* on 13 January 1958. He was now a sitting target for reviewers who found it all too easy and appealing to knock down a writer whose reputation had become that of a loutish upstart. Far from attempting to placate his potential critics, though, Amis seemed to invite hostility with *I Like It Here*. The novel's markedly thin plot followed the exploits of his most militantly philistine hero yet, Garnet Bowen, during his enforced experience of 'Abroad' and his quest for an enigmatic, possibly fraudulent, oldster novelist, Wulfstan Strether. It is a book of many Amisian postures and ironies, not least of which was the fact that it was partly based on the trip to Portugal in 1955 which Amis had taken as a condition of his Somerset Maugham Award. He had been preparing to write *Take a Girl Like You,* but instinct told him to set that aside and write another novel first. His original idea was for an anti-travelogue with Jim Dixon in the role of the author-hunter. As it was, the finished product carried all the signs of a potboiler. To those reviewers in the know it must have read like Amis's version of the primary school set-piece, 'What I Did on My Holidays'.

Even his admirers condemned *I Like It Here.* William Cooper judged it to be 'far below standard, not even bad so much as poor', and G. S. Fraser closed the book 'with a sad feeling, as if one had just watched Mr Bannister or Mr Chataway running an eight-minute or even a sixteen-minute mile'.[21] Other critics, like Penelope Mortimer and Kenneth Young, could now boast that they had never really warmed to Amis's comedy.[22] In February's *Books and Bookmen* John Foss spoke for many of his colleagues in concluding that *I Like It Here* was 'a stinker that ought never to have been published'.

There were two main features of Amis's third novel which provoked these attacks. The first was Garnet Bowen's automatic loathing of all signs of foreignness and culture. John Foss was unimpressed:

> It shows a philistinism which one previously suspected but never credited; a mocking at culture which would not have been out of place in the *Daily Express*; and a fifth-form sense of humour which rarely ventures above the level of lavatories. The word 'bum', for example, is used no fewer than eleven times in a single paragraph.

Even G. S. Fraser agreed that Amis's vulgarity and philistinism had reached unacceptable levels and that it was now time to declare that enough really was enough. The second and obviously related criticism was that Amis had covered old, tiresome and thoroughly objectionable ground in the characterization of Garnet Bowen; except for minor differences 'of name and employment', his three heroes were identical. The latest protagonist was Jim Dixon Mark III, 'Lucky Bowen'.[23]

Critics were now reading Amis's books simply as sequels to *Lucky Jim*; there had been no radical departures in his fiction to discourage this, and his first novel was by far the best known of his distinctive works. Just as *I Like It Here* was received as 'Lucky Jim Abroad', so had *Socialism and the Intellectuals* been greeted as

'Lucky Jim's Political Testament'.[24] This second heading also indicates that commentators were now treating Jim Dixon and his creator as one and the same personality. Highbrow reviewers had already begun to make moves in this direction before the publicists of Anger latched on to Amis, but with greater and wider attention, accounts of his fiction were increasingly based on the need for snappy copy rather than concern for the finer questions of authorial distance. Amis found to his dismay that journalists were more than happy to combine and confuse the fictional and the real. His heroes were assumed to be fictional *alter egos*, ventriloquist's dolls; conversely, Amis himself was promoted as a real-life version of his most famous character, with reporters highlighting his own career as scholarship boy and redbrick lecturer. A new figurehead was created – 'Lucky Jim Amis'.[25]

Amis's books had acquired the status of unquestionable documentaries of the lifestyle and attitudes of the fifties generation. Amis refused to back the pundits' cause (as the resolutely personal, even idiosyncratic, line of his Fabian pamphlet demonstrates) but he also refused to break his own rule and oppose all the opinionating about his novels by explaining what he thought he was really writing about. He had to remind himself that any publicity is good publicity, while *Lucky Jim* in particular became the victim of what Angus Wilson called 'sociological gossip'.[26]

So widespread was that gossip that eventually it would seem very odd or even affected to regard Jim Dixon simply as a main character in a comic novel. Jim was invested with an importance quite independent of the fiction to which he belonged, and it became common practice to cite him almost as a real-life figure in discussions of specific social issues. In the first issue of *Universities and Left Review* in 1957, Stuart Hall and David Marquand analysed Jim's social position and politics with as much concern and attention as E. P. Thompson analysed *Socialism and the Intellectuals*. 'Suppose Lucky Jim did join the Labour Party,' pondered Marquand. The daftest example of the character's liberation from the novel came from A. J. P. Taylor who decided that 'It was Lucky Jim who marched to Aldermaston, some thousands of him.'[27]

As it gathered its own momentum, *Lucky Jim's* social and political reputation needed less and less reference to the book and relied instead on the rapidly growing stock of fanciful opinions about what constituted 'Lucky Jimmery'.[28] Despite all the commentaries, the details of Jim's social significance remained varied and confused. Was Jim lucky or angry? A representative of social mobility or social protest? Or perhaps both? Only Jim's status as a typical product of State-sponsored opportunity was certain. Even if trend-spotters bothered to consult the novel, it would not have helped them very much, for Amis just had not had the good grace to reserve a few chapters for a careful outline of his hero's social background and significance. Which class did Jim belong to? The new middle class, the new working class, the new lower middle class, the new classless class, all were tried and tested. Certainly Jim was *not* posh. And as an Angry Young Man he must surely be angry about privilege. Or perhaps he was enraged by the Establishment in particular, or bourgeois values in general? Or maybe he was only envious of his social superiors?[29]

Many of the clichés and general confusions involved in the Lucky Jim image were gathered together by Philip Oakes for an *Evening Standard* feature on 26 September 1957:

> Lucky Jim Dixon is the first hapless hero to climb from the crib of the Welfare State. His bones are reinforced by Government dried milk. His view of the world is through National Health spectacles. And he looks back – not in anger – but with surprise, that he has been allowed to barge through the privileged ranks of bores and phonies, towards some kind of success.
>
> He is state-aided, but self-made. His accent is flat, but his wits are sharp. He has his enemies ('They are all scum,' said Somerset Maugham, remarking on the new, surging, grammar school breed). But in the uncivil war between Us and Them, he is the man most likely to move into the room at the top.

Most versions of Amis's Welfare State hero followed much more scandalized lines. 'Lust and discontent', delinquency, a complete lack of grace and sophistication, were a few of the many qualities assigned to Jim.[30] Dixon was an uncouth, barbaric, bitterly resentful, lower-class, provincial yob with a greasy chip on each hefty shoulder.

> Dixon behaves abominably; he feels – quite unnecessarily, as far as can be gathered – that he is an 'outsider' socially, and takes every opportunity to be rude. His sole escape when he feels baffled is to drink too much. He plays tricks on his colleagues, writes anonymous letters, destroys documents to give people trouble, and tries to

impersonate others on the telephone. Malicious and envious, he has in him no drop of the milk of human kindness.[31]

This condemnation of Amis's hero by Bonamy Dobrée was run-of-the-mill stuff when it was published in 1957, but when *Lucky Jim* first appeared three years earlier only one reviewer had reacted in this appalled fashion; the critic in *The Times* had described Jim as 'normal', 'intelligent', 'likeable' and 'extremely amusing', concluding that 'Mr Amis holds out no particular claims for Dixon'. Amis's own reputation had changed as well. The comic novelist of the Movement, with a taste for farce and donnish jokes, had become Lucky Amis, Socialist scholarship boy and representative of the Redbrick branch of the Angry Young Men.

How valid were the transformed reputations of Amis and *Lucky Jim*? Reading the novel now, it may seem very hard to understand what all the fuss was about. It would also have been hard to predict such heated reactions from the basic outline Amis formed for his book. He has said that, with his novels, 'situations come first'.[32] The basic scenario was a 'young man surrounded by . . . hostile powers' and the visit to the Leicester university common room gave him the idea of a redbrick location:

> What followed can most easily, and accurately, be put in note form. University shags. Provincial. Probably keen on culture. Crappy culture. Fellow who doesn't fit in. Seems anti-culture. Non-U. Non-Oxbridge. Beer. Girls. Can't say what he really thinks. Boss trouble. Given chores. Disasters. Boring boss (a) so boring girl (b). Nice girl comes but someone else's property. Whose? Etc.[33]

The narrative develops from the two major predicaments he gave his hero. Dixon is trapped in a joyless relationship with Margaret (the 'boring girl') and he has to toady to Professor Welch (the 'boring boss') to keep his job. Neither plight is deserved or of Jim's making. The 'boss trouble' started (literally) by accident: a stone Jim kicked happened to wound the Professor of English, the College Registrar narrowly avoided injury when Jim clumsily overturned his chair, and Jim has criticized a book sponsored, it transpires, by Welch. As for Margaret, she has fabricated an intense emotional relationship with Jim without his encouragement, or even his knowledge. There seems to be no way out of either trap: 'economic necessity and the call of pity' commit Jim to his job and Margaret respectively.

In developing the story of Jim's predicaments Amis created a comedy which actually dodges social themes that could have dominated the work. Instead, the novel raises issues which remain stubbornly personal. A distinct moral theme emerges – the need to find respect for oneself and for others. It is a theme which, as Amis's basic outline suggests, vindicates Jim's thorough decency.

Self-respect is associated with self-confidence in *Lucky Jim*, which is founded on the premiss that its hero does not possess enough of either. All would have been well if Jim had been able to own up to his inadvertent errors, but he was 'too frightened' to do so. He would also not have been ensnared by the scheming Margaret if he could have stood up for himself and made it clear that theirs was a purely platonic friendship. As with Philip Larkin's *Jill, Lucky Jim* is largely a story of the hero's continuing timidity. Whereas John Kemp creates a fantasy world because he is shy and overawed by his suave acquaintances, Jim Dixon lurches from one comic disaster to another in attempts at damage limitation instead of admitting and explaining his mistakes. For example: the bad impression he has made in his job means Jim has to accept an invitation to the Welches' cultural gathering, where he is roped into a chorus of madrigals because he fails to admit that he cannot read music. Finding solace in the pub, he returns home drunk and accidently burns a hole in his bedclothes. Fearful of the consequences of an open apology, Jim tries to cover up the mess and is hounded by Mrs Welch (who has to be fought off with more deceptions) for the rest of the book.

Because Jim cannot assert himself he has to keep up a series of pretences, mimicking affection for Margaret and enthusiasm for the tasks allotted to him by Neddy Welch. He reacts with abuse, but this remains silent, imagined. In the opening scene, for instance, Jim has to content himself with an unspoken commentary on Welch's prattle and a fantasy of rewarding his garrulous boss with grievous bodily harm. Another symptom of Jim's policy of mute revolt is his habit of making faces – his 'shot-in-the-back face', his 'Edith Sitwell face' his 'lascar's face', etc. – all 'designed to express rage or loathing', so that when he wants to celebrate at the end of the novel he has to make do with his 'Sex Life in Ancient Rome face'. (Jim's inhibition in making his feelings known is often shared by Charles Lumley in *Hurry on Down*; Wain's hero daydreams of kicking his landlady's dog and 'almost' or 'nearly' gives rude replies.)

As the novel develops Jim begins to show signs of confidence and decisiveness. The first turning point comes at the College Ball; he plucks up courage to ask to see Christine afterwards and riskily procures a taxi. Although he then regrets talking so frankly to her, Jim realizes that speaking his mind suddenly seems to be feasible. He even experiments with his growing self-belief by trying to put Margaret to rights, but the tactic backfires when she simply becomes hysterical. Jim's first real victory over the shags comes when he confronts Bertrand Welch, knocks him down and gives him the abuse he had (as usual) been thinking to himself.

The incident with Margaret shows that self-assurance is a personal quality which must be used carefully and properly. Naïvety leads Christine to imitate confidence but she only appears ' "prim" ' and ' "starchy" '. The self-confidence of decent chaps like Atkinson and Christine's millionaire uncle, Gore-Urquhart, is admirable, but in a shag like Bertrand it degenerates to overbearing arrogance. The diffidence of Margaret's ex-'lover', Catchpole, in fact helps to establish him as a sympathetic character, since the wrong kind of self-assertiveness, imposing and self-centred, has been shown by the shags who have oppressed Jim and consigned him to a frustrating life of boredom.

Boredom is important in *Lucky Jim* as the inevitable response to those who do not show respect or consideration for other people. The greatest bore is, of course, Neddy Welch, closely followed by Margaret and Bertrand. Bores are bores because they have no thought of others: bores are self-obsessed. Dixon puts the case against this type quite succinctly in his judgement of Bertrand: ' "Bertrand's a bore, he's like his dad, the only thing that interests him is him ... he's the only bloody runner." ' Unlike the loquaciously boring shags, the decent characters are taciturn: Jim is unused to making long speeches, Christine apologizes when she thinks she is talking too much, and Gore-Urquhart is plainly a man of few words. Another symptom of the bores' self-obsession is that they take so little account of Jim that they call him by the wrong name. Welch calls him Faulkner, Maconochie addresses him as Jackson, to Margaret he is James, and Caton and Bertrand settle on Dickinson. (It is not surprising that Jim is so pleased when

Gore-Urquhart and Christine address him by his own name.)
With such first-hand experience of the bore, Dixon is well-fitted
to become a 'boredom-detector' for fellow sufferer Gore-
Urquhart.

Far from being Maclaren-Ross's 'ignoble buffoon', Jim Dixon's
virtue is clearly portrayed within a moral context which is equally
clear, almost schematic. There are few grey areas in Amis's
characterization: there are boring shags and there are decent
chaps. Jim's enemies are completely devoted to their own dreadful interests, he and his allies are likeable, humorous and
considerate. Jim shows he is capable of the greatest altruism
when he prepares to renounce Christine out of a misplaced sense
of duty to Margaret. Critics who refused to recognize this moral
alignment and saw Jim as a despicable delinquent either had to
condemn the hero and the novel in general abuse or face up to
bewildering problems. Why did Jim come across as a thoroughly
sympathetic character? Why were the Welches so ridiculous?
Bonamy Dobrée was baffled; perhaps Amis wanted to satirize
society's vices by showing even the good characters like Neddy
Welch to be foolish and by creating a 'baboon' like Dixon as a
traditional comic hero. Jim's hooligan reputation spread first
because his farcical misadventures were misread as acts of
boorish vandalism – and then because the novel was ignored
altogether.

Similar abuse of the novel was required for it to be categorized
as a 'provincial' work. *Lucky Jim* had in fact only been treated
under the heading of the fashionable 'New Provincialism' in
general discussions about the Movement and then in comments
on Amis's own work after the publication of *That Uncertain
Feeling*. That the early critics did not tag *Lucky Jim* as 'provincial' is quite understandable, for the novel is, in a very real sense,
a 'London' comedy which mocks the pretensions of people who
prosper in a dull backwater. Much was made of the fact that
Amis lived and worked in Swansea, but he had gone there out of
necessity, not choice. Although he became very attached to
South Wales, he thinks of himself as 'a London person' and chose
to set *Lucky Jim* in the provinces partly because he wanted to use
the redbrick university background.[34] Hindsight may seem an
unfair weapon to use against those early commentators who
could have been misled by circumstantial evidence, but the

locations in his first two novels hardly celebrate the provinces. Aberdarcy is not depicted with any fondness or enthusiasm, and the unnamed town in *Lucky Jim*, as Amis says, hardly exists:

> Actually, if anybody wanted to go through *Lucky Jim* they could say, 'What are we actually *told* about this place? Where is it? What do the natives live on? Presumably it's industrial, but what industry? What is there?' It's got a hotel, it's got a railway station, it's got a cathedral, and a university . . . and it's got a place near it where a fellow has a house where madrigals are sung. And that's it. It could be anywhere.[35]

This is what Amis has called the 'deadly provincial background' of *Lucky Jim*. 'I had never had any theories about . . . the vitality of the provinces,' Amis has said – and it shows.[36]

This attitude is shared by other leading writers of the supposedly 'provincial' Movement. D. J. Enright's early novels were set in Egypt and an odd Utopian island. Of John Wain's first four novels only *The Contenders* (1958) has a secure regional location, and then for only half the book which otherwise takes place in London. The narrator, Joe Shaw, does not exactly celebrate his Potteries town: 'it's that place you stop at on the way to Manchester – the one where you look out of the train window when it's slowing down, and think, "Well, at least I don't live *here*." ' (Joe retains his childhood admiration for Brighton as an antidote.) The dispiriting glance at Coventry, also from a train window, prompts the sardonic recollections of an eventless provincial childhood in Larkin's poem 'I Remember, I Remember', which ends on a note of terse consolation: 'Nothing, like something, happens anywhere.'

'But especially in the provinces,' would be the reply of Jim Dixon, stuck in a stultifying hole he desperately wants to leave – for London. Jim's experience of the big city is an unworldly total of a dozen evenings, but his occasional visits cause painful nostalgia, even if his memories are only those of Lyons Corner Houses. London is an exotic place for Jim, as unavailable and exciting as 'Monte Carlo or Chinese Turkestan', a place to encourage poignant daydreams of escape from the boring redbrick grind. A fantasy of jumping aboard the ten-forty for a better life in London occurs to him as early as the second chapter. This daydream sharpens 'his ordinary desire to leave the provinces for London'.

This exchange constitutes an important part of Jim's sudden good fortune at the end of the novel. Critics have often missed the point and seen Jim's luck as financial. Amis has been unusually anxious to correct this misinterpretation by pointing out that Jim's salary will not change with his new job.[37] Jim's reward is not money but *London*, and the good life that beckons there – a job with Gore-Urquhart instead of lackeydom under Neddy Welch, and a relationship with Christine instead of the enforced liaison with the dismal Margaret.

Although the opinions about *Lucky Jim*'s provincialism and its hero's delinquency were clearly mistaken, the lower-class identities Amis and his fiction acquired do seem more convincing. Amis's own background certainly suits the social image of the Movement better than that of several other members of the group. (There is John Wain, for example, son of a prosperous dentist, and a student at Oxford only because his father could pay his fees; or Philip Larkin, son of Sydney Larkin, OBE, FRSS, FSAA, FIMTA, City Treasurer of Coventry; or Hampstead-raised Thom Gunn, whose father was editor of the *Daily Sketch*.) Jim Dixon, like Amis, comes from a modest background, probably lower-middle-class, with the character's career following a more suitable pattern than the author's: grammar school, provincial university (pre-emptively named as Leicester), and a humdrum Service record as an RAF corporal. Jim's lower-class origins can also be inferred from his 'flat northern voice' and even his appearance. Not for Jim the tall, reedy frame or the sensitive expression: he is 'on the short side, fair and round-faced, with an unusual breadth of shoulder'. Of Amis's first three protagonists it is John Lewis who comes closest to earning the badge of working-class membership, with his memory of 'a coach trip . . . with a party of my father's workmates'. Towards the end of *That Uncertain Feeling* Lewis can even announce that he is working in a colliery, with the 'slight' qualification that his is an office job.

Far less convincing, however, was the way Amis and his lower-class characters were held up as representatives of the rise of the meritocracy; on this issue the 'sociological gossip' about *Lucky Jim* in particular not only misrepresented the novel but also the social realities the novel was supposed to be reflecting. The assumption that contemporary fiction could be regarded as a clear and faithful mirror of society was very common in the fifties. Indeed, this helps to explain why young social realist writers, who were formed into the core of the Angry Young Men, achieved such prominence. This assumption was most clearly expressed by Geoffrey Gorer, who observed in a *New Statesman* article of 4 May 1957 that the central sexual relationships in *Lucky Jim, Look Back in Anger* and *Room at the Top* were all 'hypergamous' (i.e. the male protagonists are all involved with women of higher social standing). He proposed that this signified an increase in the real upward social mobility of lower-class men, and explained that he felt justified in generalizing from art to life because he was sure that these fictions accurately reflected social reality.

This approach to Amis's work meant that *Lucky Jim* was taken to signify the emergence of a generation of lower-class State-educated students. The reception of *Lucky Jim* helped to create the new social archetype of the scholarship boy, emblem of a meritocratic post-war society. *Lucky Jim*'s influence in this respect is shown by the publication in 1956 of George Scott's *Time and Place*. Scott claimed that, as a scholarship boy, he represented a new generation (especially of writers) and that his autobiography, published when he was only thirty-one, therefore held real relevance to the times. By 1960 the importance of the scholarship-boy phenomenon had become so generally acknowledged that Gollancz could publish *The Glittering Coffin*, the autobiographical statement of Dennis Potter, then a twenty-three-year-old working-class student at Oxford.

The problem with the cultural prominence of this meritocratic figure was that it masked a reality which was far less spectacularly egalitarian. It is true that, since the war, increased financial help (partly through ex-servicemen's grants) had made further education possible to many non-privileged students. By 1956–7 more than three-quarters of students in England were receiving State grants. However, the sociological gossips ignored the fact that these beneficiaries were mostly middle-class and that the vast majority of university entrants still came from direct-grant and public schools. By 1956 the proportion of lower-class students at university had hardly changed since the gross inequalities of the pre-war years.[38]

As a 1954 report said, the Welfare State had not provided any greater social mobility for the generation born between 1920 and 1929 – the generation of Amis and Jim Dixon. This report looked to the Butler Education Act of 1944 as holding 'a promise of change'.[39] The first Butlerites were born in 1932 and their earliest literary products – apart from those of the Angry Tinies – would be works like *Eating People is Wrong* (1959) by Malcolm Bradbury, and Potter's *The Glittering Coffin*. The image of Jim Dixon as a character whose 'bones are reinforced by Government dried milk' would require him to have been the first teenage History lecturer of modern times. Not even Jane Gaskell could have rivalled that. However, minor drawbacks such as factual accuracy were easily overcome by the journalists and critics who created this image of Jim as a Welfare State product. Their opinions *felt* right, but only helped to promote very misleading assumptions about contemporary 'egalitarianism'.

These opinions could only be extracted from the novel in the first place by the most cursory and superficial reading. On the specific issue of the Butler Act, for example, pundits had to skip over the passage when Jim Dixon actually agrees with Beesley's tirade about the dire consequences of university expansion. Beesley's speech anticipates Amis's own infamous warning that an increased university intake would mean a lowering of standards, that 'More Will Mean Worse'.[40]

Similarly, anything other than a glance over the pages of *Lucky Jim* (and Amis's other early novels) reveals that the claims for his new hero being a social rebel and protester were also very misleading. Amis's own politics were undeniably left of centre in the fifties: he stated in *Socialism and the Intellectuals* that he had always voted Labour and on several other occasions defended post-war social reform. However, he also wrote, 'I cannot pretend that the flame of my political ardour burns very bright,' and the strident socialist views ascribed to him by the *Daily Telegraph* in 1958 simply fail to ring true.[41] His Fabian pamphlet should have scotched the myths about his radicalism; writing three weeks after the height of the crises over Hungary and Suez, he admitted that he was still not moved to political commitment. Like Garnet Bowen, he thought of himself as leftish, but only really in preference to 'the other crowd'.

As with the other aspects of Amis's reputation, the political one was maintained by his publicists' eagerness to take a few details from his novels quite out of context. For example, when John Lewis says he wants to 'call for a toast to the North Korean

Foreign Minister or Comrade Malenkov' at a middle-class party, he is making a *joke* because he is annoyed by the boring patter of the guests. Jean Lewis mocks the theatrical 'honest Joe' posture her husband adopts when faced with 'upper-class types'. Likewise, Jim Dixon's pro-Labour outburst comes in reaction to the comically élitist Bertrand, and his bun theory of economic reform seems pretty tame: ' "If one man's got ten buns and another's got two, and a bun has got to be given up by one of them, then surely you take it from the man with ten buns." ' Amis's heroes do lean slightly to the left, but, as Bowen reflects, domestic politics seem too trivial to inspire anything but apathy. Amis is rightly very resentful of the interpretations of *Lucky Jim* as a statement of radical political faith. Jim's rebellion is mild, and is dictated by his particular relationship with Professor Welch. He does not want to change the social system – he wants a more enjoyable place within it. And he finds one. That he gleefully accepts his post as secretary to a millionaire businessman and finds true love with that businessman's niece hardly accords with the image of Jim as social outcast or left-wing rebel. His reward is acceptable because questions of social conscience and political principle are irrelevant. Jim has few of the scruples of Charles Lumley in *Hurry on Down*; his outlook is closer to the unashamed self-interest of Joe Lampton in *Room at the Top*.

The raw material of *Lucky Jim* certainly gave Amis the chance to write about issues of class and class conflict, or at least, as Larkin did in *Jill*, to write a novel which relies on class differences to determine characterization and narrative. After all, he created a non-U hero and placed him in a potentially U context. As Amis recalls, though, he did not want to exploit this situation to develop social or political themes. That *Lucky Jim* does not express a 'class consciousness' is indicated, Amis thinks, by the facts that he did not emphasize the Welches' social superiority, and that the Welches 'never try to make Dixon feel small in a class way'.[42] Amis is also careful to qualify his characterization of Gore-Urquhart and Christine so that they occupy the roles of upper-class benefactor and upper-class glamour girl, but refuse to meet the social requirements of these roles.

The characterization of Julius Gore-Urquhart effects an especially neat compromise. He escapes conventional class categorization by being introduced as a Scot, with a strong Lowlands accent and nationalist politics. His politics are sociologically neutral and the opposing class indicators of his accent and his hyphenated name cancel each other out. Gore-Urquhart has no definite class identity: he cannot be assumed to be either a self-made man or congenitally privileged. It is a very clever evasion by Amis. Gore-Urquhart retains the kudos of being distinguished and rich while being established as a decent sort of bloke, the perfect patron for Dixon.

The same is true of the characterization of Christine. At first she seems to fulfil all the requirements to offer Dixon a 'hypergamous' relationship. When he first meets her Dixon assumes she is 'posh', as well as beautiful and unattainable. Her appearance 'seemed an irresistible attack on his own habits, standards and ambitions: something designed to put him in his place for good'. He later complains that Christine is ' "a bit out of my class" '. These terms promise the same association between sexual desirability and higher class status made by other lower-class heroes, like H. G. Wells's Mr Polly and Braine's Joe Lampton. In *Lucky Jim*, though, Amis uses the confusion of sexual and social status to establish Christine's appeal and apparent unattainability, but refuses to continue the association which would have created a definite class theme and context. Once Christine is implicated in the upper-class role Amis steadily qualifies this so that she remains glamorous while emerging as a good sort and less out of Jim's social reach. The first hints of this qualification come when Christine pours ketchup all over her cooked breakfast and does not object when Jim eats a fried egg with his fingers. She then helps Jim in his cosmetic repairs to the burnt blankets. Christine's common streak appears again at the ball when she dances indifferently. The process of class demotion is complete when Dixon detects a 'faint cockney intonation' in her voice. Finally, he is able to speculate that she may not have much money after all. The result is that gaining Christine and a job with Gore-Urquhart does not imply that Jim has sided with the values of any particular class. Class characteristics have been used, but characterization has not been determined by class.

Lucky Jim is therefore very different in this respect from *Jill*, where a similar situation and similar personal themes are treated in a way which is clearly class-based. The working-class student, John Kemp, disowns his background when faced with the enviable assurance and wit of his well-heeled room-mate at Oxford, Christopher Warner. Kemp retreats into wish-fulfilment fantasies based on an imagined sister who enjoys an upper-middle-class upbringing. When he meets Mrs Warner he feels ashamed of his own mother and hopes passers-by will assume he is Mrs Warner's son. Kemp's cringing self-abasement is not to be taken merely as adolescent callowness: as Larkin has remarked, Kemp's background acts as 'a built-in handicap to put him one down'.[43] Thus, when John's parents arrive in Oxford they display the same nervous deference to Warner. Assurance and glamour are the prerogatives of social privilege: the lower-class outlook is marked by diffidence and, as the example of Whitbread, the dour Yorkshire scholar, serves to remind Kemp, by dull plodding.

Lucky Jim uses several class associations which recall those in *Jill*, but for different effects; the formulae and conventions of class-based fiction are present, but in such a way that themes of class conflict are avoided. If any social attitudes emerge they are those of uncomplicated aspiration. In fact, Amis takes great care to avoid creating a socially, politically concerned novel in *Lucky Jim*. Class issues would only distract attention from Amis's real concerns which are not 'social' in the ordinary sense at all.

These real concerns were ignored in the fifties. Misreadings conjured up social and political significance which would only have been hampered by attention to the novel itself. It is easy to see how the mistaken notions could prosper, for once established, Jim's reputation as an Angry Young Man, a reliable source of good copy, developed quite independently of the novel, which was relegated to the status of an occasionally consulted secondary source. Publicity creates its own momentum, its own reference points and images, and the publicized Jim offered much more scope than the 'real' Jim for journalists to indulge in social 'analysis' and pontification. *Lucky Jim* was one of the principal victims among books and plays of the time which were distorted by and for the needs of glib punditry.

5

'Class Comedy'

Kingsley Amis did deserve a radical reputation in the fifties, but
not the sociological and political ones he was awarded. The unjus-
tifiable accounts of *Lucky Jim* in particular arose from mistaken
notions of what Amis's real challenge was. Contrary to received
opinion, Amis's 'rebellion' was not that of militant social or political views given literary expression, but a distinctly literary opposition which was often expressed in cultural and social terms. 'No
"commitment" for me, except to literature,' Amis has protested.[1]
This is not the conventional disclaimer of a writer boasting his
exclusive attention to the tasks of writing, because Amis
developed a literary campaign with a force and conviction which
were noticeably absent from his apathetic political statements. If
political implications are misread in his early fiction only confused
and eventually reductive accounts are possible. But by focusing on
the literary nature of the challenge Amis was presenting in the
fifties, the author's own denials of his social significance can be
respected and innovative importance restored to his writing. This
perspective also reveals the consistency in Amis's fundamental
beliefs over the past thirty years, beliefs which are consistent with
and foreshadowed the apparently dramatic turnabout in his political sympathies.

From his earliest reviews in *Essays in Criticism* and then regularly
in his reviews for the *Spectator*, Amis maintained a resolute and
controversial opposition to the current literary orthodoxy. In his
opinion the most respected modern writers were really failures
who had simply not produced enjoyable, worthwhile writing. His
attacks were directed mostly at Modernists, and writers influenced
by Modernism, all of whom he regarded as 'modern practitioners
of a chap-fallen Romanticism'.[2]

Amis considered that one of the major faults of this decadent tradition was that it ignored 'the prime literary subject, relations between human beings'.[3] He argued for a return to the externally observed material of everyday social reality, what in his poem 'Against Romanticism' he called 'real time and place'. Rejection of social experience had led to two deplorable tendencies in modern writing. First there were novelists like Virginia Woolf who had opted for a preoccupation with the subjective. Then there were those who craved the 'uplift' of mysticism and, when transcendence failed, scurried to proclaim feelings of *ennui* and *angst*; writers who made 'off-the-peg avowals of weariness and distaste for the modern world' did so, he said, only because they were ignorant of that world and too conceited to find out about it for themselves. (A similarly hearty reaction to this temperament came from John Wain who wrote that *angst* was a 'delusion' and that sufferers needed 'to be shaken into a more robust frame of mind'.)[4]

In Amis's opinion the Modernists had ignored the obligation to their readers as well as to their proper, social subject matter. Literature had been led astray by 'losing sight of its function as a form of entertainment'.[5] Two early victims of Amis's wrath were the then-fashionable poets, Edith Sitwell and W. R. Rodgers, accused of self-indulgent obscurity.[6] Many of his subsequent attacks in the fifties were directed at those who persisted with writing which was experimental and/or ostentatious in style. 'Experiment' to Amis simply meant 'obtruded oddity'. The exhibitionist style of Dylan Thomas amounted to nothing more than 'multiplied whimsy'. Nabokov had only achieved 'a high idiosyncratic noise-level' in the ornate writing of *Lolita*.[7] Amis admired work which was accessible and entertaining. Readability was an important criterion of literary value: 'the worth of a novel has some positive correlation with its reader's willingness to turn over each successive page.'[8] As a result Amis valued humour and clarity in fiction rather than solemn attempts at profundity, and approved of middlebrow writers like P. G. Wodehouse and John Prebble, competent literary craftsmen.

These aesthetic views reveal certain moral principles at work, as the critical vocabulary suggests: verbiage is 'irresponsible', indulgent style is 'indecent', novelists should aspire to 'prose decency'.[9] These are the expressions of the ordinary bloke's morality, implying the same moral outlook which emerged in *Lucky Jim*; the selfishness of shags like the Welches and the neurotic self-concern of Margaret find their aesthetic equivalents in Modernist writers whose inaccessibility and introspection denied any consideration of their readers. Once again boredom is the response to self-obsession.

Amis's views on art and its several obligations have not just survived the shift in his political allegiance but become stronger as confidence in his own judgement has grown. In the fifties residual respect and timidity hampered the development of his views: 'I hadn't got as far as saying – to myself or anybody else – that Pound is *worthless*, that Eliot is mostly *worthless*. I was too nervous of that and too impressed by their standing.[10] Now Amis can declare that Modernism is 'a great fraud' which can prosper only under the protection of iniquitous arts subsidies. Sponsorship from organizations like the Arts Council (a 'socialist quango') only encourages artists to forget their responsibilities by freeing them from the market forces of supply and demand. A writer who does not need to please his public 'is tempted to self-indulgence and laziness'. Many twentieth-century artists 'have got heavily involved with their material at the expense of the public' which has been 'bored, baffled or outraged', reactions which for Amis confirm his argument because 'the public . . . is usually right'.[11] Amis was joined in this campaign against Modernism by Philip Larkin, whose best-known statements on the 'irresponsibility' of most modern art come in the Introduction of his book *All What Jazz* (1970), where he attacks the representative trio of 'Parker, Pound [and] Picasso' and expresses similar support in similar terms for the needs of the paying 'public', not the paid 'experts'.

Like Larkin, Amis could reject Modernism because he could dismiss questions about the nature of experience and the nature of art's relation to experience. Where others have seen necessary and vital achievements in Modernism, Amis has seen gratuitous obscurity and wilful self-indulgence. His bluff, no-nonsense stance meant that he favoured, in Pamela Hansford Johnson's words, the 'popular entertainment side' of literature instead of the 'prestige side', preferring detective novels and science fiction to the novels of Woolf and Lawrence.[12]

Amis revelled in iconoclastic judgements of literary figureheads, new and old. The one great novelist he admired without qualification in the fifties was Henry Fielding, who receives the ultimate

Amisian accolade from Garnet Bowen: 'he had been a good chap.' Amis found in his work all the virtues of realist, comic narrative and the crucial desire to entertain. At the beginning of *Tom Jones*, Fielding recommends the author to 'consider himself, not as a Gentleman who gives a private or eleemosynary Treat but rather as one who keeps a public Ordinary', a tavern keeper ready to satisfy his customers. Similarly, the title of his third collection of poems suggests that Amis chooses as his model of the artist the travelling salesman, offering his 'case of samples' in the hope that he can meet the customers' requirements. He aims to achieve this in his own fiction by writing within 'the main English-language tradition' – by 'trying to tell interesting, believable stories about understandable characters in a reasonably straightforward style: no tricks, no experimental foolery'.[13]

With such firmly held opinions about the attributes and aims of good writing, Amis had a lot to live up to in his own work. However, *Lucky Jim* does meet the demands Amis outlined and can be seen as a highly accomplished, almost exemplary, anti-Modernist novel. Its popular success is testimony to Amis's own success in using the virtues he described to achieve his fundamental aim of pleasing his public. Like all his fiction, *Lucky Jim* is an eminently accessible work, clearly written, very carefully constructed and very funny. *Lucky Jim* also shows the entertainment value of dealing with the contemporary social reality which Amis accused Modernists of ignoring. He actually depended on readers recognizing and responding to the 'real time and place' he describes, because specific social references often carry special meaning. The fact that Margaret wears a green Paisley frock, for example, or Bertrand a 'lemon-yellow sports-coat' with all three buttons fastened, classifies these characters and readers have to understand the implications of such details.

In the terms of David Lodge's valuable distinction, this technique belongs to 'metonymic' rather than 'metaphoric' fiction – to traditional realist fiction which describes ordinary social reality.[14] It is a reality Amis accepts wholeheartedly, a reality of common experience and common sense. Events and characters are not doubted or probed, but observed and judged with a confidence which Modernists had rejected as invalid. Virginia Woolf condemned descriptions of 'the fabric of things' surrounding characters and tried to render the inner reality of imagination and memory; Amis concentrates on social existence and refuses to analyse psychologies beyond a certain point; shags are shags and chaps are chaps and there's an end to it. In his first novel Amis clings to the notion of luck to save himself from the quicksand of further speculation. Jim is lucky because the comedy dictates a happy ending to unhappy predicaments. Gore-Urquhart's patronage is certainly deserved, but such benevolence owes less to recognizable circumstances than to the demands of comic convention. (As Jim himself acknowledges, he has 'hardly said two words to the man'.) Again, it is the law of comedy itself which provides Catchpole's revelations about Margaret's emotional blackmail in order to free Jim from any sense of responsibility to her. In this sense *Lucky Jim* is not lifelike at all but a novel based on the formulae found in jokes, farce or pantomime.

Margaret's characterization shows Amis at his most vulnerable because her neuroses invite less peremptory consideration than he would like. If she had Christine's looks would she be as nice a person as Christine? Dixon's speculations along such awkward lines have to be brought to a sudden halt: 'All that could logically be said was that Christine was lucky to look so nice.' And that Margaret is plain and neurotic. Catchpole's revelations also function to reassert the clear division between the clearly likeable or clearly unlikeable characters in the novel. Ambiguities and anomalies, like attractive neurotics, cannot exist.

Amis shies away from the Modernist 'indulgences' of introspection and uncertainty. Instead he offers acceptance of things as they appear to be, and, in contrast to the ambitions and anxieties of the Romanticist outlook, the axioms of the decent chap's reflections: 'All positive change was good; standing still, growing to the spot, was always bad'; 'Doing what you wanted to do was the only training, and the only preliminary, needed for doing more of what you wanted to do'; 'nice things are nicer than nasty ones'. Dixon's homespun ethics belong to the world of straightforward morality which Garnet Bowen envied Henry Fielding for having lived in, and which Amis recreates in fiction founded on the principles Bowen advocates – 'common sense, emotional decency and general morality'.

Amis's detractors would consider his return to traditional realist narrative in the 1950s to be as questionably unquestioning as the lessons Dixon learns, but *Lucky Jim* shows the advantages of working within traditional form and structure. Actually, the book follows a pattern which is not so much part of Amis's 'main English-language tradition' as timeless: a young hero in trouble gets into deeper trouble before his virtues are recognized by a benefactor and he can leave his problems behind and claim his apparently unattainable girl. All the fundamental character types of the traditional folk tale are present: the villains (the Welch family and Margaret), the donor/provider (Gore-Urquhart), the helpers (Carol Goldsmith, Atkinson, Beesley) the princess and her father (Christine and her uncle, Gore-Urquhart), the dispatcher (malevolently, in Neddy Welch), the false hero (Bertrand) and the hero (Jim).[15]

Amis takes great and unobtrusive care with the construction of his comedy within this traditional framework. The plot pivots on a series of key scenes – Neddy Welch's cultural weekend, the College Ball, and Jim's Merrie England lecture. Each of these events generates preparations and repercussions which spark off a further series of individual actions by the oppressed hero – his phone calls, his baiting of Johns, his conflicts with Bertrand and his dealings with Margaret, Christine and Professor Welch. This is a very carefully and skilfully paced comedy, in which the resolutions and revelations have all been prepared for. The slapstick sequence in the opening chapter, for example, describing Welch's atrocious car-driving, prepares for the decisive moment in the penultimate chapter when the same character's incompetence behind the wheel makes Christine miss the train which would have carried her away from Jim. Similarly, Catchpole, L. S. Caton and Michel Welch get brief mentions in the first chapter before each in turn earns his appearance (and non-appearance) money later in the novel. When the shadowy affair between Carol Goldsmith and Bertrand is finally dealt with Dixon reflects that 'the last thread was untangled'. Of course, for all the farcical problems are resolved, all the confusions clarified, the wrongs righted, and the hero and his princess can march off towards a metropolitan sunset. None of the characters is superfluous, irrelevant or forgotten. This is a totally controlled work.

Without that organizing control, traditional-realist novels can easily degenerate into a succession of separate incidents affecting the central character, just one damn thing after another. Freedom from tight construction can contribute to the appeal of picaresque or slice-of-life narratives but it can also mean that characters, incidents and details are introduced without making effective or explicable contributions to the work as a whole. What happened, for example, to Lumley's anguish about Sheila in *Hurry on Down*? His despair precedes another love and Sheila is summarily removed from the cast-list without further mention or effect, like a sacked soap-opera star. Why do minor characters like Mr Hassop's mysterious sister suddenly appear and disappear without reason in Stan Barstow's *A Kind of Loving*? Because they had real-life originals? The suspicions of fictionalized autobiography are certainly justified for William Cooper's *Scenes* series, which follows with disarming fidelity the life story of H. S. Hoff; Cooper's skill in adapting and selecting features of that story is marvellous, but occasionally events and details are mentioned or emphasized which seem more relevant to the autobiography than to the novels themselves.

In *Lucky Jim*, on the other hand, the care with which events, characters and minor details are orchestrated helps the novel to be as fully satisfying and rich in its own way as a Modernist work with its reliance on the underlying unity of symbol and image – with the advantage that readers need not have acquired particular expertise to appreciate and enjoy *Lucky Jim*. Amis showed that the traditional virtues of 'straightforward' realist storytelling were still viable and that by returning to those virtues contemporary fiction could still reach and entertain the large section of the reading public which had been spurned by the Modernists. A commitment to everyday social reality and to entertainment, with an assertively anti-Modernist fiction, was not only possible but highly effective.

However, *Lucky Jim* was a much more provocative work than loyalty to one particular literary form could have produced. This provocativeness does not even stem from conventional parody or satire, although Amis showed he was willing and able to use these techniques in his next two novels. In *That Uncertain Feeling* he presents a Dylan Thomas soundalike, Gareth Probert, Welsh bard *extraordinaire* and proud author of *The Martyr*, a verse drama which brilliantly caricatures *Under Milk Wood*. Set in Llados (a place name which recalls Thomas's naughtily reversed Llareggyb), *The Martyr* defies further specification, being chock-a-block with abstractions and capricious nonsense. In *I Like It Here*, Amis parodies an urbanely prolix style in the work of his Jamesian 'great writer', Wulfstan Strether. The two-page confrontation between Frescobaldi and Yelisaveta, principal characters of Strether's aptly-named *One Word More* (' "What is it that, my dear, would seem to be, now, the matter?" ') goads Bowen to daydream about pelting the author with ripe tomatoes. There is no such sustained and direct literary ridicule in *Lucky Jim*, the most controversial of the early novels, though Amis did take a few pot-shots at Romanticist postures of the 'Artist' in his portrayal of Bertrand as a painter of the beard-and-beret school. One slighting reference to Edith Sitwell (as the original for one of Jim's 'faces'), and Jim's dismissal of an unnamed contemporary poet are the only explicitly literary condemnations in the novel.

In fact, Amis's literary objections involved a much broader challenge in *Lucky Jim*, a challenge which meant that the book came to represent far more than a particular literary preference and that Amis gained a far more controversial reputation than his anti-Modernist stance alone would have brought. 'The Amis manner, the Amis hero, even the Amis critical technique, raise temperatures,' wrote Isabel Quigly in her *Spectator* review of *That Uncertain Feeling*; ' "Amis?" [people] say, and go red in the face.' Far more than 'a point of literary method' seemed to be at stake, a whole 'outlook' was involved.

This was so because Amis's opposition to the orthodoxy in English writing involved the content of his fiction as well as the form. This did not just mean a return to describing given social reality; much more specifically, he aimed to write about ordinary, lower-class social reality. He felt this was a new step to take at the time because, as he recalls, 'things like novels in England . . . had been the preserve of what we'll call the public school upper classes'.[16] In giving his protagonists non-privileged backgrounds and everyday problems and desires, even in giving them jobs, Amis felt that he was describing life as it was normally lived and therefore departing from the conventional fiction of the time – the fiction of privileged refinement and sensibility, of well-heeled characters and gracious settings, the fiction of garden parties, London clubs and country houses.

This dominant upper-class tradition had also accommodated the avant-garde of Modernism. The connections between privilege and experiment may look very tenuous – the élitist social conventions could be found more reliably in the traditionalist novels of writers like Angela Thirkell and L. P. Hartley; and most of the leading 'English' Modernists – including Joyce, Yeats, Conrad and Eliot – were not even actually English. But this is to forget the huge influence of the Bloomsbury Group, especially Virginia Woolf, in establishing an upper-class image for Modernism, and the already existing lower-middle-class identity of realist writing (as represented by Wells and Bennett) which made the socially élitist reputation of experiment seem all the more convincing. These class distinctions within literature had been available for several decades but they were particularly strong in the fifties. Thus in 1953, from literary evidence alone, Stephen Spender could call the *First Reading* contributors 'Lower Middle Brows', a tag which neatly conflates class and cultural categories. Conversely, anti-Modernists could attack the subjective and experimental tradition for being grounded in social privilege. Angus Wilson has put it on record that he attributed the 'over-concern with personal values' of writers like (who else?) Virginia Woolf to 'a private income and a long tradition of upper-middle-class security'. To Pamela Hansford Johnson both experiment and 'sensibility' had surrounded the English novel in a 'hush' that was decidedly 'well-bred'. William Cooper saw the Modernist themes of despair and alienation as the intellectual products of a privileged class.[17] Modernism could be regarded as a way of writing which was socially as well as aesthetically or intellectually exclusive.

The associations between social and literary élitism made Amis's own reaction coherent and comprehensive: a preference for ordinary social material went with a return to traditional formal virtues as the two halves of a whole revolt against a literary orthodoxy which was seen as both Modernist *and* upper-class. The lower-class backgrounds of his heroes were therefore the appropriate social qualifications for the anti-Modernist comedies in which they starred.

More pertinently, the felt dominance of the literature of social privilege allowed Amis creative space, the scope for originality. The social strata he described in his fiction are actually relatively prestigious (Dixon is a university lecturer, Lewis a graduate librarian, Bowen a literary journalist) but such material seemed then to be 'the most common straw', such 'ordinariness' seemed 'smelly and mean'. Even the use of the university setting in *Lucky*

Jim broke new ground, because 'varsity novels' had previously been set in Oxbridge, either comic tales of undergraduate japes or loving evocations of college life. Amis's most important original feature, though, was in his creation of bolshie, lower-class protagonists and Jim Dixon especially stood out as a new hero for a new kind of comedy. The first reviewers of *Lucky Jim* struggled to classify the novel. The one established reference (apart from *Hurry on Down*) became *Scenes from Provincial Life*, mainly because Cooper's novel also possessed a non-U hero. The novelty of this one shared feature outweighed all the obvious differences between the two works. (Indeed, when Cooper happened to hear the *First Reading* excerpt of *Lucky Jim* he called to his wife, 'Come and listen to this. Somebody's been reading *SPL*.'[18]) *Lucky Jim*'s early reviewers, however, had to resort to comparisons with the cinema. Sean O'Faolain in the *Observer* settled on 'Chaplinesque' as the best description of Dixon, Walter Allen was reminded of the Marx Brothers, John Connell mentioned Norman Wisdom and John Betjeman categorized the novel as 'a Harold Lloyd film or a Buster Keaton film in prose'.

The originality of Dixon's lower-class characterization goes some way towards explaining why his slapstick misadventures came to be interpreted as signs of loutish delinquency. It also helps to explain Amis's political and sociological reputations in the fifties: commentators latched on to the novelty of Dixon's social position and promoted him and his creator as representatives of current social reform. But since Amis was rejecting upper-class conventions, was it not the case that he was politically motivated? The question is particularly relevant for the fifties when literature, partly because it was so firmly characterized by social class, attracted an otherwise frustrated political commitment (witness too the importance to the New Left of cultural revaluation). The possibility of a political motive behind Amis's literary views seems even stronger because, as Christopher Ricks noted, it often appears that Amis dislikes things 'because they are liked by those whom he dislikes'. He himself reported that part of the reason for his antipathy to the theatre was his prejudice against theatregoers.[19] (His emphatic misogyny in the eighties is therefore a usefully provocative part of his continuing reaction to what he regards as literary and cultural chic, now represented for him by feminists and other trendy lefties.)

That Amis was, nonetheless, motivated by literary considerations in the fifties is indicated by three factors. The first is that, as *Lucky Jim* and his political statements show, Amis did not hold strong objections to the upper class. Then there is his literary journalism in which he was unwilling to make the association between privilege and experiment as clearly as Cooper and so dismiss Modernism on those grounds; he preferred to use generational rather than class terms: the pro-Modernists belonged to the 'oldster age-group' of the 'twenties and thirties' generation.[20] Even his calls for a return to ordinary material in fiction were not backed by any hints of political justification but remained steadfastly part of a literary perspective. Finally, there is Amis's own literary experience to consider. When he was rejecting the conventions of experiment and sensibility he was also reacting against his own early work:

> What I was reacting against was all the fiction and verse I'd written since the age of fifteen, all the Modernist verse . . . *The Legacy* which is Modernistic but less Modernistic than what I was writing before that. All those poems I wrote when I was sixteen. Bloody awful . . . I was bloody fortunate you see . . . If I'd been, what shall we say? Alan Pryce-Jones's son, or any other eminent man-of-letters', I'd have had a little book of poems out by the time I was eighteen. And everybody who read them at all would have said, 'Oh Christ, we don't want this do we?' Or perhaps they wouldn't . . . But I was able to get my Modernism done.[21]

Amis's misguided juvenilia continued while he was in the Army when he was still writing 'the bloody old semi-Kafka kind of stuff', 'all the pseudo-Dylan Thomas'. Very little of this early writing survived: 'All safely burnt, thank you. That's why there isn't any early Amis, if you see what I mean. It's all middle Amis.'[22] The rejection of his Modernistic novel was followed by Amis's rejection of Modernism. *Lucky Jim* was for him a radical departure into realism, the first major work of 'middle Amis's. Amis pursued the anti-Modernist campaign in his literary journalism with all the conviction and intolerance of the convert. The result in his early fiction was even more uncompromising.

Like Jim Dixon, Amis enjoys seeing a straightforward distinction between the '"two great classes of mankind, people I like and people I don't"'. This distinction is maintained by a tendency to reinforce one dislike by relating it to another. (Hence Ricks's comment.) The result is an unswerving comic prejudice. His dismissal technique can be seen in this defence of Dixon's priorities: 'It's nice to have a pretty girl with large breasts rather than some fearful woman who's going to talk to you about Ezra Pound and hasn't got large breasts and probably doesn't wash much.' Amis prefers not to tolerate such compromises as hygienic, large-breasted Pound enthusiasts or, from another article, sincere, self-effacing theatrelovers.[23] Amis found ample opportunity to apply this technique in his early novels. He is by nature a provocative writer ('I just enjoy annoying people')[24] and it was the way the available class associations appeared in his literary reaction which did most to earn him his controversial reputation. These associations involved much more than simply writing about characters who lived in digs in humdrum provincial towns, did not earn much, and occasionally expressed appropriately leftish views. Amis used and evoked deeper cultural traits and attitudes to assert the lower-class identity of his fiction and debunk the upper-class identity of the dominant literature of the time.

The most provocative result of this associative technique in his fifties fiction was the 'philistinism' of his heroes. If this was a reaction to the high-cultural refinement of the Woolfian novels of sensibility, part of Amis's assertion of ordinariness, it also implied a lower-class allegiance in the class-bound culture of the fifties, when the height of the cultural brow automatically indicated the height reached on the social ladder. So Amis presents a hero who not only eats fried eggs with his fingers but prefers beer to madrigals and is made all the more likeable for jeering at the cultural pretensions of Professor Welch and his entourage. Jim instinctively mocks anything that smacks of snooty highbrowism (his most celebrated jibe is against 'filthy Mozart') and protests his rejection of any kind of arty-fartiness: '"I can't sing, I can't act, I can hardly read and thank God I can't read music."' Even in the broadest anthropological sense, he has very few 'cultural' enthusiasms. Jim's column of likes is very short indeed: alcohol, cigarettes and tomato ketchup constitute an exhaustive list. It was mainly because culture in the fifties was so closely identified with social class, and such bolshie philistinism so original, that Jim gathered his reputation as a social rebel as well as a disgraceful boor. Eventually his anti-highbrow taunts led to talk of his suitability for Labour Party membership: in his *Universities and Left Review* article on Jim, David Marquand said that 'Every envelope he addressed would be a blow struck at Mozart.' However, Jim's sneers are not to be taken at face value, far less as politically significant: his philistinism is really a pretence. Amis deliberately awarded his hero a series of camouflaged intellectual references to show Dixon's real highbrow knowledge: 'It was a way of saying to the reader, "If you're any good, you will realize he's read these books, so don't say that he's illiterate or uneducated, because he's actually read *Principles of Literary Criticism* . . . he's read *Ulysses* . . . he's read Auden."'[25] The same act of lowbrow irreverence is put on by John Lewis in *That Uncertain Feeling*. Lewis confesses to one literary passion – for the magazine *Astounding Science Fiction* – but his plain-man pose is exposed when he treats the real low-brows, the borrowers of light romances whom he has to serve at the library, with delighted disdain.

But the philistinism of Lewis and even Dixon pales in comparison with Amis's third hero, Garnet Bowen. What had been a noticeable but secondary feature in the first two novels sustains the third. Amis is the last author to be suspected of writing fiction about his own writing, but *I Like It Here* is the work of a novelist who had temporarily run out of steam and turned for source material to the terms of his own literary reaction. It is his weakest novel but the most revealing about his provocative literary stance, for this provided the basis of the story and the characterization of the hero. Amis almost sends up the by-then-notorious philistine posture in the cultural snook-cocking which dominates the novel. Bowen is a literary hack whose choice of profession appears to be ill-judged, if only because he appears not to like literature. Special scorn is reserved for pet Amis hates like Anglo-Saxon poetry ('orang-utan's toilet requisite') and modern highbrows, repre-sented here by Wulfstan Strether, the last of the 'prancing pho-neys' of the 'great-writer period'. (Bowen dates that period as coming 'roughly between *Roderick Hudson* and about 1930 . . . Or perhaps 1939.')

But Bowen's debunking finds targets beyond authors and books. Other features of Amis's reaction are now emphasized and placed in their literary context. For example, it seemed just part of Dixon's highbrow-beating that he despised the Welches' bogus cosmopolitanism. (Celia Welch likes to think of herself as '"West-ern European first and an Englishwoman second"', priorities

advertised in the christening of her dire progeny. All too appropriately, it seems, but Michel, 'as indefatigably Gallic as his mother',
gets his come-uppance when he makes himself ill by 'stuffing
himself with filthy foreign food'.) However, Bowen's rejection or
at least suspicion of all things foreign during his enforced acquaint-
ance with the Continong is so relentless that some motives for this
Little Englandism have to be provided. Bowen finds two reasons
for his virulent insularity: 'lower-middle-class envy' of the insolent
assurance of the 'upper-middle-class traveller', and then loathing
for the 'boasting' knowledge of foreign culture habitually displayed by the literati. The affirmation of the novel's title ('Here'
means England, not Portugal) is a rejoinder to the literary cult of
Abroad.

Bowen's private theory about the success of that cult reveals
another facet of the highbrow literary identity which Amis introduced in his early fiction so he could oppose it. Bowen dismisses
the usual accounts given by cultured types of the attractions of life
beyond the Channel: '"all that stuff about the spirit being chilled
and restricted in the foggy atmosphere of Anglo-Saxon provincialism. Anglo-Saxon policemen, they mean."' 'They' being, in
Bowen's view, 'homos' who enjoy living abroad for one particular
facility:

> 'Come to the Southern shore,
> Cradle of all our values,
> Where the boys hang round your door;
> Land of the vine and olive . . .
> They'll never tell your mum;
> For a packet of fags they just pull . . .'

This theory is confirmed when he meets Wulfstan Strether's hand-
some young chauffeur: 'Oho, Bowen thought to himself. A far
from whole-hearted devotion to the pursuit of girls had sometimes
struck him as a kind of selection-board requirement for writers and
artists.' There is only one other such direct reference in the early
novels – in *Lucky Jim*, when Dixon cultivates resentment towards
'the effeminate writing Michel' – but highbrow literature's reputation for being written by and about privileged types of effete
sensibility did, I think, encourage Amis to characterize his heroes
as stridently 'normal' in their appetites and lusts; the pursuit of
women went with the drinking of beer for his new non-U heroes.

Dixon, Lewis and Bowen are all firmly heterosexual and are all men enough to prove it. Lewis especially is no slouch when it comes to arousing and satisfying a woman's desires, as this post-coital chat with Elizabeth tells us:

> She sighed and shifted her position. 'That was good, wasn't it, darling?'
> 'Yes, it was good all right.'
> 'You're quite a man, aren't you?'
> 'Oh, I don't know. It's just that you love it.'
> 'Well, don't you love it?'
> 'Yes, as a rule. I did then, anyway.'
> 'It's not it, that's not what I love. I love you.'
> 'No, you'd better not say that.'
> 'At least, of course I love it, but I love you as well.'
> 'No darling.'
> 'Listen, John, it does look as if we're going to have a marvellous time together, doesn't it? Fancy it being like that the first time.'

The dialogue may not seem terribly impressive now but Amis's descriptions of heterosexual relationships were unusually direct for the time, just one of the areas in which he tried to replace convention with writing which acknowledged ordinary reality, which showed what he thought 'everybody's like'.[26] Bowen and Strether represent the poles of the opposition Amis established between himself and what he saw as the literary orthodoxy: Wulfstan Strether, Jamesian aesthete, moneyed, aloof and gay, an old and anachronistic figure who prefers Europe to England, versus Garnet Bowen, the young provincial who stands no highbrow nonsense, a regular, lower-middle-class, beer-drinking bloke.

Left at that, the terms of Amis's literary reaction seem to be based on vague social and literary prejudices about a set of conventions and attitudes which were commonly assumed to be dominating English fiction but had few really prominent exponents. Wulfstan Strether had no convincing equivalent in real life. The novelist most usually named as a representative of the writing Amis rejected was Virginia Woolf, who died in 1941. Nevertheless, there was indeed a clear upper-class dominance in the post-war literary scene, but it was maintained by the leading critics and commentators of the day; the most visible and influential representatives of upper-class literature were the gentlemen-of-letters of literary London – the 'Mandarins'.

The Mandarins did not form any 'school' or 'movement' but they could be grouped together as literary figures who shared many tastes and values, and a privileged background which had given them the right education and then the right contacts to help them establish their literary careers, mainly in the twenties and thirties. Philip Toynbee named Cyril Connolly and Raymond Mortimer (reviewers for the *Sunday Times*), John Lehmann (editor of the *London Magazine*), Stephen Spender (co-editor of *Encounter*), Peter Quennell (ex-editor of the *Cornhill Magazine* and a prolific reviewer) and himself (the *Observer*'s principal reviewer) as leading Mandarin figures.[27] He could also have mentioned Alan Pryce-Jones, the editor of the *TLS*, or the literary editor of the *New Statesman*, Janet Adam Smith, as well as other writers and critics like Elizabeth Bowen, Harold Nicolson, Edith Sitwell and Rex Warner. Toynbee characterized these Mandarins as mostly 'younger members of, or immediate and grateful heirs to, the Bloomsbury Group' who continued to proclaim highbrow 'Bloomsbury' devotion to what Toynbee called 'the whole post-Renaissance efflorescence of the arts and philosophy of western Europe', and in particular to the Modernist work of the 'School of Paris'.[28]

By the mid fifties it was very clear that post-war social change had not ended the dominance of an upper-class intelligentsia in England. It seemed to Edward Shils that, since the English intellectual élite was still identifiable with the ruling class, its members had rediscovered the old, comfortably unquestioning confidence in established institutions and authority. At the same time the development of this conforming intelligentsia was traced by Noel Annan through a network of family associations – the Trevelyans, the Macaulays, the Huxleys, the Stephen clan, etc. – from the beginning of the nineteenth century to the present,[29] but in the London literary scene blood ties were less important than old school ties (Connolly's Eton-Balliol-*New Statesman-Horizon-Sunday Times* c.v. serves as a paradigm). However, the outcome effectively mimicked the situation Annan described: a 'close-knit class', an 'intellectual aristocracy', dominated English letters. It was inevitable, then, that literary London should attract the new catchword of conspiracy theorists. It was Henry Fairlie who rediscovered the term the 'Establishment' in a *Spectator* article in 1955 on the Burgess–Maclean spy scandal, taking it to refer to 'the whole matrix of official and social relations within which power is exercised'. Almost immediately, C. P. Snow, a self-made literary man, was describing John Lehmann's *London Magazine* as 'very much the organ of the Establishment' in literature.[30]

Only a few members of the Mandarin literary Establishment were recognized as creative writers though Stephen Spender for example had of course enjoyed prominence as one of the fashionable Macspaunday poets of the thirties, and since the war Toynbee had published two works of wholly unengaging experimental, 'poetic' prose – *Tea with Mrs Goodman* (1947) and *The Garden to the Sea* (1953). It was as opinion-formers and publicists of upper-class literary assumptions that the Mandarins held sway. To take the most important example, it was mainly because these successors to Bloomsbury were the most prominent advocates of the avant-garde that Modernism continued to be so firmly identifiable as upper-class in the fifties. Amis himself used the Mandarin association to dismiss Modernism as an outmoded cult: 'why should we have experimental writing? Because the journalists and their friends were plugging away at it in the twenties and thirties?'[31]

The connection only influenced Amis to the extent that he could use it in a passing reference; he did not react against Modernism because Philip Toynbee liked Modernism. Nor did he wage a campaign against the Mandarins in his novels. However, it often seemed as if he had done just that because the lower-class social and cultural terms of Amis's fiction had their most conspicuous counterparts in the Mandarins' collective upper-class identity. This is reflected in the way his 'rebellion' was presented at the time. Simon Raven contrasted the 'Amis-figure' with the conventionally well-bred hero of previous fiction, the 'Huxley-Hartley-Powell' figure, but Philip Oakes found a more resonant distinction by comparing Wain and Amis with Lehmann and Spender. And in Norman Shrapnel's version of the conflict, the 'Amis hero' was threatening the 'Spender hero'.[32] It was by contrast with the public image of the men-of-letters that Amis's lower-class identity appeared most appropriate and relevant.

For instance, it was the upper-class identity of the Mandarins, rather than any fictional or biographical reality, which made Amis's jibes at the highbrow literati's sexual preferences possible. This particular reputation of the literary élite was well established by the fifties – Orwell's Gordon Comstock, for instance, had derided the 'pansy crowd' of 'moneyed highbrows' in *Keep the Aspidistra Flying* (1936). In 1955 Martin Green explained that the dominance of the upper class had influenced a 'definite turn toward the feminine' in English culture. One of C. P. Snow's distinctions between the 'Two Cultures' was that, unlike the literary one, the scientific culture was marked by a 'steadily heterosexual' tone.[33]

Similarly, the provincial settings and backgrounds for the heroes of Amis's early novels were felt to be especially significant as indications of a reaction against Mandarin values because, as Toynbee himself said, the literary Establishment was 'entirely metropolitan'. The Mandarin party line on the provinces was that these were intellectual 'deserts' where sensitive souls would be isolated 'in the loneliness of being different'.[34] Oxford and Cambridge were the outposts of a literary élite firmly identified with London, or more particularly with Bloomsbury.

The 'philistinism' of Amis's heroes arrived in reaction to the high-falutin' image of 'Bloomsbury' writing but, again, that image was maintained in the fifties mainly by Mandarin critics who professed uncompromisingly highbrow tastes and assumptions. When the *Sunday Times* carried profiles of its two leading reviewers on 6 December 1953, it was hard to tell if the exercise was genuine or satirical, as one after another the clichéd enthusiasms of the privileged dilettante predictably appeared. Raymond Mortimer was acclaimed as a fervent admirer of the old masters, French cooking and avant-garde events, who had decorated the dining room of his Bloomsbury flat with French newspapers. Cyril Connolly was the committed aesthete who loved Flaubert and Henry James, hated the 'idols of the market-place', and considered despair and *angst* to be the modern writer's necessary virtues; 'Latin poetry, underwater swimming, claret, Sèvres porcelain and uncommon pet-animals are among the pleasures of which he is a connoisseur.' The pretensions of the Welches seem unassuming in comparison.

There was a special edge, then, to Dixon's and Bowen's derision of foreign culture, for, as Mortimer's choice of interior décor and Connolly's avowed passions might suggest, it was the Mandarin critics who were the most ostentatious fans of European culture. 'London,' as Spender recognized, was a 'cosmopolitan centre'.

French civilization had a particular *cachet* for the Mandarins. This was taken up by Stephen Potter in his advice on 'Writership'. Rilke and Kafka were the two 'OK-people' to use in 'Newstatesmanship', but there were even more dependably modish references: 'The absolute OK-ness of French literature, particularly modern French, and indeed of France generally, cannot be too much emphasized.'[35] Readers of *Lucky Jim* would find the names of the most convincing 'originals' of the Welches' Gallic affectation in the by-lines of review columns in the quality weeklies and Sundays.

Because the Mandarins were mainly employed as literary journalists, Amis's opposition to them was most immediately apparent in his own reviews. Like his heroes, he adopted a plain-man attitude in contrast to the Mandarin aesthetes who advertised their highbrow learning. He opened his review of *The Outsider* by remarking sardonically that Wilson had dealt with 'all those characters you thought were discredited, or had never read, or (if you are like me) had never heard of'. Where the Mandarins gushed, Amis debunked; a review of *Beowulf*, for example, provided him with the chance to consider *The Faerie Queen* and *Paradise Lost* as two other contenders for the title of most boring long poem in Eng. Lit.[36] The enthusiasms he professed in the fifties – notably for jazz and science fiction – were genuine, but they also served to demonstrate his distance from the Mandarins. An admiration for Louis Armstrong might only mean an admiration for Louis Armstrong, but in Amis's hands it means a preference for Louis Armstrong to Monteverdi, which in turn leads to a defence of scholarship-boy tastes against those of the privileged dilettante: it might be seriously argued that, for the practitioner if for nobody else, 'culture made in one's own private still is more potent than that which comes to table in a decanter'.[37] He also reacted against the style and method of Mandarin criticism. He stated his case against '*belles-lettres*' in a review of Connolly's collection, *Previous Convictions*. Connolly aspired to 'the unexacting standards of gossip and anecdote about writers', rarely allowing literature 'to come within arm's length of him'. Instead of meaningful content, the reader was offered the 'style' of 'honey-tongued Palinurus'. Amis, on the otherhand, cultivated an informal tone and actually talked about, rather than around, the books he was reviewing.[38]

He was joined by other critics of the Mandarins' belletristic approach. 'Humphry Clinker' of *Books and Art* devoted two articles (in the issues for February and March 1958) to attacking the dilettantism of 'virtuoso reviewers' with the values of the cultured and urbane amateur. *Belles-lettres*, like the Modernist tradition also associated with the Mandarins, was falling out of favour partly because it was seen, as William Cooper says, as being 'largely practised by gents'. Angus Wilson for one valued the reaction of Leavis and Snow against writers like Lord David Cecil whose 'love of literature' attitude made 'great writing into part of a gentleman's equipment for life like a visiting card or evening clothes'.[39] The case for the defence was made by Harold Nicolson who gave this self-satisfied assessment of his own qualifications as an aesthete: 'Of course I am cultured, having received an expensive education both at home and abroad, and having read and written a large number of books during the last fifty years.' For Nicolson, egalitarian notions were about as appealing as modesty, and he acknowledged that what he *would* happily concede was intellectual snobbery: 'it would be ungainly for me to pretend to be common when I am not.'[40]

Just as the *belles-lettres* of the Mandarins were obviously upper-class, so Amis's analytical, 'academic' criticism was seen as appropriately lower-class. The influence of F. R. Leavis on Amis was quickly detected, both because Leavis had conducted his own campaign against the Mandarins and their dilettantism and because this alliance fitted Amis's lower-class image. Witness Simon Raven's 'explanation' of the Leavisite mentality: 'Dr Leavis's adherents are largely state-aided young men who cannot afford a claret and Peacock approach to literature. They come from poor homes where books are luxury and must be taken seriously.'[41] It seems churlish to point out that Amis's satire in *Lucky Jim* of arty-crafty nostalgia for Merrie England, and his irreverent handling of the 'Great Tradition', discourage any such connection and that Leavis once described Amis as a 'pornographer' who had also denigrated the 'clerisy' in his fiction.[42] However, the connotations of class and opposition to the literary élite in the Leavisite label were too strong for such quibbles to be heeded.

We can now see that the terms of Amis's supposed social significance have their origin and real application in a literary context. Only with regard to his *literary* identity can Amis be properly described as 'provincial' as well as 'academic' (or 'redbrick') and as a 'lower-class' 'rebel' against the 'upper class' or the 'Establishment'. We can also see how the keywords 'provincial' and 'anti-metropolitan', which G. S. Fraser first applied to the Movement, could produce such heated responses in 1953, for those labels connoted lower-class hostility to highbrow literature in general and the Mandarins in particular.

Opposition to the Mandarins seems so thorough and so provocatively signalled in his early novels, with each major characteristic of the Mandarin identity countered and satirized, that it would be easy to construct a neat reading of Amis's early fiction as anti-Mandarin manifestos. Easy, and daft in a way all too typical of academic literary theorizing which treats 'texts' as puzzles with codes and answers. Though seldom used by many university critics, common sense is often invaluable; applied in this instance it suggests that Amis did not design those novels to attack Cyril Connolly et al., or in the hope that their 'real meaning' would be expounded by some smart-aleck thirty years later. He did undoubtedly refer to the Mandarins' collective reputation directly in some specific jibes, as in Bowen's tirade against reviewers who parade their knowledge of foreign parts; but it seems sensible to assume that Amis was mostly guided by general social images in creating the features of a lower-class identity in his fiction, and that these inevitably turned out to oppose aspects of the Mandarin reputation because this reputation was itself derived from images of the upper class. The social identity of the literary Establishment might then influence Amis by confirming the relevance of the features he chose to use. An important example of the way social images influenced Amis in his writing concerns the choice of background and setting for *Lucky Jim*. Amis was himself a Londoner with no real knowledge of the north of England, but he felt he had to depict Jim as a northerner:

Lucky Jim wasn't going to be about Bloomsbury. Nothing perhaps so tangible or explicit as Bloomsbury, but it wasn't going to be about what people did after work ... or what people did who weren't working anyway. It was going to be about somebody with a job. It wasn't going to be London for the same sort of reason. He only had to be north of England because he mustn't be London ... Non-London, non-Home Counties, non-south of England.[43]

The aversion to 'Bloomsbury' and 'London' might hint at a reaction against the Mandarins but, more convincingly, these terms surely evoked for Amis what he saw as the conventional upper-class fiction of the time. However, the motive for avoiding a background in or near London comes from the same class associations which made 'provincial' and 'metropolitan' such resonant terms in the fifties literary debates.

'Provincial' and 'metropolitan' signified 'lower-class' and 'upper-class' literary and cultural allegiances because they referred to the traditional social division of England into north and south. This division depends, of course, on prejudice and partiality.[44] Just as the 'Home Counties' label conjures up images of commuting stockbrokers rather than Kent miners, so Barnsley seems more truly 'northern' than, say, Harrogate. The caricatures involved in the north-south class divide were scorned by Orwell in *The Road to Wigan Pier*, and wryly exploited by Malcolm Bradbury in this description of James Walker's train journey in *Stepping Westward* (1965): 'the train was crossing the heavy iron bridge over the River Trent, which marked for Walker the boundary between the north of England and the south. Behind him, now, lay decency, plain speaking, good feeling; ahead lay the southern counties, all suede shoes and Babycham.'

The music-hall images of north and south were still eagerly used in the literary debates of the fifties. John Wain could still describe northern culture as more 'earnest' than southern, Anthony Hartley talked about the 'non-conformist' outlook of the new 'provincial' poets, and Spender accused young authors of 'provincial puritanism'.[45] Such clichés and generalizations maintained their value as class-loaded terms for writers who disdained sociological or biographical accuracy in evoking distinct class-cultural identities. Taken at face value, such 'social' characteristics can only seem silly or banal. For example, Spender's comment that the 'provinces are perhaps "realer" than London'[46] was not the product of research into regional discrepancies, but refers to the emerging challenge of a non-U literature more suited to the egalitarian times. As for the reputation of the 'London' highbrows as effete or homosexual, this recalls nothing so much as the Australians' or Scots' cartoon image of 'the English' as lah-di-dah Pommies or Sassenachs. Nevertheless, such connotations played a very influential part in defining the opposing factions in English letters. Literary and non-literary features had become inextricably interlinked; Amis could refer, for example, to '"style" in the pansy-travel-book sense'.[47]

Critics and hacks misread social and political significance into Amis's early fiction because of the way various class-related features appeared in the novels, but Amis's public reputation in the fifties was still important by default, since it did advertise the lower-class identity of his fiction. And Amis found other compensations, apart from the financial ones, in being labelled Angry Young Man: 'if it was boring at times to be asked by new acquaintances what I was so angry about, I was amply repaid on other occasions by seeing people wondering whether I was going to set about breaking up their furniture straight away or would wait till I was drunk.'[48]

His lower-class image made Amis a distinctive new presence in the English literary scene, prominent by contrast especially with the old guard. Crucially, this image was also considered well suited to the post-war period: as the 'Welfare Wodehouse', 'the scholarship boy's Stephen Spender', 'a fish-and-chips Waugh',[49] Amis was felt to be eminently qualified to lead the new literary 'generation' which had already begun to acquire a lower-class identity with the *First Reading* broadcasts. Other names had been mentioned in connection with the Movement, but only Amis, and to a lesser extent Wain, could be regarded as its leaders after 1954. To contemporary commentators like Massingham, it was the 'Amis group' which was challenging 'Bloomsbury'. When the editors of *Mavericks* attacked the new coterie they criticized 'the Lucky Jim attitude' of the writers, and the *Listener* critic of *The Less Deceived* described Larkin as one of 'the "Lucky Jim poets"'.[50]

In the mid fifties Amis affectively *was* the Movement and not by name or reference only. As well as being its most prominent and recognizable member when the group came to public attention, he also offered a uniquely definite, fully appropriate identity which writers like Oakes and Hartley relied on to provide characteristics which they then claimed applied collectively. (This was notably the case with J. D. Scott's 'In the Movement' article; the influence of *Lucky Jim* on Scott's group portrait is reflected in Alan Brien's parody of the piece for *Truth* a fortnight later in which provincial lecturers drink beer and burn bedclothes.) Consequently the terms of Amis's literary opposition had a very powerful influence on the development of the corporate identity of the Movement. I think this still held true after other Movement writers were able to make their own contributions to the group's image. In his study *The Movement*, Blake Morrison has shown that all the group's authors can be cited in support of several attitudes, but only Amis obviously possesses all the characteristics Morrison takes as collective. Others, like Holloway and Conquest, are far less conspicuous or, like Jennings and Gunn, sometimes depart significantly from the group identity.

Certainly the situation in the mid fifties was such that Amis's own class-referred literary reaction was taken as representative. This in turn helped to give the impression that a class division was creating the generation gap in fifties writing. This idea of a generation gap was used quite literally in a *New Statesman* satire on 8 October 1955. The article, 'Uncle and Nephews', flogged the conceit that leading authors belonged to one large family headed by uncles Evelyn and Wystan and great-aunts Edith and Virginia. An aspiring youngster is recommended to retain his unfashionable good manners, despite the success of the family's black sheep, 'Cousin Amis's. Two months later, on 30 December, the *Spectator*'s 'Dr Aloysius C. Pepper' relied on the Lucky Jim image to satirize the current literary fashion for the 'provincial-academic', so the requirements for the literary trend-follower are an impoverished, drunken appearance and a North-Midland accent.

It was no longer possible to think that the younger literary generation was distinguishable only by its minor innovations, as Harold Nicolson had assumed early in 1954. Reviewing travelogues by Michael Swan and Alan Ross in the *Observer* on 21 March, Nicolson was delighted to see these two younger authors, and particular features of their work, as representative. He detected only trivial and encouraging differences between his generation and theirs: 'the latter have better manners, are interested in architecture, manage their sex problems more quickly and, while appreciating luxury, are prepared, in a good cause, actually to enjoy discomfort.' Amis's influence would soon deny Nicolson the chance to repeat this account of reassuringly sympathetic juniors. Even in March 1954 Nicholson must have suffered from a degree of critical tunnel vision to ignore the impact made by *First Reading*.

Commentators were occasionally reluctant to explain the differences between the literary generations in terms of class, but only because they felt that post-war reform had eradicated social divisions. On 17 August 1956 a *TLS* writer asserted that, in the new egalitarian society, 'traditional class denominations are not only irrelevant but positively misleading.' This writer preferred to see the differences between young and old as the result of general social developments – there was simply a new group which had profited from improved educational opportunities and an 'old régime'. Alexander Baron likewise wanted to avoid reducing the literary 'split' to traditional socio-economic terms:

> Britain may no longer be two nations in the Disraelian, the economic sense, but culturally it consists of two nations between which there is little contact. The two nations differ in social conventions, values, tastes, emotional attitudes and forms of expression. This split governs the state of our literature.

Nevertheless, Baron then had to specify that this conflict was between the 'upper middle-class' to which literature had belonged, and the new 'middle-class intellectuals'.[51] On the other hand, the class-based nature of the opposition between Amis and the Mandarins could also renew an awareness in literary observers that England still suffered from the class division of the 'two nations'. Baron's article in *Books and Bookmen* was qualified by an editorial in June 1956 entitled 'Death Of The Mandarin', stating that the Establishment style belonged to social privilege whereas Amis and Wain heralded a literature for 'the whole nation'.

The cultural split of the 'two nations' was certainly evident in the reactions to the Movement, not so much in reviews of individual works as in general comments and surveys where opinions for or against the group were not restricted by considerations of specific content or merit. Because of Amis's influence on the group reputation, the Movement attracted the same prejudices which had bedevilled *Lucky Jim*; the Movement too was burdened with a host of social as well as literary features. In his *Spectator* article, 'Poets of the Fifties', Anthony Hartley was able to explain that the new poetry was disciplined and anti-Romantic, and, with no apparent justification, 'non-conformist', egalitarian and anti-aristocratic. Another *Spectator* article contrasted 'Bloomsbury' literary values (described in terms of foreign place-names and 'sensitivity') with the 'New Provincialism' of 'competence, entertainment value and scholarship'.[52] Without an awareness of the significance of such labels it would be hard to think why 'scholarship' should be combined with 'entertainment' and why both should be contrasted with a liking for European cities.

Since social as well as literary prejudices were explicitly involved, there was little room for compromise from either side in the conflict between the Movement and the Mandarins. Allegiances were demanded for one faction or the other. Movement supporters such as Hartley, Scott, Snow and Priestley, asserted that the old writing of experiment and upper-class values had been ousted by new authors who had come down from the provinces with works which were bang up-to-date. The arrival of the Movement also convinced its supporters that the detractors of contemporary literature were retaining their pessimism only because of their narrow and anachronistic assumptions:

> When lately the pessimists were talking about the Death of the Novel, wasn't what they were really lamenting (and shouldn't they really have been celebrating?) the passing of the Private Income Novel – that kind of novel which took over from poetry as the first-choice form of self-expression for the unhappy, sensitive young with a gift for words?[53]

Others could show little enthusiasm for the 'Amis group'. Whereas Peter Forster regarded the level of the Movement's achievement as appropriate to the economically 'egalitarian' times ('in default of peaks, we are pleasantly placed on the uplands'),[54] the lack of ambition, the replacement of spectacular accomplishment by 'mere' competence, was often less sympathetically greeted. In contrast to Forster, some commentators were tempted to equate what they saw as the drab meanness of the Welfare State with the unimpressive level of talent in its new literary group. If society lacked a leisured upper class, its art would inevitably lack the sensitivity and the 'aesthetic adventure' which, according to Cyril Connolly, only amenably privileged conditions could produce. Hence David Wright complained about the 'welfare-state mentality' in *New Lines* and criticized the contributors for accepting the world around them instead of offering a 'vision' of something grander.[55] Since the Movement had renounced Bohemian notions of the Artist as well as 'aesthetic adventure', it was also thought to have acquired the dull managerial qualities of the State bureaucracy which had supposedly supervised the ascent of the group. Wain's *First Reading* banner of 'consolidation' seemed to signify not only literary conformity but an acceptance of the social status quo. V. S. Pritchett deduced that Wain's 'consolidation' promised a 'foddering of administrators' instead of original artists, and Spender attacked the young 'academic-minded' chroniclers of 'regional life' who appeared 'all too complacent in their aims'. Spender urged aspiring writers not to follow fashion in cultivating 'the souls of officials'.[56]

Opposing social attitudes were reinforcing the different assessments of contemporary writing outlined in the first chapter. This was clearly shown in two representatively contrasting accounts of the state of English letters printed in the American *Saturday Review* on 7 May 1955. J. D. Scott praised Wain, Murdoch and Amis for following in the footsteps of Orwell and Cooper to write about contemporary social change: there was a new coherence in English fiction for the first time in nearly ten years, and it was the coherence of 'classlessness' which he welcomed. Scott compared these new 'classless' writers with novelists who persisted in working within an outmoded tradition which favoured foreign and upper-class settings, experimental presentation, 'intensity and culture'.

In the adjoining article, gloomily titled 'The Writer's Lean Life', Cyril Connolly dwelt on what he considered to be the insurmountable social problems preventing the emergence of any worthwhile talents. Connolly specialized in complaints about the writer's lot, mainly to explain why he – with all the right credentials – had not blossomed into a creative genius. This latest variation on his 'enemies of promise' theme settled for income tax as the great obstacle to literary achievement; the 'independent rentier-author' with a 'small private income' had disappeared and budding writers had been denied the means to travel abroad (self-evidently a necessary experience). Writers were 'condemned to a petty-bourgeois existence'. He noted that some younger authors had submitted to recruitment by redbrick universities but he thought little good could come of this; the only good novels produced by 'dons', in his opinion, were thrillers. Connolly prescribed that ailing writers should try to mix 'in the best available society', the class 'of power and rank'.

Considering the zest with which Amis asserted his difference from 'Establishment' writing, his actual dealings with literary London were much less belligerent than one would expect. To be sure, he was not averse to attacking individual metropolitan figures: Edith Sitwell, Dylan Thomas, C. Day Lewis and Cyril Connolly were all targets for his scorn. However, he refused to subscribe to any of the current views of the Mandarins as literary racketeers, and he parodied the conspiracy theories which envisaged 'Stephen Lehmann, permanently in session at the Café Royal, drawing up lists of new writers to proscribe and arranging for Cyril to review Philip's latest and Philip to review Cyril's latest.'[57] Literary London has been notoriously vulnerable to accusations of nepotism and cliquism and Amis's attitude seems all the more restrained when compared with *Scrutiny*'s line, which he was often presumed to be following. In the June 1951 issue of *Scrutiny*, F. R. Leavis claimed in 'Keynes, Spender and Currency-Values' that the literary 'club' was run on 'social-personal' lines and confined to 'the Axis, Eton–King's–Bloomsbury–and the relevant weekly'. A review of *Enemies of Promise* in June 1939 had given Q. D. Leavis the ammunition for her extraordinarily vehement attack on 'Mr Connolly and his set [who] are now seeing to it that the literary preserves are kept exclusively for their friends':

> We who are in the habit of asking how such evidently unqualified reviewers as fill the literary weeklies ever got into the profession need ask no longer. They turn out to have been 'the most fashionable boy in the school,' or to have had a feline charm or a sensual mouth and long eye-lashes.

It would actually have been rather odd if Amis had announced similar views about a 'social-personal' club, for his opposition to metropolitan literature had not meant exile to the literary hinterland, but had been expressed within the metropolitan network itself. The weeklies and periodicals had published his reviews, the Third Programme had broadcast his talks, the Sunday papers had (usually) praised his novels. 'The world of letters,' as Amis recalled, had indeed 'proved benign.' He recognized that he enjoyed two substantial advantages in gaining access to that world – an Oxford University education and an Oxford University First Class Honours degree.[58] Oxford was the best place for young 'outsiders' to find contacts and attention in literary London – even Cambridge lagged behind in a poor second place as a recruiting centre. The benefits of an Oxford education for the aspiring writer can be seen in the *TLS* and *Spectator* reviews of Fantasy Press pamphlets. Oxford was simply the traditional place to look for new authors – so that, for example, it was the only university visited by John Lehmann in his search for young talent for *New Soundings*.

Blake Morrison has shown that the young Oxbridge writers of the Movement had also formed a network of contacts among themselves, and it was this network rather than Mandarin talent-scouting which helped Amis to start his literary career. Two of his most useful acquaintances from Oxford were John Wain and Anthony Hartley. Wain had broadcast the *Lucky Jim* extract on *First Reading* (at a time when Gollancz was only just deciding to publish the novel) and arranged the publication of *A Frame of Mind* (which is dedicated to Wain). And it was through Hartley that Amis started to contribute poetry and his first regular reviews to the *Spectator* in 1953. At the time it was thought that the traditional Oxbridge–London connections had been destroyed by the war, but new ones had been created in their place. Malcolm Bradbury remembers that, as a student at Leicester, he looked on writers like Amis and Larkin not as 'provincials' but 'very Oxbridge insiders' who could exploit metropolitan opportunities. So effectively had they done so that as early as 1957 Charles Tomlinson saw the Movement as the 'new establishment'.[59]

For Movement writers opportunity was such that they were noticed before they had produced any noticeable achievements. The distinctive social identity of the Movement allowed it a conspicuous role in the literary scene as lower-class provincial challengers of upper-class literary London, but only because Movement writers were able to use London's literary outlets in the first place. It was just this combination of challenge and access to the literary Establishment which meant that the Movement could be promoted as a new generational group. As Walter Allen said, these new writers were 'raising the hell of a clamour at a wide-open door'.[60]

This was not quite the straightforward opposition which Movement writers claimed. Far from ignoring or attacking the metropolitan scene from outside, they relied on it; in a very real sense the Movement writers were part of the literary élitism they condemned. This is not only true of their use of the machinery of publication and publicity – their writing also shares some of the supposedly hateful Mandarin characteristics. The Movement's attitudes to both its audience and its material are often more ambiguous than its declarations allow. For example, ordinary social reality is often not celebrated in the work of Wain or Larkin, or even Amis; unlike many older writers they did not ignore that reality, but neither did they always accept it on its own terms. Just as Dixon dreams of escape to London, so in Larkin's poetry the dull normality of the 'cut-price crowd' is devalued by comparisons with either a lyrically-sensed, transcendent reality (as at the end of 'Here' and 'The Whitsun Weddings') or an impossible, even ludicrous, but powerful ideal (as offered by the advertisements in 'Essential Beauty' and 'Sunny Prestatyn'). In addition, as Blake Morrison has pointed out, the Movement's 'sense of an audience' was more ambivalent than their anti-élitist postures suggest: the characteristic 'we' of Movement poetry can imply the inclusion of the 'ordinary reader' or the exclusion of all but the initiated.

That ambivalent sense of an audience can also be inferred in Amis's work. Of course, the accent on entertainment and accessibility in his writing is consistent with his image of the writer as ordinary bloke, as entertainer/salesman aiming to please the paying public, but his relationship with his audience is not always so clearly non-élitist. Looking back on Movement poetry, Amis included himself as one of the dons who had written poetry for other dons. In an early review he assumed poets addressed, 'in the first instance', an 'inner audience' rather than the general public.[61] This restrictive notion was not confined to his poetry, for I think it is also implicit in *Lucky Jim*. Suspicions that an 'inner audience' is being addressed in the novel have led to suggestions that it is a *roman à clef*, though there are only a few specific, trivial in-jokes; Amis named his hero after Dixon Drive where Larkin had lived in Leicester, Michie after James Michie, Amis's co-editor of *Oxford Poetry*, and L. S. Caton after R. A. Caton, proprietor of the Fortune Press (the change of initials comes from Amis's and Larkin's nickname for their erstwhile publisher – Lazy Sod).

Far more important is the ambivalent nature of the implied reader in *Lucky Jim*. It might seem that Amis demands no more of this reader than that s/he should recognize that, for example, the Welches are appalling and Jim is a likeable, decent sort of bloke. However, the characterization in *Lucky Jim* can only be fully appreciated by a readership with a highly developed awareness of literary and cultural affairs, a readership which knows the significance of mocking Bertrand's 'Artist' pose, of Celia Welch's addiction to things continental, and especially of Jim's anxious denials of the cultural knowledge he does possess. Amis is addressing readers in the literary know and challenging them to toe the authorial line, so that the Welches' cultural pretensions are seen as ridiculous and Jim's anti-highbrow posture is vindicated. If the reader fails to follow the alignments presented in the novel, ludicrous misreadings, such as those of Maclaren-Ross, Maugham and Dobrée, are the result. For all its 'philistinism' *Lucky Jim* is a consciously *literary* work which on this level addresses and tests an exclusively literary readership (just as *Jake's Thing* and *Stanley and the Women* challenge readers to accept their misogyny). Amis's anti-highbrow posture could only convey its meaning in a highbrow context. This paradox in his literary stance brings together the two halves of his contradictory reputations – as an 'academic' writer, a donnish humorist, and then as a crabby, boorish philistine.

The success of *Lucky Jim* owed a lot to the originality of Amis's provocative strategy. His was a distinctive new voice, one which was taken to herald the arrival of a broad-fronted literary challenge, initially from the Movement and then, amid much more confusion, from the Angry Young Men. Amis's prominence in both groups owed ever less to his specifically literary challenge and ever more to a presumed social and political rebellion which that challenge appeared to, but did not, involve.

Not that there was no awareness of Amis as a literary influence; the success and the originality of *Lucky Jim* meant that many subsequent works by young authors were automatically and simplistically compared to it, no matter how slight the resemblance. Amis was assumed to have spawned a host of imitators. *The Small World* by W. John Morgan, *Summer in Retreat* by Edmund Ward, *Running on the Spot* by Keith Walker, *In Another Country* by John Bayley, Keith Waterhouse's *Billy Liar*, Malcolm Bradbury's *Eating People is Wrong* – these are only some of the novels said to be following in *Lucky Jim*'s footsteps. Reviewers also identified 'Lucky Jim in Fleet Street', 'Lucky Jim's Apologia Pro Vita Sua', even 'Lucky Jim, MD'.[62] In the mania for comparison, it seemed that any comic or realist account of a young man's dealings with the world around him merited the 'Lucky Jim' label.

Two authors who certainly suffered unjustly under the burden of comparison were Paul Ferris and Thomas Hinde, with *A Changed*

Man and *Happy as Larry* respectively. Ferris's first novel offers a restrained, understated depiction – very much in the manner of Hinde's *Mr Nicholas*, in fact – of the confused domestic and emotional life of the immature and irresponsible Gregory Hawkins. No matter, the hero was twenty-five and unconventional in behaviour, so Ferris was said to have created 'yet another version of the Amis-hero', 'another variant of Mr James Dixon-Porter'.[63] A similar fate awaited *Happy as Larry*; reviewers described Hinde's character as 'an existentialist Lucky Jim' and his writing as 'Amis-like slapstick' which put him 'very much in the Movement'.[64] In fact Hinde's second novel is very like his first, *Mr Nicholas*, in quietly outlining a naïve, rather gormless character failing to cope with awkward and destructive circumstances. Both Ferris and Hinde were writing quite different kinds of fiction from Amis. Ferris deliberately avoided reading *Lucky Jim*; he was influenced mainly by a short story by Paul Bowles ('Call at Corazon') and Hinde (who also had not read *Lucky Jim*), during delays and difficulties with his novel, by Dostoevsky's *The Idiot*.[65]

Nonetheless, they found themselves enrolled in the 'feeble school of Lucky Jim-ism',[66] a school remarkable only for its truancy figures. Even the notion that *Lucky Jim* started a fashion for redbrick 'campus novels' is untenable: in the fifties only Keith Walker's second-rate novel *Running on the Spot*, or, more persuasively, Bradbury's *Eating People is Wrong*, use a non-Oxbridge university setting, both with unAmisian results. Perhaps the only supportable statement about Amis's direct influence on the contemporary fiction is that he and Wain started a minor fad for using popular songs as novel titles: *There is a Happy Land*, *Eating People is Wrong*, and *The British Museum Had Lost Its Charm* (David Lodge's original title for *The British Museum is Falling Down*).

I think his influence on his contemporaries was much less direct and much more pervasive than the reviewers' simple comparisons suggest; *Lucky Jim* showed other young writers that it was possible to achieve successful results by using a straightforward, realistic, comic format and by dealing with ordinary, contemporary life. Experiment and exotica, 'style' and refinement, were no longer expected components of fiction. Before *Lucky Jim* the image of the young writer's first novel had been the precious upper-class autobiography satirized by Scogan in Aldous Huxley's *Crome Yellow* (1921):

'Little Percy, the hero, was never good at games, but he was always clever. He passes through the usual public school and the usual university and comes to London, where he lives among the artists. He is bowed down with melancholy thought; he carries the whole weight of the universe upon his shoulders. He writes a novel of dazzling brilliance; he dabbles delicately in Amour and disappears, at the end of the book, into the luminous Future.'

Lucky Jim helped to transform that image to the one gently mocked in Hilary Ford's *Felix Walking* (1958), whose narrator sums up the fashionable new hero in fiction – an ' "angry young man with a provincial University degree, and nothing but obstinacy, low comedy and a sense of decency to face the world with" '.

Amis created new fictional types in *Lucky Jim* and its successors. Charles Tansley and Leonard Bast had been replaced by Neddy Welch and Wulfstan Strether as expected objects of ridicule, Little Percy had been replaced by Lucky Jim as the new hero for a new sensibility and a new image of 'Englishness' based on lower-class decency instead of aristocratic *élan*. As well as helping to transform literary conventions, Amis was also thought to have catered for a new readership, the Welfare State's meritocrats who could supposedly identify with the new hero and his circumstances.

His challenge to the literary orthodoxy came in the form of two interlinked reactions – against the obscurities and experiments of the avant-garde and against the conventions of privilege with which the avant-garde was associated. The political connotations of Amis's literary reaction no longer apply; Amis himself has 'turned right', and his anti-Modernist views have become even more belligerent. What was a fruitful and innovative direction in the fifties has led Amis into a cul-de-sac whence he can only deliver blanket condemnations of writers who depart in any way from middlebrow traditions. People wanting to buy a safe Christmas present for Kingsley Amis would be well advised to steer clear of recent fiction.

However, the influence his stance had on the fifties was extensive. It may not be useful to look for direct imitations of his work but he, more than any other writer of the fifties, established the decade's fashion for lower-class realism. More specifically, the social aspects of his literary challenge established the terms of the decade's literary conflict – between the older men-of-letters, the Mandarins of literary London, and the rising young provincial outsiders.

6

'The Biggest AYM
in the Business'

All the highbrow disputes which surrounded *Lucky Jim* during its first two years can now be seen as a prelude to the far greater impact of *Look Back in Anger*. John Osborne's command of media attention was to become so strong in the latter part of the fifties that the earlier publicity for Amis came to look rather minor in comparison. Osborne's arrival was to have far-reaching effects: 'anger' became the literary keyword of the decade and Osborne's hero, Jimmy Porter, was readily taken to represent a general mood of dissatisfaction and dissent. From now on, the 'fifties generation' would no longer be 'lucky' but 'angry'; the uncouth social upstarts had become embittered social protesters.

Look Back in Anger also changed ideas about the English theatre, even more strikingly than *Lucky Jim* affected assumptions about contemporary fiction. It turned the social conventions in English theatre upside down, replacing the gentility of 'Loamshire' plays with the tensions and aggressions of 'kitchen sink' drama. Soon RADA elocution classes would be practising not the usual strangled, diphthonged yelps of stage 'received pronunciation' but the flat vowels of the 'North-Midlands'. *Look Back in Anger* changed the course of mainstream English drama.

When *Look Back in Anger* was first performed in May 1956, John Osborne was a twenty-six-year-old unemployed actor whose closest brush with fame and success had come four years earlier when he played the prefect Wingate in two episodes of the *Billy Bunter* series on BBC children's television. His undistinguished thespian career had followed an unsettled childhood and adolescence dominated by the death of his father when Osborne was ten and by his own ill-health. He attended a succession of schools, ending with what he calls in his autobiography, *A Better Class of Person* (1981), a 'fake public school' from which he was expelled after assaulting the headmaster. In 1947 Osborne started work as a reporter on *Gas World* but gave up trade journalism a year later to join a repertory company. He married his first wife, Pamela Lane, in 1951, in the middle of a period of his life which was spent either touring the provinces or 'resting'.

Osborne had written several plays before *Look Back in Anger*, usually in collaboration. Of these, only *Epitaph for George Dillon* (written with Anthony Creighton and eventually produced in 1958) survives, although *The Devil Inside* was performed for a week at the Theatre Royal Huddersfield in 1950 and *Personal Enemy* managed a brief run in repertory at Harrogate four years later. It was during yet another spell of unemployment that Osborne began to write *Look Back in Anger* on 4 May 1955. It took him twelve days to complete. At first it seemed that *Look Back in Anger* was heading towards an even more disheartening fate than its predecessors: 'I sent it to everyone I could think of, every agent and management, and they were not only sort of unenthusiastic, they were downright insulting, some of them.'[1] Then he saw an announcement in the *Stage* that the newly-formed English Stage Company was looking for new plays. Along with 750 other hopefuls Osborne sent off his manuscript.

The Artistic Director, George Devine, intended the English Stage Company to be a 'writers' theatre' which would help to revive contemporary drama. The English theatre had been languishing since the beginning of the fifties; in March 1956 Angus Wilson took it for granted that 'The standard of English plays is lamentably low,'[2] and indeed, Devine's ambition to create a writers' theatre faced one major problem – a lack of writers. Devine's main hopes for the English Stage Company's first season rested on plays by an American and two novelists – Arthur Miller's *The Crucible*, Nigel Dennis's stage adaptation of *Cards of Identity*, and Angus Wilson's *The Mulberry Bush*. It was in a forlorn attempt to discover new talent that Devine had placed the advertisement in the *Stage*. Of all the manuscripts that were submitted, only *Look Back in Anger* was accepted for performance. Osborne received £25 from the ESC for an option on his play, which he soon found being welcomed as part of an eagerly anticipated initiative. In the *New Statesman* T. C. Worsley reported that the ESC's forthcoming season at the Royal Court was 'one of the most exciting and important events in the English Theatre for a great many years', and that the ESC's directors were certain they had made 'a real discovery' in their new playwright, 'Paul' Osborne.[3]

'The first night of *Look Back in Anger*' – that extraordinary evening on 8 May 1956 which started a theatrical revolution, when Jimmy Porter's tirades were let loose on a shocked and unsuspecting world . . . Osborne has noted that the number of people who claim to have witnessed that historic performance is curiously high: 'I mean, the number of people who've said to me that they were there, I think if they had all been there they'd have filled the Albert Hall.'[4] And in reality the atmosphere at the opening performance of *Look Back in Anger* was not electrifying – there were no demonstrations of joy or howls of protest. For the *Sunday Times* critic, Harold Hobson, the occasion was 'entirely unmemorable' and for Osborne himself 'it just seemed a rather dull, disappointing evening'.[5] However, there was at least one member of that first-night audience who was far from disappointed – the *Observer*'s young drama critic, Kenneth Tynan:

> one began to respond within ten minutes to this blazing figure on stage who was spraying out all the ideas and thoughts one had half-articulated the previous ten years . . . At the end of it one walked out serenely glowing, surrounded by disgruntled middle-aged faces, knowing that something very heart-warming had happened and that one was dying to be on the street with the news.[6]

Osborne remembers the first-night notices as being 'depressing', 'dismissive' and 'carping'. Only John Barber in the *Daily Express* and Derek Grainger in the *Financial Times* welcomed the play with any enthusiasm. The *Evening News* critic thought it was 'the most putrid bosh' and Milton Shulman wrote in the *Evening Standard* that *Look Back in Anger* achieved 'only the stature of a self-pitying snivel', but most critics agreed with the *Manchester Guardian*'s Philip Hope-Wallace, who judged this to be a 'strongly felt but rather muddled first drama'. Osborne could not even claim any notoriety from this reception, for the consensus among Fleet Street reviewers seemed to be that he was a dramatist to watch who had written a play with obvious flaws; even Shulman followed his attack with the qualification that Osborne showed 'considerable promise'. In the playwright's own words, this response 'didn't sell any tickets'.[7]

Then came Tynan's acclaim in Sunday's *Observer*:

Look Back in Anger presents post-war youth as it really is, with special emphasis on the non-U intelligentsia who live in bed-sitters and divide the Sunday papers into two groups, 'posh' and 'wet'. To have done this at all would be a signal achievement; to have done it in a first play is a minor miracle. All the qualities are there, qualities one had despaired of ever seeing on the stage – the drift towards anarchy, the instinctive leftishness, the automatic rejection of 'official' attitudes, the surrealist sense of humour . . . the casual promiscuity, the sense of lacking a crusade worth fighting for and, underlying all these, the determination that no one who dies shall go unmourned.

Osborne had spoken for everybody in the country between twenty and thirty years old, declared Tynan – 6,733,000 people. He had certainly spoken for Kenneth Tynan: 'I doubt if I could love anyone who did not wish to see *Look Back in Anger*. It is the best young play of its decade.' The notion of Osborne's spokesmanship was taken up by T. C. Worsley in the *New Statesman* on 19 May and, during *Look Back in Anger*'s second short run, by a typical *Times* fourth leader on the 26th, which roundly dismissed the claims that Osborne had expressed the mood of his generation; the danger was that posterity would assume that Jimmy Porter was representative, for young people were really not 'cross' or 'embittered' but polite, considerate, serious, restrained: 'Where the prodigies celebrated by Mr Evelyn Waugh in 1930 or thereabouts organized parties in balloons and swimming baths, the youth of today visits prisons and reads Kierkegaard.'

On the same day that *The Times* was summing up contemporary youth, Colin Wilson, who had indeed read a great deal of Kierkegaard and a lot more besides, was being heralded in the *Evening News* as 'A Major Writer'. Osborne was completely overshadowed by Wilson's sudden fame. Interest in *Look Back in Anger* was picking up slightly and extra performances were arranged for the second week in June, but a report in the *Daily Mail* on the 9th that it was a box-office success came too soon. Even when Osborne began to attract much greater comment early in July as an 'angry young man' and a leader of Daniel Farson's 'Post-War Generation', *Look Back in Anger*'s weekly takings averaged just £950. Not until the BBC televised the extract from the play on 16 October did it begin to show a profit, as weekly takings leapt to £1,300, then £1,700. And it was only after the middle of October that Osborne began to match Colin Wilson's success and become really well known as 'the angriest young man of them all'.[8]

Predictably, he denounced the AYM label, describing it as a 'cheap journalistic fiction', a 'journalistic swindle'.[9] Nonetheless, unlike Amis, he also seemed happy to validate his press reputation. He did not deny his 'anger' or the contemporary significance of his play during the early *Panorama* interview, and in his *Daily Express* article on 18 October 1956 he even exploited the catchphrase himself, warning that he might 'mellow with the autumn and become less of an angry man – a bit grumpy, perhaps, but less angry. I doubt it.' A month later he confessed in the *Daily Mail* that he was really angry about the refusal of 'nearly everyone' to recognize the problems in society.[10] Osborne appeared to be playing the part the press had given him. Whether it was giving a vitriolic speech at the Arts Theatre Club, or kicking up a stink about his accommodation in Moscow, or agreeing that there were lines of 'undoubted obscenity' in *The Entertainer*, he could be relied upon to provide journalists with the right story.[11] Fleet Street editors pestered him for contributions, for he was sure to provide the 'lively copy' expected of him.[12] Osborne even included appropriate references in *The Entertainer* (written in eleven days) to Suez, rock 'n' roll, U and non-U, and scholarship students.

It was principally because Osborne was so conspicuously wrathful that the reputation of the Angry Young Men was maintained with such conviction in 1957.[13] Far less clear were the nature and motivation of his protest. Tynan had identified him as a spokesman of the 'non-U intelligentsia' and mentioned the anarchic, 'instinctive leftishness' of Jimmy Porter, but those political hints had gradually grown fainter. By the time of the Suez Crisis, Osborne's controversial image rested much more on his reputation as an outspoken critic of womanhood. When the *Daily Mail* commissioned an article by Osborne for 14 November it was not on the current political upheaval but on the topic of 'What's gone wrong with WOMEN?' 'Britain's Most Provocative Playwright' announced that society's problems were caused by a domination of 'feminine' attitudes – lack of 'imaginative vitality', hostility to idealism, indifference to anything but personal suffering, etc., etc. Three days later, when news of his impending divorce was reported on the front page of the *Mail*, Osborne's reputation as one who shared Jimmy Porter's volatile and acerbic relationships with the opposite sex could be taken as confirmed. Helped by the handy political and social references in *The Entertainer* and the growing opinions about the AYM as a group of rebels and outsiders, the emphasis shifted back to social protest in 1957, but for all the commentaries and analyses of his work, the reasons for his anger remained as uncertain as the supposed message to society in *Lucky Jim*. Nor could that uncertainty be dispelled by Osborne's essay in *Declaration*, since his freebooting ire found such a variety of victims that his standpoint was even more difficult to detect.

Disagreements about the causes of Osborne's protest were reflected in the amorphous corporate identity of the 'group' he now effectively led. The Angry Young Men continued to be as vaguely and variously defined as when Farson and Barber first announced their existence. This was shown in Fleet Street's two cartoon series about the AYM. Flook's life as a young angry in the *Daily Mail* was actually a vaguely Bohemian one, but 'Trog' was inspired to write his strip by *Look Back in Anger* itself. Flook's new friend is Len Bloggs, a much-aggrieved skiffle performer who lives in provincial digs, sneers at the posh Sunday papers, gatecrashes bourgeois parties and delights in berating his wife, who alternates between worrying about Len and ironing his clothes. However, the storyline has to fall back on familiar legends of Bohemia: Len becomes successful and Flook accuses him of throwing 'his idealism away with his duffle coat', but Len is soon ousted by an Eskimo calypso singer, learns the error of his ways, and returns to a *Look Back in Anger*ish conclusion and argumentative marital bliss.

A less distracted version of literary developments came in the chequered career of the *Daily Telegraph*'s very own angry young writer, Eric Lard. Lard made his first appearance in Peter Simple's 'Way of the World' column on 3 January 1957 and his exploits were given regular coverage until the end of the decade. Lard emerged as a faithful follower of literary fashion, changing as the AYM image changed, basing most of his controversial career on the reputation of Osborne but having to acquire a new image whenever a new author influenced the hazy image of the group. Thus, on 5 April 1957, Lard sees his friend James Glowtcher rival Braine's success with *No Room in the Dustbin*, a novel starring the acned but sexually irresistible Drabworth lavatory attendant, Ron Cladge. On 3 May, Lard and Glowtcher enjoy amazing commercial success with 'Angry Young Men Ltd' and 'Tantrum Products', the latter marketing a clockwork model of Lard and 'Joe Redbrick', 'the engaging cuddly toy with his turtle-neck sweater, leather-patched tweed jacket and blue jeans'. Omitted from *Declaration*, Lard plans his own manifesto, *Proclamation*, on 14 November, but since Osborne has attacked almost every other institution, Lard has to single out the National Playing Fields Association for condemnation. He continues to take his lead from Osborne for several months afterwards, attacking Fleet Street, the Monarchy, Suez, T. S. Eliot, Algeria and the London commercial theatre. Amis exerts a brief influence as Lard denounces Abroad and belletrist Julian Birdbath, and then, as the AYM begin to be replaced by other literary news, Lard tries out a Behanish pose, a new identity as a Beat, and a brief return to Osborne-style controversy with a musical play, before planning to end the fifties on a high note with a Nabokovian censorship scandal.

Like his fictional counterpart, John Osborne seemed to cultivate a freelance indignation which was all the more lucrative for being unrestricted by any coherent set of principles or beliefs. Name a topic, any topic, it seemed, and he would lambast it. But even if critics who were bamboozled by Osborne's tirades had closely analysed the text of *Look Back in Anger* their problems would not have been solved. The small army of commentators who worried over *Look Back in Anger* in the fifties did not misrepresent the play in their exegeses of its social protest, so much as the play misrepresents itself.

At first sight it appears that *Look Back in Anger* is staged in the battleground of the class war. The play opens with Jimmy Porter lounging about in his grubby attic flat, giving one of the posh Sunday papers a piece of his mind and then moving on to castigate his upper-middle-class wife Alison, and her upper-middle-class friends and family. This initial situation, plus the very fact that Jimmy was twenty-five years old, led most of the first-night critics to treat Osborne's hero as if he were supposed to be a socially and politically significant figure as a representative of the younger generation. (Moreover, Stephen Williams reported in his *Evening News* notice that he had been told that such was indeed Osborne's intention.) Most first judgements were therefore based on whether or not the critics considered Jimmy Porter acceptably typical. Only a couple of reviewers, most notably Tynan, enthused about Jimmy as 'the voice of the young';[14] the majority were puzzled or, like Stephen Williams, offended by the idea. Several reviewers dismissed Jimmy Porter as a tedious neurotic, typical only of tedious neurotics.[15] To Robert Wraight of the *Star* Osborne's hero looked like 'a caricature of the sort of frustrated left-wing intellectual who . . . died out during the war', a description which echoes Helena's insight in the play that Jimmy was 'born out of his time'. Philip Hope-Wallace told his readers that he simply could not believe Osborne had spoken for a new 'lost' generation. Most first-night reviews reported that *Look Back in Anger* offered passion and invective without amounting to much – there was 'a fine flow of savage talk', thought Cecil Wilson of the *Daily Mail*, but it all became fairly boring because no reasons or explanations for Jimmy's constant temper had been given.

Look Back in Anger appeared to present some kind of social protest but in a way that left most of its reviewers bewildered. Just why was Jimmy so resentful? asked Milton Shulman. What did he want from life? Kenneth Allsop continued the questionnaire in *The Angry Decade*. Why were Jimmy and Alison living in the Midlands if neither belonged there? Why was Jimmy running a sweet stall, of all things, since he had a university degree and this was a time of full employment? Why should Alison's mother have assigned detectives to follow her son-in-law? Why did Alison have to spend her weekends doing so much ironing? Such questions and complaints were greeted with derision, first of all by Tynan in his *Observer* eulogy of the play, then by Osborne himself in his *Declaration* essay, when he castigated the quibbles of 'deluded pedants', 'fashionable turnips' who wanted things spelled out for them and just could not appreciate art: 'I can't teach the paralysed to move their limbs.'

No, but that is the response to a different issue. In asking such questions early critics were not being risibly dull and incompetent. *Look Back in Anger* is a realist work and it needs to be accepted as realistic, believable. The queries of the 'fashionable turnips' would be irrelevant to a play by Beckett, Simpson or Pinter, but Osborne has made much of social elements in his characterization and then failed to account for the inconsistencies and oddities in the social detail. For example, he stresses the fact that Jimmy is non-U and, to all intents and purposes, an enemy of the bourgeoisie, but Jimmy also mentions that his father's last months were subsidized by monthly cheques from his family, that some of his mother's relatives are 'posh', and that his mother was concerned with 'smart, fashionable minorities'. If social class is to be an issue, and one way or another that seems to be the idea, then it is not being turnip-headed to expect the apparent contradictions and curiosities in Jimmy's background, and elsewhere in the play, to be there for some purpose or to be accounted for. But they remain puzzling and pointless.

When *Look Back in Anger* is not unbelievable it is hackneyed – we have Alison, the wife who suffers in silence, Helena, the proud beauty who succumbs to Jimmy's emotional power and vitality, Cliff, the understanding friend, Alison's upper-middle-class father, neatly cast as a Colonel, Alison's upper-middle-class brother, felicitously christened Nigel, Hugh's mother, a charwoman with a heart of gold, Alison's memories of the 'guerrilla warfare' exercised by Jimmy and Hugh when they gatecrashed upper-class parties and behaved shockingly.

Several of these clichés seem to strengthen the presence of a political theme in the play. In the opening scene Jimmy notes the pronouncements of a ludicrously right-wing bishop who had described class distinctions as proletarian propaganda and called on all Christians to help make H-bombs. Porter's next Tory victim is Nigel, 'The Platitude from Outer Space', and another platitude he does appear to be, a bowler-hatted, ex-Sandhurst 'chinless wonder' and, of course, a Conservative MP whose political meetings suffered the militant attentions of Jimmy and Hugh. When Alison reflects that these two comrades regarded her as 'a sort of hostage from those sections of society they had declared war on', she is merely nurturing a notion that has already taken firm root – her husband is a radical figure engaged in some sort of radical protest.

However, once a few more threads of consistency have been unravelled in the jumble of information and declamation in the play, these first impressions turn out to have been very misleading. Osborne's own Porteresque performance in *Declaration* as well as the presentation of his hero within the play itself indicate that Jimmy's tirades are to be taken seriously as severe indictments of society, but author and character only really share an enthusiasm for aggressively striking quasi-political attitudes. Osborne has given his hero the appearance of someone who refuses to compromise principles, scoffs at convention and holds fast to socialist idealism; and indeed, Jimmy *is* perpetually enraged – by the quality Sunday newspapers, the book reviews in the quality Sunday newspapers, Sundays, 'yobs' who go to the cinema on Sunday nights, Tories, the upper middle class, women, church bells . . . but his verbal assaults become so indiscriminate that they can only demonstrate that he gets easily het up. Which, it seems, is Jimmy's real aim and ideal:

> Oh heavens, how I long for a little ordinary human enthusiasm. Just enthusiasm – that's all. I want to hear a warm, thrilling voice cry out Hallelujah! (*He bangs his breast theatrically.*) Hallelujah! I'm alive! I've an idea. Why don't we have a little game? Let's pretend that we're human beings, and that we're actually alive.

The invective, it transpires, is not directed against social injustice at all, but against reticence, apathy and complacency. Social class remains an issue in the play only because these evils are associated with the bourgeoisie, and good, honest human feeling with the working class. Jimmy attacks Alison for being 'phlegmatic' and 'pusillanimous', Helena for her 'delicate, hot-house feelings', and admires 'common as dirt' Cliff for his 'big heart' and Hugh's working-class mother for her tearful appreciation of Alison's photograph. The acknowledged exception to the class-emotion rule is Alison's friend Webster, whose 'bite, edge, drive' and 'enthusiasm' Jimmy finds 'exhilarating'. Osborne acquired his insights into the class division in emotional response during his childhood: he describes in *Declaration* how his mother's family of Cockney publicans would bawl and brawl the night away whereas his father's more genteel relatives were grave and restrained.

The supreme importance of the virtues of energy and emotion is there in *The Entertainer* as well. The great moment in the life of Archie Rice came when he heard an 'old fat negress' singing in a Canadian bar:

> I wish to God I were that old bag. I'd stand up and shake my great bosom up and down, and lift up my head and make the most beautiful fuss in the world. Dear God, I would. But I'll never do it. I don't give a damn about anything, not even women or draught Bass.

Archie's tragedy is not the allegorically political one of lost pride and grandeur, as it often appears and is often assumed to be. It is that he can no longer care or respond – he is 'dead behind the eyes'. 'I want,' Osborne professed in *Declaration*, 'to make people feel, to give them lessons in feeling.' The political references in *Look Back in Anger* are soon made redundant. As it turns out, Jimmy Porter's protest is against the repression of feeling and his predicament is a deeply personal and emotional one. Hence the title of the play. Jimmy looks *back* in anger, and the 'strawberry birthmark' he insists on thrusting in the faces of his companions is not the scar of some radicalist grudge but a stigma of the suffering he experienced when he was ten years old and for twelve months took care of his father who was dying from wounds received in the Spanish Civil War:

> Every time I sat on the edge of his bed to listen to him talking or reading to me, I had to fight back my tears. At the end of twelve months, I was a veteran . . . You see, I learnt at an early age what it was to be angry – angry and helpless. And I can never forget it. I knew more about – love . . . betrayal . . . and death, when I was ten years old than you will probably ever know all your life.

Jimmy has cultivated the rage and bitterness he felt at his father's deathbed ever since. Perhaps it is a legacy of his mother's callous treatment of her dying husband, but Jimmy reserves special fear and loathing for women. He thinks Alison is a 'refined sort of butcher', like 'some dirty old Arab, sticking his fingers into some mess of lamb fat and gristle'; she has 'the passion of a python' and when they make love she 'devours' him as if he were 'some over-large rabbit'. Jimmy's insults are rather unconvincing, for Alison is rarely anything but passive and Helena too is successfully dominated after Jimmy shrugs off her useless opposition. In any case, 'butchering' is Jimmy's prerogative, for he has nothing but contempt for emotional 'virgins' like Alison and Helena who cannot boast the educative pain of witnessing a spurned parent's slow demise. Jimmy's relationship with both women is dictated not just by hatred of women in general but by his desire to goad them into satisfactorily painful response, to make them *feel*. Alison is especially provocative: her 'happy, uncomplicated life', her ignorance of anguish, her never having had 'a hair out of place, or a bead of sweat anywhere' – all this is contributory negligence and she is obviously asking for it:

> Oh, my dear wife, you've got so much to learn. I only hope you learn it one day. If only something – something would happen to you, and wake you out of your beauty sleep! If you could have a child, and it would die. Let it grow, let a recognizable human face emerge from that little mass of indiarubber and wrinkles. Please – if only I could watch you face that. I wonder if you might even become a recognizable human being yourself. But I doubt it.

Alison merits more detestation when she leaves Jimmy, and her farewell note makes, as he puts it, a 'polite, emotional mess' of her rejection of him. Even the news that Alison is pregnant cannot move him for he has just returned from another deathbed vigil. Eleven hours alone supervising the death of Hugh's mum, the certain absence of any flowers from Alison and her certain absence from the funeral where Jimmy will be all on his own deny her any sympathy. She is a 'cruel, stupid girl'. Helena reacts to this with predictable upper-class horror and slaps Jimmy, but his own suffering and despair are so powerfully profound that Helena finally overcomes hidebound convention and manages the only response true emotion demands: she kisses him passionately. Curtain.

Things are looking up for Jimmy several months later in Act III: he has Helena deeply in love with him and doing his ironing for him now, and while she may still have a bit to learn on the subject of real feeling, she obviously comes nearer the mark than the contemptible Alison. Then comes the twist. Alison returns looking 'ghastly' after a miscarriage or an abortion. Not that Jimmy cannot cope with that: 'I don't exactly relish the idea of anyone being ill, or in pain. It was my child too, you know. But (*he shrugs*) it isn't my first loss.' Anyway, he still resents the criminal lack of flowers at Hugh's mum's funeral. Yet all is not lost for Alison, who has been learning the lessons of suffering as recommended by Jimmy:

> I was wrong, I was wrong! I don't want to be neutral, I don't want to be a saint. I want to be a lost cause. I want to be corrupt and futile! . . . All I wanted was to die. I never knew what it was like. I didn't know it could be like that! I was in pain, and all I could think of was you, and what I'd lost. I thought: if only – if only he could see me now, so stupid, and ugly and ridiculous. This is what he's been longing for me to feel. This is what he wants to splash about in! I'm in the fire, and I'm burning, and all I want is to die! It's cost him his child, and any others I might have had! But what does it matter – this is what he wanted from me! Don't you see! I'm in the mud at last! I'm grovelling! I'm crawling! Oh, God –

The Colonel's daughter has been brought to her knees and her edifying degradation qualifies her for reconciliation with her hero. Jimmy and Alison can retreat into the poignant pretence of being a bear and a squirrel.

Critics have often winced at the Porters' furry escapism but their sentimental fantasy world requires far less suspension of disbelief than much else in the play; as Osborne has pointed out, a glance over a newspaper's Valentine's Day messages would show the squirrels and bears business to be fairly mild documentary realism. Alison's final lines – 'Poor bears! . . . Oh, poor, poor bears!' – with the shift from irony to tenderness, are, for me, among the best in the play and make for a daring and moving end to a work which has produced several moments of real tension and surprise. Whatever else is lacking in *Look Back in Anger*, the play does prove that the young Osborne possessed an acute sense of melodrama: most scenes end on a truly histrionic note – Alison left mouth a-tremble, Alison walking out on Jimmy, Helena kissing Jimmy, Alison returning to Jimmy. There is also the startling opening to Act III which replicates the beginning of the previous two Acts, only with Alison's place at the ironing board occupied by Helena. Such moments, together with the general claustrophobic atmosphere created by Jimmy's incessant taunts and harangues, could have formed the basis for a play of real force and power centred on an infuriating and destructive protagonist who displays utter selfishness in obsessive resentment. But *Look Back in Anger* is undermined by one fundamental contradiction which makes the queries about its social details and even the strange case of the vanishing political protest seem paltry.

There is, it appears to me, an extraordinary discrepancy between intention and effect. For the play to work, Jimmy need not be seen as a rebel or a representative spokesman since the 'political' theme has been mislaid and might soon be forgotten in the play's emotionalism, but he certainly does need to be seen as sympathetic and his appalling attitudes and behaviour do eventually have to be vindicated. Jimmy is not supposed to be beyond criticism and quite a few of his jeers and jibes are clearly intended as excessive and needlessly hurtful. Yet he cannot be treated as the villain of the piece without producing responses as damaging and inappropriate as the 'happy, hearty laughter' which greets the performance of *Look Back in Anger* in Amis's novel *Russian Hide-and-Seek* (1980). To regard Jimmy as anything other than spell-binding, impossible, dangerous – even sometimes cruel, yes, but tortured and brave and impassioned, a complex soul whose pain and torment only those who have suffered much can really understand – is to make a nonsense of the whole work, which only succeeds if the audience takes Jimmy as seriously as he is taken by the other characters in the play. Why else did Alison marry him if not for the sheer power and appeal of his burning personality? Why does she return, grateful that at last she can deserve his love, even at the cost of her unborn child and future infertility? Why does Helena suddenly kiss him passionately and fall in love with him? Why are all the characters, including Alison's father, so *enthralled* by him? Unless some Svengali effect is to be inferred, it must be because, as Alison recalls, he is simply irresistible: 'Everything about him seemed to burn . . . his eyes were so blue and full of the sun . . . Jimmy went into battle with his axe swinging round his head – frail, and so full of fire.' There is no suggestion that Jimmy is an ironic creation, like Pechorin in Lermontov's *A Hero of Our Time*; he has been invested with great importance and Osborne has been quick to react to the more dismissive accounts of his hero as a neurotic or a misfit. The character who so dominates the play has been depicted with great sympathy, even empathy.

In 1959 Pamela Lane was reported as describing *Look Back in Anger* as an autobiographical work, a judgement with which Osborne is said to have agreed,[16] and which a reading of *A Better Class of Person* tends to support. The recollections of Jimmy's early relationship with Alison, for example, frequently chime with Osborne's account of his own first marriage and there is a definite parallel between the circumstances (though not the cause) of the death of Osborne's father and that of Jimmy Porter's. Of course, Osborne did not run a sweet-stall or attend a 'white-tile' university, and one can only hope that Jimmy and Alison's relationship had no real-life foundation, but an autobiographical basis to the play helps to explain a few of its otherwise redundant and 'unrealistic' details: Jimmy's recollection of being hounded by detectives hired by his mother-in-law comes from Osborne's personal experience, and the unnecessarily unorthodox background of the not-so-working-class hero seems to be based on that of Osborne's own family. Far more importantly, an interpretation of *Look Back in Anger* as a very self-indulgent emotional fantasy can account for the glamorized presentation of Jimmy. Even if he is not the young Osborne's idealized self-projection, he might as well be.

However, I do not think it is necessary to be a card-carrying repressive or a shallow upholder of good form to think that Jimmy Porter is entirely unglamorous and unadmirable; that all the noise and fuss he makes from living at great emotional pressure and what-have-you, amounts to nothing more than relentless self-pity and self-concern. Jimmy's ranting finds its closest literary parallel in

the histrionics of Violet Elizabeth Bott, and the play's main elements – Jimmy telling everybody just what he thinks of them,
Jimmy being the only one to care about the deaths of his father and
Mrs Tanner, Jimmy being kissed by Helena, Jimmy finally accepting the grovelling pleas of Alison – are reminiscent of nothing so
much as the curses and door-slamming, nobody-understands-me,
you'll-be-sorry-when postures of adolescent daydreams.

The same air of adolescent melodrama is to be found in many of
Jimmy's monologues. One of the usual things to say of *Look Back
in Anger* is that it contains high-quality invective but Jimmy's
speeches are often marred by excruciating lines: 'Helena, have you
ever watched somebody die?'; 'Either you're with me or against
me'; 'I'll make such love to you, you'll not care about anything else
at all'; 'It's no good trying to fool yourself about love. You can't fall
into it like a soft job, without dirtying up your hands. It takes muscle
and guts'; 'it isn't my first loss'; 'the pain of being alive'. These lines
are not deliberately bad to highlight some flaw of self-dramatization
in Jimmy's character: they ask to be taken at face value. So too with
the similarly heartfelt monologues in *The Entertainer*, such as this
passage for Jean when she follows Jimmy's example and lets rip with
some fervent idealism:

> Have you ever got on a railway train here, got on a train from
> Birmingham to West Hartlepool? Or gone from Manchester to Warr-
> ington or Widnes? And you get out, you go down the street, and on
> one side maybe is a chemical works, and on the other side is the
> railway goods yard. Some kids are playing in the street, and you walk
> up to some woman standing on her doorstep. It isn't a doorstep really
> because you can walk straight from the street into her front room.
> What can you say to her? What real piece of information, what
> message can you give to her? Do you say: 'Madam, d'you know that
> Jesus died on the Cross for you?'

The depiction of the decaying music hall and the dead patter of
Archie Rice help to make *The Entertainer* a better play than *Look
Back in Anger*, but again, as in Jean's outburst, meaning and
relevance are often displaced by superficial melodrama. The
general impression is all that counts. Especially in *Look Back in
Anger* the result is merely a series of effects, as in a pretentious pop
song; the play lacks credibility not so much because of the hackneyed
or anomalous social details but because it presents glamorized
emotional histrionics rather than any believable emotional reality.

Archie Rice describes the condition of *Look Back in Anger* rather well:

> Why, we have problems that nobody's ever heard of, we're characters out of something that nobody believes in . . . we're so remote from the rest of ordinary everyday, human experience . . . We're too boring. Simply because we're not like anybody who ever lived . . . we do nothing but make a God almighty fuss about anything we ever do.

In the ordinary course of events *Look Back in Anger* would probably have disappeared, though not quite without trace, after its first three nights. That it survived to become the most discussed theatrical work of the fifties is due in the first place to the enthusiasm of Kenneth Tynan. Tynan was thrilled by the play because it *appeared* to offer the politics and passion he longed to find in contemporary drama. The gestures in the play and the very fact that the hero ranted and raved were enough, so he delightedly acclaimed Osborne as 'the voice of the young'. When reports started circulating that Osborne was indeed a spokesman for his generation *and* an angry young man, the initial doubts and queries about *Look Back in Anger* were swept aside. Critics no longer questioned the play: its social significance and – as Osborne grew famous – its author's talent were taken for granted.[17]

And for all its faults and flaws, *Look Back in Anger* is an important work, because it did effect a breakthrough in English theatre. The breakthrough was not achieved by any experimental structure or form: it is to all intents and purposes a traditionally conceived three-Act play. Osborne has claimed innovation in the fact that people are mentioned in the play who never turn up, but he was anticipated in that technique to much greater purpose and effect – by the fairly well-known creator of a character called Godot. But *Look Back in Anger* was simply the first play in a long time to be performed in or near the West End with a dingy setting and a hero who was more or less lower-class and prone to violent rhetoric. For all that these were postures and gestures, Jimmy's social and emotional protest had real force and relevance in the context of the contemporary drama. There had been a vogue, led by T. S. Eliot and Christopher Fry, for verse drama in the late forties, but for the most part 'Loamshire' theatre had been the order of the day, and the most successful playwrights in the fifties had been purveyors of polite, upper-middle-class drama, like Terence Rattigan and

William Douglas-Home. In *The Angry Decade* Kenneth Allsop wrote that Jimmy became a folk hero not because he explored or personified any particular social plights or views but because there existed, at last, in the English theatre a character who displayed a 'vitriolic articulateness about fairly ageless states of mind'. Since those states of mind remain unclear, the judgement is more accurate if pruned to 'vitriolic articulateness': that was all that mattered. Reflecting on the 'upsurge' of 'proletarian drama' in the last three years of the fifties, Tynan was convinced that it was *Look Back in Anger* which 'breached the dam' so that there followed 'a cascade of plays about impoverished people'.[18]

Although he did his best to live up to his reputation as an Angry Young Man in the fifties, castigating Tories, women, the monarchy, people who liked sport, people who liked gardening, theatre critics, Fleet Street, the H-Bomb, etc., Osborne was not a social rebel or protester and, as Harold Hobson has said, it was by being misunderstood that *Look Back in Anger* was placed at the head of the new tradition of kitchen-sink, 'political' drama.[19] Like Amis, Osborne has been regarded as having 'turned right' since the fifties, but his views remain as idiosyncratic as ever. He still obviously delights in vituperation and has denounced, among other people and things, the National Theatre, the Common Market, feminists, Concorde, Bob Geldof and the Band Aid appeal, Peter Hall, Jill Bennett, his mother and his daughter. How relevant or interesting or dignified Osborne's splenetic outbursts have been is questionable but they have often kept him in the public eye when his works have attracted attention mainly for their dreadful reviews. His reputation, which plummeted after *The World of Paul Slickey*, still rests on *Look Back in Anger* and *The Entertainer*. Probably his best-known play after those two is *Luther* (1961) which, with its handy background for History A-level, has found some continuing success as a school text. But one recent work has brought Osborne more widespread praise and attention – oddly enough an autobiography of his early years.

7

'Outsider In'

For most of his literary career Colin Wilson has remained on the fringe of English artistic and intellectual life. But for eighteen months in 1956 and 1957 he was one of the most famous writers in England, a leader of the new literary generation, a twenty-four-year-old author who helped to inaugurate the era of the AYM.

When his first book, *The Outsider*, appeared on 28 May 1956, the acclaim was so spectacular that Wilson became a national celebrity overnight. This success was all the more extraordinary considering the nature of Wilson's book. *The Outsider* was an apparently abstruse philosophical work speculating about the principles of genius and the meaning of life and packed with recondite literary and mystical allusions and quotations. Wilson's fame as philosopher was quite unique in the mid fifties, far outstripping that of the fashionably daunting Jean-Paul Sartre. Now a home-grown intellectual star – and a self-confessed 'Existentialist' what's more – had burst upon the scene to astounding praise and publicity.

In contrast to the relatively orthodox apprenticeship of Kingsley Amis, Colin Wilson was himself an 'outsider' to the literary world. *The Outsider* was his first published work of any kind. Reviewers were flummoxed: 'What sort of man is Mr Colin Wilson?; 'Who is Colin Wilson?' Answers would soon be found as reporters eagerly gathered details about the young author's background – not a difficult assignment, for Wilson has always shown immense enthusiasm in broadcasting the details of his autobiography for the benefit of enthralled contemporaries and future fans. Readers who wish to familiarize themselves with his life and intellectual development may consult the 18,000-word autobiographical preface to *Religion and the Rebel*, the four-page self-portrait in Allsop's *The Angry Decade*, Sidney Campion's biography *The World of Colin Wilson*, published when the subject was only thirty-one, the autobiography *Voyage to a Beginning* (1969), and the essays Wilson has added to subsequent editions of *The Out-sider*. My own account must be brief.

Colin Wilson was born in Leicester in 1931. His father worked in a local boot and shoe factory and struggled to make ends meet for much of the thirties. Wilson managed to win a scholarship to the Gateway Secondary Technical School, but came bottom of his class in his first year and completed his formal education when he was sixteen. For the next two years he worked as a warehouseman, a laboratory assistant at his old school, and as a clerk, before being conscripted into the RAF. His was to be an abbreviated experi-ence of National Service, for he wangled a discharge by claiming to be homosexual. Wilson's superior officers might have suspected his fraudulence in 1951 when he married his first wife, Dorothy Betty Troop. He still had no desire to settle into respectability and an ordinary career; he was determined to take temporary, menial jobs so he could concentrate his energy and ambition on his spare-time writing. Ever since leaving school Wilson had pursued an ambitious course of self-education and literary training with a dedication strengthened by an unwavering faith in the importance of his task and his own talent. Marriage, a move to London, and then the arrival of a baby could not weaken Wilson's resolve. He continued to read widely, kept a voluminous journal, and worked when he could on a million-word novel based on the story of Jack the Ripper.

He managed to hold down a job in a plastics factory in Finchley for eighteen months, but the strain of the constant moves from one set of furnished rooms to another told on his wife, who returned to Leicester with her young son. The separation was to prove final. Wilson struggled on in London, enduring more casual jobs, but also gaining encouragement from the friendships he was forming with a few other aspiring writers who drifted in and out of the city's Bohemian scene. It was through a connection with an anarchist discussion group in Dollis Hill that he met Bill Hopkins and Stuart Holroyd. Wilson soon established firm friendships with both after he discovered that they shared his ideas and his dreams of spec-tacular literary achievement. But even modest achievement looked far off so long as he could only read and write in the evenings.

In 1954 Wilson decided he had to devote his full time and attention to his novel. He saved a little money, gave up his job in another plastics factory and bought a rucksack and sleeping bag. That summer and autumn he spent his days writing his novel in the British Museum and his nights sleeping rough on Hampstead Heath. This regime ended only when the colder weather eventually forced him to find digs in New Cross.

He has recalled that it was here, alone, on Christmas Day 1954, cut off from family and friends, that the thought came to him that he was in the same situation as many of his favourite fictional characters, suffering an isolation imposed by some sort of deep compulsion. Stuart Holroyd had already shown him the first chapters of a critical book he was writing. Now, recording his thoughts in his journal, Wilson reflected that he too had the starting-point for a book. He began to work on his new project as soon as the British Museum reopened on 27 December, and by the end of the afternoon had written the first four pages of what was to become *The Outsider*.

This new work was based on the ideas and quotations Wilson had been jotting down in his journal since early adolescence when he had first became obsessed with basic questions about the meaning of life. He intended it to demonstrate his theory that the vast majority of people experienced only a mundane, dulled awareness and that a few rejected the commonplace and aspired to a far more intense insight. In his autobiography he describes his excitement on realizing that his own convictions were shared by his favourite authors: 'As I began to see this clearly, all the non-stop reading of my teens began to fall into place . . . Shaw, Eliot, Hulme, Christian mysticism, Eastern mysticism, Dostoevsky, Tolstoy and Nietzsche and the rest . . . all were saying the same thing in different ways.'

He now called on his personal canon of writers and thinkers to develop his long-cherished ideas. He made quick progress: he had to take another job but still managed to write most of his book by the middle of 1955. Although Secker & Warburg were already expressing interest in his novel, Wilson chose to send an outline of his work and a short excerpt to Gollancz, since he admired Victor Gollancz's own anthology of spiritual writing, *A Year of Grace* (1950). It was a shrewd move. Victor Gollancz had turned to religion after the Second World War when he suffered a breakdown, and the theme of spiritual quest in *The Outsider* brought Wilson a very enthusiastic response.

He delivered his completed manuscript in the autumn of 1955 and collected an advance of £75. Jon Evans at Gollancz had retitled it *The Outsider*, setting aside Wilson's suggestion, *The Pain Threshold*. The catchy new title was emblazoned across a dust-jacket carrying a commendation from Edith Sitwell who wrote that this was an 'astonishing' book and that Wilson would be 'a truly great writer'. Sitwell's opinions were backed up by a 137-line blurb stressing the book's importance and the startling precocity of its author. There was, however, more than a touch of desperation about the hype; both Jon Evans and Victor Gollancz shared Sitwell's enthusiasm, but they anticipated modest sales at best for such an obviously uncommercial work. The initial printing of 5,000 copies seemed extremely optimistic.

The first sign that this estimate was very wrong came in a pre-publication notice which Gollancz had been promised in the *Evening News*. John Connell's piece on Saturday 26 May was headlined 'A Major Writer – and He's 24'. Connell predicted a rumbustious début for this sensational young author: 'I think he will shock the arid little academic philosophers a good deal, and one or two of the more fashionable critical mandarins may wince at his coming.'

On the contrary, to the astonishment of everyone but themselves, the next day the two most fashionable critical Mandarins of them all devoted their important lead reviews to eulogies of *The Outsider*. Philip Toynbee in the *Observer* claimed that Wilson had written 'an exhaustive and luminously intelligent study', and in the *Sunday Times* Cyril Connolly declared *The Outsider* to be 'one of the most remarkable first books I have read for a long time'.

Wilson had arrived. When *The Outsider* appeared in the bookshops the following day the first 5,000 copies sold out. The second impression was snapped up three days later. Meanwhile, the *Evening News* had celebrated publication day by carrying a feature on the prodigious new writer, 'The Inside Story of the Outsider'. Exciting stuff it was, too, for Wilson revealed all about his devotion to matters intellectual, the struggles he had faced and, best of all, the nights he had spent on Hampstead Heath in his sleeping bag. With a biography as thrilling as the ovation for his book, he had become a gossip columnist's dream. On Saturday 2 June the *Mail*'s diarist, 'Tanfield', reported that the young author had been so busy giving interviews to the press that he had eaten nothing but chocolate bars all week. Like his rival, 'William Hickey' in the *Express* highlighted the sleeping-bag episode and then scooped the discovery that the sometime vagrant was 'Flabbergasted' at his success. The next day the quality Sundays carried their own features on Wilson. The *Observer*'s 'Pendennis' grouped Osborne and Wilson together for a double portrait and, to complete an extraordinary week for the young philosopher, 'Atticus' announced that the *Sunday Times* had commissioned a series of articles from him.

The reviews which followed in June reinforced Wilson's sensational reputation. The *Daily Telegraph*'s John Applebey hailed *The Outsider* as 'provocative, illuminating, adult', and Mary Scrutton in the *New Statesman* judged it to be a 'really important' work. Elizabeth Bowen described Wilson as 'brilliant' and herself as 'thunderstruck' at his learning. V. S. Pritchett announced on the Home Service that *The Outsider* was 'brilliant', 'dashing, learned and exact'. Even more enthusiastic was Kenneth Walker's review in the *Listener* where *The Outsider* was said to be 'masterly', 'the most remarkable book upon which the reviewer has ever had to pass judgement'.[1]

It seemed inevitable that a few critics would react against this acclaim. Kingsley Amis, Burns Singer and the *TLS* reviewer were all less than sympathetic.[2] In his *New Statesman* column on 7 July, J. B. Priestley doubted the lasting worth of Wilson's ideas, but still thought the praise he had received was well-deserved. John Applebey's only objection was that the author's 'tricks of sophistication' suggested he might be 'no more than a writer's writer', but it was clear from the outset that exclusive appreciation would not be one of Wilson's problems. By 13 July Daniel Farson was able to declare in his *Daily Mail* feature that *The Outsider* had enjoyed 'the most rapturous reception of any book since the war'. Two American reports described Wilson's début with awe; *Time* said it was 'causing a run on critical superlatives in highbrow London's literary marketplace', and Harvey Breit in the *New York Times Book Review* said simply that Wilson had 'walked into literature . . . like a man walks into his own house'.[3]

With such spontaneous critical and popular success Wilson had quickly outgrown any conventional highbrow reputation and become a fully-fledged celebrity. Even the *Daily Express* recommended his book. He posed in his sleeping bag on Hampstead

Heath for a photographer for *Life* and on 17 August was interviewed by Daniel Farson for ITV's *This Week*. This programme, which also established Farson in a career as one of the fifties television personalities, followed on from his *Daily Mail* articles on the 'Post-War Generation' where he acclaimed his new friend as a 'genius', a 'rare person – a man with a vision'. John Barber's riposte for the *Daily Express* established Wilson as one of the new Angry Young Men, a reputation which Wilson was to retain, if only because of the connotations of his book's title and his own fame. Even John Osborne, with his new public image as the original angry young man, could not rival Wilson's fame during the summer of 1956. For a while, indeed, media interest in Osborne was dependent on Wilson's far greater initial impact – his appearance in the features by 'Pendennis' and, more importantly, Farson, and therefore Barber, came as a result of the publicity breakthrough which Colin Wilson had made.

Osborne could certainly not match the level of immediate financial success which Wilson enjoyed. In August Gollancz placed advertisements for *The Outsider* which ran: 'Printings are so rapid that we are not certain whether the one in hand is the eighth or ninth'. It was a favourite Gollancz tactic – release impressions of a thousand copies and catalogue each one to dress a book up as a bestseller. But in the case of *The Outsider*, appearance had become reality. By October 20,000 copies had been sold in hardback, translation rights already sold to five countries, and the American edition selected as a Book of the Month. There was even talk of producing an LP, with the author and Anthony Quayle reading key passages. He had earned £4,000 in royalties by September and a total of £20,000 within a year of *The Outsider*'s publication, a remarkable sum for the period.

Wilson's fame and fortune grew as he was courted by editors for articles and reviews. The first of these appeared in the *Sunday Times* (as promised by 'Atticus') where he contributed two lead reviews and an article on Shaw. With invitations from the *Daily Express* and *Reynolds News* as well as journals like the *Listener* and the *London Magazine*, many other pieces followed. The BBC also went out of its way to secure his services, and he was able to voice his beliefs and opinions regularly over the airwaves.[4]

Despite all this success, it was clear that, unlike his book, Wilson himself had not sold out: he could still be lauded as a genuine Outsider, an intellectual who had renounced bourgeois values and committed himself to a truly Bohemian appearance and lifestyle. In the large photograph which accompanied John Barber's article in the *Express* on 26 July, Wilson appeared dressed in a T-shirt, cooking over two primus stoves in his seedy Notting Hill flat – a 'classic rebel in classic setting', said the caption approvingly. *Time* was anxious to give a comprehensive account of Wilson's Bohemianism in the feature of 2 July:

> He lives in a two-room London slum flat overlooking a garden of weeds, feeds on sausages, beer and chocolate biscuits, and sleeps on an inflatable green rubber mattress. Wilson is tall and thin, favors black-and-white turtle-neck sweaters, beaver-colored corduroy pants and brown leather sandals. His pale blue eyes stare through horn-rimmed glasses at neat rows of worn, secondhand books and a door covered with hieroglyphics and an Einstein formula.

Yes, Wilson was 'a proper Outsider'.

His personal appearance had become as familiar as the title of his book. Cecil Beaton photographed Wilson for his 1957 collection *The Face of the World*, and parodists and cartoonists latched on to the distinctive look with glee. Soon the horn-rimmed glasses, lank hair and inevitable polo-necked sweater were adorning caricatures of the celebrity philosopher. Wilson provided the essential components for a new literary type, as the cover illustration for the November 1957 issue of *Twentieth Century* demonstrates; three generations of writers are represented, the youngest by an author wearing the mandatory costume of Wilsonian spectacles and sweater and holding an (Amis-inspired) glass of beer. He was offering a new literary image at a time when one was badly needed. Poets tended to look like bank officials, complained the *Evening Standard*'s fashion journalist, Amanda Marshall, on 9 February 1956. She could find literary glamour only in the attractive individual appearances of W. S. Merwin and Elizabeth Jane Howard, but no really *artistic*-looking writers.

According to a *News Chronicle* feature on youth fashions, published on 12 May, a fortnight before *The Outsider*, the elements of Wilson's personal style would identify him as a Bohemian. But it was Wilson's own image which gave late-fifties Bohemianism a specific identity and style; until his arrival there was no fixed image of young arty types, although they were beginning to be associated with the new espresso bars. The *News Chronicle* reporter, for instance, could only refer to jazz trumpeter Humphrey Lyttelton before resorting vaguely to Sartre and Saint Germain to evoke a Bohemian milieu.

Wilson's appearance (in both senses) changed all this. Young Wilson clones were soon haunting the new espresso bars and by 11 March 1957, Wilson's influence on young men's 'ungroomed' style was being lamented by the luckless Amanda Marshall. Pipes were out and polo-necked sweaters were in. Wilson was the mentor and model, *The Outsider* the handbook and badge, for a cult of coffee-bar Existentialists with *angst* in their pants. An advertisement even appeared in the personal columns of the *New Statesman* from an 'Outsider, 24. . .' offering other Outsiders a share in his caravan.

According to Malcolm Bradbury, Wilson did belong to a distinctive Bohemian subculture, but one that ended with the appearance of the espresso bars which were usually assumed to be the Bohemian's natural habitat. In Bradbury's opinion the espresso bar clientèle mimicked the attitudes and appearance of a small group of genuine drop-outs, like Colin Wilson, which flourished during and after the Second World War. In a *Punch* article of 1958, Bradbury nicknamed this group 'the sugar-beet generation' (since its members often relied on casual work during the sugar-beet harvest), and in another article, co-written with a bona fide Bohemian, Dudley Andrew, light-heartedly described the history of the 'Beets'.[5] They classified the Beets as a 'semi-literary and artistic group', working-class and provincial in origin and connected with Fitzrovia, the literary Bohemia of wartime London. Bradbury based his accounts on his experience between 1953 and 1955 of Nottingham's bed-sitter community which developed around the Art School, the University and the Playhouse. Through this community Bradbury met Dudley Andrew himself, and such writers as Willis Hall, Alan Sillitoe, B. S. Johnson, and Colin Wilson, three years before *The Outsider* was published. (It was a community Bradbury later depicted in his television Play for Today, *Love on a Gunboat*.)

The Beets' creative pretensions far outstripped their achievements, so the group remained largely unnoticed and unchronicled in contemporary writing. One account appears in Roland Camberton's novel, *Scamp* (1950), but this depicts the late-forties aftermath of Fitzrovia. The only novel about the Beet lifestyle was

Noel Woodin's *Room at the Bottom*, but the Beets also gain a brief mention in Bradbury's own first novel, *Eating People is Wrong*, when Professor Treece stumbles across the Bohemians of the Mandolin Espresso Bar and is told that they are 'pseudo-writers, pseudo-painters, pseudo-philosophers' who share a 'strain of thinking, which is all perfectly connected and rather widespread'. This has all remained 'underground', and only Colin Wilson has been able to find public attention.

Not quite: in 1957 two other Beet Bohemians made their mark – Wilson's friends, Bill Hopkins and Stuart Holroyd. Michael Hastings and John Braine (who used the Notting Hill flat as a London base) were also associated with Wilson, but it was Hopkins and Holroyd who were rightly seen as his principal colleagues, and Wilson used his own fame to promote his chums' literary careers. Gollancz published Holroyd's *Outsider*-like credo, *Emergence from Chaos*, in June 1957, and again covered the dust-jacket with an excited summary which compared Holroyd with Wilson and noted, just in passing, that at twenty-three Holroyd was even younger than his predecessor. Hopkins was an elderly twenty-nine when his first novel *The Divine and the Decay* was published by MacGibbon & Kee in December 1957, but he had already contributed to *Declaration*. Hopkins owed his premature prominence to Wilson, who had also assured *Books and Art* readers in October 1957 that his colleague was a genius. Questioned in the following month's issue, Hopkins had agreed.

Unfortunately for Hopkins and Holroyd, their talents were not allowed to shine for long. Their own *putsch* on literary London was appallingly timed to coincide with the dramatic decline in Wilson's reputation, which inevitably dragged them down in its wake. Wilson's fall from grace did not mean a mere disappearance from public view – it could be studied in the full glare of press interest. The first of a series of scandals broke on 5 December 1956 when the *Daily Express* reported that, in a speech to a spiritualist society in Knightsbridge, Wilson confessed *The Outsider* was a fraud. Wilson replied that his remarks had been completely misrepresented, but the denial could not wipe away the smear. A week later *Time* and *Newsweek* carried the *Daily Express*'s original story. The incident was not very damaging in itself, but it did signal a change in press attitudes to Wilson. For over six months he had enjoyed the attentions of journalists anxious to outdo each other in their praise for the new genius. Now another, even more fruitful angle could be taken for their stories. Victor Gollancz was alive to the danger and sent Wilson a six-page letter warning him to avoid further indiscretions.

Neither Gollancz nor Wilson could prevent the next slur, a *Sunday Pictorial* story about his marriage which appeared on 16 December. Wilson might be 'widely hailed as the greatest literary genius of the century', conceded the *Pictorial*, but few knew about his murky past. Mrs Betty Wilson told *Pictorial* readers about her hardship since her famous husband had stopped paying maintenance money for her and their five-year-old son, despite his huge windfall from *The Outsider*.

This exposé was also denied by Wilson but it only turned out to be the prelude to a far greater scandal about his domestic life in February the next year. The story involved Wilson, his girl-friend Joy Stewart, and her parents. Mr and Mrs Stewart had come across one of Wilson's diaries and been horrified to read a series of pornographic fantasies. Wilson later claimed that these were really details of research for a forthcoming novel, but the Stewarts assumed otherwise and resolved to rescue their daughter. They stormed into Wilson's flat. 'Aha, Wilson!' announced Mr Stewart, 'the game is up!' He then brandished the instrument demanded by tradition – a horsewhip. His wife, meanwhile, busied herself by thumping the young philosopher with her handbag. Unfortunately for Wilson a spectator at this full and frank exchange of views was his supper guest, Gerald Hamilton, an ageing roué enjoying a brief spell in the limelight as the 'original' of Christopher Isherwood's Mr Norris. Hamilton did not spectate for long, since he could spot a lucrative scandal when he saw one, and he slipped off to telephone Fleet Street.

The following day, 20 February 1957, the incident was reported in the *Daily Express* and the *Evening Standard* and was front-page news for the *Daily Mail*. On the twenty-first the *Express* and the *Mail* interviewed the combatants and the *Mail* somehow managed to carry a photograph of Mrs Stewart (obligingly) wielding her handbag. The day after that, the *Express* and the *Mail* interviewed Wilson and Joy Stewart in Devon where they had fled, the *Mail* carried a photograph of Wilson's wife and child, and the *Standard* carried a satire on the whole fiasco by Wolf Mankowitz.

And there the whole episode seemed ready to end. But no. In

an attempt to justify his anachronistic intervention Mr Stewart had given journalists a sample of the diaries, which included the remark, 'I am the most serious man of our age'. Now Wilson sought to rectify the bad impression the extracts might have given: in a gesture more generous than wise he handed the journal over to the *Daily Mail*. Current obscenity laws ruled out the printing of any pornographic material but the excerpts which did appear on the twenty-third probably hit Wilson's reputation harder than the initial scandal had done and certainly confirmed the impression that he enjoyed unusual self-confidence: 'The day must come when I'm hailed as a major prophet . . . I must live on, longer than anyone else has ever lived . . . to be eventually Plato's ideal sage and king.' Naturally enough, these statements found a less than sympathetic audience; three days later the *Daily Mail* published readers' letters attacking Wilson alongside a reassessment of *The Outsider* by Kenneth Allsop.

This was not the first time Wilson had made public his self-belief. During his television interview with Farson the previous year, he had said that he assumed he was a genius, with a frankness that the *Daily Sketch* TV critic for one failed to find endearing: 'Colin (I'm A Genius) Wilson Gives Me A Pain', declared the headline for Herbert Kretzmer's column on 18 August. In another interview with Farson a month later, Wilson had announced that he intended to lead a renaissance in English literature. Questioned about the new young talents, he had replied, 'Frankly . . . there are none. Except myself, of course.' Wilson repeated the performance when he told Farson in October 1957 that both he and Bill Hopkins were geniuses. (Farson later greatly regretted the 'vile' part he played in his friend's downfall.)[6]

Another well-publicized controversy about Wilson in September 1957 could only supply his opponents with more ammunition. Wilson had complained to the *Daily Mail* that a play he had written, *The Death of God*, had been rejected by Ronald Duncan and George Devine of the English Stage Company. It was an awkward situation for Wilson, who had already let it be known that this masterpiece would be presented at the Royal Court and that he had Olivier in mind for a part (as God?). Duncan was quoted in the *Mail* on 28 September as explaining that the play was simply too bad to be put on the stage: 'the main inspiration seems to be a TV children's hour serial.' This theatrical contretemps was

151

also reported by the gossip columnists of the *Express* and *News Chronicle* and inspired the *Telegraph*'s 'Peter Simple' to verse:

> There was a young man in a pique
> Whose play was found lacking in chic.
> Such sensitive plants
> Should stick to Gollancz,
> Where prophets are hailed every week.[7]

Reflecting on all the hullaballoo he caused in 1957 Wilson judged that 'the personal publicity was a mistake' but 'not always avoidable'.[8] This does not square with Wilson's conviction at the time: 'Any real man of genius must be prepared to take on the most difficult forms of self-expression, such as the newspapers.'[9] As a self-confessed man of genius Wilson actively encouraged press attention. He had sent his letter of protest to the Royal Court to the *Daily Mail*, for example, and had of course handed over his personal diaries to the same newspaper. On that earlier occasion he had made a deal with *Daily Express* reporters for their exclusive coverage of his flight from London, which was supposedly taken to escape publicity. He had even scuppered the *Express*' scoop by sending the *Daily Mail* newsdesk a postcard announcing his return to London: 'I thought it only fair to let them know too.' Several years later Wilson justified his talent for publicity as a product of his magnanimity: 'I can't find the heart to send [reporters] back to their editors, empty-handed.'[10]

Whether it was mainly a result of Wilson's own naivety or of a malicious press, the notoriety he suffered from the scandals actually did not do as much damage to his literary standing as one might assume, for Wilson's highbrow reputation had already declined dramatically by the time the popular press began to ridicule him. Indeed, that ridicule had been sanctioned by a growing reaction against Wilson's initial spectacular success.

The Outsider continued to sell astonishingly well throughout the latter part 1956 and 1957, but critical enthusiasm had proved short-lived. The unflattering reviews of later critics, notably A. J. Ayer in the October issue of *Encounter* and Raymond Williams in *Essays in Criticism* three months later, were echoed in America where *The Outsider* and its reputation were greeted with bewilderment. Meanwhile, Wilson had become a regular butt of humorists who realized that the book's title and display of learning made very promising material. On 11 July 1956 Geoffrey Gorer produced a name-dropping extract from 'The Insider by C*L*N W*LS*N' for Punch. On 24 August Lionel Hale's parody 'The Backsider' appeared in the Spectator. The previous week the New Statesman's Weekend Competition was titled 'The Offsider' and invited readers to write a piece in the style of a collaboration by 'Messrs Angus, Sandy and Colin Wilson'.

The two namesakes produced their own satires in 1957. Several years earlier, while assistant superintendent of the British Museum Reading Room, Angus Wilson had encouraged the young Colin in his writing, an interest which led to a dedication to him in The Outsider. Judging by the title story in Angus Wilson's collection A Bit Off the Map, patronage had turned to hostility, for the tale presents, in the declamations of Huggett, a cutting parody of Colin Wilson's beliefs. On 13 October the Sunday Times published Sandy Wilson's satire 'Types of Today', including the biography of the much-acclaimed young genius Reg Glupton, 'unkempt nineteen-year-old son of a Cricklewood glazier'. The article was accompanied by a photograph of the gormless Reg sporting the famous Wilsonian spectacles, hair and sweater.

The parodies were, of course, signs rather than causes of a general critical rethink about Wilson's status and abilities, the main impetus for which had come not from the few later reviews attacking The Outsider, nor even from the scandals involving its author, but from Wilson's own journalism. Months before the publication of the diary extracts, he had already demonstrated a curious talent for the regular production of somewhat unorthodox statements. Articles and reviews by Wilson were much in demand in 1956 and 1957 but where other young writers might have used such opportunities to establish a literary career, he seemed able only to contribute to his own ruin.

His first attempt at literary journalism was a Sunday Times review, published on 17 June 1956, of Maurice Nicoll's Psychological Commentaries on the Teaching of Gurdjieff and Ouspensky, vol. 5. An impressively esoteric choice, but Wilson used his column space to ponder whether Gurdjieff and Nicoll himself were geniuses. His second contribution appeared on 22 July, launching Shaw as a mystic, an opinion treated very coolly the following week by Sunday Times regular, Raymond Mortimer. The paper printed only one more review – on 5 August, and titled, not too appropriately perhaps, 'No Nonsense'. The series which 'Atticus' had proudly announced turned out to be very short-lived.

Other pieces Wilson wrote also failed to impress. A *London Magazine* article of August 1956 provoked Elizabeth Jennings and R. W. Gaskell to castigate what had been a vague and pretentious outline of his basic ideas. Another *London Magazine* piece in January 1957 gave Donald Davie the chance to note in the next issue that 'Mr Colin Wilson's activities become steadily more embarrassing'. Wilson's declaration in a *Listener* review that D. H. Lawrence was a 'second-rater' with a 'trivial mind' prompted Maurice Cranston and Geoffrey Gorer to attack Wilson's general attitude to literature. Wolf Mankowitz then responded to Wilson's denunciation of contemporary writers in *Reynolds News* with a denunciation of Colin Wilson.[11]

His appetite for opinions that might euphemistically be termed odd appeared to be insatiable. In an article in the *Daily Express* on 14 September 1956 he declared that death was almost impossible for someone who did not want to die: 'People die because they want to.' 'And why do people die? Out of laziness, lack of purpose, of direction.' Another of his debatable assertions was widely mocked towards the end of 1956. Invited to speak at an *Encore* symposium on current drama at the Royal Court on 18 November, Wilson took the opportunity to reassess Shakespeare as a 'thoroughly second-rate mind', a mere producer of 'good quotes': 'In Shakespeare, in point of fact, these things, the sort of things you find stuck on your calendars, occur all over the place. For the most part, it's absolutely commonplace and absolutely second-rate.' He was ridiculed by Wolf Mankowitz during the symposium, and afterwards by a jaunty 'Peter Simple' who found that once again Wilson had inspired the Muse:

> Shakespeare, Mr Wilson notes,
> Was a hack who churned out quotes.
> Poor old Will, he never tried a
> Method used in 'The Outsider':
> Though his plots might be on loan,
> His quotations were his own.[12]

Wilson's remarks proved to be even more ill-advised when the critic John Carswell reacted to that judgement of Shakespeare by examining the 'good quotes' Wilson had used so liberally in *The*

Outsider. In a letter to the *TLS* on 14 December, Carswell revealed that a sample of 249 lines of quotations in Wilson's book had yielded 82 major errors and 203 minor errors, an average of over one error per line. In his *Sunday Times* review Cyril Connolly had noticed many 'minor inaccuracies' in *The Outsider* but had been content to ascribe these to Wilson's incompetent typing; by now, though, the climate of opinion had changed. Coming as it did when reports were circulating that Wilson had confessed *The Outsider* to be a fraud, Carswell's revelation was taken to be a serious blow to his reputation. The *News Chronicle*'s gossip columnist interviewed him about the current swing of critical opinion on 17 December; Wilson's explanation that mistakes had occurred because he had written his book in a 'white heat of inspiration' failed to bolster his crumbling credibility.

So, even before Wilson was ambushed by Mr Stewart and the scandalmongers, the original acclaim for *The Outsider* was dwindling so fast that by the end of 1956 the book which had caused such a sensation in May could earn only one mention in the *Sunday Times* 'Books of the Year' survey, and that was Arthur Koestler's nomination of it as 'Bubble of the Year'. The same day, 23 December, in the *Observer*'s listing of the books of 1956 only Philip Toynbee mentioned *The Outsider*, taking the chance to qualify his earlier enthusiasm and to damn *The Outsider* with distinctly fainter praise:

> I would like to do an act of impenitence by reiterating my admiration for Mr Colin Wilson's *The Outsider*. I doubt whether this interesting and extremely promising book quite deserved the furore which it seems to have caused. But the very fact that it has aroused so much controversy suggests that Mr Wilson's thesis deserves attention.

It was an odd line to take, especially since his own eulogy had done so much to give *The Outsider* such attention. Toynbee's admiration was even less evident by 26 May the next year when he reviewed Holroyd's *Emergence from Chaos*, which he thought superior to *The Outsider*, a book now definitely devalued: a year to the day after he had acclaimed it as 'a real contribution to our understanding of our greatest predicament', Toynbee found that its virtue lay in its 'disorderly passion'.

Despite his impenitence in the earlier exercise in backtracking, Toynbee was clearly responding to the current revaluations of *The*

Outsider. By August 1957, for example, a *Books and Bookmen* reviewer was explaining *The Outsider*'s undeserved success as being the result of Wilson's youth and the misguided but influential praise of the hapless Philip Toynbee. In the February 1957 number of *Twentieth Century*, W. John Morgan relegated Wilson to the status of a media 'personality', like 'Miss Nancy Spain or Mr Gilbert Harding, or even Champion the Wonder Horse'.

Victor Gollancz was only too aware that Wilson's literary reputation was at a low ebb when he published the sequel to *The Outsider* in October 1957. In contrast to *The Outsider*, *Religion and the Rebel* carried no promotion of the author and his importance (despite the plethora of available commendations) other than an endorsement from Herbert Read, who stated rather lamely that he considered this to be a better book than Wilson's first. The fame and acclaim might never have existed. Nobody anticipated another 'masterly' survey, except the evidently ill-informed *Sunday Dispatch* journalist who awaited Wilson's second critical success.[13] Kenneth Allsop's prediction was more astute: 'Ever since *The Outsider* appeared . . . there has been an ominously growing ambush awaiting Colin Wilson's next book . . . The ambush may still take place. The rotten eggs may be about to fly about his shaggy head.' As it turned out, *Religion and the Rebel* was indeed greeted with a barrage of rotten eggs. Only the very earliest reviews – Allsop's in the *Daily Mail* on 19 October and Kenneth Young's in the *Daily Telegraph* the previous day – were at all favourable. Yet if, as Allsop had predicted, any retraction took place, then it was done by proxy: of the original champions of *The Outsider*, only Toynbee took it upon himself to review the sequel. As 'Pharos' remarked in the *Spectator* on 1 November, many critics were noticeable by their absence. Clearly, reading *Religion and the Rebel* was for some, as Janet Adam Smith confessed, 'a highly embarrassing affair'.[14]

For others it was a golden opportunity to set the record straight, and editors were liable to appoint reviewers who could be relied on to attack Wilson unreservedly. Critics like Anthony Hartley and Keith Waterhouse would have been identifiable as unsympathetic, and Raymond Mortimer, Wolf Mankowitz and Maurice Cranston, who had all attacked Wilson previously, were assigned to review his second book.

Relatively charitable reviews appeared in newspapers and

magazines which had not been implicated in Wilson's success. Comparatively lenient criticisms were made in *The Times* and the *TLS*, by Iris Murdoch in the *Manchester Guardian* and A. J. Ayer in the *Spectator*.[15] Elsewhere Wilson was panned. His second book was described as a 'mixture of banality and incomprehensibility', 'half-baked Nietzsche', 'a suet pudding full of other men's currants'. Toynbee now remembered *The Outsider* as 'clumsily written and still more clumsily composed', and concluded his recantation by condemning *Religion and the Rebel* as a 'vulgarizing rubbish-bin'.[16]

More attacks on Wilson, and on Holroyd and Hopkins, came from reviewers of *Declaration*, published a week before *Religion and the Rebel*. The *TLS* critic described Wilson's work as 'a literary Madame Tussaud's' and derided his pretensions and his career as a press celebrity. To Iain Hamilton, Wilson and his two associates were 'woolly bleaters' and Peter Green gave the trio a new label – 'the Spotty Nietzscheans'.[17] When *Religion and the Rebel* was published in the United States in November, *Time*, ever-alert to changing moods, carried a scathing review. A photograph of the author was slotted alongside the review with a caption deftly summarizing the change in the young philosopher's status: 'Egghead, scrambled'.

Wilson may have been voted 'Most Publicized Author of the Year' by *Books and Bookmen*, but another of the magazine's awards was less ambiguously unflattering; *Religion and the Rebel* was definitely 'Flop of the Year'.[18]

For several months Wilson persisted with his enthusiastic approach to press relations. He telephoned the *Sunday Dispatch* gossip columnist to say that Gollancz had advised him to cut his losses and take a job. He also told reporters that he was quite satisfied with the reception of his second book since any criticism was encouraging for a young writer. He even obliged journalists by holding a press conference in a Fleet Street espresso bar where he explained that both books were second-rate – compared, that was, to his great creative work-in-progress on Jack the Ripper. Reporting this incident, a *Manchester Guardian* columnist pitied Wilson for having become 'a ridiculous figure'.[19]

That conclusion was to be rubbed in by several merciless satirists. Alex Atkinson acclaimed Wilson in the December issue of *Books and Art* as the author of 'two of the funniest books of this generation'. On 25 October an *Evening News* reporter nominated Wilson one of the five people she would like to see sent into space and, to round off a miserable twelve months, *Daily Mail* readers voted him one of their 'Comics of the Year' on 31 December.

Wilson's intellectual standing after 1957 can be gauged by the off hand treatment his work received at the BBC whence invitations had once come unsolicited. In 1959 Wilson's agent assured P. H. Newby that Wilson had written several 'superb' radio features on Strindberg. Newby declined the offer: 'The moment does not seem quite right for it.'[20]

His demotion was reflected in the popular press coverage as well as in literary circles. The *News Chronicle*, for example, still gave Wilson a little attention, but even its very limited interest in his attempts to regain his lost reputation was unusual. A filler reported his collaboration on a book with Hopkins and Holroyd (only Wilson's effort was published, in 1959, as *The Age of Defeat*), and another item previewed the première of his play, *The Metal Flower Blossom*, performed by (how are the mighty fallen) an amateur group in Plymouth. In 1959 the gossip column carried a story about his plan to establish Colin Wilson Productions Limited, a company which would stage his own rejected plays and be funded, he said, by John Braine and Shelagh Delaney.[21] Needless to say, this remained a plan.

On the whole, Wilson could only attract press attention by providing journalists with such 'newsworthy' bits and pieces. The *News Chronicle* managed to report his tie-less entrance into the Athenaeum to meet Aldous Huxley on 20 October 1958, and news of a minor traffic offence he had committed was briefly reported in the London evening papers on 2 July. One more incident earned Wilson headlines in the daily newspapers, but the story only confirmed his later reputation as a reliably ludicrous nincompoop. Reports that he had burnt his hands and hair after mistakenly pouring petrol on a fire made Wilson front-page news for one more time on 19 January 1959. It was all too symbolically appropriate for 'Peter Simple'. Two days later the *Daily Telegraph* printed his epitaph for Colin Wilson as a literary celebrity.

> I strove with many for the love of strife,
> Nietzsche I loved and next to Nietzsche, Shaw.
> I warmed both hands before the fire of life,
> It blew me up – as all the papers saw.

8

'Egghead, scrambled'

When *The Outsider* appeared Colin Wilson was heralded as showing the promise, even the achievement, of a great writer. For a few months afterwards he had been lionized by the highbrow and popular presses alike, only to see his fame turn to notoriety and his second book rubbished by the critics. As Kenneth Allsop said in *The Angry Decade*, 'Wilson's parabola, 1956–7, was spectacular.'

It seems that Wilson's antics embarrassed his enthusiasts into shifty silence, or a hostility which was supported by other critics only too eager to put him in his place. Certainly, the dramatically different receptions of *The Outsider* and *Religion and the Rebel* cannot be explained by a dramatic slump in standards. The fundamental similarity of the two books is hardly surprising, since *Religion and the Rebel* is a direct sequel to *The Outsider*. Indeed, as Wilson revealed in a letter to the *London Magazine* in April 1958, he had originally planned the two books as one work and Gollancz had advised the division into separate publications.

In fact, both works are equally flawed and equally objectionable. Although the attacks on *Religion and the Rebel* were caused by a critical backlash, reviewers were not really being unfair. The real puzzle is how *The Outsider* could have been praised at all, for the acclaim was entirely undeserved.

Both books are based on the pet theory which Wilson had been cultivating since his early adolescence: that exceptional people rebel against the shams and delusions of society. However, these 'Outsiders' are not social rebels in the fashionable sense of the term. Wilson's Outsiders are spiritual heroes who have rejected everyday assumptions and routine living as hollow and meaningless – they 'see too deep and too much'. Outsiders seek a greater intensity, a transcendent awareness of Reality, Purpose, the Truth. Wilson argues that these goals can be achieved by developing an 'Existentialist' or 'religious' attitude, a theme which he pursues more vigorously in his second book. Despite Wilson's odd terminology, the general impression given in both books is that he has come up with a particularly crass version of the Romanticist notion about the artist-genius alienated by temperament and vision from the vast and bovine majority.

But this may do Wilson an injustice, because a general impression is all he conveys. Instead of attempting some straightforward exposition of his 'philosophy', he uses the ploy of describing the lives and works of writers and visionaries whom he regards as the great Outsiders. These figures are supposed to offer 'concrete examples' of outsiderliness, 'the basic data' for Wilson's own quest for the meaning of life. As a result, both books are stuffed with literary, philosophical and religious references. Barbusse, Wells, Hesse, Nietzsche, Dostoevsky, George Fox, Sri Ramakrishna, Gurdjieff and T. E. Hulme are some of the writers dwelt on in *The Outsider*; Rimbaud, Shaw, Swedenborg, Pascal and Kierkegaard among those featured in *Religion and the Rebel*.

Wilson's early admirers were much impressed by his apparent familiarity with so many great and often exotic figures, but the mere inclusion of so much 'basic data' indicates that the treatment will be at best superficial. Wilson tried to give the appearance of prodigious mastery, but even in his less brief accounts he uses his 'concrete examples' only for crude summaries of plot, characterization or biography; consequently, an examination of four novels by Henry James can take up less than two pages. When he considers the work of Hermann Hesse, he allots seventeen pages to outlining the stories and heroes of five novels. And that, apparently, is a 'full analysis'. Wilson is a little more generous with his space in *Religion and the Rebel*, treating himself, for instance, to an extended eulogy of his great hero, Shaw. Nevertheless, the second book too has all the depth of a children's encyclopaedia; a typical passage is the 'closer analysis' of Cardinal Newman's *Essay in Aid of a Grammar of Assent* – yet another facile résumé which comes to a satisfied halt after barely two pages.

But Wilson is plainly not interested in analysis of any kind. What obviously does interest him a great deal is the accumulation of references. He is devoted to comparisons and catalogues which could only be bewildering and pointless if the aim were not to show off how many books he has read. In *The Outsider*, just for example, we learn that *Vala* was 'Blake's own way of writing *The Brothers Karamazov*'. Confused? Then try another reflection on Blake, where Wilson shows how lightly he wears his learning: 'Blake, in common with another great English mystic, Traherne, achieved a "Yea-saying" vision that brings Van Gogh's blazing canvases to mind.' The agglomerative technique was an essential part of Wilson's name-dropping equipment and he practised it to perfection. So, when he comes to describe Stavrogin in Dostoevsky's *The Devils*, Wilson is able to offer this slapdash recipe: 'Conceive him as a Russian combination of Evan Strowde and Oliver Gauntlett, add a touch of Pushkin's Eugene Onyegin and you have a reasonably accurate picture.'

Another advantage of the state-and-list method is that the results are more or less irrefutable, since meaning has to be inferred. The disadvantage is that such statements possess little or no meaning in the first place. Witness Wilson's triumphant description of Nietzsche in *The Outsider*:

> Nietzsche's temperament was less devotional, more intellectual, than Blake's; there is a fundamental similarity all the same, and it would be more accurate to regard Nietzsche as a Blakean Christian than as an irreligious pagan. Always provided, of course, we know what we mean by a Blakean Christian (unfortunately, it is beyond the scope of this book to study Blake's conception of Christianity).

The final parenthesis comes as something of a surprise, for judging by the rest of the book, that study need not have taken too much space.

The same criticism applies to *The Outsider* and *Religion and the Rebel* as a whole; Wilson relies on his summaries, digests and comparisons supposedly to demonstrate and develop his exposition, but in fact these function to conceal the absence of any coherent development in the argument – indeed, the absence of any argument whatsoever. (It is an approach Wilson has adapted and refined throughout his prolific career.) The method is the same in both books. First he makes some sort of grand declaration (e.g., 'The Outsider tends to express himself in Existentialist terms'), then he announces the relevance to this point of a book which is then dealt with in a callow summary and said to be amazingly similar to other works which generate more summaries and comparisons and therefore still more summaries, until Wilson finally decides to pull up short with series of weird and wonderful generalizations, *preferably in italics*, which he claims are the conclusions of his acute and thorough analysis. The following example from *The Outsider* gives an indication of the Wilson method in its final stages:

> we can see at a glance that we have here a strange group of men – Blake, Kierkegaard, Nietzsche, Dostoevsky: two violently unorthodox Christians, one pagan 'philosopher with a hammer', and one tormented half-atheist half-Christian, all beginning from the same impulse and driven by the same urges. Since we can see plainly, after our painstaking analysis, that this impulse is fundamental in the Outsider, it is not a bold step to assert that *these men held basically the same beliefs*. The differences that seem to separate them are only differences of temperament (imagine Blake's reaction to Kierkegaard's *Diary of the Seducer*, or Nietzsche's to Dostoevsky's *Life of Father Zossima*!); the basic idea is the same in all four.

So what are the common 'basic idea', 'impulse' and 'urges'? He has shunned the dull business of explanation, despite his claims in both *The Outsider* and *Religion and the Rebel* that his aims are 'painstaking', 'scientific' 'analysis' and 'definition'.

Perhaps Wilson is joking, though, because he openly scorns 'the intellectual-critical approach' of the 'ascetic scholar'. 'Intellect is not enough,' he announces in *The Outsider*; far better the insights of 'the intuitional thinker'. Unfortunately, Wilson shows little consistency or reliability in his intuitional thought, giving the impression that freedom from intellectual-critical demands simply means that he could write whatever came into his head. Just as Freud and Russell are intuitively dismissed in brief abuse, so Lamarck's discredited theory of evolution can be intuitively preferred to Darwin's. In *The Outsider* Wilson decides that *Notes from Underground* was written 'when no other "Outsider" literature existed', then declares two pages later that Kierkegaard had anticipated Dostoevsky and Blake had anticipated Kierkegaard. In *Religion and the Rebel*, intuition inspires Wilson to attack 'Pastor' Russell as a 'cranky messiah', but to admire Russell's Jehovah's Witnesses when their ideas coincide with those of Swedenborg, whom Wilson happens to like. Bill Hopkins actually defended the results of such spontaneity in his *Declaration* essay: 'A visionary has the prerogative of freely contradicting himself while still retaining his influence.' What Wilson actually does retain is puerile pontification masquerading as analytical expertise throughout two books of fatuous polemic which lack the attractions of either an objective critique or a personal manifesto.

This was not the opinion of the enthusiasts who praised *The Outsider* for its 'admirable' diagnosis and 'authentic ring of criticism'. In reality the absence of any authenticity in Wilson's performance is made all the more conspicuous by the spectacular assertions which litter both books. These are often startlingly unorthodox, as when Wilson promotes Gurdjieff and Shaw in *The Outsider* to be 'major prophets of Nietzschean rank'. Even if such declarations could be regarded as 'bold' and 'refreshing', the majority of Wilson's opinions are clearly nothing more than oafishly facile. 'Art is thought,' he avows in *The Outsider*. 'Reason . . . made the Victorians self-sufficient.' Dogmatic nonsense is no less a hallmark of *Religion and the Rebel*: 'A man is more alive than a cow, just as a cow is more alive than a tree.' 'Jesus . . . had more in common with Hitler than with Ramakrishna.' Such insights are, like Wilson's Victorians, self-sufficient. Wilson relies heavily on what Stephen Toulmin has called 'portmanteau definitions'. Toulmin compares these definitions to belts: the shorter they are, the more elastic they need to be.[1] But Wilson's statements only stretch credibility.

By the time *Religion and the Rebel* appeared the critics were ready to condemn Wilson's talent for gross simplification, whereas the supporters of *The Outsider* had actually enjoyed his 'illuminating' certainty. Somehow V. S. Pritchett had managed to commend Wilson as a 'subtle, patient writer' who was not only 'dashing' but 'learned and exact'. And even when Toynbee and Connolly noticed that Wilson was prone to 'hasty' and 'pontificating' statements, they considered this was unimportant – 'scarcely worthy of mention', according to Kenneth Walker in the *Listener* – in the light of his overall achievement.

Even more charity must have been required for Wilson's early fans to overlook the way he treats the works of his great Outsiders. He can indulge in all his generalizations and comparisons only because he steadfastly ignores the individuality of the 'concrete examples', which were apparently written only to provide him with a useful motto. When he 'examines' Hesse's *Steppenwolf* in *The Outsider* he is therefore annoyed at the difficulties presented by 'the stage scenery: the overblown language, the Hoffmannesque atmosphere'. Once 'stripped of its externals of stagy scenery and soft music', though, a moral is found. Similarly, Wilson is gratified to discover that 'the lesson' in Dostoevsky's *The Idiot* is identical to that in Hesse's *Demian*. It seems that Wilson's self-education had involved nothing more than speed-reading a lot of books for suitable maxims and snippets.

This impression is strengthened by the impatience Wilson shows when a writer does not meet his demands. Special scorn is reserved for what he terms 'Humanism', and its exponents – Russell and Darwin are two hated examples – are easily swept aside as myopically rational. Nor are the more inspiring Outsiders safe from facile contempt, for Wilson dismisses pessimism and despair as signs of weakness and inadequacy. In chapter 4 of *The Outsider*, for instance, he sees Van Gogh, T. E. Lawrence and Nijinsky as failures because they got depressed. The positive thinking praised by Toynbee and Walker only reveals his philistinism conscientiously at work. Wilson feels 'let down' by Hesse's *Siddhartha* because there is no 'successful solution' to the Outsiders' problems. Nijinsky's *Diary* is 'unpleasant', as is *Notes from Underground* – 'so unnecessarily unpleasant as to be barely readable': 'The nasty taste it leaves in the mouth is due to its failure as a work of art, its obsessive caterwauling about the weakness of human nature etc.'

Fascinated by artists but not at all interested in art, Wilson must have needed patience as well as Listerine to persevere with his reading. In *Voyage to a Beginning* he reveals that he admired poets not because they wrote poetry but because they were 'determined to live more fully than others'. This sub-Romantic prejudice explains the lives-of-the-artists emphasis in his first two books. Both are full of thumbnail biographies in which Wilson can demonstrate his affection for the tantalizing anecdote. For example, in *Religion and the Rebel* Wilson relates that Boehme read the Scriptures on the advice of a mysterious stranger, of possibly supernatural origin. Particularly in this second book, Wilson's brief lives slide all too easily into such nose-tapping allusions to his Outsiders' beyond-our-ken experiences. Maybe Hegel had a mystical revelation, someone said Wittgenstein had an inexplicable rapport with birds, perhaps Swedenborg did possess paranormal powers . . .

This desire to personify attitudes and ideas resulted in his most distinctive creation – the figure of the Outsider. Wilson invested this figure with the requirements and aspirations of what he maintained was an 'Existentialist' philosophy. Early reviewers of *The Outsider* were so attracted and convinced by Wilson's eponymous ideal that they often expounded their own versions of the Outsider mentality. When it came to the sequel, however, Wilson was vilified for only offering twaddle – although this was obviously a repeat performance, relying on the same terms and tactics. Once again, critics of the second book got it right: meaning *is* outside Wilson's scope, as Raymond Mortimer said in the *Sunday Times*. In both books the Outsider remains an elusive character, as impossible to describe with confidence as it is to decide what Wilson's brand of 'Existentialism' contains.

One thing, though, is clear: whatever else it is, his Existentialism, embracing Shaw, Sri Ramakrishna, Plato and Swedenborg, bears little relation to what is normally understood by the term. 'Existentialism' serves as a meaninglessly flexible, conveniently trendy label in *The Outsider*, but Wilson warms slightly to the task of explanation in the sequel. Here he defines his Existentialism as a philosophy of the Will and of action, opposed to 'mere logic and reason', and adds that it 'might as easily be called religion'. Alas, just what he means by religion is also extremely vague, and he freely uses words like 'visionary', 'prophet', 'mystic', 'artist' and 'poet' as if they were interchangeable. Daunting terms, but the necessary spiritual awareness of 'Existentialism' looks pleasingly accessible: in the second book Wilson assures us that deep emotional and spiritual experience are 'practically the same thing'; in *The Outsider* a 'visionary' is given as someone who sees 'the world as positive', so Wilson duly grants visionary status to drunks and those who have just eaten a good meal.

It looks as if the young genius showed uncharacteristic wisdom in skirting precision. Perhaps that is why early admirers like Toynbee and Walker sympathized with his refusal to explain his ideas of religion in *The Outsider* ... Wilson certainly does not make the mistake of clarifying the nature of his Outsiders, for a term that can embrace so many diverse figures, from Gurdjieff to Wells's Mr Polly, must depend on lax and fanciful use. As with the rest of Wilson's definitions, the Outsider is described in statements involving other terms which would themselves require a couple of volumes of explanation. In the first book, for example, he specifies that someone is an Outsider 'because he stands for Truth', and that the Outsider's 'first business is self-knowledge'.

Wilson indulges in grandiose blethering while basic questions, which presumably only ascetic scholars could be dull enough to ask, go unanswered. For instance, can Outsiders be found in all societies or are they products of particular environments? Most reviewers of *The Outsider* followed Gollancz's blurb which claimed that Wilson had diagnosed 'the malaise of the soul of mankind in the mid-twentieth century'. 'A representative theme of our time,' declared Toynbee. Only in *Religion and the Rebel* did Wilson begin to view his Outsiders in the vaguest historical perspective, stating that they 'appear like pimples on a dying civilization' such as contemporary society, unlike more enlightened eras like the Middle Ages and the seventeenth century. The inclusion of George Fox (1624–91), Thomas Traherne (1637–74), Jacob Boehme (1575–1624), Blaise Pascal (1623–62) and Nicholas Ferrar (1592–1637) as Outsiders means that Bill Hopkins' defence of his visionary colleague would again be particularly useful. But Wilson's commitment to self-contradiction and issue-fudging makes any defence impossible and such tributes as Toynbee's, to the 'explanatory treatment' in *The Outsider*, very strange indeed.

More important still, much confusion surrounds Wilson's account of what kinds of people become Outsiders. His category seems to include almost anybody who takes his fancy. This suspicion may be confirmed by 'developments' in Wilson's later work. In *Order of Assassins* (1972) he sees murderers like Jack the Ripper as 'Outsider-criminals' with close affinities to the 'Outsider-artist'. There are numerous mentions in *The Outsider* of poets, prophets, visionaries and so-on, but only towards the end of the sequel does Wilson finally state that his ideal Outsider is the 'artist-philosopher', since the 'mere artist or thinker' is too narrow-minded. Are these artist-philosophers born or made? Both, seems to be the eyebrow-raising answer, for he regards his Outsiders as either born geniuses or ordinary folk who have battled to gain their higher awareness. In *Religion and the Rebel* he apparently believes that sheer laziness prevents someone from becoming a genius and that an artist achieves greatness at 'the tremendous price of will-power and sweat'. However, this Stakhanovite view contrasts with his attraction to the Romanticist notion of the artist blessed and cursed by natural genius. Thus, Wilson discloses, Boehme possessed 'the natural gifts of a true poet'.

Whether the difference between Outsiders and others is achieved or somehow innate, it is certainly decisive. Wilson readily took to appalling extremes the Romanticist views about the magnificent superiority of the caste of artist-priests. In the first book he describes the Outsider as a higher type of being who rightly holds others in 'a Swiftian contempt': 'The common mob, the philistines and money-changers, are "flies in the market-place"', 'ants in a formicary', and the humanist is the most irritating of these 'insects', these 'human lice'. 'The average man is distinguished from dogs and cats mainly because he looks farther ahead: he is capable of worrying about his physical needs of six months hence, ten years hence.' Such descriptions of Insiders are common. The animal imagery seems to be less the product of simile-hunting than of Wilson's view that ordinary people exist on more or less the same level as 'caged animals'. In *Religion and the Rebel* he states that people are 'apes', little better than cows.

One reason for the widespread hostility towards *Religion and the Rebel* was the clearer social implications of Wilson's outlook. Only men of genius could have true religious insight, he thought, so for those who belonged to the 'lower form of life', 'myths and parables and ceremonies' were to be provided. 'The religion of the majority has to be simplified and coated with sugar.' Wilson is attracted to the idea of political dictatorship but finds the dangers to Outsiders too strong, and rejects the option only on these grounds. Nevertheless, he is sure that 'the Outsiders must achieve political power over the hogs'. In his later work Wilson has even estimated the number of Outsiders in a society; the 'dominant minority' comprises five per cent of the population and the remaining ninety-five per cent of humanity are necessary only as passive objects of the élite's dominance. However, the geniuses, the true Outsiders, are 'probably .005 per cent of the five per cent'.[2] By this calculation there are about 150 people, apart from himself, worth Wilson's admiration in Britain today.

This aspect of his ideas was already quite apparent in *The Outsider*; among its reviewers, A. J. Ayer inferred a Nietzschean slant to his concept of the Outsider, and both Raymond Williams and J. B. Priestley objected to his contemptuous dismissal of the

'Insiders'. This attitude was obviously not important to, or noticed by, critics like John Connell who praised Wilson's 'bracing sanity' and the 'strength and wisdom' of his conclusions. No such opinions were expressed of *Religion and the Rebel* and critics like Young and Mankowitz condemned the Nazi-like posture Wilson had adopted. What did he see himself as, wondered Raymond Mortimer: 'An English Luther or Hitler?' Hostility to Wilson's Fascistic inclinations was reinforced by critics of *Declaration*. He shied clear of political themes in his own essay, but Holroyd and Hopkins made disturbing statements, similar to those in *Religion and the Rebel*, about the 'Will to Power' and the need for a 'new leadership'. Wilson's reputation as the leader of this trio meant that he was included in reviewers' attacks on the Fascism of the 'Spotty Nietzscheans'.

Reviewers of *Declaration* were certainly justified in grouping Wilson, Holroyd and Hopkins together, for the beliefs they shared even included assumptions about their own genius. It was a preposterous conviction of his own talent which had encouraged Wilson to start and continue writing, a conviction confirmed when he gave the manuscript of his novel to Bill Hopkins, who was able to reply: 'Congratulations; you are a major writer! Welcome to our ranks!'[3] Wilson's claims for himself and his colleagues were already notorious, of course, and now Hopkins showed that he too was keen to advertise his self-confidence, stating in *Declaration* that he intended to 'stand up higher than anyone else and discover the escape route to progress'.

The appearance of their credos together in *Declaration* made it clear to the public at large that the three great minds thought alike. Holroyd and Hopkins also despised the 'humanist-scientific' intellectual tradition and called for an altogether more inspiring and ambitious outlook, free from nitpicking rationalism. Writers – such, presumably, as themselves – were given responsibilities of truly Wilsonian grandeur: they were to become 'the pathfinders to a new kind of civilization' and a new capacity for religious belief. Like Wilson, Hopkins and Holroyd refused to stoop to specifics: 'I do not mean any belief in particular,' Hopkins assured, 'but rather belief divorced from all form whatsoever. The form is an arbitrary matter.' According to Holroyd in *Emergence from Chaos*, 'A religion is anything that a man can live by.' (Would 'humanist-scientific' convictions count? Or a passion for Glasgow Rangers?)

Unconcerned about the precise form of their 'religious Existentialism', they were more particular about their political requirements, which also closely follow Wilson's. Democracy had failed to create the right kind of civilization, opined Holroyd, who noted that all the great civilizations of the past were hierarchical. He recommended government to be placed 'in the hands of an expert minority', always providing that this was the proper sort of minority, of course, not tyrannical but moral and visionary in character. If this 'expert minority' was to be anything like Hopkins' conception of the 'new leadership', which the powers of the irrational and unspecified belief would create, then *Declaration*'s critics were right to be worried.

Hopkins' vision of political domination appears in his first and only novel, *The Divine and the Decay*, whose main character, Plowart, Wilson praised as an Outsider hero.[4] Plowart fully deserves this description: he decries 'absurd philosophies like humanism [and] social systems like democracy', and venerates favourite Outsider authors like Dante, Pascal and Shaw. Plowart also stresses the importance of the power of the Will and religious belief. Like Wilson's, Plowart's religion is rather unconventional, since he professes a hatred of lesser human beings and 'ludicrous virtues like compassion'. With this hero, Hopkins creates his own stunningly ill-written fantasy about the Outsiders' political power over the human lice. Plowart is leader of the New Britain League which is 'recruiting thousands of young, ardent men and women to bring a new epoch to life and a new name of fire to the scroll of history'. Even if this could be mistaken for something along the lines of the Young Liberals, Hopkins leaves no doubt about his hero's politics: Plowart's aim is 'dictatorship' and he compares himself to 'Lenin, Hitler, Mao Tse-tung'.

Wilson praised *The Divine and the Decay* in the highest terms: 'the most important book that's been published in England over the past thirty years, maybe since *Ulysses*'. In a vain attempt to make the novel more acceptable, and with a characteristic disregard for consistency, Wilson even claimed that Plowart was not supposed to be an admirable hero.[5] Reviewers of the novel assumed otherwise. This was a 'statement of neo-Fascist nihilism', an 'adolescent power-fantasy' which 'ought to have been published in Hitler's Germany'. To G. S. Fraser, *The Divine and the Decay* ('not a work of literature') indicated the possible formation of 'a half-educated, angrily self-important Fascist intelligentsia'.[6]

Hopkins' novel was reissued in 1984, complete with a new title (*The Leap!*), a blurb announcing a cult following and a forth-coming major film of the book, and a Foreword from Colin Wilson (who compares Hopkins to Nietzsche and acclaims Plowart as an 'alpha' hero who wishes to be a 'god', not a 'worm'). There is also an Author's Preface. Here Hopkins reflects on the critics' unanimous attacks on his novel first time round, finding comfort, as Wilson has done, in a conspiracy theory – the 'barrage of abuse' was, of course, 'orchestrated' . . . According to Hopkins, another conspirator was Howard Samuel, a left-wing property millionaire and owner of the publishers MacGibbon & Kee; he claims that Samuel had commissioned *The Divine and the Decay*, but was so horrified by the reviews that he ordered the destruction of all remaining copies of the novel.

Hopkins says that after the dreadful reception of his novel, two other works-in-progress – *Time of Totality* and *The Titans* – were also destroyed, this time by accident, in a fire at his house.[7] While this seems to belong to the dog-ate-my-homework brand of explanation, Hopkins' literary career *had* gone up in smoke, meta-phorically if not literally. He published a few articles after 1957, mainly in *Time and Tide*, and enjoyed a brief literary resurgence in 1965 as Bob Guccione's first Editorial Director at *Penthouse*. Not a taxing post, one would have thought, but he was replaced after the first issue, which carried a symposium of writers, including Wilson and Holroyd. (Wilson went one better than Hopkins as Contributing Editor for the first *two* numbers of *Penthouse*.) He wisely opted for a life outside literature, and became an antiques dealer.

Holroyd was a little more successful after the débâcle of 1957, publishing an autobiography, *Flight and Pursuit*, in 1959 when he too contributed a column for a short while to *Time and Tide*. He also enjoyed one more moment of fame when his play *The Tenth Chance* was produced at the Royal Court on 9 March 1958 under the direction of Osborne's friend, Anthony Creighton. The play ran for only one night, but it still managed to provoke a brawl among the more famous members of the audience. Towards the end of the performance, the novelist Elaine Dundy marched ostentatiously out of the theatre, followed by her husband, Kenneth Tynan. Christopher Logue shouted out to explain that the play was 'rubbish' and Wilson yelled back that Logue should leave as well. After the curtain fell the action switched to a nearby bar where Holroyd's team of Wilson, Hopkins and Michael Hastings faced their adversaries Logue and Tynan. John Osborne was a gleeful spectator as Wilson squared up to the *Observer*'s theatre critic: 'We'll stamp you out, Tynan. You wait.' A scuffle broke out and ended with Logue being shoved under a table. The fracas was front-page news in the *Express* next day, and Holroyd and Logue were interviewed about their differences of opinion on BBC TV's *Tonight*.

Another well-known figure had attended the sole performance of *The Tenth Chance* – Oswald Mosley. Mosley obviously disagreed with Tynan's verdict that the play was 'sadistic spinach' about salvation through torture, for he reviewed *The Tenth Chance* very favourably in his Fascist journal, the *European*. The first contact between Mosley and the Spotty Nietzschean trio had been made by Wilson himself soon after the publication of *The Outsider*, of which Mosley later wrote a fifteen-page eulogy for the February 1957 *European*. (He took a shine to Wilson's ideas and wondered if Wilson himself might end up as a 'saint'.) Through his friends in Fleet Street, Farson and Allsop, Wilson also met another thirties Fascist, Henry Williamson, with whom Wilson says he 'established a bond of sympathy' based on their mutual admiration of Mosley.[8] When Wilson expressed this admiration in print in the December 1959 issue of *Twentieth Century* he was vehemently attacked by Bernard Levin in the *Spectator* and in Bill Connor's 'Cassandra' column in the *Daily Mirror*.[9] He defended himself by claiming he was a socialist and did not support Mosley's politics, but this only followed his original remarks that Mosley was a 'likeable' and 'sincere' chap who owed his notoriety to his followers, not his policies, and that Mosley's intention to stand for Parliament was 'an excellent idea' which Wilson himself had suggested. That article was published just two months after the General Election in which Mosley had stood for the Spotty Nietzscheans' local constituency of North Kensington in an attempt to inaugurate a Fascist renaissance with his Union Movement. It was a particularly noisome and provocative campaign ('something of an error', Wilson admitted) as Mosley showed great sincerity in pursuing a vigorous anti-immigrant line after outbreaks of racial violence in the constituency – the race riots in Notting Dale in

August 1958 and then the murder of West Indian Kelso Cochrane on Whit Sunday 1959.

But a couple of years earlier there had already been signs that Wilson might be able to take up the hints made in *Religion and the Rebel* about turning his ideas 'to some more practical form', because Bill Hopkins had directed his talents towards the founding of a new political party – the Spartacans. Plans for Hopkins' new order had been laid by October 1957 and the Spartacans were launched in May 1958 with Holroyd and Wilson as founder members. Perhaps now Wilson would find a political platform for his social policies – for example, that the mentally ill should be shot. The Spartacans' numbers soon swelled to forty or fifty, there were plans for a series of Spartacan *Essays*, and Mosley tried to enlist the Spartacans' support for his General Election campaign. But it was not to be. Although Hopkins also admired Mosley, he declined his offer and even with a spearhead of three self-appointed geniuses, the Spartacans failed to brand history's scroll with their new name of fire, and soon disappeared altogether.

The decline and fall of the Spartacans went unnoticed, for Wilson, Holroyd and Hopkins had already been exiled from serious attention, a situation which remains more or less unchanged today. Wilson has plodded on as a full-time writer in a prolific career (approximately sixty books to date) noteworthy for an unshakeable devotion to the spurious and the half-baked. His obsessive quest for something grander than normality has led him to investigations of 'psychology' and the paranormal, subjects he has tackled with all the thoroughness and insight promised by *The Outsider* – none. He shares several of his enthusiasms with Holroyd, who returned to authorship in the seventies with a sex manual as well as books on parapsychology and the like. They even collaborated on a coffee-table book, *Mysteries of the Mind* (1978), and Wilson provided another Introduction, this time for Holroyd's most ambitious book to date – *Prelude to the Landing on Planet Earth* (1977). This is a report on the communiqués of the Council of the Supergalaxy given to Uri Geller's mentor, Andrija Puharich, and Sir John Whitmore through an implant in the versatile brain of medium Phyllis V. Schlemmer (with the help of the etheric body of Dr Lyall Watson). Evidently, the Supergalactic Council advised Puharich and Whitmore to avert global war in November 1974 by beaming psychic rays at the Kremlin. The two heroes were then informed via Ms

Schlemmer of the real history and purpose of the Earth. The human race actually contains two types: the original inhabitants of this planet – the blacks – and the rest, who are really 'seeded' souls of the universe, first embodied here in 32,400 BC, to establish civilizations like Atlantis (whose citizens were reincarnated as dolphins). Subsequent astral ambassadors have included Jesus Christ, Nostradamus and Uri Geller. Proof that all this information is not fraudulent comes when Holroyd listens to recordings of Ms Schlemmer and then sees a house plant jumping off a shelf.

As Holroyd says, this is not 'inherently implausible'. Nor are Wilson's theories about a dominant minority, poltergeists, the occult, the preservative effects of the Great Pyramid, telepathic snakes and so forth, inherently implausible. But Wilson and Holroyd's pretence of intellectuality cannot hide the sorry fact that they are either unable to question and justify claims which stand in blatant need of questioning and justification, or unwilling to pass up the chance of making a bit of money out of books which are, by all other standards, valueless. If the speculations of Wilson and Holroyd are eventually found to be correct – if, for example, there *is* a psychic ether, or if the Ancient Egyptians *were* visited by extraterrestrials, or if human beings *have* yet to find an extra dimension of mental freedom – then they will have expressed revolutionizing truths not by good judgement or uncanny intuition, but by an outrageous fluke.

By the end of 1957 an observer would not have needed supergalactic powers of premonition to see that Wilson, Holroyd and Hopkins would find it rather difficult to recover intellectual respect. Reviews of *Declaration* had become obituaries for the public demise of the threesome who were now treated as symptoms rather than analysts of the contemporary malaise:

> the 'sickness of the world' so dear to them is reflected less in the content of their effusions than in the fact that those effusions are published, attract the attention of journalists, and get the length of being discussed by people who know damn well that they do not need to look at this stuff *sub specie aeternitatis* to recognize it for the drooling that it is.[10]

This view was loudly echoed in reviews of *Religion and the Rebel*. In his *Books and Art* notice of December 1957, Anthony Hartley wrote: 'I cannot for the life of me take Mr Wilson seriously as anything except a pimple on the cultural body.'

Various social and cultural ailments were diagnosed in the attempts to explain how and why Wilson had enjoyed such a huge and undeserved success. One obvious theory was that he had been praised so highly simply because he was so young: he was a product of the media's obsession with youth and the new youth subculture, a highbrow counterpart of the new rock 'n' roll idols, 'the literary Elvis Presley', 'a kind of philosophical Tommy Steele'.[11] Just as his fame was blamed on the popular press, so the popularity of The Outsider was blamed on a gullible public of half-educated teenagers.

However, these explanations ignored the uncomfortable truth that Wilson had not started his career as a cult author but as the darling of the most prominent literati of the day. It was they who had acclaimed him and they who were directly responsible for his success.

Why, then, did such a patently bad and objectionable book as The Outsider receive such praise?

In an extremely charitable mood one could find several mitigating explanations for the astonishing misjudgements of The Outsider – pressures of deadlines, the attractions of Wilson's youth and his apparently prodigious achievement as a self-taught writer, the air of philosophizing and the ostentatious display of learning . . . But this is to condescend to experienced reviewers and to ignore the fact that critics like Connolly and Toynbee had spotted Wilson's inadequacies and errors, only to treat them with remarkable leniency.

There were, however, a few critics who immediately realized that The Outsider did not merit such sympathy. A division in critical opinion was apparent from the beginning, and it is by looking at the two factions that the real reasons for Wilson's success, and its implications, can be appreciated. The detractors fall into two select groups. One was the small band of academic reviewers – A. J Ayer, Raymond Williams and the TLS critic – who were prepared to give critical analysis rather than praise a performance. The other critics of The Outsider – Burns Singer in Time and Tide, J. B. Priestley in the New Statesman and Amis in the Spectator – were young and/or middlebrow. Their objections were not based on any comprehensive fault-finding; Priestley actually thought Wilson's success was, to some extent, welcome and well-deserved. Rather, these three – and Amis especially – showed that they had little or no time for his basic ideas and the tradition he invoked, and were not susceptible to any initial glamour.

On the other side, Wilson's promoters can also be broadly characterized by distinctive allegiances. Edith Sitwell, Philip Toynbee, Cyril Connolly, Rex Warner, John Lehmann (who readily gave Wilson column-space in the *London Magazine*) and Elizabeth Bowen all belonged to the older, pre-war generation and all can be classed as Mandarin. (Two other prominent supporters deserve a mention: V. S. Pritchett, though not of Mandarin stock himself, was a similar belletrist, and Kenneth Walker, who gave Wilson that extraordinary acclaim in the *Listener*, was a devotee of mysticism and Gurdjieff.) Commentators of the day assumed that Wilson's rise to fame was, like Amis's and Osborne's, propelled by opposition to this older generation. On the contrary. Wilson owed his success to the Mandarins and for two main reasons; first, they were obviously susceptible to the *sort* of nonsense he wrote, and second, he seemed to offer the kind of young talent they desperately wanted to find.

Although Wilson's working-class Bohemianism seemed to promise a direct contrast to upper-class aestheticism, he did in fact have several basic affinities with the Mandarins; his method and presentation were ideal for Mandarin consumption. His intuitive, assertive approach and his cultural self-advertisement have much in common with the dilettante manner of, say, Cyril Connolly. In Connolly's work too, confident opinions and *aperçus* jostle with lists of marvellous references, revealing a desire to impress rather than inform. Here, for instance, from *Enemies of Promise* (1938) is Connolly on Firbank:

> Firbank is not epigrammatic, he is not easily quotable, his object was to cast a sheen of wit over his writing. Like all dandies, like Horace, Tibullus, Rochester, Congreve, Horace Walpole, and the youthful Beckford, like Watteau and Guardi, he was obsessed with the beauty of the moment, and not only the beauty, but the problem of recording that beauty, for with one false touch the description becomes ponderous and overloaded, and takes on that unreal but sickly quality often found in modern paganism. Firbank, like Degas, was aware of this and, like Degas, he used pastel.

It is not surprising that Connolly, for one, thought that Wilson possessed 'a quick, dry intelligence, a power of logical analysis', whereas Ayer and Williams were able to recognize the wholesale deficiencies of this kind of smug waffle.

Another feature of Wilson's work which was incorrectly assumed to have met with Mandarin incomprehension and even hostility was his range of esoteric references. His unconventional learning and opinions gleaned from autodidactic enthusiasm, were, so this theory goes, daring, exciting, 'un-English'. In fact *The Outsider*'s appeal lay not so much in the novelty of its sources and ideas as their popularity with Wilson's earliest eulogists. In this respect, I think *The Outsider* can be compared to a book which had great critical success half a century earlier. Compton Mackenzie's *Sinister Street* (1913) described, with great indulgence, such a range of core upper-class experiences that it was bound to appeal to privileged readers who could identify with aspects of Michael Fane's life. The variety of Wilson's anthology of Outsiders was likewise inclusive enough to guarantee the interest of any readers with a predilection for the European Romanticist literary tradition, and this certainly included the Mandarins.[12]

More appealing still was the use Wilson made of his dabblings in the works of the great and good. To reviewers who could mistake name-dropping for 'learning' and 'intellectual analysis', Wilson seemed somehow to be able, at a prodigiously early age, to conduct a wondrously well-informed inquiry into the 'big questions' of the human condition. And this at a time when it looked as if the days of the great sages, like Whitehead and even Shaw, had gone for ever. Speculation on a grand scale about grand themes seemed to have been made impossible by the progress of arcane, pernickety and exclusive academic specialisms. This tendency was most evident in current English philosophy which was dominated by the tedious ordinary-language philosophy of Austin and (if only by name) the Logical Positivists, principally Ayer, who concentrated on 'demolishing metaphysics' and on 'the overthrow of speculative philosophy'.[13] The narrow, iconoclastic empiricism of Ayer in particular found a literary parallel in the work of the Movement writers. They too had refused to deal in transcendental themes or great issues about the human condition, and focused on resolutely mundane realities. (This very general similarity encouraged blithe assumptions about the Movement authors being influenced by

Logical Positivism.) With the public dominance of the Movement in literature and Logical Positivism in philosophy, there was a great need for more ambitious and inspiring speculation. *The Outsider* met that need.

On 20 December 1959 the *Observer* published an article by Philip Toynbee in which he tried to summarize the general intellectual 'myth' of the decade. He distinguished between two opposing tendencies in the intellectual scene, one secular and the other transcendental. The first showed 'a revulsion against loose thinking, pretentious writing' and '[a] determination to accept the limitations of our knowledge and to pay fitting respect to the commonplace and the everyday'. The second, more dated, tradition aspired to greater metaphysical heights and produced what Toynbee nicknamed 'Blue Sky' works. Current academic philosophers and historians and the Movement authors were secular, and writers like Jung and Arnold Toynbee – and Colin Wilson – were transcendental. It was an astute and fair-minded account, but Toynbee had made his own preferences much clearer in another *Observer* article which appeared three years earlier on 20 May 1956; here he acknowledged the workmanlike achievements of authors like Amis who were dealing with everyday reality, but called for talents more sublime: 'Visionaries are needed.'

One week later Colin Wilson appeared from nowhere and Toynbee could acclaim a sensational prodigy who had beaten the French at their own game and made 'a real contribution to our understanding of our deepest predicament'. At last. To Mandarin eyes it looked as if Wilson had bridged the widening gap between literature and philosophy and tackled profundities with comprehensive learning. He seemed to boast such a depth and breadth of knowledge that he could even muster a few gratifying references to physics and mathematics. And not only was his book tenaciously ambitious, it also came packaged with that spine-tingling title and the glamorous brand-name – 'Existentialism'.

Clearly, the Mandarins were also ill-equipped to qualify their enthusiasm for *The Outsider*. Two months before he praised Wilson's book, Toynbee had asserted the advantages enjoyed by the 'indulgent' literary journalists who knew a little about a lot and could be forgiven occasional errors, compared with the new 'academic' critics who were too specialized and intolerant.[14] However, the welcome for Colin Wilson exposed the shortcomings of, in

Amis's phrase, 'vacuous belletristic enthusiasm' as practised by the Mandarin book reviewers,[15] who were masters of no trade, including – on this showing – that of reviewing books. They managed to detect a few errors in *The Outsider*, but exercised indulgence; they mistook name-dropping for learning, bombast for boldness; they did not question what Wilson's philosophy actually involved, far less why on earth it was called Existentialism; and when Wilson claimed the achievements of careful argument and explanation, they were more than happy to take him at his word. Nor did the Mandarins object to his vulgar notion about the contrast between the élite questers for Truth and the brainless masses. No doubt if Wilson had shown more tactful continence in his journalistic career, and followed *The Outsider* with a tirade about a society which preferred Bingo to Plato, or some such nonsense, then lack of talent and worth would have been no obstacle to his continued success.

The Mandarins' eagerness to laud *The Outsider* also stemmed from the grudges and anxieties they held about recent specifically literary developments. These anxieties were in turn ultimately caused by the major problem facing any writer, young or old, in the post-war period – the legacy of Modernism. How was it possible to advance within a tradition that appeared already to have reached its limits? How could one emulate the achievements of the great practitioners of literary extremism? The odds against anything other than failure were forbiddingly high, as John Wain acknowledged: 'A writer setting up business in the 1950s is like a batsman going out to the wicket as fifth or sixth man, to follow a succession of giants who have all made centuries.'[16]

Wain, Amis and the other Movement writers had coped with the burden of Modernism by simply refusing to shoulder it. The Movement's rejection of experiment in favour of traditional virtues and forms was deplored by the Mandarins, whose fears for the future of literature in the inhospitable post-war climate had grown as the fifties wore on. As well as seeming to represent threats to upper-class social and cultural values, the Movement was regarded as promoting a regrettably regressive literary programme which, in Mandarin opinion, consigned contemporary writing to be second-rate.

The Mandarins expected young writers to revive the literary scene with the innovation of an avant-garde. Yet the only group to appear by the mid fifties was a bunch of young conservatives whose aims seemed as bland and uninspiring as the label they had been given. The Movement's banner of 'consolidation' hardly promised the shock of the new. The Mandarins' problem was that they wanted young writers to display a Modernist-style rebellion against the literary status quo, but since the Movement writers saw Modernism as the established and outmoded tradition, their challenge had taken the form of a return to pre-Modernist virtues. These older writers wanted a kind of reaction against convention which would really have been conventional; John Lehmann, for example, saw no literature of protest in 1955 and discounted the 'Wain-Amis-Murdoch' school[17] which *had* rebelled – against the values and expectations of people like John Lehmann.

The irony of this situation was lost on those who pined for a Modernist avant-garde. The arrival of the Movement only highlighted the absence of a more exciting 'revolutionary' group:

> for the first time since the 1870s we have no *avant-garde* in English writing. Experiment – or the fruitful exploration of other men's experiments – belongs to the middle-aged; the young, we are told, murmur 'consolidation', which in effect means playing for safety. That this is a healthy condition of literature I cannot believe.

To Jocelyn Brooke, the 'intellectual climate' of 1955 was 'a great deal bleaker and less stimulating' than in the twenties and thirties because there was 'no *avant-garde* to flutter anybody'.[18]

The Movement had not just dashed Mandarin hopes of being fluttered. The Mandarins resented the modesty of the new group's aesthetic ambitions principally because they saw these as self-imposed limitations which showed that the Movement writers could not qualify, and did not want to qualify, for consideration as sublimely gifted artists. The Movement had frustrated – and then increased – the Mandarins' fundamental desire to have the contemporary literary scene revived and vindicated by a special kind of saviour, one which was much discussed in the fifties – the genius.

Even the emergence of an avant-garde would not have satisfied John Lehmann by 1954: 'It is the genius one waits for, the writer who is going to be head and shoulders above his contemporaries.' It was useless to expect any such figure to emerge from the Movement. 'The new genius when he shows his face will certainly have nothing to do with "consolidation".'[19] Only with the appearance of a genius could the fifties be saved from its manifest inferiority to the Modernist Golden Age. For Mandarins like John Lehmann, the legacy of the Modern Classic status of Joyce, Woolf, Yeats, Lawrence, Eliot and others overshadow any less ambitious accomplishment; each 'minor' work, each 'ordinary' talent, could be unfavourably compared to the great Modernist achievements and increased the need for a genius to appear. Stephen Spender resented even the controversy the *First Reading* group had aroused in 1953: the only movements worthy of attention were those containing writers who proclaimed their own genius. In March 1954 Spender published his 'Letter to a Young Writer' in *Encounter*; in this epistle he dismissed the Movement and fantasized about his ideal young author (fondly christened 'Henry James Joyce Junior') who would have the soul of a Rilke or a Van Gogh.

According to Spender, 'the only new writers left in England are the old ones', and the last 'new writer' was Dylan Thomas.[20] Thomas had been the best candidate in the post-war years for the exalted position of resident genius, and his death in 1953 had left a void which the young provincials were obviously not going to fill. Movement writers were well enough equipped, though, to retaliate against the resentful dismissals. Indeed, an important feature of their collective identity was hostility towards Thomas and the veneration which followed his death.[21] If the Mandarins longed for major new talents, then the Movement mocked that longing. Amis in particular was provocatively untroubled by the absence of great writers: 'these days – not that it worries me at all – geniuses are thin on the ground'; 'There is some ground for equanimity in looking forward to an era of minor literature.'[22] Such remarks would be especially galling to Cyril Connolly, who had stated in *The Unquiet Grave* (1944) that 'the true function of a writer is to produce a masterpiece . . . and no other task is of any consequence.'

With the publication of *The Outsider* the Mandarins suddenly thought they had a possible masterpiece on their hands and in the unknown Colin Wilson a possible genius. Wilson was no creative experimentalist but his apparent adoration of the Modernists and their Romantic predecessors and his supposedly prodigious achievement more than made up for that. Better still, he had dealt with a favourite Mandarin theme and ideal – the artist as genius

Outsider. His *idée fixe* also involved the conviction that he himself possessed a sublime intelligence, a delusion of grandeur which was cruelly endorsed by the tremendous ovation for *The Outsider*. Wilson stumbled towards his fall from grace when he began to make this belief in his own genius public, but that was what the Mandarins really wanted to believe. If Wilson had only shown more restraint, the Mandarins could have satisfied their desire to welcome him as a true Outsider, for Wilson's Bohemian image and Romanticist ideas provided just the right antidote to the image promoted by the Movement (particularly Amis) of the writer as ordinary tax-paying citizen. Until he ruined his reputation, Wilson gave Mandarins the chance to indulge in great expectations which had been denied by the Movement writers, whose aspirations seemed as unassuming as their collective image, thereby confirming the prejudice that a dull, mediocre society spawned only dull, mediocre art and artists. This view can be seen at its most hackneyed in David Wainwright's *Evening News* feature on Wilson the day *The Outsider* was published: 'It has been feared that the Welfare State has killed the thoughtful man by too much kindness, seducing him from the wholehearted pursuit of his meditative ideal. Thank God, it hasn't.'

As this suggests, the Mandarins' susceptibility to the glamour of the genius was shared by the popular press. The thrilled reactions of the Mandarins to Wilson were echoed by journalists like Connell, Barber and the *Time* feature-writer who all hyped Wilson as a spectacular talent. The most enthusiastic account came from Daniel Farson in his second *Daily Mail* feature: 'I have just met my first genius. His name is Colin Wilson.' Farson portrayed a miraculously precocious, dynamic thinker: 'Wilson's strength is his clear, clean vision, moving straight ahead. He analyses the heart of the situation simply. When he writes, he types rapidly without corrections; at the end it looks as if a professional typist has done it, not a word has to be changed.'

Unfortunately for the Mandarins, it soon emerged that their 'major writer' possessed talents only for attracting scandal and ridicule. They had acclaimed not a post-war genius but a young author who presented an embarrassing parody of the Romanticist values and temperament the Mandarins held dear. In *Hurry on Down*, John Wain anticipated reality in his satirical characterization of Froulish, the self-advertising would-be writer whose masters are 'Dante, Spinoza, Rimbaud, Boehme, and Grieg'. Just as the Mandarins enthused about the 'School of Paris', so Wilson pontificated about his own canon of great artists; where the Mandarins valued the spectacular and the ambitious, Wilson proclaimed his single-minded commitment to grand themes; in place of the Mandarins' cultural élitism, Wilson offered a pseudo-intellectual Fascism; the Mandarins were desperate for a genius to appear and Wilson proposed himself as 'a major prophet', 'the major literary genius of our century'; with Holroyd and Hopkins, he was even able to provide his own sad version of an avant-garde.

Thirty years on, all the hype and embarrassment are remembered dimly, if at all. In 1978 Picador were able to reissue *The Outsider* as a period masterpiece, a 'superb ... bestseller', its cover decorated with eulogies to prove it. Perhaps the débâcle of *The Outsider* made the Mandarins more wary of searching for the genius of our times and the book with the Answer, but it is interesting to find Toynbee up to old tricks twenty years later, greeting the seventies' equivalent of *The Outsider*, Robert Pirsig's *Zen and the Art of Motorcycle Maintenance*, as 'a work of great, perhaps urgent, importance' 'which seems to reach the very heart of our present psychological and spiritual anguish'.[23]

The lasting effects of the fiasco of Colin Wilson's glory and damnation would be felt by Wilson and his two colleagues, not the Mandarin critics who acclaimed him. As Alvarez noted, the careers of *The Outsider*'s 'original boosters' were not directly affected; those in the profession of letters were not obliged to offer explanations, let alone resignations, for errors of judgement even on this scale.[24] However, Wilson's reception did serve to widen the literary generation gap. Many of the new writers had shown that, unlike their elders, they were not vulnerable to Wilson's confidence trick; Amis, Singer and Williams had contributed three of the few hostile reviews of *The Outsider*, and Morgan, Mankowitz, Jennings and Davie had attacked either the book or the prodigy himself in the following months. He was also an easy target for younger writers' satires; Andrew Sinclair (in *The Breaking of Bumbo*), Angus Wilson and Malcolm Bradbury all parodied the Spotty Nietzschean Bohemians in their fiction, and Tynan and Anderson derided Wilson & Co. in *Declaration*.

Kingsley Amis capitalized on Mandarin embarrassment, scorning those who craved 'uplift' as well as experiment in their reading with perky reminders about the cult of Colin Wilson.[25] He was joined by Anthony Hartley who, in his review of *Religion and the Rebel*, mocked those in the London literary world who had fallen over *The Outsider* 'with a sickening squelch'. Likewise, Keith Waterhouse blamed Wilson's success on the older dilettante critics of the 'one-notices-certain-omissions-in-the-index school', whose incompetence would have meant praise for *Religion and the Rebel* if that had been published first and a reaction against *The Outsider* if that had been the sequel. Connolly and Toynbee, the two 'original boosters' named by Alvarez, were rightly singled out as most responsible; Raymond Williams ridiculed the 'Sunday thinkers' and, later, Bernard Bergonzi remembered the day when Colin Wilson was 'invented by Messrs Toynbee and Connolly'.[26]

Other Mandarins who endorsed that initial acclaim were not engaged in some kind of conspiracy to publicize *The Outsider*, nor were they merely parroting the tributes of the fashionable Sunday thinkers; London's literati hailed *The Outsider* because of shared inadequacies and anxieties, and shared hopes that Colin Wilson could help to justify and restore highbrow values and priorities just when these were under threat from the Movement. Ironically, the Mandarins' enthusiasm for Wilson only helped to strengthen the position of the young writers who opposed them. Even more ironic was the fact that their praise had been so spectacular that it attracted the attention of the popular press and led to the media's invention and promotion of the Angry Young Men. Wilson was hardly a social protester, but his youth, his fame and the title of his book earned him an 'angry' reputation along with John Osborne. The Mandarins' initial welcome for Wilson had made a decisive contribution to the creation of the decade's literary myth, started by the emergence of the Movement – the myth of the appearance of a whole generation of lower-class radicals committed to attacking the social and literary Establishment.

9

'Working-class Novelist'

Looking back on Anger certain names automatically come to mind as epitomizing the fifties generation: John Wain, Kingsley Amis, John Braine, John Osborne . . . One more writer can surely be added to the roster – a writer whose first two books, *Saturday Night and Sunday Morning* and *The Loneliness of the Long-distance Runner*, strike the same note of importance and success as *Lucky Jim* or *Look Back in Anger* and resonate with as much period significance. But if Alan Sillitoe seems to belong by right to the canon of fifties writers, the fact is that he has been 'canonized' by hindsight. Critics have usually assumed that his first works immediately made a great impact, but when *Saturday Night and Sunday Morning* appeared in October 1958 it was to a noticeably restrained critical welcome. A similarly unspectacular impression was made by *The Loneliness of the Long-distance Runner* when it was published a year later. As it turned out, Sillitoe did enjoy the greatest popular success of all the fifties' new writers, but he found his fame in the sixties and through the cinema. His was an intriguingly delayed success.

The rewards that success brought made dramatic changes to the life of an author. Born in Nottingham in 1928, Alan Sillitoe endured a childhood marked by real hardship, for his father remained unemployed for nearly the entire span of the thirties. Having failed the eleven-plus (twice) Sillitoe left school at fourteen and started the first of a series of jobs in local factories, working for a while as a capstan-lathe operator, like Arthur Seaton in *Saturday Night and Sunday Morning*. When he was called up for National Service in 1946, he entered the RAF, an institution which gave him his first set of underwear and then a posting to Malaya as a wireless operator. Sillitoe used his experiences there, together with much of his early autobiography, for Brian Seaton's story in his third novel, *Key to the Door*. [1]

He has recounted that his was a very unbookish background: 'It is almost true to say that I read nothing that was adult till I was twenty.' Two cherished exceptions were *Les Misérables* and *The Count of Monte Cristo*, which he read many times after hearing serializations of them on the radio. He came across a few more novels while he served with the RAF, but discoveries such as Tolstoy's *Kreutzer Sonata* were rare and random. Sillitoe's own early efforts at literary expression were equally sporadic. When he was fourteen he tried his hand at verse, and then dreamt briefly of becoming a writer while he composed biographies of his cousins, who were army deserters. The ambition was soon forgotten after his mother found his notebook and, realizing the dangers of this diligent documentary, burnt it.

On completing his National Service in 1948, Sillitoe was told that his demob X-ray had revealed tuberculosis. It was only now, condemned to eighteen months' convalescence in hospital, that he began to read and write seriously. His first attempt at a novel was over 400 pages long and took seventeen days to complete. He gave it the title of *By What Road* and, with great hopes, entered it in a competition for new novels run by Eyre & Spottiswoode. It was returned without comment. Undaunted, Sillitoe gave his profession as 'writer' in the passport he acquired when he left England in January 1952 with Ruth Fainlight. However premature, Sillitoe's self-classification did indicate how he would spend the next six years, though not how he would earn a living, in the south of France for a year and then Majorca. Surviving mainly on his RAF pension of forty-five shillings a week and occasional work teaching English, Sillitoe wrote constantly – poems, stories, a travel book and seven novels – sending his manuscripts back to London, receiving only rejection slips in return. His perseverance and the difficulties he faced for most of the fifties can be judged from the fate of a uniquely accepted piece, 'Kedah Peak'. This was adapted from a narrative he had written in hospital in 1948, and he submitted it as a radio talk to the BBC in January 1953. The Talks Department accepted the piece and asked when he could arrange to give the broadcast. A national audience and a fifteen-guinea fee awaited Sillitoe in London, but he simply could not afford the trip and the BBC would not consider anyone else giving the talk. Other pieces were rejected, and the BBC grew impatient until, eventually, he raised enough money for the journey. After a four-year delay Sillitoe had his first notable success as a writer when 'Kedah Peak' was broadcast on the Home Service on 10 April 1957.

His determination was rewarded again in 1957 when Howard Sergeant's Outposts press printed 250 copies of a pamphlet of poems, *Without Beer or Bread*. It was completely ignored by the reviewers but most of the copies were sold. Sillitoe had been encouraged in his versifying by Robert Graves, whom he had met in Majorca. Graves also offered advice about his fiction, suggesting that he should turn from his singularly unsuccessful fantasy narratives and have a go at writing a realistic novel set in his own background in Nottingham. He was able to follow this advice a year later when he realized that a group of his realistic short stories involved the same central character. He drew up a chapter scheme and started his new novel – the eighth – in the autumn of 1956, finishing the first draft six months later and calling it *The Adventures of Arthur Seaton*. This work acquired a new title, *Saturday Night and Sunday Morning*, during the laborious process of revision and pruning which was completed by August 1957.

Even before Sillitoe had finished his final draft there were signs that this novel was bound for success where the previous seven had failed. Tom Maschler had been given an early draft by Sillitoe's agent and was so keen that his firm, MacGibbon & Kee, publish the novel that he travelled to Majorca to discuss the manuscript with Sillitoe. But still publication eluded him: Maschler was overruled and MacGibbon & Kee rejected the book. When it did the rounds of the other London publishers, the hopes which Maschler's enthusiasm had raised were soon dashed. One publisher rejected it outright, another thought the descriptions of working-class life failed to ring true, a third did not like the ending, a fourth considered it too long . . . Sillitoe's agent told him that perhaps he ought to accept failure yet again and start on yet another book. The last hope lay with W. H. Allen who had been sent the typescript in a final, token gesture. They expressed cagey interest but refused to give an acceptance unless Sillitoe could prove he was not a one-work wonder. Fortunately he was able to show them the manuscript of *The General*, and W. H. Allen finally accepted *Saturday Night and Sunday Morning* in April 1958. Sillitoe celebrated the end of his nine-year literary apprenticeship by blowing a little of the ninety pounds he received from his advance on lunch in a Lyons corner-house.

W. H. Allen selected *Saturday Night and Sunday Morning* to head their autumn list of 1958 and announced in their promotional material that it was 'the best first novel we have seen in years'. When it was published in October it seemed that Sillitoe was indeed going to be another headline-hitting author of the fifties; in that month's issue of *Books and Bookmen* he was picked out as the season's most promising new writer and the *News Chronicle* carried a profile-cum-review where *Saturday Night and Sunday Morning* was said to be as important as *Lucky Jim* and *Look Back in Anger*. *Reynolds News* published a similar feature by Brian Glanville two months later and a column-length biography of the new author even appeared in the *News of the World*.[2] But somehow the novel failed to take off. This is not to say that it was not noticed or suffered bad reviews – the cool response in the *TLS* stands out as exceptional. Praise came from John Wain in the *Observer* and reviewers in the *Daily Telegraph*, *Sunday Times* and *New Statesman*.[3] However, for the most part, critics in the quality press had given Sillitoe a few compliments tucked away at the bottom of columns mainly devoted to other books. The impact *Saturday Night and Sunday Morning* had made is indicated by its mention in the *Observer* on 23 November as one of the 'outstanding' novels of 1958 – along with twenty others. When Sillitoe received an Authors' Club Award for his novel the following year, it marked the highlight of a début which had turned out to be quite respectable but not remarkable.

This pleasing, conventional success was followed by the publication of *The Loneliness of the Long-distance Runner* in September 1959. This volume collected some short stories, like 'Uncle Ernest', which Sillitoe had failed to have published in the early fifties, and others which were more recent. One of these was the long title story. Sillitoe had had the first idea for this during his visit to England to give his BBC broadcast. He was staying at the time in a cottage in the country. One day a cross-country runner passed his window and Sillitoe jotted down the famous title phrase in his notebook. He thought no more of it until he came across the notebook again a year later, when he sat down and immediately wrote the first 8,000 words of the Borstal boy's monologue.

It was this story which attracted most interest and helped the collection to gain rather more critical attention than *Saturday Night and Sunday Morning*. Sillitoe's new work received top billing in *The Times* and the *New Statesman* and even managed to oust Kerouac's *The Dharma Bums* into second place in John Bowen's *Sunday Times* column.[4] Reviewers were also less inhibited in their tributes: the stories were 'outstandingly talented', 'vigorous and original', 'exceptional'.[5] Sales were boosted when *The Loneliness of the Long-distance Runner* was recommended by the Book Society, and Sillitoe's reputation as a promising new writer was confirmed when his stories won the Hawthornden Prize. Growing interest was shown when Kenneth Tynan gave *Saturday Night and Sunday Morning* a belated mention as a 'Book of the Year' in the *Observer* on 27 December 1959. Two days later the *Daily Mail* carried a feature by Kenneth Allsop, suggesting that Sillitoe would come to be regarded as a major writer of the fifties.

Signs that Allsop's prediction would very soon be realized came in 1960 when Sillitoe's work suddenly made a far greater impression. 'Success!' declared an *Evening Standard* headline on 2 August, 'It won't change Mr Sillitoe.' But there was a great change in his literary career that week, when *Saturday Night and Sunday Morning* appeared in paperback. Pan Books were printing 150,000 copies of the novel and expected sales to reach 250,000 in the following months. This was not a rash forecast since the print-runs were timed in preparation for the general release of the film of *Saturday Night and Sunday Morning*, premièred in Leicester Square on 26 October 1960.

Starring Albert Finney as Arthur Seaton, Karel Reisz's film followed on from the version of *Room at the Top*, which had made the initial breakthrough, to establish a brief but memorable period in the early sixties when the New Wave in the English cinema saw contemporary novels and plays about working-class life adapted for the screen. Like *Room at the Top*, the film of *Saturday Night and Sunday Morning* was awarded an X-certificate and rave reviews. Only now did Sillitoe experience the routine of media attention, television appearances, press interviews. This had fairly predictable results. The day after the première, the *Daily Mail* reported the now-fulfilled maternal faith and modest, hardworking life of Mrs Sylvina Sillitoe. Less respectfully, the *Mail*'s 'Paul Tanfield' sneered at the rebelliousness of Arthur Seaton's creator and impersonator, for both Sillitoe and Finney ('stalwart defenders of the working-class') made a point of not wearing formal evening dress at the première-night party: 'Success has not gone to their heads. Just to their bank balances.' The following year Evening Standard readers had to be reassured that Sillitoe 'bears no resemblance whatsoever to Albert Finney', and Kenneth Allsop stressed that Sillitoe had had to endure long years of hardship to gain his present wealth.[6]

A year after the première, the film was said to be 'breaking all sorts of records' at the box-office.[7] Continuing success had been assured by official condemnations; the film's reputation for frank sex scenes was confirmed when it was banned in Warwickshire, and more useful outrage was provided by Lieutenant-Colonel Cordeaux, Conservative MP for Central Nottingham, who attacked the film in February 1961 for giving the impression that local workers were 'ill-behaved, immoral, drunken teddy-boys'. Seen the film? Now buy the book ... By the time the Lieutenant-Colonel was objecting, 750,000 copies of the paperback had already been sold and another impression of 125,000 copies was in the pipeline. Within a year of its release by Pan, Saturday Night and Sunday Morning, which in hardback had sold 8,000 copies in two years, was to become one of the first five million-selling paperbacks in Britain, along with the Penguin Odyssey, Lady Chatterley's Lover, The Dam Busters and Peyton Place.[8]

Alan Sillitoe was benefiting from an important development in the publishing industry whereby the period between hardback and paperback publication had been cut from at least five or six years to just one or two. Pan also published The Loneliness of the Long-distance Runner in October 1960, only thirteen months after its appearance in hard covers. The general public could respond to current media coverage in a way that had not been possible with many other writers in the fifties. For example, by the time Penguin published Hurry on Down in 1960 the momentum of publicity for Wain's novel had long been lost.

It was only in the early sixties, with the phenomenal popular success of Saturday Night and Sunday Morning in film and paperback, that Sillitoe was added retrospectively to the list of the most famous young writers of the fifties. Surveys of writing of the previous decade could now be relied on to name him alongside

Wain, Braine, Osborne and Amis as an Angry Young Man. Clearly he did offer journalists and critics ideal material for the degree and kind of enthusiasm with which both groups had greeted his predecessors. Why, then, did his début not follow the same pattern? Why was he not recognized as bolstering the fifties' literary myth until after that myth had lost its immediate relevance? As early as October 1961, John Coleman, reviewing *Key to the Door* in the *New Statesman*, remembered Sillitoe's first novel being greeted with loud applause. This account seemed convincing and appropriate: the only trouble is that it is wrong.

One of the main reasons for surprise at the generally lukewarm reception of *Saturday Night and Sunday Morning* in 1958 is that it tackled a subject which had mostly been ignored or abused in English fiction – working-class life; it was rightly welcomed by the *Daily Telegraph*'s Peter Green as 'that rarest of all finds: a genuine, no-punches-pulled, unromanticized working-class novel'. As had been the case with *Lucky Jim*, Sillitoe's originality defied reviewers' attempts to find comparisons. The setting in working-class Nottingham meant that a few reviewers gave knee-jerk mentions of D. H. Lawrence, and John Wain, more convincingly, was reminded of Philip Callow's recent novel, *Common People*; but other critics floundered after references.

Alan Sillitoe was not quite a pioneer, of course: Jack Common and Philip Callow were two other working-class authors in the fifties. But he still had very few mentors to guide him over the terrain of a working-class fiction – he had found only Robert Tressell's *The Ragged Trousered Philanthropists*, Arthur Morrison's *A Child of the Jago*, Walter Greenwood's *Love on the Dole*, the first half of *Sons and Lovers* . . . 'it was a very sketchy map I walked over'.[9] A map which had in fact been drawn up mainly by xenophobic tourists. In writing a novel about the working class Sillitoe faced a baleful set of literary conventions which had not improved since George Orwell's observations of 1940:

> If you look for the working classes in fiction, and especially English fiction, all you find is a hole. This statement needs qualifying, perhaps. For reasons that are easy enough to see, the agricultural labourer (in England a proletarian) gets a fairly good showing in fiction, and a great deal has been written about criminals, derelicts and, more recently, the working-class intelligentsia. But the ordinary

town proletariat, the people who make the wheels go round, have always been ignored by novelists. When they do find their way between the covers of a book, it is nearly always as objects of pity or as comic relief.[10]

Sillitoe was determined to help give working-class readers the chance of finding their lives honestly and fully portrayed in contemporary fiction.[11] He succeeded in creating two memorable characters in Arthur Seaton and the long-distance runner, Smith. The presentation of Seaton is especially good, conveying the constant swaggering and the fantasies of destructive protest of someone whose main concern is always to come out on top but who knows he is ruled by 'Them' in authority.

'They' have to remain a vague force, since Sillitoe was committed to dealing with uncompromisingly working-class contexts. What's more, unlike *Jill* or *Room at the Top*, Sillitoe's early fiction did not show working-class characters climbing the social ladder. Force of habit must have led John Holloway to consider that marriage would shove Seaton into the middle class, for that is a blatant misreading of the end of *Saturday Night and Sunday Morning*. Sillitoe criticized D. H. Lawrence for depicting just such a renunciation of the working class in *Sons and Lovers*, and recalled: 'I wanted to write a novel about a working man who, though not necessarily typical of the zone of life he lived in, belonged to it with so much flesh and blood that nothing could cause him to leave it – not even his mother.'[12] Despite its rarity value, only a few reviewers really appreciated this 'insider's' portrayal of working-class life. Most of them dismissed the new author with a polite nod.

This is even more surprising when one realizes that Sillitoe seemed to arrive, as Colin Wilson had done, at a very favourable moment and to meet a very definite literary demand. While setting a fashion for realist accounts of lower-class life, the publicity for the Movement and the Angry Young Men had also highlighted the continuing absence of genuine working-class fiction in England.[13] Worries about this lack became well enough established for the *TLS* to take up the theme; on 12 September 1958 a leader article announced that 'the thing we most need is an imaginative insight into the amount of sheer manual skill which is necessary to keep our civilization running'. One month later *Saturday Night and Sunday Morning* appeared, but the need was evidently more apparent than real.

Highbrow enthusiasm might also have been anticipated for Sillitoe since he made his début at a time when there was growing debate about political commitment in literature. For more than a decade after the war the common assumption had been that writers renounced politics after the thirties, and this was only encouraged by the tepid political views of the Movement. 'Commitment' was not so much unfashionable as apparently redundant in a period (it was thought) of prosperity, social reform and an absence of 'good, brave causes'. Young intellectuals suffered from 'an excess of moderation', complained yet another trend-sanctioned *TLS* leader of 1 February 1957. *Declaration* only proved how dismissible was the supposed social protest of the AYM who appeared to have replaced political awareness with naivety or self-interest. Commitment seemed to be one of those exciting notions which are found among French intellectuals, not their unmercurial English counterparts.[14]

Yet there were early signs that Commitment was evolving out of the nebulous Anger into the latest literary fashion. In the autumn of 1956 the film journal *Sight and Sound* carried Lindsay Anderson's call to arms, 'Stand Up! Stand Up!', which attracted such interest that a follow-up questionnaire was published in the issue for spring the next year, with reflections on political commitment in culture by John Berger, Kingsley Amis, Spike Milligan, Colin Wilson and others. The *London Magazine* latched on to the theme and format in May 1957 with a symposium of various writers' attitudes to politics. The rehabilitation of literary commitment was assured with the rise in 1957 of a culturally orientated New Left around two new journals – the *New Reasoner* and the *Universities and Left Review*. (They amalgamated in December 1959 to form the *New Left Review*.) Books associated with the New Left also appeared: *The Uses of Literacy*, *Culture and Society* and *Conviction* led the revival of a noticeably literary radicalism. *Saturday Night and Sunday Morning* was published only a few weeks after *Culture and Society* and *Conviction*, when the question of commitment was both well-grounded and fresh. The *Universities and Left Review* had already tried to lionize Braine, Amis and Osborne as fellow radicals, but his apathetic reviews denied Sillitoe the attention of the young intellectuals of the New Left.

In fact Sillitoe's early fiction offered both the New Left and the literary pundits much more relevant material than did the other

AYM. For a start, he gave a convincing account of the changing social conditions of workers rather than of a small group of upwardly mobile young professionals. In *Saturday Night and Sunday Morning* he described a new working-class prosperity which had begun with the full employment and higher wages of the war effort. 'War was a marvellous thing in some ways,' reflects Arthur Seaton, 'when you thought about how happy it had made so many people in England.' Compare this with Cyril Connolly's complaints in *Horizon* about post-war deprivation. Austerity, after all, is relative. Equally, the Seatons now enjoy relative affluence which allows Arthur's father the luxuries of television and cigarettes and his mother freedom from worry and debt. Arthur spends freely and owns one hundred pounds' worth of clothes bought from his wage of fourteen pounds a week.[15]

Sillitoe also contrasts this new affluence with Arthur's staunchly extremist political views. At first sight these might look outdated, but this anarchistic hero could – should – have been taken as a timely reminder that relative prosperity had not produced a classless equality. Seaton and the long-distance runner can hate the society they live in because there are still forces of power and privilege to hate. Similarly, the prospects of social mobility and educational opportunity were still completely alien to much of the population;[16] it is hard to imagine Arthur pining for scholarships or toiling at correspondence courses in accountancy. In *The Loneliness of the Long-distance Runner* Sillitoe also provided a very necessary reminder that deprivation and hardship had not ended with the thirties. As he himself remarked in the magazine *Anarchy* in April 1964, the Welfare State had done little for what he estimated were the five million people in England who still lived in real poverty. The Smith family in the title story only come across enough money for a brief spending spree when they receive industrial compensation for the death of the hero's father. The society of 'haves and have mores' was a figment of ill-informed imaginations; the Welfare State had produced reforms which were, in the final analysis, cosmetic. Sillitoe's early fiction could have at least shown the literati how prejudiced were their assumptions about 'Universal Welfare'.

The accuracy and relevance of the social background in these two books surely provided ideal material for commentators to repeat their performance over the similarly endowed *Lucky Jim* and advertise Sillitoe as a spokesman of the new working class. Instead there were only curt assumptions that Sillitoe was evoking 'working-class psychology' or 'the working-class spirit'.[17] He also gave critics the chance to sensationalize him as an Angry Young Man – only more so. The tenor of Peter Green's opinion that *Saturday Night and Sunday Morning* made *Room at the Top* look like 'a vicarage tea-party', was echoed in Graham Hough's remark that Amis's 'Lucky Jim larks' paled in comparison with *The Loneliness of the Long-distance Runner* and the *Sunday Express* critic's description of Smith as a real 'Outsider', not a 'phony' one.[18] Yet it is not these comments but their very rarity that is perplexing. The receptions of *Look Back in Anger*, *Lucky Jim* and *Room at the Top* were precedents which should have guaranteed Sillitoe similar attention, for his fiction contained elements which were even more sensational.

For example, the descriptions of Arthur's sexual exploits are at least as frank as those which helped to earn Braine the interest of Fleet Street. The story of Arthur's adulterous goings-on with two sisters, which eventually lead Brenda to a gin-bath abortion and Arthur to suffer the brutal reprisal of Winnie's husband, was pretty daring for those pre-*Chatterley* days. So much so that Sillitoe's screenplay for *Saturday Night and Sunday Morning* fell foul of the censor; some of the fight scenes had to be toned down and the plot altered to make Brenda's abortion unsuccessful. (The censor's reader was very perturbed at the 'slap-happy and success-ful termination of pregnancy' – 'very dangerous stuff'.)[19] If the author of *Take a Girl Like You* could be nicknamed 'Kinsey Amis' and Jim Dixon be considered 'a randy and feckless bachelor',[20] it seems odd that Sillitoe's novel did not gain a controversial reputa-tion for explicit sexual content. Likewise, the condemnation of 'obscenity' in *I Like It Here*, which has Bowen punctuate a diatribe with the word 'bum', would promise a heated response to the 'bastards', 'arses' and 'boggers' which pepper Sillitoe's dialogue. But reviewers were not to be disturbed.

Then again, if Somerset Maugham could condemn Jim Dixon's pranks as the actions of a despicable lout, why did the monologue of a virulently unrepentant Borstal inmate not arouse great protest or at least interest? Dixon, Porter and Lampton had all been vilified as barbarians, but they seem positive gentlemen beside Sillitoe's heroes. Maugham lambasted Dixon for enjoying six pints of beer in an evening, an exploit which becomes wimpishly restrained in comparison with Seaton's thirteen pints, seven gins and assaults-by-vomit in the opening chapter of *Saturday Night and Sunday Morning*. (Seaton's performance is only bested in fifties fiction by Joe Lampton's binge of twenty pints and half a bottle of gin in *Room at the Top*.)

Even more shocking were the political views of Sillitoe's heroes. Dixon's bun analogy and even Jimmy Porter's attacks on the upper middle class are put firmly in the shade by the violently anarchistic fantasies of Arthur Seaton who daydreams about machine-gunning all sorts of figures of authority, from taxmen to trade unionists. It pleased some critics to think that Arthur has been tempered or reformed by the end of the novel,[21] but this hardly squares with his final prophecy – 'trouble for me it'll be, fighting every day until I die'. (Anxiety to retain the force of his protagonist's anarchistic temperament persuaded Sillitoe to write the screenplay, which he feared might otherwise turn Arthur into a safe stereotype.) The anarchistic outlook receives even more militant expression in the 'Them' versus 'Us' social philosophy of the long-distance runner who, cherishing a reflex hatred of authority and privilege, cultivates his own up-against-the-wall daydream of revolution.

Other stories in the second book confirm Sillitoe's desire to focus on deprivation and resistance, even if this means writing about the thirties instead of the less melodramatic underprivilege of the fifties. His characters are often victims, in one way or another, of an unjust and unequal society. There is 'Uncle Ernest', for example, emotionally wrecked by the First World War and then by the police who end his soul-saving friendship with two young girls; or the blasé suicide in 'On Saturday Afternoon', driven to self-destruction by unemployment and the break-up of his marriage. None of the other characters rivals Smith's extremism but Sillitoe does occasionally yield to the temptation of giving them Political Statements. For example, young Colin and Bert cheer themselves up at the end of 'Noah's Ark' by yelling anti-war, anti-Tory songs and then, to the tune of 'rule Britannia':

> 'Rule two tanners
> Two tanners make a bob,
> King George nevernevernever
> SHAVES HIS NOB!'

It is a hand-me-down ardour which strikes a note as false and intrusive as Smith's own reflection about how he shared and shared alike with his partner-in-crime, 'just like the comrades my dad was in'.

This clearly promises some sort of radical political commitment from Sillitoe himself. Here again, Sillitoe seems to offer the right stuff for media attention of the sort that bypassed all finicky literary consideration to identify Amis with Jim Dixon. Such a manoeuvre would have been just as misleading, because neither Seaton nor Smith is a political paragon. Sillitoe has remarked on Seaton 'mouthing his rebellious platitudes',[22] and Smith's admiration of Communist Hungary is plainly not calculated to credit him as the most acute of social rebels. Even so, these characters' political convictions could well have been identified with their creator's own very radical views. Sillitoe's political commitment is revealed in the propagandist aims he had for his writing; art, he declared, was to be used 'as a hidden persuader' in a campaign he outlined for all 'writers of the Left' to oppose the cultural forces which brainwashed people into passive acceptance of the old values of 'the Right'.[23] In a letter to Owen Leeming of the BBC, he referred to his disappointment at the reception of his short stories: '*The Loneliness of the Long-distance Runner* wasn't taken in the way I hoped it might be, though there's still time for the poison to work. But the gates of Thebes are strong.'[24] Sillitoe's political beliefs are difficult to classify on conventional party lines; he said in 1960 that if he were to join a particular party he would choose the Communists,[25] but a more accurate label might be that given to describe Brian Seaton's politics in *Key to the Door* – 'socialist-anarchist'. This category can encompass his inclination to admire the Soviet Union, his support for the anti-Polaris marches in 1961, and a decade later, his refusal to fill in a Government census form.

If such views were too extreme for the middlebrow press, then journalists still had the chance to do to Sillitoe what they did to Colin Wilson and hype his biography. The early profiles in the *News Chronicle* and *Reynolds News* show that he had great appeal and curiosity value as an 'authentic' working-class novelist. Even better, though, is the content of that biography: impoverished background, illness, romance, travel, help from a famous mentor, eleventh-hour reprieve from failure. As interviewers have since demonstrated, these ingredients can easily be whisked up into a classic years-of-struggle yarn. It is a story which also lends itself to a striking autobiographical reading of *Saturday Night and Sunday Morning*. Sillitoe has always had to stress that this is wrong-headed, that voluntary exile in Majorca helped him to distance himself from his material. Recall the media inventions of Lucky Jim Amis, Outsider Wilson and Braine at the Top, and it will come as no surprise to discover that Sillitoe and his novel have inspired similar biographical cartoons.

This kind of media interest began when *Saturday Night and Sunday Morning* was published, only to fizzle out until the film was released. It may seem perverse to niggle that another author did not suffer the abuses and distortions of AYM publicity, but the significance of Sillitoe's reception lies in its restraint.

One possible explanation is that the timing of his arrival was not quite so propitious as it looked. *Saturday Night and Sunday Morning* was published a year after *Declaration*, when media enthusiasm for controversial young writers was well on the decline. In addition, unlike Colin Wilson or John Osborne, Sillitoe did not project a spectacular personal image (Brian Glanville wrote in *Reynolds News* that he looked like a 'young violinist' or a 'friendly marmoset') and was not young enough, unlike Shelagh Delaney, to rekindle popular press interest. Further, Fleet Street's literary attention in October 1958 was occupied with promoting Brendan Behan's *Borstal Boy*. As a result, Sillitoe's novel did not rate a filler paragraph in the *Daily Mail* whereas *Borstal Boy* received an admiring lead review on 18 October alongside a large cartoon of Behan, the roaring-boy celebrity, *Books and Bookmen*'s 'Character of the Year.'

Still more to the point, however, an important feature of the other young writers' publicity is that their popular press coverage had been sanctioned by highbrow enthusiasm. In Sillitoe's case this was just not noticeable or sustained enough for other journalists to follow the example of David Holloway's early profile in the *News Chronicle* and hype Sillitoe as an exciting new writer. The explanation for the delay in Sillitoe's fame as an Angry Young Man can therefore be found in the critics' lack of interest.

Unlike Amis, Sillitoe had to compete with other writers for highbrow attention. The autumn lists in 1958 contained several notable new novels – Doris Lessing's *A Ripple from the Storm*, Iris

Murdoch's *The Bell*, Lawrence Durrell's *Mountolive* – which could relegate *Saturday Night and Sunday Morning* to brief notices. But this still fails to account for the curiously muted critical response. Sillitoe *was* noticed, and praised, then quickly passed over by reviewers who had every reason to give him far more than routine compliments. This indifference was, I feel, largely the result of middle- and upper-class reviewers' ignorance and prejudice when faced with fiction describing working-class life.

Symptomatic of this was the critics' concentration on Sillitoe's working-class subject matter at the expense of any mention of his art. They even overlooked stylistic or formal features in *Saturday Night and Sunday Morning* which might have come in for criticism; its structure, for example, though not as loose as in the less successful of Sillitoe's later novels, does betray its origins as a group of short stories: some episodes, like the sudden introduction of Sam in the fourteenth of the sixteen chapters, are not really integrated. On the other hand, his technical accomplishments were also ignored – the deft shifts through first-, second- and third-person narrative in the portrayal of Arthur Seaton, or the careful evocations of time passing which give a fine background to the changes in the hero's life.[26]

But Sillitoe's fiction was discussed briefly for its documentary value ('Politicians of all parties, please note,' requested the *Sunday Times*) and not appreciated on its own aesthetic terms. The critics could not see beyond the working-class characters and setting. This myopia was all the more disabling because working-class life was clearly so alien to them; much was made of his accuracy and observation, but these qualities were taken on trust. To critics like John Wain the novel *felt* right: 'I know nothing about the interior life of a typical lathe operator, and not very much about his exterior life; but I felt confident, reading Mr Sillitoe's book, that I was getting a truthful account. It felt solid and accurate.'[27] These first critics did not seem anxious to correct their ignorance, and their reviews were marked by a concern not to offend rather than genuine enthusiasm at finding working-class life treated as valid literary material. Praise often came wrapped in hackneyed condescension, of the same brand as John Lehmann's gush about 'the real vitality of working-class life, in all its earthiness and its poetry'.[28] The *News Chronicle*'s David Holloway was touched by the simple world of Sillitoe's novel, a world apparently unstained by the sophisticated or the adult: 'its characters are the people who live, laugh and fight there'. Alternatively, the *Manchester Guardian* critic could marvel at Sillitoe's ability to tap vital proletarian energy: 'His book has a glow about it as though he had plugged in to some basic source of the working-class spirit.'

His style was described in similar clichés; presumably the vital energies of his subject matter had galvanized his pen and typewriter. 'Vivid' description was his hallmark to several critics, including the *New Statesman*'s Maurice Richardson, who also considered the novel's style to be 'effectively clear and blunt, as if it had been written with a carpenter's pencil on wallpaper'. Other reviewers borrowed their literary terminology from the physical attributes of manual labour: Sillitoe's stories were 'tough' and 'sturdy', his novel 'robust'. (Two contemporaries who suffered the same treatment were Philip Callow, who was said to write with 'complete simplicity and natural strength', and Bill Naughton – a 'true proletarian artist' whose 'robust' work was 'forceful' and 'sturdily original'.) These terms deny intellectual or aesthetic sophistication, yet reviewers were unable to ignore Sillitoe's obvious literary talent. The paradox could be resolved – Sillitoe was a 'born writer' blessed with 'instinctive accuracy'.[29]

These critics had nothing more than a passing interest in what one of Shelagh Delaney's reviewers was happy to call 'the lower sort of human situation'.[30] Hence too the readiness to label Sillitoe, his characters and his writing as 'working-class' and leave it at that. Sixty or seventy per cent of the population could be considered quite adequately under the one category. This contrasts with the anxiety to place members of the much more familiar middle class with far more precision. (George Orwell, for instance in *The Road to Wigan Pier*, described his family background as 'lower-upper-middle class'.) The deliberations over the exact social identity of Jim Dixon show the ability and the need to place individual characters within a finely-graded structure. Many contemporary novelists also relied on the established implications of appearance and behaviour to 'classify' their characters. Take the wearing of suede shoes, for instance; this was a sure sign that the offender was a rather dodgy sort, a bourgeois spiv perhaps, or (even worse) an effete smoothie. Thus, Lewis suspects the suede-shoed Whetstone of homosexuality in *That Uncertain Feeling*; Vin Salad's wide-boy pretensions are betrayed by his 'light suede strap shoes' in *Anglo-Saxon Attitudes* (1956), whose upper-middle-class Jasper Stringwell-Anderson wears similar (though *orange*) foot-wear for part of his costume as a 'vulgar sort of dandy'. At a party in *Hurry on Down* Charles Lumley encounters 'a young man in grey suède shoes': 'Charles caught sight of those shoes and decided that he now knew all he wished to know about one guest at least.'

This use of detail is, of course, often an essential technique for realist writers, including Sillitoe himself. In *Saturday Night and Sunday Morning* Arthur's Teddy Boy suits, Robboe's 'ancient Morris' and semi-detached house, and Mr and Mrs Robin voting Liberal and sending their sons to the Scouts all help to place these characters in social gradations which obviously do exist within the umbrella category, 'working class'. The point is that Sillitoe's reviewers could not identify these distinctions, whereas critics had been ever-eager to practise just that sort of decoding in discussions of the Movement and Angry Young Men. The majority of these reviewers were undoubtedly pleased to see a working-class writer making his mark, but they were not really bothered about the social and literary issues he raised. Even the melodramatic political views of his heroes could not stir up interest in the highbrow literary world which had been greatly affected by enthusiasm or resentment provoked by the Movement. The various postures of that group of writers had been quite innocuous by comparison but these had been adopted in territory which was much more visible because closer to home. Sillitoe was effectively dismissed as a marginal curiosity, a welcome addition to the scene perhaps, but hardly inspiring or significant.

The result was that polite interest was replaced by the more heartfelt reactions of prejudice and boredom, as soon as Sillitoe's work had become familiar. When he returned to the Seaton family in *Key to the Door*, published in October 1961, several reviewers were quite open in their contempt for his tiresome whim of writing about that beastly working-class family. The *TLS* critic joshed Sillitoe for creating his own clichés and considered that the Seatons' Nottingham speech just did not have the dignity of 'dialect'. (Quaint 'dialects' can be found in rural areas, but only 'ugly' or 'lazy' 'accents' in industrial towns.) In his *Sunday Times* review, Cyril Connolly gave a few snooty observations of the 'small, closed world' Sillitoe described, a world where people evidently drank in pubs and worked in factories and often 'copulated'. John Davenport in the *Observer* advised Sillitoe to stick to short stories because his material was simply too mundane to avoid becoming boring in a long novel.[31]

Davenport also indulged in a couple of swipes at the idea that there was a current development of the 'working-class novel' – a 'meaningless', 'silly', 'limp phrase' of 'inverted snobs' who would bully 'us' into accepting their 'dull criteria'. Resentment such as this, and the fundamental indifference of the sort which greeted *Saturday Night and Sunday Morning*, indicate that there actually was no attempt to herald a new working-class fiction in the late fifties. On the evidence of the numbers required for the promotion of the Movement and the AYM, the appearance of Philip Callow, Bill Naughton, Keith Waterhouse and Alan Sillitoe was more than enough to generate talk of a new 'proletarian' trend. In hindsight perhaps this does not look like a formidable quartet; Sillitoe's own reputation has declined a little as his novels have too often become disappointingly rambling exercises in emotional, political and verbal indulgence. Only Keith Waterhouse has proved exceptionally gifted. Nevertheless, the pundits could easily have expounded the various supposed social significances of the latest 'Northern' group. Indeed, at the time Keith Waterhouse was worried about the dangers of critics doing just that, and spotting a new 'school' of working-class writers.[32]

There undoubtedly was a development of working-class writing in the late fifties, one which carried on into the early sixties when Stan Barstow, Barry Hines and David Storey made their debuts. By then the working-class author had become something of a culturally fashionable figure, though not nearly as fashionable as the Liverpudlian pop star or the Cockney photographer. P. D. James could introduce the character of Ernie Bales, young Nottingham playwright, in *A Mind to Murder* (1963); the successful author Wilf Cotton, son of a Yorkshire miner, turns up in Barstow's *The Watchers on the Shore* (1966), and a cigar-smoking 'novelist from the north' makes a cameo appearance in Sillitoe's own novel *The Death of William Posters* (1965). But the new literary type found acceptance through its novelty rather than through publicity. 'Proletentiousness: A tendency, especially in modern literary and artistic circles, to boast of real or imagined working-class origin.' This entry deserved to win a *New Statesman* competition for neologisms on 22 June 1962, because the pun itself referred to a trend which was only vaguely familiar, and certainly not established in the same excited, dominating manner as the Anger of the fifties had been. Fortunately, Keith Waterhouse's wish was fulfilled: working-class fiction was 'allowed to take its place quietly as an additional and lively scene in the literary landscape'. Unfortunately, the reasons for that are less heartening.

10

'Decade Talk'

Alan Sillitoe's early work and reception highlight several fallacies in the received opinions at the time – and since – about literature and society in the fifties.

First, his fiction reveals how mistaken were the assumptions about post-war egalitarianism. Encouraged by the publicized fashion for upwardly mobile heroes, some critics were ready to assume that 'the majority receive almost equal shares', that this was a 'semi-Marxist Welfare State' which had rendered class distinctions 'essentially obsolete'.[1] The appearance of Seaton and Smith alone should have been enough to discredit such fanciful notions.

Second, the emergence of a genuinely working-class writer confirms that the attempts to promote the Angry Young Men as proletarian outsiders were thoroughly misguided. Ironically, the late addition of Sillitoe to the fifties canon has helped to maintain the myth of a 'working-class "angry" literature' in the fifties.[2] The irony can be appreciated by the simple method of reading the canon itself. Jimmy Porter may strike the attitudes of a working-class hero but his sweet-stall part-ownership was the occupation of a pretentious drop-out. Joe Lampton comes from a working-class background but his success story describes his escape from the depressingly unprosperous fate of 'Len or Sid or Cliff or Ron'. Although his contemporaries often assumed otherwise, Amis was adamant that Jim Dixon was not working-class but came from a 'white-collar background'.[3] Another writer supposedly establishing a fashion for 'working-class naturalism'[4] in the fifties was John Wain, but he, like Philip Larkin in such poems as 'Here', 'The Large Cool Store' and 'The Whitsun Weddings', evidently saw the working class as 'them', not 'us'. So, when Charles Lumley visits Rosa's working-class home, he thinks and behaves with the unease of a well-intentioned but patronizing anthropologist, protesting a little too much about the 'genuine dignity' he observes in Rosa's father.

For all the fuss they created, the work of the most famous new writers of the fifties made only very limited sorties down the social scale, usually describing the lower-middle instead of the upper-middle or middle-middle class. The contrasting receptions of Amis and Sillitoe suggest that a condition of attracting immediate publicity for extending literature's social range was that such an extension should not depart too far from the class which most literati belonged to and were used to reading about. Characters and settings could be demoted one or two places in the social hierarchy – a redbrick education instead of Oxford, a career in an ordinary profession rather than any glamorous or inherited position – but more adventurous raids on the inarticulate would not be acclaimed by critics who much preferred more familiar territory. Innovations had to be made within the existing highbrow context and on its terms. Hence the effectiveness of Amis's various cultural postures: it was thrilling and controversial to find a hero who cursed Mozart or another who preferred science fiction to Jane Austen, but only mildly interesting to come across characters who apparently did not read at all and would regard higher education as the property of alien privilege. The writers implicated in the Movement and the AYM could be accepted and absorbed by the literary Establishment, but Sillitoe was a far more convincing 'outsider'.

His early work also highlights the absence of real social protest in the AYM; the virulent, anarchistic declarations of Seaton and Smith, and Sillitoe's own radical social views, contrast with the writing of his more celebrated contemporaries. Kingsley Amis was half-heartedly left-wing in the fifties and happy in *Lucky Jim* to assume an 'innocence in ambition', concerned with a challenge which was not political but literary. John Braine was preoccupied with price-tags, not politics, and his hero clambers up the social ladder unencumbered by a social conscience. As for Colin Wilson and his colleagues Hopkins and Holroyd, conventional politics seemed too trivial; only a brand of pseudo-Fascism could appeal to them, with its call to the elect and contempt for the rest. It was John Osborne who did most to maintain the impression that the new literary fashion was for protest, but he offered a manner, a style of revolt, not genuine and informed dissent. Not, of course, that this was a promotional drawback – the media required, even preferred, only the appearance and connotations of rebelliousness. The AYM could command headlines and column space where writers associated with the New Left could not.

If the individual AYM showed little or no real sense of social or political commitment, far less can any common programme of dissent be detected. *Declaration* made that very clear at the time; with no identifiable cause or motivation, 'Anger' remained as nebulous as the characterization of the *Telegraph*'s Eric Lard, open to a wonderful variety of interpretations and explanations. Even the sense of a lower-class identity could be lost as the AYM slogan became increasingly popular: the 'Angry Young Woman' identified by 'William Hickey' in September 1956 was peeved débutante Lynn Mallet; two years later the *Daily Mail* reported that a sociologist had diagnosed the cause of young men's anger as that scourge of adolescence – pimples.[5]

Much of the anxiety and ingenuity which commentators showed in their accounts of the Angry Young Men could have been avoided if Osborne had chosen a different title for his play. The novelist Elizabeth Montagu pointed this out in a letter to the *Spectator* on 25 October 1957: 'Had he called it *Look Sideways in Passion* or *Look Forward in Protest*, would whoever-they-are now be known as "The Passionate Young Men"? "The Protesters"? Or "The Entertainers"?' While these suggestions carry as much conviction as the official tag, the 'anger' of its title was crucial for the promotion of the supposed group. As with the christening of the Movement, the title had to be loose enough to accommodate a very vague identity, and this label had both appealingly rebellious connotations and no specific reference. Hence nobody could be sure what the Angry Young Men were angry about. This vagueness also helped the popular press to promote a trend which would have been less melodramatic and pervasive if it had been tied down by a specific cause. It was also difficult to question the slogan's validity – sceptics could always be referred to the highly visible (and equally unspecific) wrath of John Osborne or Jimmy Porter. Moreover, it would have been odd if there seemed to be no justification for the AYM's relevance and representativeness; it is a strange young generation that unanimously voices satisfaction with society. Hence Lindsay Anderson dismisses the idea of the Angry Young Men as 'a most extraordinary journalistic invention', but adds 'I don't mean that there was no basis in reality'.[6]

In fact, the lack of any basis in reality for the myth of literary anger in the fifties explains why the myth did not survive, far less prosper, in the sixties. During a decade marked by greater opportunities for self-assertion by young people and eminently fashionable anti-Establishment protest, the literary 'rebels' of the fifties seemed to be displaced and even hostile. If in some quarters the AYM retain a reputation as 'the most articulate precursors' of the 'Underground or hippie counter-culture',[7] it can only be said that leading ex-Angries were particularly anxious to disown their 'influence': 'these f. . . . . . happenings' (John Osborne, 1968); 'We support America in Vietnam unequivocally' (John Braine, Kingsley Amis and others from the 'Fascist Beasts' Luncheon Club', 1967); 'We mustn't let the rebels walk all over us' (Kingsley Amis, 1975).[8] Conventional wisdom sees the AYM rapidly settling into comfortable middle age, their earlier protest a passing phase of callow youth, easily remedied by maturity and prosperity, like acne. A far more convincing account, which needs no recourse to such clichés, is simply that the later views of the leading AYM confirm the spurious nature of their earlier reputations.

In contrast to the Angry Young Men, the Movement does still seem valid as a literary grouping of the fifties. The label itself may have been invented, but some sort of movement definitely existed before it was given publicity and then official status with a capital letter. A core of shared friendships and opinions preceded, and prepared the way for, John Wain's decisive promotion on *First Reading*. G. S. Fraser's early tabulation of the group's social features misrepresented or ignored many writers on Wain's broadcasts, but it did serve to denote a genuine and genuinely shared outlook among some of the contributors. The impression of coherence was strengthened when Fraser's choice of characteristics (provincial, academic) was detected in Movement writing, and when individual Movement authors supported each other in print. Similarities in their work were sufficiently plain for Wain, Amis and Gunn to be bracketed together as early as 1953, before the *First Reading* controversies. Indeed, A. Alvarez was able to produce an identikit Movement 'poem', constructed from one or two lines from the work of eight of the nine *New Lines* contributors.[9]

With the Angry Young Men, on the other hand, it is clear that not only the label but the entire notion of the grouping was completely unjustified. The writers named did not know each other before the group was created, and when they did comment on one another's work it was usually to criticize. The bickering was most obvious in *Declaration* but had been apparent from the start. Amis ridiculed *The Outsider* in his *Spectator* review and declared unhappy astonishment at comparisons between himself and 'glum chums' like Osborne. Wilson denounced 'insiders' like Amis and Wain for reflecting 'second-rateness'. Osborne sneered at *The Outsider*: 'I'm told it is a very good reference book – such a wealth of bibliography.'[10]

One qualification must be made, however, for once the idea of the AYM had developed, it seemed that a few writers were willing to play up to their reputations, and even, like Osborne, to exploit the label imposed on them. Hastings decided he was angry about tailors' wages and conditions; Braine stated that 'I, and other Angry Young Men, choose to live in the provinces'; and Wilson agreed he could be justifiably regarded as angry since he was furious about unambitious writing.[11]

The AYM were invented by the media. The idea was advanced in the *Daily Mail*, the label was taken from a press officer's chance remark about one writer, and the reputation was decided by the application of that label in the *Daily Express*. From then on the 'Angry Young Men' were good copy. Fleet Street's literary bent in the fifties may seem extraordinary now, but it would be wrong to get too nostalgic about these good old days when the popular press treated writers with real interest and respect. It is true that literature still held a little more effective prestige value for middlebrow newspapers like the *News Chronicle*, the *Express* and the *Mail* than is the case today, and that a few journalists like Daniel Farson and Kenneth Allsop could indulge in – indeed, make successful careers out of – their desire to be in the literary swim. But the focus could remain on the new writer's *works* for only a short while, and even then those works had to be misrepresented as provocative, contentious, outrageous, antiEstablishment, and so on. Most of the coverage of the AYM – especially of Colin Wilson's scandals and John Osborne's dedication to controversy – now looks like a dry run for Fleet Street's slalom downmarket towards its reliance on news and features about pop stars and the characters/actors of TV soap.

So, even if all the writers concerned had followed Kingsley Amis' example and refused to play Fleet Street's game, the promotion of the AYM – the writers, the grouping and the reputations – would have carried on regardless. The whole story of the rise and fall of the AYM can be told as a media event. Once created by the press, they were pushed into a publicity spiral, with all the inevitable results. Initial interest brought the writers and the group more attention because they were already recognizable, and each new story made them more familiar and paved the way for even more stories. Interest developed into prurience, so that the hype soon involved scandal and then, of course, condemnation of the fame it had created as undeserved. Thereafter the publicity quickly wound down and coverage was reduced to a few smaller individual stories, and stories describing the end of the coverage . . .

A similarly self-generating cycle explains the transience of the AYM as a literary phenomenon. Individual works were announced as significantly alike. Attempted interpretations and explanations became assumptions which soon became clichés. When their column-filling value had been exploited the clichés were summarily dropped. The Angry Young Men, the outsiders who looked back in anger, the lucky Jims who found room at the top, were literary punditry's novelty product, at most a manufactured fashion. The product soon lost its appeal and the fashion changed.

If there was any substance at all behind the myth, it must be sought in the reasons for the initial attention before the promotion process took over. The real significance of the AYM is that English literature had appeared to be, as Amis says, predominantly upper-class, and several prominent new writers in the fifties were more or less lower-class. This one characteristic loomed so large that all other differences were ignored, and, encouraged by misreadings of *Lucky Jim*, Jimmy Porter's diatribes and the title of Colin Wilson's book, social protest was inferred and then taken for granted. It was because of the originality and supposed significance of a supposed lower-class background and material that the leading young writers in the fifties found fame. This explains why most of them are still recognized only by their first works. Of the original 'Angries' only Kingsley Amis has enjoyed a really successful career since the fifties; the reputations of Osborne, Braine,

Wesker, Hastings, Delaney and especially Colin Wilson have declined not because critics are jealous or unappreciative of their talents but because they are not particularly talented writers who struck it lucky when literary merit was not a criterion for literary prominence.

Paradoxically, the very rarity as well as the novelty of lower-class writers in the fifties made their numbers seem overwhelming. The illusion of a widespread movement was perpetuated by the commentators' technique of mentioning the same few names in supposedly abbreviated lists: 'Amis, Wain, Braine and the rest'; '*Lucky Jim, That Uncertain Feeling, Look Back in Anger, Room at the Top* (to mention no others)'; 'the professional AYM, like Kingsley Aimless, Colic Wilson and John Heartburn'.[12] Well, who are these unfortunates, always known but never named?

It was easy – and facile – for received opinion to relate the apparent emergence of a barrage of lower-class authors to catch-penny declarations about contemporary social change. Thus inter-preted, the AYM became the spokesmen of a new up-and-coming class. Eventually, the very popularity of their books – itself caused by the discussion and controversy inspired by assumptions of their representative status – was taken as clinching proof that these new writers had appealed to, and now represented, a new readership.

It might be possible, of course, to ignore such drawbacks as the immediate response to Jimmy Porter, articulated by Helena in the play, that he was indeed 'born out of his time', or Amis's denial of representative status for his hero ('Jim is a man in a book, not a "generation" '),[13] and regard the advent of Porter, Dixon and Lampton as reflecting post-war social reform. However, any claims, such as Tynan's for Osborne's hero, that the AYM spoke for a whole class, or even a whole generation, have to be qualified. A. S. Byatt may remember her fellow undergraduates at Cambridge following the *Lucky Jim* fashion and rejecting previous images of 'varsity privilege,[14] but as Sillitoe's fiction could have reminded opinionators, the population was not composed entirely of scholarship boys and redbrick students. Far better to take an opinion poll on trust than the extremely partial and exaggerated accounts of literati whose concept of the 'young generation' appeared to exclude all those who had not pursued an Arts or Humanities university course.

As is illustrated in the reputations of Amis and Osborne, the accounts of the fifties literary generation also relied on extremely simplistic assumptions about the relationship between the fictional and the real. Novels and plays were discussed for their documentary value, writers were acclaimed for sociological insight, articles were written about the Jim Dixons and Jimmy Porters of the Welfare State. But correlations between literary works and the society in which they are written and first read are surely much more subtle and complex than this. Straightforward connections can certainly be traced in the fifties, but they concern social developments which affected literature directly – the relaxation of the obscenity laws, for example, or the importance of radio (especially the Third Programme) and then television in advertising new writing. The reception of Amis in particular shows that most of the more ambitious claims about books' social significance in the fifties had to ignore what the books and the society were actually like.

The faults are compounded if a whole grouping is invented on the basis of a common social significance. The individuality of each writer, each book, is ignored, the relationships between these and society are reduced to manageable banalities. As books become tracts, writers become clones. Any one of the AYM's various social reputations could be valid only if a monotonous unity of shared cause and effect were possible. Malcolm Bradbury satirizes the blank assumption of just such a unity in *Stepping Westward* when his novelist hero, James Walker, reflects on his membership of the fashionable group of writers in the fifties: 'He belonged, after all, to a generation of literary men all of whom, thanks to a common educational system and a common social experience, had exactly the same head, buzzing with exactly the same thoughts.' In the absence of genetic engineering the AYM identity could only gain the coherence which journalists required through misrepresentation and fantasy. The heroes' composite portraits had to gloss over inconvenient facts like Joe Lampton starting his vocational training as a POW, or Jim Dixon attacking the new university intake which he was supposed to represent. Similarly, the conventional ideas about the writers themselves had to ignore the basic drawback that none conformed to the Butlerite–redbrick career pattern of the 'typical' Welfare State product. Neither Wilson nor Braine had attended university, Sillitoe left school at fourteen, Osborne had a thespian background and was expelled from a minor public school, Amis and Wain were Oxford graduates . . .

If generalizations about social significance are to follow rather than sidestep the biographical and literary data, a whole range of competing possibilities could be deduced from the same few writers and books. If selective prejudice could promote Anger as representative, why not read *Lucky Jim* and *Room at the Top* as key works of the Conforming Young Men? Or, noting that Porter, Lumley and Lewis all refuse orthodox professional advancement, why not discuss the attitudes of the Non-conforming Young Men? Or again, looking at the biographies of the central fifties authors, a 'common educational system' seems much less important than a common experience of the National Health Service. Sillitoe began his literary self-education as a tubercular convalescent in a sanatorium, Braine turned *Born Favourite* into *Room at the Top* in the same condition and circumstances, while the hospital scenes in the latter halves of *Hurry on Down* and *Eating People is Wrong* reveal where Wain and Bradbury found the time to finish their first novels. Were the fifties dominated not by Butlerites but Bevanites? Should this be known as the decade of the Ill Young Men?

But Anger went unquestioned, and a handful of writers were assumed to be reflecting in their books and lives the results of post-war social change and attitudes produced by that change – to be expressing views which were waiting to be expressed. Perhaps there is some truth in these assumptions, but again opinion polls would have to be consulted, and again these assumptions could lead to as many versions of what was being represented as there are circumstances and views described in each selected work. My own impression is that the great publicity of the myth of the Angry Young Men actually created the reality the writers were supposed to be reflecting. Hence, for example, the emergence of the scholarship boy as a significant social figure during the controversies surrounding *Lucky Jim*; as Amis says, the scholarship boy 'had been there but he hadn't been noticed before'.[15] Alternatively, in a more straightforward manner, there was the vogue for Bohemianism among part of the espresso-bar clientèle following Colin Wilson's fame. It seems to me that the promotion of the AYM as social representatives functioned as self-fulfilling prophecy.

If a dominant spirit special to the decade is to be found among new writers of the fifties, it would be better to avoid assumptions of shared social and political importance and look instead for a literary *Zeitgeist*; it is in a *literary* context that the work of the supposedly Angry writers can be most properly and fruitfully discussed. Amis can be appreciated for debunking and helping to replace a set of outmoded and élitist fictional conventions and values. *Look Back in Anger* retains some importance as the play which performed a similar service for the English theatre, countering country-house drama and drawing-room *politesse* with non-U subjects and vehement, contemporary rhetoric. John Braine can be regarded as detailing issues of class conflict, social ambition and sex with a new candour. Colin Wilson of course is the exception, for his success is best understood as the result of his meeting the unsatisfied demands of critics whose values were being challenged, explicitly and implicitly, by the most prominent new writers. The AYM have no viable identity as a group of social rebels, but they do share with the Movement a reaction against upper-class and/or experimental writing. The lower-class realism of several other 'fifties' writers – Cooper, Sillitoe, Delaney, Wesker, Waterhouse, Braine – might seem to strengthen the view that Amis, Osborne and Braine can be taken to represent a generational literature which reacted against the literary orthodoxy represented by the Mandarins. New writing in the fifties appears to have been dominated by anti-Modernism.

'What will be the general myth of the fifties?' asked Philip Toynbee in the penultimate week of the decade, but the myth was already so well established as to look hackneyed and tiresome. Although the 'Angry Decade' was a very misleading title for the period, the specifically literary identity does seem secure; we know what Malcolm Bradbury means when he says he is 'a prototypical figure from 1950s fiction' and that *Eating People is Wrong* is 'a very fifties novel'.[16] There is an accepted canon of the decade's authors and an accepted view of the development of fifties writing. If it is unusually thorough, an account will begin with William Cooper conveniently inaugurating a new fashion in 1950 with *Scenes from Provincial Life*. The redirection towards anti-Modernism is said to be established in 1953 and 1954 with the emergence of the Movement and the trio of picaresque novels, *Lucky Jim, Hurry on Down* and *Under the Net*, before the realist cause gains more adherents in the theatre after the breakthrough of *Look Back in Anger*, and in the novel with Braine, Sillitoe, and, it is usually assumed, a host of others.

The reaction against experiment acquired such publicity in the fifties that it has affected the reputation of post-war English literature as a whole, which has often been accused of parochialism, insularity and backwardness, of writing as if the Modernists had never written, ignoring problems of existence, perception and narration, and resting content with minute accounts of class distinctions and other cosy social realities. It seems to many English critics that the avant-gardes of Europe and the Americas have, by humiliating contrast, continued to make energetic and exciting progress. Various reasons have had to be advanced to explain or excuse English literature's apparent refusal to acknowledge the Modernist or post-Modernist condition. One theory has it that traditional writing survives in England because the traditional social framework has survived upheavals like the Industrial Revolution and the Second World War, while other countries suffered greater and more enlightening trauma. Other explanations look to the 'English national spirit' or some such; this is said to involve an outlook which is comfortable, liberal, unextreme, empirical, opposed to doctrines, manifestos and fancy theories.[17]

These grand generalizations may all hold some truth but, as an appraisal of the anti-Modernist views of Amis and others shows, an immediate and evident reason for a rejection of the avant-garde in England was that it was implicated in a moribund, socially élitist literature. The class associations which could condemn Modernism also gave its post-war opponents the chance to appear every bit as rebellious and explorative in the social content of their work as an avant-garde would have done in novelty of presentation. Amis was able to declare that 'the adventurous path is the one that leads away from experiment'.[18]

Yet, despite the obvious dominance of anti-Modernist writing in the fifties, this account of the decade's literary identity (let alone that of post-war English literature in general) faces several major objections. First of all, anti-Modernism was, of course, not unique to the period; the realist tradition of a more accessible 'middlebrow' literature had continued to find many more practitioners and a much greater audience than Modernism even while the latter was developing – often more conspicuously in theory than in practice – its highbrow dominance. In addition, the coexistence of the traditional and the experimental continued in the fifties. This was also the decade when Samuel Beckett gained widespread attenton, effectively as a new writer, with his trilogy and particularly with *Waiting for Godot*. Lawrence Durrell made a similarly delayed impact with the *Alexandria Quartet*. N. F. Simpson and Harold Pinter could have been pigeon-holed as English representatives of the Theatre of the Absurd. The publication of *The Comforters* in 1957 could have given Muriel Spark a reputation as one of 'England's' metafictional novelists.

Far from being acceptably comprehensive, the myth fails to accommodate innovative writers of the time who with hindsight are considered much more worthy and important than most of the apparent leaders of their generation. William Golding, for instance, enjoyed 'what you might call a Third Programme success' until *Lord of the Flies* was filmed and became popular as a school textbook in the early sixties.[19] The relatively quiet débuts of Geoffrey Hill and Ted Hughes, as well as those of Golding, Pinter, Spark, and of Iris Murdoch and Doris Lessing too, support Malcolm Bradbury's contention that 'most of the important books that were written in the fifties were not the ones that we normally mention', and that these show more metaphorical emphases.[20] It is too easy to exaggerate the dominance in the fifties of social realism, a mode which was publicized at the time because of the practitioners' class, real or assumed.

New writers who did not have the right social qualifications lingered in the shadow of their 'representative' contemporaries. Considering the other new talents and trends which appeared, the received version of the fifties generation seems repugnantly exclusive. For one thing, as its label indicates, the tendency associated with the Angry Young Men was a noticeably masculine one. Iris Murdoch, Doris Lessing and Elizabeth Jennings were briefly incorporated – more rather than less misleadingly – in the decade's groupings but other new women writers of the period were merely overlooked. Anxieties about late-forties fiction might have been partly allayed by the arrivals of Elizabeth Taylor and Barbara Comyns, and in the early fifties Elizabeth Jane Howard, Penelope Mortimer and Brigid Brophy all produced notable new work but received no acclaim comparable to that of their male colleagues. Then again, as indeed the *First Reading* broadcasts showed, other poets emerged at the same time as the Movement, offering different new directions. Edith Sitwell was able to provide a list of young poets (including Silkin, Hill and Causley) whom she admired for not following the Movement's lead. Howard Sergeant and Dannie Abse could produce *Mavericks*, an anti-*New Lines* anthology of new poets like Michael Hamburger and J.C. Hall who shared a 'primary Dionysiac excitement' far removed from 'consolidation'. The young poets Alan Brownjohn and Charles Tomlinson protested that the Movement did not represent the best work of their generation.[21]

These and other writers were denied the kudos of spokesmanship, which, given the inanities and misreadings involved in the creation of the accepted version, they could easily have been awarded.The rise of the meritocracy was not inherently, necessarily, *the* social trend of the decade or the only one which might be thought to be reflected in new writing. Another literary myth of the fifties could well have been manufactured in the same way as Anger.

For example, it is possible to construct a generational trend which gives the impression that fifties literature and society was dominated by a religious revival. Let us follow the example of the period's literary pundits and take the university as the institution providing the measure of the latest generational fashion. 'Religion at Oxford Ousts Marxism', ran a *Sunday Times* headline on 3 June 1956. The article asks if the students' new preference may not point to a national religious revival among the young. Once again, the state of the world and the *Zeitgeist* (a different one this time, of course) are invoked as reasons and causes. Once again, a connection can be made between this presumed fad and a few interesting works by writers who gained reputations as acute monitors of social and cultural change. In Angus Wilson's short story 'Such Darling Dodos', Robin and Priscilla, representing the thirties generation, find their social concern is outdated when they meet a pair of post-war Oxford undergrads who have renounced politics and turned to God. In *Socialism and the Intellectuals* Amis remarked that church-going was obligatory for the intellectually fashionable student, and in his novel *A Travelling Woman* (1959) John Wain describes the huge and influential success of a book by the sage-like Edward Cowley, *The Discovery of Faith*. With the AYM myth as our precedent, this seems ample justification to look around for writing that could be included as examples of a religious literary generation. An array of impressive new talents could be cited as members of, say, the Metaphysical Movement: Beckett, Golding, Spark, Murdoch, Hill and Pinter could all be nominated, however inaccurately, as writers belonging to a 'group' concerned with God, the death of God, or whatever. This alternative 'generation' could also have incorporated Colin Wilson on the much sounder basis of *The Outsider*'s content, not merely its title.

The reasons for that alternative not being created and accepted have nothing to do with its blatant silliness, which is no greater than that of the concept of the AYM. Religion could not become the literary theme of the fifties because religion was already associated with writing of the forties, and 'decade talk' requires dramatic and punctual changes in the *Zeitgeist*. And the fifties could not be seen as religious as well as angry because decade talk also requires only a single defining trend. Consequently, in *The Angry Decade* Allsop has to leave out writers he admires, like Lessing, MacInnes and Golding, because they have not been influenced by the 'mental mood' of 'dissentience' and have not described 'the psyche of the Fifties', even though he thinks they have dealt with issues specific to the period and that they are better writers than many of the AYM, whom Allsop takes as 'representative' but then criticizes for not representing fifties society in any coherent or comprehensive manner.

The appeal of a distinctive literary definition for the period was too powerful for the generation to be questioned or ignored. And as time has passed the contemporary attractions of self-definition have been replaced by those of convenience: 'Angry Young Man', 'fifties writing' and suchlike terms retain their currency because they make teaching and talking and writing about literature easier and more dramatic, as well as giving the gratifying impression that one's finger is firmly on the pulse of cultural change.

Malcolm Bradbury defends period identities as 'good organizing fictions'[22] and indeed has been able, so far, to write his own novels by and about each of four decades, so that his most recent, *Rates of Exchange* (1983), reflects the currently accepted intellectual vogues for economics, linguistics and structuralism. But how valid really is such decade talk in literary history? It seems to me that the period fiction of the fifties at least has organized very little, ignored all the contradictions and complexities of actuality, and created an identity which can only be totally misleading or banal. Even if we want to accept lower-class, anti-Modernist realism as the dominant, distinguishing tendency of the decade, so many qualifications and reservations are needed to make it at all feasible that the only available generalizations are too general to be useful. The dramatic accounts of shared challenges and rebellions have to be reduced to a drab statement along the following lines: in this period there were some new writers who came from non-upper-class backgrounds and described non-upper-class life in realist, anti-Modernist work.

If there is as little real basis as this for the myth as it was formed at the time, the myth must ultimately owe its existence to a system which operates more or less independently of the reality which the system's favoured products help to create. Of course, the raw material for the fabrication of a myth must be available: rival cohesions were not asserted, so that the Movement and the Angry Young Men could be awarded the prize as generational groups; the distinctive lower-class identities of both groups meant that they were conspicuous in a predominantly upper-class literary context; and these class identities meant that the groups were felt to be appropriate in the context of post-war social change. However, this raw material could only gain generational significance because it was ready to be processed by the myth-making machinery.

As the development of the Movement's representative status clearly shows, the machinery requires literary distinctiveness and the opportunity for this to be noticed. A decade's 'generation' therefore requires national (i.e. metropolitan) recognition as a generation and has to be defined against the preceding generation. If literature can initially be divided into two categories, the metaphoric and the metonymic, it follows that mainstream (i.e. metropolitan) literary chronology will be characterized by an oscillation from period to period between these two poles. The Modernist twenties follow pre-war realism and are succeeded by the thirties which revert to political realities. The forties are seen as returning to neo-Romanticism and the fifties as being firmly realist. Sure enough, the literary myth of the sixties is one of experiment and engagement – à la Alvarez and *The New Poetry* – with the extreme and the subjective. Social causes are usually invoked to justify the selection of these identities, but if the Second World War could witness a retreat into the subjective, why did the Cold War or the thirties' political tensions not realize similar generational trends? The literary *Zeitgeist* is determined rather by the swing of a metropolitan pendulum.

Perhaps the absence of convincing decade talk in the seventies, and, notwithstanding the attempts to find a 'Martian' or 'ludic' school of poets, the apparently pluralist eighties, are signs that access to and recognition through the metropolitan system is now less straightforward than it used to be. University expansion has reduced the overweening importance of Oxbridge to literary London. (If any English universities are to be singled out as present suppliers of new talent, they would probably be Hull and East Anglia.) Much more significantly, metropolitan-based 'English' 'mainstream' culture has itself been challenged by writers from previously marginalized cultures. There has been the growing importance of regional centres – notably Liverpool and Newcastle – in the sixties and, more recently, the importance of poets from Northern Ireland, the 'Glasgow Group', Afro-Caribbean writers and, most striking of all, the developments in women's writing.

In the fifties, however, the old myth-making machinery could still clank and whirr into action and a few not too dissimilar writers could be fabricated into a generational grouping which was eagerly expected and readily accepted. As usual, other quite different and often more talented new authors had to be excluded and the works of their 'representative' contemporaries had to be mangled and distorted to make them representative. What was new in the 1950s, though, was the vigour and extent of the promotion campaign for the decade's literary generation. The Angry Young Men were marketed by unprecedented media hype. The period's literary myth of anti-Establishment protest and anti-Modernist realism was established with such force that it has served to confirm myths of post-war social equality and opportunity and to highlight inferiority complexes about the reactionary and parochial nature of post-war English writing.

On the plus side, several young writers became household names as literary delegates of the fifties. Paperback publication, television and film adaptations meant that their books and plays, which had already achieved remarkable commercial success, could reach a huge audience. As a result, for readers and viewers alike, lower-class social reality gained new literary and cultural validity and became an expected component of imaginative work. New literary images of Englishness were broadcast: the élitist model of the gentleman had been challenged and replaced in what was made to seem a cultural takeover bid. The 'fifties generation' survives in its original caricature form mainly in the cartoon world according to Eng. Lit., for as the fifties gave way to the sixties another generation had to be found and Amis for one could breathe a sigh of relief: 'Sometimes I would meditate on how nice it would be if one's novels were read as novels instead of sociological tracts, but then one morning the whole shooting-match just softly and silently vanished away, and there we all were, reduced to being judged on our merits again.'[23]

Notes

One: 'In the Movement'

The title for this chapter was the headline for an unsigned article by J. D. Scott in the *Spectator* on 1 Oct 1954, p. 399.

1 Angus Wilson, *The Wild Garden* (London, Secker & Warburg, 1963), p. 105; Doris Lessing, 'Spotlighting Suburbia', *Books and Bookmen*, Oct 1955, p. 21.
2 Personal interview with William Cooper, 23 Nov 1984; C. P. Snow reviewed *Scenes from Provincial Life* in 'English, French, Jamaican', *Sunday Times*, 5 March 1950, p. 3, and Pamela Hansford Johnson in 'Young Man's Fancies', *Daily Telegraph*, 14 March 1950, p. 6.
3 Personal interview with William Cooper.
4 'Current Periodicals', *TLS*, 25 Aug 1950, p. 538; see Robert Hewison, *In Anger: Culture in the Cold War 1945–1960* (London, Weidenfeld & Nicolson, 1981), p. 19.
5 John Lehmann, 'A Literary Magazine On The Air: Problems and Findings', *BBC Quarterly* 7 (1952), p.77.
6 'The English And The American Novel', *TLS*, 29 Aug 1952, p. xii; three years later J. D. Scott made a similar attack on the typical post-war first novel in 'The British Novel: Lively As A Cricket', *Saturday Review*, 7 May 1955, p. 23.
7 See the early reviews and articles in Kerry McSweeney (ed.), *Diversity and Depth in Fiction: Selected critical writings of Angus Wilson* (London, Secker & Warburg, 1983).
8 Pamela Hansford Johnson, 'The Sick-room Hush over the English Novel', *Listener*, 11 Aug 1949, pp. 235–6
9 Russell recalled his encounter with Snow in *The Pearl of Days: An Intimate Memoir of The Sunday Times* (London, Hamish Hamilton, 1972), p. 222, and Snow's anti-Modernist 'Credo' appears on pp. 223–5; an account of Snow's anti-Modernist reviews is given by Rubin Rabinovitz, 'C. P. Snow as Literary Critic', *The Reaction against Experiment in the English Novel, 1950–1960* (New York, Columbia University Press, 1967).
10 Angus Wilson, 'Sense and Sensibility in Recent Writing', *Listener*, 24 Aug 1950, p. 279.

11 Donald Davie, 'The Earnest and the Smart: Provincialism in Letters', *Twentieth Century*, Nov 1953, p. 387.

12 Cecil King, *Strictly Personal* (London, Weidenfeld & Nicolson, 1969), p. 133; Robert Hewison gives a brief account of *Encounter*'s funding in *In Anger*, pp. 60–1.

13 Blake Morrison gives an excellent summary of the Movement's early work in *The Movement: English Poetry and Fiction of the 1950s* (Oxford, Oxford University Press, 1980), pp. 10–54; a checklist of the Fantasy Press series is included in John Cotton's booklet, *Oscar Mellor: The Fantasy Press* (Hitchin, Dodman Press, 1977).

14 Philip Oakes, *At the Jazz Band Ball* (London, André Deutsch, 1983), p. 223.

15 Anthony Hartley, 'Critic Between the Lines', *Spectator*, 8 Jan 1954, p. 47; Donald Davie, 'Augustans New and Old', *Twentieth Century*, Nov 1955, p. 468.

16 Walter Allen, 'New Novels', *New Statesman*, 30 Jan 1954, pp. 136–7; George Scott, 'A bright first novel about a very bright young man', *Truth*, 5 Feb 1954, p. 185.

17 Anthony Quinton, 'A Refusal to Look', *Listener*, 22 July 1954, p. 139; Stephen Spender, 'A Literary Letter From London', *New York Times Book Review*, 10 Jan 1954, p. 14, and 'Speaking Of Books', *New York Times Book Review*, 1 Aug 1954, p. 2.

18 J. D. Scott, 'A chip of literary history', *Spectator*, 16 April 1977, p. 20.

19 Spender, 'Speaking Of Books', p. 2; John Lehmann, 'Foreword', *London Magazine*, March 1954, p. 12; Cyril Connolly, 'The Writer's Lean Life', *Saturday Review*, 7 May 1955, pp. 19–21, 63.

20 John Raymond, 'Two First Novels', review of Françoise Sagan, *Bonjour Tristesse*, and Brian Moore, *Judith Hearne*, *New Statesman*, 21 May 1955, p. 727.

21 T. R. Fyvel, 'Problems of the Modern Novelist', *Listener*, 21 April 1955, p. 709; Scott, 'The British Novel', p. 46.

22 John Raymond, 'New Novels', review of *Academic Year*, *New Statesman*, 5 Feb 1955, pp. 189–90.

23 John Wain, 'What The Critics Missed In My Book', *Books and Bookmen*, Dec 1955, p. 15.

24 Edmund Wilson, 'Is It Possible to Pat Kingsley Amis?' Review of *That Uncertain Feeling*, *New Yorker*, 24 March 1956, p. 129

25 J. B. Priestley, 'The Newest Novels', *New Statesman*, 26 June 1954, p. 826.

Two: 'The Angry-Young-Man Club'

The title for this chapter was originally the headline in the *Daily Express*, 4 Sept 1956, p. 6, for an unsigned article.

1 John Osborne referred briefly to Fearon's chance remark in an interview on *Desert Island Discs*, BBC Radio 4, 27 Feb 1982; my account is mainly based on information kindly given by Barbara Fearon in letters of 28 May and 5 June 1985; the earliest use of Fearon's remark I have traced is in an article by Thomas Wiseman, 'Angry Young Man', *Evening Standard*, 7 July 1956.

2 J. B. Priestley, 'The Future of the Writer', *London Magazine*, June 1954, p. 63.

3 W. A. S. Keir, 'A Cold Blast from the North', *Twentieth Century*, Sept 1956, pp. 195–6.

4 Daniel Farson, 'Two Lost Generations', *Books and Bookmen*, Sept 1956, p. 15.

5 For an example of how a whole series of cultural and social changes has been assigned origins in a dramatic turnabout in this one year, see Phyllis Bentley's imaginative account in '*O Dreams, O Destinations*' (London, Victor Gollancz, 1962), p. 267:

> From 1956, the date of Kingsley Amis's novel *Lucky Jim* and John Osborne's play *Look Back in Anger*, there took place a complete change of style, a complete break in the century. Clothes, shoes, hair-dressing, furniture, not to mention economics, manners and morals, all changed violently, and these changes were symptoms of a deep psychological change, a re-orientation of outlook.

6 Alistair Davies and Peter Saunders, 'Literature, politics and society', in Alan Sinfield (ed.), *Society and Literature 1945–1970* (London, Methuen & Co., 1983), p. 28.

7 These versions of events appear in Robert Hewison, *In Anger: Culture in the Cold War 1945–1960* (London, Weidenfeld & Nicolson, 1981), p. 129, and Blake Morrison, *The Movement: English Poetry and Fiction of the 1950s* (Oxford, Oxford University Press, 1980), p. 248.

8 Kingsley Amis describes his reactions to Suez in *Socialism and the Intellectuals*, Fabian Tract No. 304 (London, Fabian Society, 1957); Paul Johnson, 'Lucky Jim's Political Testament', review of *Socialism and the Intellectuals*, *New Statesman*, 12 Jan 1957, pp. 35–6. On 1 Feb 1957 a *TLS* editorial, 'Sensibility And Sense', complained that young writers seemed too 'committed . . . to a sceptical and empirical attitude' to be aroused by any political causes.

9 Osborne's nomination was made by Thomas Wiseman, 'My Top Ten of 1956', *Evening Standard*, 22 Dec 1956, p. 5; 'Atticus', *Sunday Times*, 30 Dec 1956, p. 3.

10 Wiseman, 'My Top Ten of 1956', p. 5.

11 Letter received from John Braine, 23 July 1986.

12 Richard Lister, 'Mr Braine joins the young men in revolt', *Evening Standard*, 19 March 1957, p. 12; see also John Davenport, 'New Novels', *Observer*, 17 March 1957, p. 14, and R. G., untitled review of

Room at the Top, *Punch*, 17 April 1957, p. 517.

13 David Holloway, 'Small Town Casanova', *News Chronicle*, 14 March 1957, p. 6.

14 Braine was hailed as 'the new apostle of success' by Robert Pitman, 'It's cash, cash all the time for the man at the top', *Sunday Express*, 9 Feb 1958, p. 6.

15 These were the headlines for articles by Robert Pitman, *Sunday Express*, 9 Feb 1958, p. 6, and Thomas Wiseman, *Evening Standard*, 21 June 1958, p. 5.

16 John Braine, 'Chucking My Job: The Best Thing I Ever Did', *Daily Express*, 20 July 1957, p. 4; Braine's *Reynolds News* articles were 'Way to the Top', 10 Nov 1957, p. 3, 'My Desk–a hospital bed', 17 Nov 1957, p. 3 and 'When I saw the dazzling dawn of SUCCESS', 24 Nov 1957, p. 3. Cyril Aynsley, 'Never A Christmas Like It Before–For Six People To Whose Lives 1957 Brought Dramatic Change', *Daily Express*, 24 Dec 1957, p. 4; 'Bookmarks', 'Careful Young Man', *Books and Bookmen*, Sept 1957, p. 21.

17 John Scott, 'Very Little Room at the Top', *Observer*, 1 Feb 1959, p. 26; Ernestine Carter, 'Room at the Top', *Sunday Times*, 31 Aug 1958, p. 19.

18 Alastair Buchan, 'Look Back in Sorrow', *Observer*, 2 Dec 1956, p. 8; John Golding, 'Looking Back in Anger', *New Statesman*, 22 Dec 1956, pp. 816–17; 'Look Back In Calmness', *Sunday Times*, 30 Dec 1956, p. 6.

19 Alex Bannister, 'Anything But Lucky Jim', *Daily Mail*, 2 Aug 1956, p. 4; Howard Whitten, 'Lucky Jim punishes Kent', *Reynolds News*, 8 June 1958, p. 14.

20 John Brophy, 'Angry Young Dubliner', review of Mary and Padraic Colum, *Our Friend James Joyce*, *Time and Tide*, 21 March 1959, p. 342; Milton Shulman, 'The Mellow Old Man delivers a counterblast', review of J. B. Priestley, *The Glass Cage*, *Evening Standard*, 27 April 1957, p. 8; Len Ortzen, 'Angry Young Muslims', *Twentieth Century*, Aug 1959, pp. 63–72.

21 John Osborne, 'You've Fallen For The Great Swindle', *News Chronicle*, 27 Feb 1957, p. 4.

22 The composite impression of Anger was satirized by Alan Sillitoe in *The Death of William Posters* (London, W. H. Allen, 1965) when he has Myra remember reading 'a book (or was it books?) called *Hurry on Jim* by Kingsley Wain that started by someone with eighteen pints and fifteen whiskies in him falling downstairs on his way to the top'. (p. 166).

23 Teddy Boy references to Jimmy Porter came from, for example, Christopher Hollis, 'Keeping Up With the Rices', *Spectator*, 18 Oct 1957, p. 504, and Derek Stanford, 'Beatniks and Angry Young Men', *Meanjin* 17 (1958), p. 414; the assessment of Porter and Dixon was

made by James Gordon, 'A Short Directory to Angry Young Men', *Good Housekeeping*, Jan 1958, p. 93.

24 Lister, 'Mr Braine joins the young men in revolt', p. 12.

25 Kenneth Tynan, 'The Men Of Anger', *Holiday*, April 1958, p. 93.

26 J. D. Scott, 'Britain's Angry Young Men', *Saturday Review*, 27 July 1957, p. 11.

27 'Sensibility And Sense', p. 65; Anthony Hartley and Kenneth Allsop opted for the explanation that the AYM were protesting at the lack of good, brave causes in *A State of England* (London, Hutchinson, 1963), pp. 86–7, and *The Angry Decade* (London, Peter Owen, 1958), pp. 20–1, respectively.

28 Gillian Freeman, 'The Last Of The AYM?', review of William Camp, *Prospects of Love*, *Reynolds News*, 9 June 1957, p. 8; Chris Chataway, 'Angry Young Men? "Moaners" Is How I Describe Them', *News Chronicle*, 25 Feb 1957, p. 4.

29 V. S. Pritchett, 'These Writers Couldn't Care Less', *New York Times Book Review*, 28 April 1957, pp. 38–9.

30 Stanford, 'Beatniks and Angry Young Men', p. 416; John Barber, 'Angry Young Men fight it out in bar', *Daily Express*, 10 March 1958, p. 1.

31 Tom Maschler quoted Amis's letter in the Introduction to *Declaration* (London, MacGibbon & Kee, 1957), pp. 8–9.

32 'Not the Cream But The Top Off The Milk', *TLS*, 8 Nov 1957, p. 674; Henry Fairlie, 'Slobbering Sentimentality', *Tribune*, 25 Oct 1957, p. 9; Angus Wilson, 'Protest Meeting', *Observer*, 13 Oct 1957, p. 18.

33 Daniel Farson, 'A Few Dusty Mice Drink To Declaration', *Books and Bookmen*, Dec 1957, p. 4; Morrison, *The Movement*, pp. 238–41

Three: 'When the Angry Men Grow Older'

The title for this chapter was the title of an article by Stephen Spender in the *New York Times Book Review*, 20 July 1958, pp. 1, 12.

1 J. G. Weightman, 'Out of the Mouths', review of *Declaration*, *Twentieth Century*, Dec 1957, p. 535.

2 Peter Quennell, 'L'Affaire Minou', *Spectator*, 25 Jan 1957, p. 110.

3 Peter Chambers, 'The Fantastic Fairyland of Jane Gaskell', *Evening Standard*, 27 Aug 1957, p. 10.

4 Letter received from Helen Griffiths, 6 Nov 1984; Amanda Marshall, 'Where are the schoolboy novelists?' *Evening Standard*, 15 Oct 1957, p. 8; 'Bookmarks', 'Making Good', *Books and Bookmen*, Jan 1958, p. 30.

5 J. W. Taylor, Cartoon, *Punch*, 18 Dec 1957, p. 715; Alex Atkinson, 'The Peckham Prodigy', *Books and Art*, Nov 1957, pp. 41–2. Other

parodies include Brian Parker, 'A Genius in the House', *Punch*, 30 Oct 1957, p. 505, and 'Christmas Shopping Guide', *Punch*, 4 Dec 1957, p. 660.

6 Paul Rock and Stanley Cohen have analysed the manufacturing of the Teddy Boy scare by the popular press after the 'battle' of St Mary Cray in April 1954. Their article, 'The Teddy Boy', appeared in Vernon Bogdanor and Robert Skidelsky (eds.) *The Age of Affluence, 1951–1964* (London: Macmillan, 1970), pp. 288–320.

7 Tom Baistow, 'This youth cult makes me sick', *News Chronicle*, 4 Dec 1957, p. 5.

8 William Salter, 'Youth on the March', *New Statesman*, 26 Oct 1957, pp. 531. See chapter 8 for more opinions of Wilson as a literary pop star.

9 'More Angry Young Men', *Listener*, 3 July 1958, p. 8; Henry Brandon, 'Beat Generation', *Sunday Times*, 15 June 1958, p. 19.

10 Quentin Crewe, 'Find A New Joke, Mr Amis', *Evening Standard*, 14 Jan 1958, p. 10; Penelope Mortimer, 'The Old and the Young', *Sunday Times*, 12 Jan 1958, p. 9.

11 This account of developments in the theatre is based on information provided in Robert Hewison, *In Anger: Culture in the Cold War 1945–1960* (London, Weidenfeld & Nicolson, 1981), pp. 141–9.

12 W. A. Darlington, 'Joan Littlewood's Year', *Daily Telegraph*, 28 Dec 1959, p. 9.

13 'Two Tastes Of Honey For Girl Playwright', *News Chronicle*, 5 Dec 1958, p. 7; Mary Watson, 'When Should They Start Dating?', *Evening News*, 30 May 1958, p. 5.

14 'William Hickey', 'Life With Behan', *Daily Express*, 1 June 1957, p. 7.

15 Felix Barber, 'Humour Rides The Storm', *Evening News*, 15 Oct 1958, p. 3; Robert Pitman, 'Mr Behan of Dublin makes the potted plants shake', *Sunday Express*, 12 Oct 1958, p. 6.

16 A. Alvarez, 'Exile's Return', *Partisan Review* 26 (1959), pp. 285–7. The first issue of *Universities and Left Review* appeared in Spring 1957.

17 Recalled by Raymond Williams in 'The reasonable Englishman', review of Richard Hoggart, *An English Temper*, *Guardian*, 8 April 1982, p. 16.

18 Graham Greene and John Sutro, Letter, *Spectator*, 10 Feb 1956, p. 182; the idea for the allegorical portrait of Gordon was forwarded by A. Livesey, Letter, *Spectator*, 17 Feb 1956, p. 214, and Greene reported censorship proposals mooted at the inaugural meeting of 'The John Gordon Society' in the *Spectator*, 6 March 1956, p. 309.

19 'The First Edition Of Lolita', *Evening News*, 6 Nov 1959, p. 1.

20 John Carpenter, 'Salford's Shelagh wakes up to a £90 bill', *Evening News*, 11 Feb 1959, p. 4; John Carpenter, 'Shelagh waits', *Evening News*, 17 Feb 1959, p. 4.

21 Osborne, interviewed by Roy Plomley, *Desert Island Discs*, BBC Radio 4, 27 Feb 1982.
22 Derek Monsey, 'Mr Harvey has a way with the women', *Sunday Express*, 25 Jan 1959, p. 17; John Waterman, 'Mr Harvey puts an X in Yorkshire', *Evening Standard*, 22 Jan 1959, p. 13; Frank Jackson, 'Here's a film that's torrid and true', *Reynolds News*, 25 Jan 1959, p. 7.
23 A more striking change in the status of an original work happened to *The Entertainer* when Four Square Books published John Burke's novel of the film of the play in 1960.

Four: 'Beginning with Amis'

This chapter's title was the headline for David Wright's review of *That Uncertain Feeling* in *Time and Tide*, 27 Aug 1955, p. 1114.

1 Kingsley Amis, 'Oxford and After', in Anthony Thwaite (ed.), *Larkin at Sixty*, (London, Faber & Faber, 1982), pp. 28–9.
2 Personal interview with Kingsley Amis, 30 Nov 1984; Gollancz was quoted by Kenneth Allsop, 'Prophet who sells sermons by the millions', *Daily Mail*, 26 Oct 1960, p. 10.
3 This was recalled by P. H. Newby in an interview with Kate Whitehead. I am indebted to both for allowing permission to cite this recollection.
4 J. Maclaren-Ross, 'High Jinks and Dirty Work', *Sunday Times*, 24 Jan 1954, p. 5; 'Standing Alone', *The Times*, 27 Jan 1954, p. 8; John Metcalf, 'New Novels', *Spectator*, 29 Jan 1954, p. 132; A[nthony] P[owell], untitled review of *Lucky Jim*, *Punch*, 3 Feb. 1954, p. 188; John Betjeman, 'Amusing Story of Life at a Provincial University', *Daily Telegraph*, 5 Feb 1954, p. 8.
5 Personal interview with Amis.
6 Rex Warner, untitled review of *That Uncertain Feeling*, *London Magazine*, Dec 1955, pp. 75–6; Philip Oakes, 'Recent fiction', *Truth*, 26 Aug 1955, pp. 1077–8.
7 See, for example, Philip Toynbee, 'Class Comedy', *Observer*, 21 Aug 1955, p. 9; Isabel Quigly, 'New Novels', *Spectator*, 2 Sept 1955, pp. 316–7; 'Social Misfits', *TLS*, 16 Sept 1955, p. 537.
8 John Connell, 'Booby's Progress', *Evening News*, 27 Aug 1955, p. 4; Elizabeth Bowen, 'An African Boyhood', *Tatler*, 7 Sept 1955, p. 416.
9 J. Maclaren-Ross, 'New Novels', *Listener*, 8 Sept 1955, p. 391.
10 Peter Quennell, 'Bird Men *Are* Just a Flight of Imagination', *Daily Mail*, 26 Aug 1955, p. 6.
11 Stephen Spender, *The Struggle of the Modern* (1963, repr. London, Methuen, 1965), p. 58.
12 Wright, 'Beginning with Amis', p. 1114.

13 Personal interview with Amis.
14 Kenneth Tynan, 'The Voice of the Young', *Observer*, 13 May 1956, p. 11; T. C. Worsley, 'A Test Case', *New Statesman*, 19 May 1956, p. 566; the 'unlucky Jim' description was used by Derek Grainger, 'Look Back In Anger', *Financial Times*, 9 May 1956, p. 2, and supplied the title for John Beavan's review in *Twentieth Century*, July 1956, pp. 72–4.
15 Colm Brogan, 'Lucky George', *Spectator*, 6 July 1956, pp. 36, 38. J. G. Weightman thought that many intellectuals were, like Colm Brogan, forming hostile views of redbrick universities based on the reputation of *Lucky Jim* ('The Uneasy Don', *Twentieth Century*, Feb 1956, p. 139); J. B. Priestley, for example, had berated 'the new and deliberate loutishness among so many of the younger lecturers in provincial universities' in *Journey Down a Rainbow* (co-written with Jacquetta Hawkes), (London, Heinemann-Cresset, 1955), p. 91
16 Arnold Kettle, 'Some of My Best Friends are Intellectuals', review of Kingsley Amis, *Socialism and the Intellectuals*, *Daily Worker*, 12 Feb 1957, p. 2.
17 Two of Amis's television appearances in the fifties were on BBC's *Monitor* when he was interviewed by Simon Raven on 2 Feb 1958 and on ITV's *The Western* on 4 Nov 1959; popular press interest in Amis is shown in items such as 'William Hickey's' coverage of his move to Peterhouse College, Cambridge in the *Daily Express* on 1 March 1961, p. 3, and a report in the *Sunday Dispatch* of his sabbatical year in the United States by Christopher Lucas, ' "Lucky Jim" Barnstorms Princeton, US', 12 Oct 1958, p. 14; Hilary Amis, 'Why I married Lucky Jim', *Daily Mail*, 20 Feb 1958, p. 8.
18 Kettle, 'Some of My Best Friends are Intellectuals', p. 2; Kingsley Amis, 'Amis replies to Kettle', *Daily Worker*, 14 Feb 1957, p. 2; Kingsley Amis, 'The group *I* don't belong to', *Daily Express*, 7 Jan 1957, p. 4; *Reynolds News* announced the serialization on the front page (*What Did* Kingsley Amis *Say*?', 20 Jan 1957), and published two extracts–'The Egg-Heads and I–and the way we look at Socialism', 20 Jan 1957, p. 3, and 'Something to get angry about', 27 Jan 1957, p. 3.
19 Personal interview with Amis.
20 Ivon Adams, 'Lucky Face', *Star*, 26 Sept 1957, p. 12; Anthony Carthew, 'Redbrick Life', *Daily Herald*, 27 Sept 1957, p. 6; Harold Conway, 'Lucky Jim! It's Fun, Fun, Funny', *Daily Sketch*, 27 Sept 1957, p. 12.
21 William Cooper, 'It's not so funny, Mr Amis', *News Chronicle*, 15 Jan 1958, p. 6; G. S. Fraser, 'New Novels', *New Statesman*, 18 Jan 1958, p. 77.
22 Penelope Mortimer, 'The Old and the Young', *Sunday Times*, 12 Jan

1958, p. 9; Kenneth Young, 'A Trip Abroad for Lucky Jim', *Daily Telegraph*, 17 Jan 1958, p. 13.

23 Simon Raven, 'The Kingsley Amis Story', *Spectator*, 17 Jan 1958, p. 79; Angela Milne, 'The Lucky Touch of Success', *Sketch*, 29 Jan 1958, p. 126.

24 David Wright, 'Lucky Jim Abroad', *Time and Tide*, 18 Jan 1958, p. 75; Paul Johnson, 'Lucky Jim's Political Testament', *New Statesman*, 12 Jan 1957, p. 35.

25 This literary chimera was discussed by Elizabeth Berridge, 'Is There A Chill Wind Blowing Through The Literary Palm Courts?', *Books and Bookmen*, Nov 1956, p. 11.

26 This phrase was employed by Angus Wilson to deride those who were apparently reading novels as sources of trite sociological interest; 'Mood of the Month–III', *London Magazine*, April 1958, p. 44.

27 A. J. P. Taylor, 'Look Back at the Fifties: (i) Backwards to Utopia', *New Statesman*, 2 Jan 1960, p. 5.

28 This phrase comes from Mary Scrutton, 'Comments on a Case-History', *Twentieth Century*, Feb 1956, p. 165.

29 These opinions come, respectively, from Kenneth Tynan, 'The Men Of Anger', *Holiday*, April 1958, p. 93; David Marquand, 'Lucky Jim and the Labour Party', *Universities and Left Review* 1 (1957), p. 58; Christopher Hollis, 'Keeping Up With the Rices', *Spectator*, 18 Oct 1957, p. 504.

30 These qualities were identified by, respectively, Simon Raven, 'Dies Irae', review of Paul Ferris, *A Changed Man*, *Spectator*, 7 Feb 1958, p. 179; Allsop, *The Angry Decade*, p. 21; 'Time To Stand And Stare', review of Michael Swan, *A Small Part of Time*, *TLS*, 5 July 1957, p. 408.

31 Bonamy Dobrée, 'No Man's Land', *Sewanee Review* 65 (1957), l. 314. Dobrée's hostility might be partly explained by the fact that he was widely rumoured to be the 'original' of Professor Welch.

32 Kingsley Amis, 'Situations come first–themes later', *Morning Star*, 16 May 1965, p. 4.

33 Kingsley Amis, 'Real and made-up people', *TLS*, 27 July 1973, p. 847.

34 Amis, quoted by Kevin Byrne, 'The Two Amises', *Listener*, 15 Aug 1974, p. 219; personal interview with Amis.

35 Personal interview with Amis.

36 Amis, quoted by Clive James, 'Kingsley Amis–A Profile', *New Review*, July 1974, p. 22; Amis, quoted by Pearson Phillips, 'How the angry brigade got lucky', *Observer*, 17 Sept 1978, p. 35.

37 See, for example, the Letters Amis has written to correct reviewers who have made this mistake: *Listener*, 29 July 1954, p. 179; *London Magazine*, Dec 1957, p. 55; *Observer*, 13 Oct 1968, p. 11, and 19 Sept 1982, p. 26.

38 See J. E. Floud et al., *Social Class and Educational Opportunity*, (London, Heinemann, 1956), pp. 122–3.

39 D. V. Glass and J. R. Hall, 'Social Mobility in Great Britain: A Study of Inter-Generation Changes in Status', in D. V. Glass (ed.), *Social Mobility in Britain* (London, Routledge & Kegan Paul, 1954), p. 217.

40 Kingsley Amis, 'Lone Voices', *Encounter*, July 1960, p. 8; Amis had complained about the poor standards of university entrants in a Letter, *Twentieth Century*, March 1956, pp. 286–7.

41 Amis first defended the Welfare State in a Letter, *Listener*, 13 May 1954, p. 829, and then in a remark to Daniel Farson, 'I Meet A Genius With Indigestion', *Daily Mail*, 13 July 1956, p. 4. The confession of his relative apathy came in his *Daily Express* article 'The group *I* don't belong to', and the misleading impression of his political extremism was given by 'Peter Simple', in 'Amis Go Home', *Daily Telegraph*, 3 July 1958, p. 10.

42 Personal interview with Amis.

43 Larkin, Interview with *Paris Review*, in Philip Larkin, *Required Writing* (London, Faber & Faber, 1983), p. 63.

Five: 'Class Comedy'

The chapter title was the headline for a review of *That Uncertain Feeling* by Philip Toynbee, *Observer*, 21 Aug 1955, p. 9.

1 Kingsley Amis, untitled contribution to James Vinson (ed.), *Contemporary Novelists* (London, St James Press, 1972), p. 46

2 Kingsley Amis, 'Communication and the Victorian Poet', *Essays in Criticism* 4 (1954), l. 399.

3 Kingsley Amis, 'Anglo-Saxon Platitudes', review of *Beowulf*, trans. David Wright, *Spectator*, 5 April 1957, p. 445.

4 Kingsley Amis, 'Fresh Winds from the West', *Spectator*, 2 May 1958, pp. 565–6, and 'New Novels', review of Godfrey Smith, *The Flaw in the Crystal*, *Spectator*, 19 March 1954, p. 336; John Wain, 'What The Critics Missed In My Book', *Books and Bookmen*, Dec 1955, p. 15.

5 Kingsley Amis, interviewed by Walter Allen, in *We Write Novels*, BBC Third Programme, 23 June 1955.

6 Kingsley Amis, 'Emily-Coloured Primulas', *Essays in Criticism* 2 (1952), 342–5, and 'Ulster Bull: The Case of W. R. Rodgers', *Essays in Criticism* 3 (1953), p.470–5.

7 Kingsley Amis, 'Thomas the Rhymer', review of Dylan Thomas, *A Prospect of the Sea*, *Spectator*, 12 Aug 1955, p. 227, and 'She Was a Child and I Was a Child', review of *Lolita*, *Spectator*, 6 Nov 1959, p. 635.

8 Kingsley Amis, review of Bernard Fergusson, *The Rare Adventure*, *Spectator*, 29 Oct 1954, p. 534.

9 These remarks occur, respectively, in Amis' reviews of Gwyn Thomas, *The Stranger at My Side*, *Spectator*, 23 July 1954, p. 126; 'Is the Travel-Book Dead?', review of Laurie Lee, *A Rose for Winter*, and Peter Mayne, *The Narrow Smile*, *Spectator*, 17 June 1955, p. 774; and 'Waving the Leek', review of Gwyn Jones (ed.), *Welsh Short Stories*, *Spectator*, 6 July 1956, p. 33.

10 Personal interview with Amis, 30 Nov 1984.

11 Amis quoted by Michael Davie, 'Lucky Jim discovers there's life after 60', *Observer*, 25 April 1982, p. 16; Amis, *Comment*, Channel 4, 1 May 1984; Amis, Introduction to his *Collected Short Stories* (London, Hutchinson, 1980), p. 11; Amis, *An Arts Policy?*, Centre for Policy Studies pamphlet (London, 1979).

12 Amis stated this preference to Walter Allen on *We Write Novels.*.

13 Amis, untitled contribution to *Contemporary Novelists*, p. 46.

14 David Lodge, *The Modes of Modern Writing: Metaphor, Metonymy, and the Typology of Modern Literature* (London, Edward Arnold, 1977).

15 These are the classifications made by V. I. Propp in his *Morphology of the Folk-tale*, as detailed in Terence Hawkes, *Structuralism and Semiotics* (London, Methuen & Co., 1977), p. 69.

16 Personal interview with Amis. See also Amis's comment that characters with Jim's background were 'under-represented in the then standard English novel'. (Kingsley Amis, 'From the Fifties: Lucky Jim', *Radio Times*, 30 Nov 1961, p. 23.)

17 Angus Wilson, 'If It's New and Modish Is It Good?', *New York Times Book Review*, 2 July 1961, p. 1; Pamela Hansford Johnson, 'The Sick-room Hush over the English Novel', *Listener*, 11 Aug 1949, p. 236; William Cooper, 'Reflections on some Aspects of the Experimental Novel', in John Wain (ed.), *International Literary Annual* 2 (London, John Calder, 1959), pp. 35–6.

18 Personal interview with William Cooper, 23 Nov 1984. In fact, Amis *had* read Cooper's novel and admired it for at last portraying a 'hearteningly recognizable' world. (Kingsley Amis, 'What Marriage Did for Our Joe,' review of *Scenes from Provincial Life* and *Scenes from Married Life*, *Observer*, 29 Jan 1961, p. 28.)

19 Christopher Ricks, ' "I was like that myself once"', review of Amis, *What Became of Jane Austen?*, *Listener*, 26 Nov 1970, p. 739; Kingsley Amis, 'That Certain Revulsion', *Encore*, June–July 1957, p. 10.

20 Amis' remarks come from 'She Was a Child', p. 635, and 'In Defence of Dons', in *Literary Opinion* 3 BBC Third Programme, 9 June 1954, respectively.

21 Personal interview with Amis. In a Letter to the author of 24 July 1986 Amis qualified the 'Modernist' classification of his early work. An early poem, 'Prelude', written in the summer of 1939, he remembers as a 'suburbanite's Waste Land', but a more typical effort is probably 'He

Reads Immortality In The Eyes Of A Virgin', published in the City of London School magazine in 1940, which, like many of the poems in *Bright November*, is not experimental in any way but terribly melodramatic and intense along the usual adolescent-Romantic lines.

22 Personal interview with Amis.

23 Amis, quoted by Dale Salwak, 'An interview with Kingsley Amis', *Contemporary Literature* 16 (1975), p. 8; Amis, 'That Certain Revulsion', p. 10.

24 Personal interview with Amis.

25 Ibid.

26 Ibid.

27 Philip Toynbee, 'Young mandarins for old', review of Robert Hewison, *In Anger*, *Observer*, 5 April 1981, p. 28.

28 Toynbee, ibid.

29 Edward Shils, 'The Intellectuals:– (I) Great Britain', *Encounter*, April 1955, pp. 5–16; N. G. Annan, 'The Intellectual Aristocracy', in J. H. Plumb (ed.), *Studies in Social History: A Tribute to G. M. Trevelyan* (London, Longmans, Green, 1955), pp. 241–87.

30 Henry Fairlie, 'Political Commentary', *Spectator*, 23 Sept 1955, p. 380; C. P. Snow, 'The Periodical Press: 5. Monthlies and the Less Frequent', *Author* 66 (Autumn, 1955), p. 4.

31 Amis, 'In Defence of Dons',

32 Simon Raven, 'The Kingsley Amis Story', *Spectator*, 17 Jan 1958, p. 79; Philip Oakes, 'A New Style in Heroes', *Observer*, 1 Jan 1956, p. 8; Norman Shrapnel, 'Spender hero–Amis hero', review of *I Like It Here*, *Manchester Guardian*, 4 Feb 1958, p. 4.

33 Martin Green, 'Home Thoughts From Abroad and Vice Versa', *Quixote* 7 and 8 (1955–6, pp. 42–51; repr. in *A Mirror for Anglo-Saxons* (London, Longmans, 1961), p.15; C. P. Snow, 'The Two Cultures', *New Statesman*, 6 Oct 1956, p. 413. See J. G. Weightman's contrast between the *Lucky Jim*-inspired image of redbrick students as boors and the opposing caricature of privileged university aesthetes as 'delicate sodomites with the right vocabulary' ('The Uneasy Don', *Twentieth Century*, Feb 1956, p. 139). These class-culture-sexuality connotations die hard, as Peter Porter's jibe at images of 'England's effete literary Establishment' shows ('A land fit for conservatives', *TLS*, 30 July 1971, p. 892).

34 Toynbee, 'Young mandarins for old', p. 28; T. C. Worsley, 'Horizon', *New Statesman*, 10 Dec 1949, p. 694.

35 Stephen Spender, 'A Literary Letter From London', *New York Times Book Review*, 10 Jan 1954, p. 14; Stephen Potter, *Some Notes on Lifemanship* (London, Hart-Davis, 1950) – chapter 5 on 'Writership' includes accounts of 'Newstatesmanship', 'Rilking', and literary Francophilia.

36 Kingsley Amis, 'The Legion of the Lost', review of *The Outsider*, *Spectator*, 15 June 1956, p. 830, and 'Anglo-Saxon Platitudes', p. 445.

37 Kingsley Amis, 'Editor's Notes', review of John Lehmann, *The Whispering Gallery*, *Spectator*, 7 Oct 1955, p. 459.

38 Kingsley Amis, 'Connolly in Court', *New Statesman*, 6 Dec 1963, pp. 836, 838; Amis stamped his laconic hallmark on his first review for the *Spectator* ('Talk About Laugh', 20 Nov 1953, p. 595) when he announced that the humour of *Thurber Country* 'will prevent me from flogging my review copy'.

39 Personal interview with William Cooper; Angus Wilson, 'If It's New And Modish Is It Good?', p. 12. Cecil's title made him a favourite target for anti-Mandarins; John Raymond was another who singled him out for attack, enrolling him in the 'Yum-Yum charm school of literary enjoyment that is the logical and deathly end-product of the mandarin tradition'. ('Talking Turkey,' review of John Wain, *Preliminary Essays*, *New Statesman*, 10 Aug 1957, p. 179.)

40 Harold Nicolson, 'Urbanity', *Spectator*, 28 March 1958, p. 384.

41 Simon Raven, Letter, *London Magazine*, Oct 1955, p. 68; G. S. Fraser was the first to presume a Leavisite influence on the *First Reading* contributors (see his first Letter about the broadcasts to the *New Statesman*, 1 Aug 1953, p. 132), and Walter Allen invoked Leavis' name in his review of *Lucky Jim* ('New Novels', *New Statesman*, 30 Jan 1954, p. 136).

42 Robert Conquest recalls that Leavis condemned Amis as a 'pornographer' upon Amis' appointment at Peterhouse College (Conquest, 'Profile', *Listener*, 9 Oct 1969, p. 485); the Leavises later condemned Amis in print in *Dickens the Novelist* (London, Chatto & Windus, 1970) in a long and irate footnote on p. 141.

43 Personal interview with Amis.

44 I had thought it unnecessary to add this point, until, just before I wrote this passage, the Conservative Government's Junior Health Minister, Ms Edwina Currie, criticized 'Northerners' for excessive crisp-eating and other dietary crimes.

45 John Wain, Letter, *Encounter*, June 1955, p. 68; Anthony Hartley, 'Poets of the Fifties,' *Spectator*, 27 Aug 1954, p. 260; Stephen Spender, 'On Literary Movements', *Encounter*, Nov 1953, p. 67.

46 Spender, 'A Literary Letter From London', p. 14.

47 Kingsley Amis, 'What Marriage Did for our Joe', *Spectator*, 29 Jan 1961, p. 28.

48 Kingsley Amis, 'Lone Voices', *Encounter*, July 1960, p. 11.

49 John Metcalf, 'New Fiction,' review of W. D. Pereira, *Time of Departure*, etc., *Sunday Times*, 25 Nov 1956, p. 7; J. G. Weightman, review of *Socialism and the Intellectuals*, *Twentieth Century*, Feb 1957, p. 180; Sam Hynes, 'Random Events and Random Characters',

review of *I Like It Here*, *Commonweal*, 21 March 1958, p. 642.

50 Hugh Massingham, 'British Intellectuals on Strike', review of
Socialism and the Intellectuals, *New Republic*, 4 March 1957, p. 10;
Howard Sergeant and Dannie Abse (eds.), *Mavericks* (London,
Editions Poetry and Poverty, 1957), p. 9; 'The Listener's Book
Chronicle', *Listener*, 15 Nov 1956, p. 809.

51 Alexander Baron, '"You Can't Help Laughing"', *Books and
Bookmen*, Feb 1956, p. 9.

52 'The New Provincialism', *Spectator*, 1 April 1955, p. 396.

53 Richard Lister, 'New Novels', review of James Lord, *No Traveller
Returns*, etc., *New Statesman*, 24 Sept 1955, p. 373.

54 Peter Forster, 'Novel and not so Novel', *Books and Bookmen*, July
1956, p. 9.

55 David Wright, 'A Small Green Insect Shelters In The Bowels Of My
Quivering Typewriter', *Encounter*, Oct 1956, p. 76–7.

56 V. S. Pritchett, 'First Stop Reading!' *New Statesman*, 3 Oct 1953,
p. 379; Stephen Spender, 'Speaking Of Books', *New York Times
Book Review*, 1 Aug 1954, p. 2, and 'Letter to a Young Writer',
Encounter, March 1954, p. 5.

57 Amis, 'In Defence of Dons'.

58 Amis, 'Lone Voices', p. 10; Salwak, 'An Interview with Kingsley
Amis', p. 1.

59 Personal interview with Malcolm Bradbury, 8 Dec 1983; Charles
Tomlinson, 'The Middlebrow Muse', review of *New Lines*, *Essays in
Criticism* 7 (1957), p. 216.

60 Walter Allen, 'Words In Spate', review of Dylan Thomas, *Quite
Early One Morning*, *New Statesman*, 6 Nov 1954, p. 586.

61 Amis, interviewed in Peter Firchow (ed.), *The Writer's Place:
Interviews on the Literary Situation in Contemporary Britain*,
(Minneapolis, University of Minnesota Press, 1977) pp. 22–43; Amis,
'Communication and the Victorian Poet', p. 386.

62 These classifications were made by John Metcalf, 'The Little
American Girl', review of Marshall Pugh, *A Wilderness of Monkeys*,
Sunday Times, 19 Jan 1958, p. 7; Paul Johnson, 'Counter-
Revolutionaries', review of George Scott, *Time and Place*, *New
Statesman*, 30 June 1956, p. 768; and Robert Frith, 'Lucky Jim, MD',
review of Dr Hamilton Johnston, *The Doctor's Signature*, *Books and
Art*, Nov 1957, p. 34.

63 Simon Raven, 'Dies Irae', *Spectator*, 7 Feb 1958, p. 179; Henry
Drown, 'New Novels', *Time and Tide*, 8 Feb 1958, p. 171.

64 Francis Wyndham, untitled review of *Happy as Larry*, *London
Magazine*, May 1957, p. 77; J. I. M. Stewart, 'New Novels', *New
Statesman*, 26 Jan 1957, pp. 108–9.

65 Both authors insisted in correspondence that their books could not

have been influenced by Amis's fiction. Letter received from Paul Ferris, 27 March 1983 and 29 May 1983, letter received from Thomas Hinde, 1 Feb 1984.

66 The phrase comes from an unsigned article, 'An Anti-Creep Movement', *Books and Bookmen*, April 1957, p. 3.

Six: 'The Biggest AYM in the Business'

The title of this chapter was the title for a review by John Osborne of Vladimir Dudintsev's *Not By Bread Alone*, in *Books and Art*, Oct 1957, pp. 7–8.

1 Osborne interviewed by Roy Plomley, *Desert Island Discs*, BBC Radio 4, 27 Feb 1982.

2 Angus Wilson, 'The Novelist and the Theatre', *Observer*, 18 March 1956, p.16.

3 T. C. Worsley, 'A Writer's Theatre', *New Statesman*, 24 March 1956, p. 272.

4 Osborne interviewed by Ian Hamilton, 'Still Angry After All Those Years', *Bookmark*, BBC2, 10 April 1986.

5 Harold Hobson and Osborne recalled the play's first night in interviews on 'Still Angry After All those Years.'

6 Kenneth Tynan's recollections were broadcast on 'Still Angry After All Those Years.'

7 Osborne recalled his reaction to the first-night reviews in his appearance on *Desert Island Discs*.

8 *Look Back in Anger*'s weekly takings are detailed by John Russell Taylor, *Anger and After: a guide to the new British drama* (London, Methuen, rev. edn. 1969), p. 35; Osborne–or rather, in this case, Jimmy Porter–was described as 'the angriest young man of them all' by James Gordon, 'A Short Directory to Angry Young Men', *Good Housekeeping*, Jan 1958, p. 93. The appearance of *Look Back in Anger* on television and news of Osborne's suit for divorce combined to give him as much media attention as Colin Wilson. On 22 March 1957, Osborne eventually matched Wilson by being interviewed on ITV when he appeared in conversation with Bernard Braden on *Contact*.

9 John Osborne, 'You've Fallen For The Great Swindle', *News Chronicle*, 27 Feb 1957, p. 4.

10 John Osborne, 'What's gone wrong with WOMEN?', *Daily Mail*, 14 Nov 1956, p. 10; in his review 'The Biggest AYM in the Business', Osborne also applied the catchphrase to Dudintsev.

11 These events were reported by, respectively, 'William Hickey', 'Angrier Than Ever', *Daily Express*, 16 April 1957, p. 4; Nigel Harris and David Steel, 'Young Men–But Not Angry', *Reynolds News*,

11 Aug 1957, p. 7; Robert Wraight, 'Is Sir Larry's Play Obscene?',
    Star, 13 Sept 1957, pp. 1, 16.
12 See, for example, Osborne's dutifully heated and contentious articles,
    'What's gone wrong with WOMEN?', 'You've Fallen For The Great
    Swindle', and 'I want more fighting talk', *Reynolds News*, 17 Feb 1957,
    p. 3. Osborne was soon rewarded for his stirring performances in print
    with a position as guest television critic for the *Evening Standard*, from
    4 to 9 March 1957.
13 For example, Christopher Hollis was beginning to doubt the validity of
    the AYM label after reading *Lucky Jim* and meeting Colin Wilson, but
    revived his enthusiasm for the new literary protesters after
    interviewing Osborne for the *Spectator*: 'Keeping Up With the Rices',
    18 Oct 1957, pp. 504–5.
14 The phrase appeared as the headline for Tynan's review of *Look Back
    in Anger* for the *Observer*; only Derek Grainger and John Barber, in
    the *Financial Times* and *Daily Express* notices of the play, had
    anticipated Tynan in hailing Osborne/Porter as representatives of the
    younger generation.
15 See, for example, Cecil Wilson, 'This actor is a great writer', *Daily
    Mail*, 9 May 1956, p, 3; Robert Tee, 'So Angry–And Distasteful',
    Daily Mirror, 9 May 1956, p. 16; and Derek Monsey, 'Miss Robson's
    Wavelength', *Sunday Express*, 13 May 1956, p. 10.
16 Reported by Bill Hopkins, 'John Osborne: From Anger to Elegance at
    £3,000 a week', *Lilliput*, April 1959, pp. 21–9
17 For example, as Allsop noted in *The Angry Decade*, *The Times*
    greeted *Look Back in Anger*'s return to the Royal Court in March 1957
    with obedient enthusiasm, praising its 'air of desperate sincerity' and
    comparing Osborne to the young Noël Coward as the voice of his
    generation, whereas the first-night reviewer for *The Times* had
    dismissed the play, summing up that it had 'passages of good violent
    writing, but its total gesture is altogether inadequate'.
18 Kenneth Tynan, 'Look Behind the Anger', *Observer*, 27 Dec 1959,
    p. 7; Arnold Wesker has said, 'Seeing *Look Back in Anger* sparked me
    to write *Chicken Soup with Barley*.' (In Ena Kendall, 'A Room Of My
    Own: Arnold Wesker', *Observer Magazine*, 20 Jan 1985, pp. 32–3.)
19 Hobson made this point on 'Still Angry After All Those Years.'

Seven: 'Outsider In'

The title of this chapter appeared as a heading in the *Times Educational
Supplement* for an item on Colin Wilson on 13 July 1956, p. 934.

1 John Applebey, 'Looking at Life–and Finding it All a Sham', *Daily
    Telegraph*, 8 June 1956, p. 8; Mary Scrutton, 'Outsiderismus', *New*

Statesman, 16 June 1956, p. 700; Elizabeth Bowen, 'Dwellers in the Wilderness', *Tatler*, 27 June 1956, p. 697; V. S. Pritchett, review of *The Outsider* on *Talking of Books*, BBC Home Service, 24 June 1956; (Kenneth Walker,) 'The Listener's Book Chronicle', *Listener*, 7 June 1956, p. 767.

2 Kingsley Amis, 'The Legion of the Lost'; *Spectator*, 15 June 1956, pp. 830–1; Burns Singer, 'The Heavenly Disease', *Time and Tide*, 9 June 1956, p. 686; 'Chosen Few', *TLS*, 8 June 1956, p. 342.

3 'Intellectual Thriller', *Time*, 2 July 1956, p. 62; Harvey Breit, 'In And Out Of Books', *New York Times Book Review*, 1 July 1956, p. 8.

4 Examples of Wilson's contributions to the popular press are his untitled article in the *Daily Express* on 14 Sept 1956, p. 6; 'I Hate the Mob Mentality', *Reynolds News*, 3 Feb 1957, p. 3; and 'The Frenchman', *Evening Standard*, 22 Aug 1957, p. 10; the BBC sent its first invitation to Wilson to make a broadcast on 22 June 1956 and his first talk, *What I Believe*, was transmitted on 30 Sept.

5 Malcolm Bradbury, 'Notes from the Provinces', *Punch*, 31 Dec 1958, pp. 867–9; Malcolm Bradbury and Dudley Andrew, 'The Sugar Beet Generation: A Note in English Intellectual History', *Texas Quarterly* 3 (Winter 1960), pp. 38–47.

6 Daniel Farson, 'Two Lost Generations', *Books and Bookmen*, Sept 1956, p. 18; Daniel Farson, 'My Genius', *Books and Art*, Oct 1957, pp. 24–5; Farson reflected on the results of his interviews with Wilson in his autobiography, *Out of Step* (London, Michael Joseph, 1974), p. 135.

7 'William Hickey', 'Out goes the Outsider's first play', *Daily Express*, 28 Sept 1957, p. 3; 'John London', 'Slanging-match', *News Chronicle*, 30 Sept 1957, p. 3; 'Peter Simple', 'Out of Court', *Daily Telegraph*, 1 Oct 1957, p. 10.

8 Colin Wilson, 'The Writer and Publicity; A Reply to Critics', *Encounter*, Nov 1959, p. 13.

9 Wilson, quoted by Farson, in 'My Genius', p. 24.

10 Wilson, quoted by Farson in *Out of Step*, p. 136, and by Sidney R. Campion, *The World of Colin Wilson: A Biographical Study* (London, Frederick Muller, 1962), p. 215.

11 Wilson's articles and the responses to them were as follows: 'A Writer's Prospect–II', *London Magazine*, Aug 1956, pp. 48–55, and R. W. Gaskell and Elizabeth Jennings, Letters, *London Magazine*, Oct 1956, pp. 54–7; review of Crawford Knox, *The Idiom of Contemporary Thought*, and J. P. Hodin, *The Dilemma of Being Modern*, *London Magazine*, Jan 1957, pp. 63–6, and Donald Davie, Letter, *London Magazine*, Feb 1957, p. 61; 'The Brainless Superman', review of Graham Hough, *The Dark Sun*, *Listener*, 6 Dec 1956, p. 951, and Maurice Cranston, Letter, *Listener*, 13 Dec 1956, p. 1001,

Geoffrey Gorer, Letter, *Listener*, 20 Dec 1956, p. 1037; 'I Hate the Mob Mentality', p. 3, and Wolf Mankowitz, 'Go second-class–you'll be first-rate', *Reynolds News*, 10 Feb 1957, p. 3.

12 A transcript of the symposium was published in *Encore*, June–July 1957, pp. 13–35; 'Peter Simple', *Daily Telegraph*, 27 Nov 1956, p. 8.

13 Alan Brockbank, 'Colin Wilson finds a New Religion', *Sunday Dispatch*, 15 Sept 1957, p. 4.

14 Janet Adam Smith, 'Little Wotting at Little Gidding', *New Statesman*, 26 Oct 1957, p. 536.

15 'Eight Self-Starters Without A Single Engine', *The Times*, 24 Oct 1957, p. 13; Iris Murdoch, 'Concepts or Blood', *Manchester Guardian*, 25 Oct 1957, p. 6; A. J. Ayer, 'Folie de Grandeur', *Spectator*, 25 Oct 1957, p. 550.

16 These quotations are from, respectively, Anthony Hartley, 'The Cult of Colin Wilson', *Books and Art*, Dec 1957, p. 51; Raymond Mortimer, 'Not Angry Enough', *Sunday Times*, 20 Oct 1957, p. 6; George Malcolm Thomson, 'The Outsider Finds It Hard to Be Original', *Evening Standard*, 22 Oct 1957, p. 14; Philip Toynbee, 'Unhappy Sequel', *Observer*, 20 Oct 1957, p. 18.

17 'Not The Cream But The Top Off The Milk', *TLS*, 8 Nov 1957, p. 674; Iain Hamilton, 'Enough of Their Guff', *Spectator*, 18 Oct 1957, p. 520; Peter Green, 'Child's Guide to the AYMs', *Time and Tide*, 2 Nov 1957, p. 1370.

18 'Credits and Discredits Of 1957', *Books and Bookmen*, Jan 1958, p. 3.

19 Bromley Abbott, 'To Work!', *Sunday Dispatch*, 1 Dec 1957, p. 2; 'John London', 'So satisfied', *News Chronicle*, 23 Oct 1957, p. 3; 'Our London Correspondence', *Manchester Guardian*, 30 Oct 1957, p. 6.

20 Jean Leroy, Letter to P. H. Newby, 6 Jan 1959; P. H. Newby, Letter to Jean Leroy, 27 Jan 1959. Both letters held in the BBC Colin Wilson file.

21 The three items were reported in the *News Chronicle*'s 'John London' column: 'Inkpen assignment', 10 Sept 1958, p. 3; 'Blossoming', 26 Sept 1958, p. 3; 'Wanted–£5,000', 26 Feb 1959, p. 3.

Eight: 'Egghead, scrambled'

The title of this chapter was the caption to a photograph of Colin Wilson in 'The Tohu-Bohu Kid', review of *Religion and the Rebel, Time*, 18 Nov 1957, p. 123.

1 Stephen Toulmin, *Foresight and Understanding: An enquiry into the aims of science* (London, Hutchinson, 1961), p. 18.

2 See Wilson's Postscript to *The Outsider* (1967; repr. London, Picador, 1978), pp. 304–5, and *Order of Assassins: The Psychology of Murder* (London, Hart-Davis, 1972), p. 153.

3 Cited by Sidney R. Campion, *The World of Colin Wilson: A Biographical Study* (London, Frederick Muller, 1962), p. 111.

4 Wilson reviewed Hopkins' novel on *Just Published*, BBC West of England Home Service, 22 Dec 1957.

5 Wilson, *Just Published*; Wilson denied Plowart's status as a Fascist hero in his review of *The Angry Decade*, 'So I may try to be a Hitler!', *News Chronicle*, 28 May 1958, p. 6, and in a Letter to the *TLS*, 15 Nov 1957, p. 689.

6 These quotations are taken, respectively, from the following reviews of Hopkins' novel: 'Social Allegory', *TLS*, 20 Dec 1957, p. 769; Graham Hough, 'New Novels', *Encounter*, Feb 1958, p. 86; Robert Waller, in *Just Published*; and G. S. Fraser, 'New Novels', *New Statesman*, 30 Nov 1957, p. 748.

7 Hopkins related the accidental incineration of his masterpieces to Peter Firchow, *The Writer's Place: Interviews on the Literary Situation in Contemporary Britain* (Minneapolis, University of Minnesota Press, 1974), p. 181.

8 Wilson, quoted by Daniel Farson, *Henry: An Appreciation of Henry Williamson* (London, Michael Joseph, 1982), p. 150; in this book Farson describes his and Allsop's admiration for Williamson, and then their introducing Wilson to him, pp. 146 ff.

9 Colin Wilson, 'The Month', *Twentieth Century*, Dec 1959, pp. 492–8; Bernard Levin, 'Spoiling the Broth', *Spectator*, 1 Jan 1960, pp. 6–7; 'Cassandra', 'The Dart of Colin Wilson', *Daily Mirror*, 10 Dec 1959, p. 6, 'My Undear Outsider', *Daily Mirror*, 15 Dec 1959, p. 4, and 'Mosley and Wilson', *Daily Mirror*, 21 Dec 1959, p. 4.

10 Iain Hamilton, 'Enough of Their Guff', *Spectator*, 18 Oct 1957, p. 520.

11 Kenneth Allsop, 'Now, Colin . . . Let's See Your Genius', *Daily Mail*, 26 Feb 1957, p. 6; Keith Waterhouse, 'Grasshopper, what are you sounding now?', *Tribune*, 1 Nov 1957, p.13.

12 For example, Nijinsky and T. E. Lawrence (two of the three figures central to chapter 4 of *The Outsider*) had enjoyed a vogue following among English aesthetes (see Martin Green, *Children of the Sun: A narrative of 'decadence' in England after 1918*, rev. edn. London: Constable, 1977). The inclusion of mystics as well as artists was especially gratifying to critics like Toynbee and Bowen, and Cyril Connolly confessed his interest quickened on reading the title, because he had earlier suggested this for the translation of Camus' novel, *L'Étranger*.

13 A. J. Ayer, *Language, Truth and Logic* (London, Victor Gollancz, 1936), p. 44.

14 Philip Toynbee, 'Academics & Journeymen', *Observer*, 25 March 1956, p. 17.

15 Kingsley Amis, Letter, *Spectator*, 8 July 1955, p. 47.

16 John Wain, 'A Writer's Prospect–IV', *London Magazine*, Nov 1956, p. 60.
17 John Lehmann, 'Foreword', *London Magazine*, Sept 1955, p. 11.
18 Walter Allen, 'Phoenix In A Mirror', *New Statesman*, 23 Jan 1954, p. 102; Jocelyn Brooke, 'The Wrong Side of the Blanket', *London Magazine*, July 1955, p. 51.
19 John Lehmann, 'Foreword', *London Magazine*, March 1954, pp. 11–12.
20 Stephen Spender, 'A Literary Letter From London', *New York Times Book Review*, 10 Jan 1954, p. 14.
21 Blake Morrison describes Movement antipathy to Thomas in *The Movement: English Poetry and Fiction of the 1950s* (Oxford, Oxford University Press, 1980), pp. 145–54.
22 Kingsley Amis, 'Grave and Gay', review of Alberto Moravia, *A Ghost at Noon*, etc., *Encounter*, April 1955, p. 78, and 'Art and Craft', review of John Lehmann (ed.), *The Craft of Letters in England*, *Spectator*, 13 July 1956, p. 69.
23 Philip Toynbee, 'Voyage of discovery', *Observer*, 27 Oct 1974, p. 30.
24 A. Alvarez, 'Exile's Return', *Partisan Review*, 26 (1959), p. 285.
25 Kingsley Amis, 'Fresh Winds from the West', *Spectator*, 2 May 1958, p. 565, and 'She Was a Child and I Was a Child', review of *Lolita*, *Spectator*, 6 Nov 1959, p. 635.
26 Raymond Williams, 'The New Party Line?', *Essays in Criticism* 7 (1957), p. 75; Bernard Bergonzi, 'Catholic Herald', review of Colin Wilson, *Man Without a Shadow*, *New Statesman*, 1 Nov 1963, p. 623.

Nine: 'Working-class Novelist'

The title for this chapter comes from the heading of an anonymous *Books and Bookmen* review of *Saturday Night and Sunday Morning*, Oct 1958, p. 16.

1 Several autobiographical essays appear in Sillitoe's collection *Mountains and Caverns* (London, W. H. Allen, 1975), including 'The Long Piece', pp. 9–40, a collation of various other autobiographical accounts; he also describes his family background in *Raw Material* (London, W. H. Allen, 1972).
2 'Working Class Novelist', p. 16; David Holloway, 'Our Al's an author now', *News Chronicle*, 15 Oct 1958, p. 6; Brian Glanville, 'Bread and cocoa memories for Alan Sillitoe', *Reynolds News*, 7 Dec 1958, p. 6; 'Life And Love In A Not So Big City', *News of the World*, 30 Nov 1958, p. 9.
3 'Blessings In Disguise', *TLS*, 7 Nov 1958, p. 646; John Wain, 'Possible Worlds', *Observer*, 12 Oct 1958, p. 20; Peter Green, 'A Tapestry of

Human Passions', *Daily Telegraph*, 17 Oct 1958, p. 15; Richard Mayne, 'Short Reports', *Sunday Times*, 12 Oct 1958, p. 18; Maurice Richardson, 'New Novels', *New Statesman*, 18 Oct 1958, pp. 539–40.

4 'New Fiction', *The Times*, 8 Oct 1959, p. 15; Pamela Hansford Johnson, 'New Novels', *New Statesman*, 3 Oct 1959, p. 448; John Bowen, 'On Making Gestures', *Sunday Times*, 20 Sept 1959, p. 18.

5 These assessments occur in, respectively, Francis Wyndham's untitled review of *The Loneliness of the Long-distance Runner*, *London Magazine*, March 1960, p. 65; Graham Hough, 'New Novels', *Listener*, 1 Oct 1959, p. 542; W. G. S., 'Short Stories', *Books and Bookmen*, Oct 1959, p. 29.

6 Thomas Wiseman, 'Everybody got me wrong, says Mr Sillitoe', *Evening Standard*, 1 Sept 1961, p. 8; Kenneth Allsop, 'I Starved . . . For Saturday Night and Sunday Morning', *Daily Mail*, 16 Feb 1961, p. 10.

7 Wiseman, 'Everybody got me wrong', p. 8.

8 The book's sales by 1961 were reported by Allsop in 'I Starved . . .', p. 10; its place in the bestsellers' hall of fame was detailed in J. A. Sutherland, *Fiction and the Fiction Industry* (London, Athlone Press, 1978), p. 176.

9 Sillitoe, 'The Long Piece', p. 37.

10 George Orwell, 'Charles Dickens', in *Inside the Whale* (London, Victor Gollancz, 1940), pp. 11–12.

11 See Alan Sillitoe's essay, 'Both Sides Of The Street', *TLS*, 8 July 1960, p. 435.

12 Sillitoe, 'The Long Piece', p. 37.

13 See, for example, Edward Shils, 'The Intellectuals:–(1) Great Britain', *Encounter*, April 1955, p. 14, and W. John Morgan, 'Furnaces Untapped', *Listener*, 5 April 1956, pp. 361, 363.

14 'The notion of commitment . . . is a characteristically French rather than English notion.' ('The Writer And The Idea', *TLS*, 26 April 1957, p. 257.) Never one to scorn a cliché, Paul Johnson said he had to live in Paris to find his political awakening and 'capacity for outrage'. ('A sense of outrage', in Norman Mackenzie (ed.), *Conviction* (London, MacGibbon & Kee, 1958), p. 208.

15 Arthur's self-limited piecework wage was good but not out of the ordinary. The average weekly earnings for an adult male in manufacturing industry were £13.5s.5d in October 1958. See Ferdynand Zweig, *The Worker in an Affluent Society* (London, William Heinemann, 1961), p. 2.

16 The new opportunities for social mobility were noticeably absent for the children from the thirty per cent of families headed by semi-skilled and unskilled workers. See Mark Abrams, 'Social Change in Modern Britain', *Political Quarterly* 30 (1959), p. 156, and J. E. Floud et al., *Social Class and Educational Opportunity* (London, William Heinemann, 1956), p. 122.

17 These phrases are taken from Wain, 'Possible Worlds', p. 20, and Ray

Perrott, 'Miss Murdoch rings the bell', review of *Saturday Night and Sunday Morning, Manchester Guardian*, 4 Nov 1958, p. 4.

18 Hough, 'New Novels', p. 542; Dee Wells, 'One boy's private war', review of *The Loneliness of the Long-distance Runner, Sunday Express*, 20 Sept 1959, p. 6.

19 Alan Sillitoe recounted the screenplay's difficulties with the censor in 'Writing and Publishing', *London Review of Books*, 1–14 April 1982, p. 8; the censor's reader's report was quoted by Ann Shearer, 'The Changing Image III', *Guardian*, 25 Feb 1985, p. 10.

20 Peter Forster, 'Benefit of the doubt for Mr Amis', review of *Take A Girl Like You, Daily Express*, 22 Sept 1960, p. 14; Simon Raven, 'The Kingsley Amis Story', *Spectator*, 17 Jan 1958, p. 79.

21 See, for example, J. R. Osgerby, 'Alan Sillitoe's *Saturday Night and Sunday Morning*', in G. R. Hibbard (ed.) *Renaissance and Modern Essays* (London, Routledge & Kegan Paul, 1966), pp. 215–30; and Allen Richard Penner, *Alan Sillitoe* (New York, Twayne, 1972), p. 76.

22 Alan Sillitoe, 'My Israel', *New Statesman*, 20 Dec 1974, p. 890.

23 The quotations come from Sillitoe's articles, 'Proletarian Novelists', *Books and Bookmen*, Aug 1959, p. 13, and 'Both Sides Of The Street', p. 435.

24 Sillitoe's letter to Owen Leeming is dated 17 Dec 1959 and held in the BBC's Alan Sillitoe file.

25 Reported by Patricia Lewis, 'Next stop for Sillitoe–Tangier', *Daily Express*, 27 Oct 1960, p. 16.

26 References to the changing seasons and the 'Big Wheel of the year' have (inevitably) led a few university critics to suspect that mythic Themes are waiting to be discovered behind the novel's realism. One critic has read *Saturday Night and Sunday Morning* as a reworking of *The Waste Land*, with Arthur's fondness for angling triumphantly interpreted as a sign that he is really the Fisher King (Osgerby, 'Alan Sillitoe's *Saturday Night and Sunday Morning*'). Another critical detective has claimed that Graves' White Goddess myth is the novel's major structuring device–a notion which eventually explains that Aunt Ada represents the Eternal Feminine, that Sam is an envoy of the Sun-God, and that Brenda's gin-bath abortion is 'an hilarious [*sic*] parody of Graves' account of the "cauldron-ritual" ' (Hugh B. Staples, '*Saturday Night and Sunday Morning*: Alan Sillitoe and the White Goddess', *Modern Fiction Studies* 10 (1964), pp. 171–81).

27 Wain, 'Possible Worlds', p. 20. See also David Holloway's remark in his review of *Saturday Night and Sunday Morning* in the *News Chronicle*: 'It is not necessary to know anything about the setting to be sure it is absolutely genuine', and Pamela Hansford Johnson declaring in the *New Statesman* that she read *The Loneliness of the Long-distance Runner* with 'a sense of absolute trust'.

NOTES

28 John Lehmann, Letter, *Listener*, 12 April 1956, p. 405.
29 Penelope Mortimer, 'A White Hope?', review of Philip Callow, *Common People*, *Sunday Times*, 10 Aug 1958, p. 7; 'How's Poor Ould Ireland?', review of Bill Naughton, *Late Night on Watling Street*, *TLS*, 26 June 1959, p. 381; Green, 'A Tapestry of Human Passions', p. 15, and Perrott, 'Miss Murdoch rings the bell', p. 4. This line was also followed by Sillitoe's publishers, W. H. Allen–the blurb to *The Loneliness of the Long-distance Runner* introduced him as a 'born writer'.
30 Philip Hope-Wallace, review of *A Taste of Honey*, *Time and Tide*, 21 Feb 1959, p. 216.
31 The reviews of *Key to the Door* cited here are: 'Scenes From Provincial Life', *TLS*, 20 Oct 1961, p. 749; Cyril Connolly, 'Mild-and-Bitter Rebel', *Sunday Times*, 15 Oct 1961, p. 31; John Davenport, 'Leaden Days Of Youth', *Observer*, 15 Oct 1961, p. 29.
32 Waterhouse expressed his misgivings in a Letter to Walter Allen, 27 March 1960, quoted in a Letter received from Keith Waterhouse, 26 January 1984. He made his comments in reply to an article by Allen, 'The Newest Voice in English Lit Is From The Working Class', *New York Times Book Review*, 20 Dec 1959, p. 4. Waterhouse wrote that working-class writers 'are being currently overpraised for their observation to the exclusion of any other qualities', and that he was afraid of 'a terrible reaction' to writers like himself in the near future as a consequence.

Ten: 'Decade Talk'

The chapter title headed an article by Rayner Heppenstall in the *New Statesman*, 14 April 1956, pp. 377–8.

1 These quotations come from, respectively, an *Encounter* editorial, 'This Month's *Encounter*', June 1956, p. 2; Nigel Dennis, 'Lucky Jim & His Pals', *Time*, 27 May 1957, p. 106; and 'New Patterns Of Society', *TLS*, 17 Aug 1956, p. xxviii.
2 See, for example, Stanley S. Atherton, *Alan Sillitoe: A Critical Assessment* (London, W. H. Allen, 1979), p. 16; and Ronald Hayman, *The Novel Today: 1967–75* (London, Longman, 1976), p. 29.
3 Dale Salwak, 'An Interview with Kingsley Amis', *Contemporary Literature* 16 (1975), p. 10.
4 The phrase was used by John Fowles to describe what he remembered as the majority of novels published around 1953, in Sally Beauman, 'Exile in a World of Imagination', *Sunday Telegraph Magazine*, 4 Oct 1981, p. 66.
5 'William Hickey', 'An Angry Young Woman Says: I'm Leaving

242

England', *Daily Express*, 27 Sept 1956, p. 4; Montagu Smith, 'Pimples cause the angry young man', *Daily Mail*, 25 Sept 1958, p. 9.

6 Lindsay Anderson, 'A year of my own', *The Colour Supplement*, BBC Radio 4, 23 Sept 1984.

7 David Glover, 'Utopia and Fantasy in the Late 1960s: Burroughs, Moorcock, Tolkien', in Christopher Pawling (ed.), *Popular Fiction and Social Change* (London, Macmillan, 1984), p. 187. The same strange idea was advanced by Arthur Marwick in *British Society Since 1945* (Harmondsworth, Penguin Books, 1982), p. 86.

8 John Osborne interviewed by Kenneth Tynan, in 'Osborne', *Observer*, 7 July 1968, p. 21; Kingsley Amis, John Braine et al., Letter, *The Times*, 3 Feb 1967, p. 11; Kingsley Amis, 'We mustn't let the rebels walk all over us', *TV Times*, 16–22 Aug 1975, p. 6.

9 One of the earliest groupings of the Movement poets was made by G. S. Fraser and Iain Fletcher in their Introduction to *Springtime* (London, Peter Owen, 1953), p. 10; Alvarez offered his composite poem in his Introduction to *The New Poetry* (Harmondsworth, Penguin Books, 1962), p. 20.

10 Kingsley Amis, 'The Legion of the Lost', *Spectator*, 15 June 1956, pp. 830–1 and Amis, quoted by Daniel Farson, 'I Meet A Genius With Indigestion', *Daily Mail*, 13 July 1956. p.4; Colin Wilson, 'I Hate the Mob Mentality', *Reynolds News*, 3 Feb 1957, p. 3; John Osborne, 'The Things I wish I could do . . . by the Theatre's Bright Boy', *Daily Express*, 18 Oct 1956, p. 8.

11 Michael Hastings, 'I Accuse!', *Daily Express*, 4 Sept 1956, p. 6; John Braine, 'The Month', *Twentieth Century*, Feb 1958, p. 171; Colin Wilson, 'Speaking Of Books', *New York Times Book Review*, 17 Feb 1957, p. 2.

12 These quotations are taken from, respectively, 'Give Them A Cheer', *Books and Bookmen*, April 1958, p. 3; Geoffrey Gorer, 'The Perils of Hypergamy', *New Statesman*, 4 May 1957, p. 566; and Ritchie Calder, 'When *We* were angry we *Did* something about it', *News Chronicle*, 13 Aug 1957, p. 4.

13 Kingsley Amis, Letter, *Listener*, 29 July 1954, p. 179.

14 A. S. Byatt made this recollection on *Bookmark*, BBC 2, 20 Feb 1985.

15 Personal interview with Kingsley Amis, 30 Nov 1984.

16 Malcolm Bradbury interviewed by Christopher Bigsby, in Bigsby and Heide Ziegler (eds.), *The Radical Imagination and the Liberal Tradition* (London, Junction Books, 1982), p. 62; Malcolm Bradbury, Introduction to *Eating People is Wrong* (London, Secker & Warburg, 1976), p. 3.

17 John Holloway, for instance, forwards the idea that England has lacked Modernism-inducing crises in 'English culture and the feat of transformation–1,' *Listener*, 12 Jan 1967, pp. 47–9, and Malcolm

Bradbury tries out the notion of English society as an unalienating *'Gemeinschaft'* in *The Social Context of Modern English Literature* (Oxford, Basil Blackwell, 1971), p. 21; Bernard Bergonzi gives his version of 'the ideology of being English' in *The Situation of the Novel* (London, Macmillan, 1970), pp. 58–9.

18 Kingsley Amis, 'In Defence of Dons' in *Literary Opinion*, No. 3, BBC Third Programme, 9 June 1954.

19 William Golding, interviewed by Owen Webster, 'Living with Chaos', *Books and Art*, March 1958, p. 15, and in a Letter received from Golding 26 Jan 1984.

20 Personal interview with Malcolm Bradbury 8 Dec 1983.

21 Edith Sitwell, 'Young Poets', in *Mightier Than The Sword: The PEN Hermon Ould Memorial Lectures 1953–1961* (London, Macmillan, 1964), pp. 74–6; Dannie Abse, Introduction to *Mavericks* (London: Editions Poetry and Poverty, 1957), p. 9; Alan Brownjohn, 'Movements And Movers', *Truth*, 11 Feb 1955, pp. 171–2; Charles Tomlinson, 'The Middlebrow Muse', review of *New Lines, Essays in Criticism* 7 (1957), pp. 208–17.

22 Personal interview with Bradbury.

Index